FRIENDLY FIRE

Patrick Gale was born on the Isle of Wight in 1962. He spent his infancy at Wandsworth Prison, which his father governed, then grew up in Winchester. He now lives on a farm near Land's End. As well as writing and reviewing fiction, he has published a biography of Armistead Maupin, a short history of the Dorchester Hotel and chapters on Mozart's piano and mechanical music for H.C. Robbin Landon's *The Mozart Compendium*. His most recent novels are *A Sweet Obscurity* and *Rough Music*.

Also by Patrick Gale

FRIENDLY FIRE

Patrick Gale

Illustrations by Aidan Hicks

FOURTH ESTATE • *London* and *New York*

First published in Great Britain in 2005 by
Fourth Estate
A Division of HarperCollins*Publishers*
77–85 Fulham Palace Road
London W6 8JB
www.4thestate.com

1 3 5 7 9 10 8 6 4 2

A catalogue record for this book is available
from the British Library

ISBN 0-00-715100-4

Typeset in Sabon by Palimpsest Book Production Ltd,
Polmont, Stirlingshire

Printed in Great Britain by
Clays Ltd, St Ives plc

For Aidan Hicks

I know nothing of these things.

Is this sheltered place the wicked world
Where things unspoken of can be?

(*The Turn of the Screw*,
MYFANWY PIPER)

MICHAELMAS TERM
(thirteen years, ten months)

The first time Lucas came to Sophie's attention, he was wearing a dress. Towards the end of her first month at the school, Sophie paused one night in Flint Quad and was transfixed by what she saw through one of the male chamber windows. Music was playing, Bryan Ferry singing 'Love is the Drug' which was what had pulled her up short in the first place as it was a song with good associations for her. A girl in a soiled, purple silk ball gown was showing an older boy how to jive. Girls were banned from all male chambers after sundown, one of those rules whose wisdom was swallowed as unquestioningly as peasants accepted folklore in a werewolf film.

As the lawbreaker mouthed instructions, the boy whirled her around, held her by one hand then another, twirled her this way and that. Each was concentrating too hard to smile. A bored lack of interest was *de rigueur* so nobody but Sophie appeared to be watching them. Two boys were attempting to toast crumpets on a cluster of candles. A third played air guitar. A fourth and fifth played a wild, improvised game involving a fives glove and a softened pack of butter.

Then the dancers' manoeuvres caused the girl to be spun out in such a way that her eyes momentarily met Sophie's through the barred window and Sophie saw it wasn't a girl at all.

Tatham's had been founded in the fourteenth century by a wealthy and pragmatic bishop to train up priests to replace those lost to the Black Death, the costs being met entirely at his gift. As the school expanded over the centuries and began to take on fee-paying, less ambitious students, the band of charity boys remained in the original medieval buildings, Schola, and became marked out as Scholars, as opposed to the often inaptly named Commoners who were housed elsewhere. Scholars had to pass a far harder exam to gain entrance to the school and had at most times to wear a coal-black clerical uniform, complete with gown and sleeved jerkin so there should be no mistaking their ambivalent rank; at once intellectually exalted and socially obliged.

The school was peculiar in having admitted a very few female Scholars, on the same terms as the male ones, in every year's intake since the seventeenth century. This practice had its origins in a group of serving-women educated to the point of being able to read Greek by a group of Scholars who had entered into a bet on the subject. Most of these Xenophon-parsing maids vanished into nunneries or marriage but one took it upon herself to pass on her outlandish knowledge to the offspring of the man then Master of Schola, blessed with five daughters. One of these went on to write formidable texts on poverty, marriage and the proper cultivation of vegetables.

In honour of that story, the female Scholars, who sat the same exam and wore much the same uniform as their male equivalents, were members of Schola, housed amongst the boys but apart from them. They had their own chamber, dormitories and studies in a corner of Flint Quad. Their staircase had its peculiar touches of gentility: a small, secluded rose garden, proper bathrooms and a live-in chaperone, usually a retired member of the domestic staff, rarely with any Greek and known as Nurse. They were allowed to visit a male chamber in pairs, in daylight. They could receive calls only from boys approved and overseen by Nurse, and only in the afternoon. And they were known as Daughters.

Since 1970 daygirls had also been admitted on a fee-paying basis as Commoners but only to the sixth-form. They were extremely social and had nothing to do with the Daughters. Inevitably, with the cost of fees spiralling ever skyward, more and more well-off parents had taken to hothousing their sons in prep school so as to win them scholarships and a free path to university but attitudes towards the education of women remained sufficiently conventional for few such parents to risk putting their daughters at the same social disadvantage during their formative years.

Boys and girls studied together but were kept separate in class, any girls having to sit in the front row. Teachers addressed boys by their surnames, girls as Miss Whatever. Outnumbered by nearly twenty-five to one, girls found their femininity negated by their own desire for invisibility and by the inevitably high profile given to any mixed-sex friendship. Younger for their age, boys in a class tended to clump assertively together, girls to form quietly scornful twos and threes. The only other girl in Sophie's div – the name given to a general class – was Kimiko Matsubara, a painfully shy Japanese, who clung to her like a lemur between lessons but had no small talk. This suited Sophie, who was naturally independent and cautious, as it gave her the appearance of a friendship without the emotional commitment.

Even as the school boasted of the psychological healthiness of being mixed-sex, an unspoken horror of pregnancy was evident in its every policy decision. There were stories, myths effectively, of couples who had been caught, disgraced and expelled. The Daughters' rose garden was said to be haunted by the ghost of a baby, secretly delivered, stifled and buried there under a magnificent bush of Great Maiden's Blush. To hear it cry was to be in imminent danger of disgrace oneself.

Boys could visit if Nurse was present and approved. Girls' daylight visits to boys, in pairs, were only possible on securing a handwritten permit from Nurse explaining their visit's purpose. This was a highly effective deterrent; it was peculiarly difficult to find a pretext for a visit that did not shrivel into paltry deceit when carefully repeated by her as she formed it in her respectable, school-report hand.

'Miss Tyler, accompanied by Miss Legg, wishing to consult Nicholas Macdonald Hay concerning the life cycle of the flea.'

'Miss Legg, accompanied by Miss Crosbie, wishing to consult Magnus Fisher concerning the bowing of Brandenburg Number 3.'

And all this accompanied by knowing looks and laughter. Sophie had witnessed the process often enough to know it was not for her. Besides, not knowing the boy's name, she would have had to have found a boy in his house she knew, however tenuously, then staged a visit on a trumped-up pretext in the hope of glimpsing the boy who mattered. He was a Commoner, about her height, and he looked good in a dress. That was all she knew.

She contented herself with glimpsing him in Brick Quad or on the path to Stinks, the science blocks, between lessons, looking in vain for a moment when he might talk to someone she already knew.

Then she found that he swam. She had always liked swimming, not just because it was free but because it required no coordination of limb, eye and ball. Best of all, for a girl uncomfortable with her body, who hated sweating, it brought the merciful illusions of being clean, cool and almost bodiless. Once she was up to her neck in water, that was. There remained the hell of pulling on a swimsuit and passing gingerly from changing room to pool through sanitizing shower and footbath and the merciless gaze of others. With her hair tugged up in a regulation rubber cap, however, and her eyes hidden in hideous goggles, she knew she was unrecognizable even before she reached the water.

She saw him by chance. She happened to have finished a length and be turning just as he walked through the boys' footbath and took his place in a lane four over from hers. He dived in with unsplashy efficiency and was immediately hidden from view amid all the bobbing heads and windmilling arms. But she knew he was there, sharing the water with her. She swam on and on, exhausting herself until the rowdies and paddlers began to queue up for the start of Rec Swim. She scanned the remaining length-swimmers in his lane as she walked to the girls' changing room and realized he must have left while her back was turned.

Her breakthrough sighting of him, a few weeks later, came during that year's Junior Play, a modish staging of Louis MacNeice's radio drama, *The Dark Tower*, complete with daringly loud Pink Floyd soundtrack. He played the hero's mother, in false eyelashes, somebody's not-quite Chanel suit and a long blonde wig. Someone in the make-up department had tried to age the wig with white powder, clouds of which came off whenever he moved his head. Sophie recognized him only when he patted the sofa beside him bossily and said the line, 'Now, Roland, sit here by me on the sofa. We'll look at them backwards.'

He reappeared, dancing, in a black Eton Crop wig and a knee-length beaded dress as part of the partying crowd in a later scene. For some reason she couldn't fathom they were all shouting, 'And we shake the bag! And we shake the bag!'

Once the lights came up at the end she was able to look up his name in the programme. Lucas Behrman. As was her instinct, she immediately translated the two words into a picture to fix them in her memory: a man with a blazing lantern in his hand and a bear walking beside him. Light Bearman.

She glimpsed him a couple more times between classes but there seemed to be no predictability to his movements. And now the carol service was upon them and Illumina, the end of term festivities, and she was beside herself, only discreetly. She thought about him all the time, even during a maths test, and her scores began to slip, which shook her.

Then Kimiko Matsubara quietly, almost apologetically, reported that he was in Middle Part and the boarding house known as Dougal's. She even had his home address.

'Whatever makes you think I'd be interested?' Sophie snapped. 'You're the one in love with him, clearly. Why should I care? How'd you find out, anyway?'

'There's a little book of names and addresses. You can consult it at Jago's.'

Jago's was the school's stationers and booksellers, which printed the school newspaper and notepaper as a sideline, and this little book.

Sophie dismissed Kimiko with suitable scorn then ran round to see the book for herself, horrified that nobody had thought to point it out to her in her first weeks at the place. It was a tiny paperback, bound in blue sugar paper with the school's crest and the term and the year on the front. Oh yes, old Miss Jago told her, Short Roll was produced every term. That term's print run had long since sold out, of course, but Miss Cullen was welcome to consult the browsing edition. This was a much-thumbed and defaced copy dangling on a thin chain at one end of the shop's only counter.

The listings started with the Warden, governing body and staff then descended from the specialized empyrean of the upper sixth to the most junior Commoners. After that, to her dismay, came a comprehensive listing of everyone's names and addresses, in alphabetical order, staff as well as pupils, embarrassing middle names and all. It was a primer in social distinctions. Some were suddenly revealed as grand, with a surname that matched their house, or even village. The less fortunate might live somewhere with a telltale suburban plural in the address – The Rowans or Four Winds. One of the more retiring dons had to squirm before the public exposure of his being a secret Beverly. Sophie had no middle names which, she realized looking at the list, made her odd.

Lucas Daniel Behrman, she read and memorized, placing the lantern-bearer and his bear in a circle of lions. *17 Tinker's Hill*. A local boy. Day pupils were a rare novelty and the fact was recorded with an asterisk beside the D that showed he was in Dougal's. Thanks to hours spent walking and bicycling its leafy streets, Sophie had developed a taxi driver's mind-map of the city's districts. Tinker's Hill was smart – private houses on an unadopted road, each different from its neighbour. It was expensive but not as smart as its residents hoped. The houses were visible from the pavement, after all, were nearly all postwar and, with names like Shangri-La and Marble Halls, a local byword for new money. Sophie was relieved at this; she felt it gave Lucas a certain social vulnerability to offset her own, although it could hardly match it.

Her address was displayed with brutal honesty. *Wakefield House*. Her first, irrational impulse was to tear out the page with her name on but she realized the address had been there all term and no one had passed comment so perhaps nobody had realized its significance.

But he was local. He would know or would easily find out. Until now she had told no one. Not that she was ashamed. Not exactly. But she preferred not to stand out or seem in any way odd. Having skimmed a few Mallory Towers novels out of idle curiosity, she had dreaded the first girlish interrogation but it never came. The few girls who were interested in status symbols, houses, cars, fathers' jobs, previous education, university plans, were so only in relation to themselves and could easily be diverted into describing their own backgrounds at length. If they then remembered their manners sufficiently to ask about her again, Sophie could shrug and say something like, 'Oh, nothing so exciting. The usual, really,' or 'So normal it makes me yawn.'

To be ordinary was fine, so long as one had the modesty to admit it. Perhaps in reaction to an ethos of excellence, smugness was perceived as the cardinal social crime in boys and girls alike. It amazed her to hear how some people rattled on about their family and possessions and pony and this and that, blithely handing over ammunition to be used against them the moment they were out of earshot.

Wakefield House was the town orphanage, not long renamed a children's home. It had been her address, her home indeed, since she was five but she suspected she had been in care longer than that. She knew nothing about her parents, if they were loving but dead or the reverse. For a long time she had toyed with the idea that both were dead and that she had been too old or unappealing an infant for anyone to want to adopt her. Since arriving at Wakefield House, however, she had annual conversations with a social worker so had been able to confirm each year that, no thank you, she was happy where she was and did not wish to be considered for either fostering or adoption.

The novels she had read that featured orphans had got it wrong. She did not long for her flesh-and-blood parents or lie awake at night weeping, because Margaret and Kieran, the childless, forty-something couple who ran the home, were ideal parent substitutes. Paid to put children at the centre of their lives but as calmly affectionate towards their charges as they were with one another. They were warm, funny, just sensible enough not to be dull and always to hand. Other people complained of fathers so wedded to their work they were rarely at home but Kieran was so wedded to his, he rarely left it.

There was some swapping of rooms whenever children left

but Sophie had always turned down offers of a change, electing to stay in the same small bedroom above the kitchen extension. There she could hear balls being kicked in the yard or Margaret and Kieran murmuring as they worked down below, but the view from her window was away over rooftops, up the hill from the river, towards the cathedral. When she wanted to be private and alone, which was most of the time, she could be there and lose herself in a book yet have just enough sounds from the house to feel anchored somewhere safe.

She remembered virtually nothing from before she came there, perhaps because of the lack of pictures or keepsakes that might have locked early memories in place. She remembered a small blue room with a window filled with the whirling leaves of a wind-stirred tree and, she was sure, remembered the sensation of sitting on her mother's lap, one hand resting on the back of her mother's fingers as they traced the words in a book. Books were her principal memory. Whenever she tried to think back to the time before Wakefield House, it was the rustling of pages and dim, mysterious smells of paper and glue that came to her. Her only photograph of that time was of herself as a serious toddler, learning to walk, propping herself upright with the big volumes at the bottom of a wall of closely filled bookshelves. If she looked very closely, she could make out the shadow of whoever took the photograph but they were hunched down so it was impossible to discern more than that it was a person with two legs.

She could not remember not reading. The great gaps in her early memories were filled with narratives shared by millions of other children: Ali Baba, Babar the Elephant, Ferdinand the Bull, Orlando the Marmalade Cat, Winnie the Pooh, Alice. Especially Alice, for whom she retained a deep affection; a girl who, like herself, seemed to spring into fiercely cogitating being

12

without the assistance of a family or even much of a home life. She had arrived at school already a keen reader, apparently, and had quickly adopted the practice of reading far ahead of any unambitiously short passage prescribed for homework. Absorbing and remembering the contents of a book was for her as simple a task as looking through glass and she found most tests and exams a matter of consulting her near-photographic recollection of the page on which a piece of information was set out. It was only when she encountered autistic children and observed their baffling combination of chronic detachment and total absorption that she recognized elements of autism in herself. She compared her ease of understanding with her contemporaries, and saw how they muddied their perceptions by trying to interpret what they perceived before they had fully perceived it. Their thoughts and personalities got in the way. Sophie's understanding, she realized, was more neutral, as detached as a camera lens from whatever passed through it. She could become passionately identified with narrative, but information – a maths theorem, the various meanings of a new word, the principal rivers and products of the British counties – plainly presented, stowed itself in the drawers of her memory like so many squarely ironed handkerchiefs and could be brought out again exactly as it went in.

Like other small children at Wakefield House, she began her schooling at St Boniface's, the Church of England primary that served the parish. Depending on their ability, children from there went on to either to the city's secondary modern or to one of its single-sex grammar schools. Being bright for her age, she was put in for the eleven-plus on the assumption that she would go on to the girls' grammar but she startled her teachers by scoring one hundred per cent. Telling her this over supper,

Kieran joked that she was Tatham's material. When she asked what Tatham's was, he explained about the old school and its scholarships. Seeing her interest, he took a group of them on a Sunday walk over there.

The Chapel tower was just visible from her bedroom. It seemed to stick up to one side of the cathedral and she had always assumed it was just another church, not part of a school. As Kieran led the others through its high doors, Sophie stood in Flint Quad, transfixed. House martins were swooping down from their nests under the eaves, almost brushing the four quadrants of flints that divided its paths and gave it its name. Scholars lolled on battered sofas and armchairs they had dragged out into the sunshine. Some wore the black uniform, some sports clothes or jeans. Some played cards or chess, others kicked footballs against ancient buttresses. She saw all this and felt herself claimed.

'They have a special exam,' Kieran explained. 'You can take it at twelve or thirteen but you have to have Latin or Greek, algebra, all sorts. Stuff they don't teach at St Bonnie's.'

'But if I did learn it,' she asked, 'could I do the exam?'

'Sure. Anyone can. We'd just have to enter you. Hey! Wilf! Put that back where you found it. Now.'

Necessarily dependent on whatever entertainment could be had for nothing, she had long been dividing her free time between the city baths, to which the council gave Wakefield House children free passes, and the city library. This was her home from home. She knew her way around it, how to read the Dewey Decimal System, how to consult the deep drawers of card catalogues, how to order books she couldn't find. She tried looking under Tatham's, Exams and Scholarships and eventually found several bound volumes of past Tatham's scholarship papers and a syllabus. Greek was not essential but Latin

14

was and French (which she had barely begun) and areas of maths and history that were a mystery to her.

It was daunting but she was methodical and she had two years. She also had a supporter on the staff at St Boniface's who agreed to let her work on at her own pace provided she continued to participate in some classes too. She suggested they put Sophie in for the exams at twelve as a trial run and was almost as astonished as Sophie when Sophie was summoned for an interview and offered the last available scholarship. It was only when everyone congratulated her that Sophie understood they had never expected her to succeed and had been supporting her purely out of kindness.

Financial assistance was discreetly found through the county council to buy her uniform and pay her a modest monthly sum of pocket money. Any books she needed were provided under the terms of the scholarship, second-hand. She had far fewer possessions than most other pupils and was certainly the only Daughter to arrive on her own with her things crammed into an army surplus rucksack. Even the pupils who came from overseas, passed through a succession of International Aunts and stewardesses, arrived with trunks. And most Scholars were dropped off by at least one parent, some by entire, gawping families. Margaret offered but Sophie hated fuss and Margaret was showing signs of fretfulness so Sophie insisted she would be fine on her own, said her round of goodbyes at home and presented herself at the Porters' Lodge on foot.

Armed with the knowledge of Lucas Behrman's div, it was easy enough to track him down. Div was the class in general culture and essay-writing, common to all parts of the school and designed to round out the specialized knowledge of the scientists and classicists in particular. One's position in the school was indicated by one's div class, from lowly JP4 to the exalted heights of A1, the most senior classics div. All divs met at the same time so it was simply a matter of pretending she needed to be excused just towards the lesson's end then racing across from her div room to his, on the other side of Brick Quad.

She arrived just in time to see him come out. Seeing him in male clothes, house tweed jacket and sensible shoes, it was hard to imagine him in a dress. But there was something very neat and self-contained about him. He was not gossiping or horsing around like the others but was studying the blurb on the back of a novel by someone called Mary Renault, moving within the crowd but not of it. She saw at once how he had learnt, as she had, the knack of being overlooked when it suited him, of switching himself off like a torch.

The Chapel clock was striking and a groundsman was raking a last load of fallen leaves across the grass. Lucas had dark brown hair and the kind of pale complexion that must betray every emotion. She stood in his path on purpose but he stepped silently around her, murmuring, 'I'm so sorry,' and without making eye contact. Watching him go, she felt breathless until Kimiko arrived at her side, releasing her from the moment with her questions and the chance to escape into familiar scorn.

The Michaelmas term ended with Illumina, a pyromaniac's delight. This was the lighting of a giant bonfire on Schola Field, the playing field nearest the school's historical centre and of hundreds of candles tucked into holes in the ancient walls on three of the field's boundaries. The Chapel bells rang out carol tunes, smuggled bangers and sparklers were lit, even the

occasional rocket. Under cover of darkness and in the knowledge that no meaningful punishment would be handed out on
the last night of term, a harmless carnival anarchy was loosed
on the air along with the tang of gunpowder.

This and the thought of being reunited with their families
sent Kimiko and the other Daughters into an outbreak of sickly
nostalgia – a kind of reverse homesickness in which they could
hardly bear to leave school since it meant leaving one another.
Sophie pretended to join in so as not to seem cold but her mind
was elsewhere, riding an imaginary bicycle up and down his
street, looking for places from which to watch him unobserved
and excuses to knock on his door. She was consumed by a
fantasy in which she saw his mother – who of course looked
like him as the mother in the play – let slip a gold bracelet
while hurrying in from the snow, thus giving Sophie the reason
to call and be warmly welcomed.

CHRISTMAS HOLIDAYS
(thirteen years, eleven months)

Christmas in Wakefield House was a happy but moderate business. To avoid wild expense or upsets caused by favouritism, it was agreed that the children draw names from a pudding basin, then buy just one present each, for whoever's they drew. Anything else – cards, decorations and so on – they were encouraged to make themselves to save money.

Sophie had a pact with Wilf that they each folded the paper with their name on it into a triangle rather than a rectangle so that it would be easy to spot. Then they went shopping together so that each could be sure of getting exactly the present they wanted. It was unspontaneous perhaps but, like many people from unstable backgrounds, they hated surprises and it was preferable to the torture of knowing someone you despised had drawn your name and would be buying you something hideous.

Wilf was two years older than her and had an older brother's protective instincts towards her but he was far less bright, which lessened the gap between them. He was actually a William but his nickname – arising from his mumbled delivery of Will Franks – had stuck long after the original scurrilous tease had been forgiven and forgotten. His mother was in prison for armed robbery and assault, following a raid on a supermarket that had gone horribly wrong. He despised his mother and was counting on her not being released until he was sixteen and independent. He adored Margaret and was always hanging around the kitchen, jealous of the younger children's claims on her attention, so she was always happy to send him off on errands with Sophie to help him.

He bought Sophie a dynamo kit for her bicycle because people at school kept nicking her batteries. She bought him a new *Dark Side of the Moon* cassette because his first one had got tangled in a tree during a fight. They bought Margaret paper chains and tinsel in Woolworth's. Then, on the pretext of wanting to see how rich people had decorated their houses, she pedalled furiously ahead and led him up to Tinker's Hill.

In the fading light, they passed bungalows and sprawling haciendas, a Tudorbethan manor and twin mock Georgians that seemed more garage than house. Sophie pointed out details; twinkling lamps, a Father Christmas climbing a chimney, a hedge lit with fairy lights, a wishing well converted into an outdoor crib. Her mind, however, was on counting the numbers as she did so.

Number seventeen, unnamed, was one of the older houses on the hill, a white 1930s structure with elegant lines and curved metal windows painted a cheerful green. Standard bushes formed a guard of honour along a path of curious green stone chippings, which Wilf pointed out were like the sort one saw in a cemetery. There was a glimpse of a swimming pool, a cover pulled over it.

'Why've we stopped here, Soph?' Wilf asked. 'All they've got is that spastic lantern thing.'

He was right. She hadn't noticed at first but there were no decorations, not even a holly wreath. There was merely a branched lantern, a sort of pyramidal candelabrum really, glowing in an upstairs window.

'Maybe they're Jehovah's Witnesses?' she suggested.

'Too rich,' he said. 'Jehovahs are never rich coz they don't believe in saving. Do Mormons do Christmas? The Osmonds are Mormons. They're rich. Look. They're coming home. They've got a Jew's Canoe.'

'What's that?'

'Mercedes. Definitely not Jehovahs. Nice one.'

He stood openly staring in a streetlamp's glare at the big black car as it slowed to turn in. Sophie hastily backed her bike into the shadows, barking a shin, and watched from behind a tree. The Mercedes pulled in and stopped in front of the garage. A man in a dark blue overcoat got out, unlocked the garage and flicked a switch which set the car gently turning on a concrete turntable until it was facing the way it had come in. (Wilf let out a low whistle of admiration.) Then the man stepped back into the car and reversed it into the garage.

The garage light was on and, for a few seconds before the man shut the door, Sophie had a glimpse of a small woman in a hat and fur coat and Lucas Behrman in a suit and a smaller version of his father's overcoat. Their clothes were more elegant than anything Sophie had seen at close quarters, like clothes in a film, but it was the absurd luxury of the turntable and the

formal restraint with which mother and son had remained in
the car until it was safely inside that had told her most strongly
these were people of another race entirely.

'So who are they?' Wilf asked as they wheeled their bikes
on up the hill. 'Who lives there?'

'No one,' she said. 'Just a boy at school. I was curious, was
all.'

'Do you fancy him?'

'Don't be a wally. Did you see what he was wearing? Will
that dynamo make my bike slower?'

'Not so as you'll notice. Race you back?'

'Okay.'

She had worried that Wakefield House would feel strange
after a term away and that the others might have begun to
resent her in her absence. Margaret and Kieran seemed pleased
to have her back however and, far from feeling envious, the
others continued to show only incomprehension and pity, as
though her scholarship landed her in a kind of prison, like ordinary school only harder and even more dull. Just once or twice,
one of them mocked something she said when she unwittingly
lapsed into laconic Tatham's idiom or forgot herself and said
actually or *gorgeous*.

The scant four weeks of holiday flew by in an orgy of
afternoon television and long lie-ins with a book and a bowl
of cereal; luxuries forbidden at school. Along with the usual
drum of Quality Street and hamper of Christmas food, the
town council gave them Twister, a game they played so
obsessively and in such fits of laughter that Margaret
threatened to get rid of it because she worried it was stopping them sleeping properly. But it was only a craze. They
had one most holidays, like a benign bug passed around the

house. Once it had been Racing Demon, banned when a girl reverted to bedwetting from too much excitement, another time it was Slinky races on the stairs. By Easter, Twister would be just another battered game in the toy cupboard, as unfashionable as Kerplunk or Go.

The first day of each term brought chaos to Jago's as every boy and girl joined in great queues to buy stationery and collect and sign for the set texts and textbooks assigned to their classes. The books were piled up neatly on thick mahogany shelves kept empty for the purpose but few pupils were sure of which classes they had been put in beyond their div. This meant that most students had to consult crazily arcane lists to find out then take a note of that information to Miss Jago who sat at a high clerk's desk at the shop's cavernous rear, where she presided over the term's reading lists, then take their list of books to one of the queues for a sales assistant.

Being given books was one of the best parts of the scholarship for Sophie and she wanted to relish the moment this time without being jostled in a scrum. She also had a mind to read some of the books in advance and so steal a march on her peers. But when she called in soon after Christmas, Miss Jago told her firmly that the lists were never made public before the start of term. It was as though the old woman had sussed that Sophie was planning a kind of cheat.

'If you're a local girl, though, and you want to beat the queues, try calling in on the last day of the holidays. We've usually got the lists together by then.'

So Sophie contented herself with reading ahead in Greek, a subject in which she was still struggling to catch up, and physics, which was proving elusive. She knew she had done well in her first term and would be moving up the div ladder a little.

'Ah yes,' Miss Jago said as she took her name two weeks later. 'Miss Cullen.' She liked to pretend she knew everyone by sight or at least by reputation. She had the new term's div and form listings before her and was enjoying her access to knowledge not yet made public. 'A double remove. You'll be joining Master Behrman, here, in the Middle Part. So that means Eysenck's *Introduction to Psychology, Seven Types of Ambiguity, The Golden Bough*. Huh. Long read. *The Secret Agent* and *Metamorphosis*. Keep you going. Science and maths books as for last term. For French ditto but you'll need *Les Mains Sales*. Greek as for last term, Latin ditto. Oh. English. Yes. *Henry V*. Sign here please. And enjoy them.'

Sophie hadn't recognized him at first because his duffel coat and stripey scarf were so far removed from the most recent, elegant image she had of him. But perhaps the suit and cashmere overcoat were his teenage equivalent of a smaller boy's clip-on bow tie and flannel shorts; enforced party wear.

He pushed back his hood. 'Hello,' he said. 'Lucas Behrman.'

'I know,' she said. 'I'm Sophie. Cullen.'

'I've seen you around with that Japanese girl.'

'Kimiko Matsubara.'

'That's the one.'

He blushed and looked down at their respective book heaps. He was shy. She would never have predicted that. Or perhaps the blush was for another reason.

'How did you wangle second-hand copies?' he asked. 'New ones cost a mint. My father always complains.'

'I'm a Daughter. We don't pay so the school gets us second-hand stuff whenever it can.'

'Oh. Of course. Sorry.'

They walked together, she wheeling her bike, chatting of

neutral school subjects until she began to break off, explaining that she lived in the other direction. Which was when he invited her back for coffee.

'Lucas, your father's not in for supper so I thought it might be nice if we – Oh. Hello.' She broke off, seeing Sophie in the hall with him. It was Audrey Hepburn, or as good as: petite, brown-haired, immaculately groomed without seeming artificial. She held out a hand and searched Sophie's face with the huge, kind eyes of a Disney mouse. 'I'm Heidi,' she said. 'Lucas's mother.'

'Sophie,' said Sophie. She noticed Heidi's hand was small and soft then saw that she was in stockinged feet.

'Sorry,' Lucas said. 'No shoes. It's a house rule.'

Flustered, Sophie stooped to unlace her shoes and copied Lucas in putting them on a low rack beside the front door. She saw how the house had deep cream carpet everywhere. It flowed from room to room and up the stairs, lapping the wainscots. Back at Wakefield House there were only rugs here and there which slid about on dark-stained floorboards or dull lino.

'I think it helps people relax,' Heidi said. 'Shoes indoors, especially men's shoes, are a bit like wearing armour to bed. Would you both like coffee? I just made some.'

Real coffee, brewed in a gurgling percolator. Buttery Dutch shortbread. Proper coffee cups with saucers. Sophie could hardly breathe.

'I apologize for the kitchen, Sophie.'

'It's lovely.'

'It's a museum piece. Same age as the house. It's all coming out later this year, once Mr Perfectionist here will make up his mind.'

'Mum!' Lucas groaned.

Heidi caught Sophie's eye, taking her into her confidence in a we-girls-understand way at once intoxicating and appalling. 'Twenty brochures was it? Thirty? You'd think something in there would be right for him. But the finishes were wrong or the drawers or the way the cupboards met the floor. My son the architect.'

'Mum!'

'Sorry, angel.'

'Sophie's in my class from next term,' Lucas explained. 'We just found out in Jago's. She lives on the other side of town.'

'Oh. That's nice. Are you a day student too, Sophie?'

'Er . . . No. I'm a Daughter. We have to board.'

'That must be hard.'

Until now Sophie would not have agreed but, seeing the comforts Lucas came home to every night, she hesitated.

'It's not too bad,' she said.

'I bet your mum misses you.'

'Actually she's dead,' Sophie blurted out. 'And, well, my dad's not very well so it's probably better this way.'

Heidi's face was all concern and she reached out to touch Sophie gently above the elbow. 'That must be very tough for you,' she said.

'It's fine, Mum,' Lucas said. 'You can see she's fine about it. Haven't you got a patient or something?'

Again that girls-together smile. 'Aren't I terrible? He never brings anyone home, you see. You're extremely honoured, Sophie. Now don't let him bully you. If you want more coffee and biscuits, help yourself and do stay to lunch. The fridge is groaning.'

'Well I –' Sophie began but the doorbell rang.

'I'm gone,' Heidi said and left them. Through the half-open

door, Sophie saw her let in a tall, unhealthily thin girl with long, lifeless hair half across her face. She led her into another room and shut the door behind them. Apparently the girl wasn't offered biscuits or coffee.

'She's a shrink,' Lucas explained. 'Cutters and skellies mainly. Dad's a QC.'

He might have been talking Urdu but she nodded as though she understood and accepted a top-up of the coffee that was so much more delicious than anything on offer at home, even though it was making her heart race.

Going up to someone's room was all very well when you were smaller, because you naturally were showed your host's toys and settled down to play with them. Thirteen and three-quarters was too old for play, however, and nothing mention-able had yet suggested itself as a substitute. Lucas's room was an odd mixture. There were photographs of animals on the walls, taken from magazines – seals, a hippo, a foal – which surely dated from his childhood. There was a *Times* wall chart of the night sky and, leaning against the wall on a chest of drawers, a couple of recent David Bowie albums.

'Do you like him?' she asked.

'Yes,' he said carefully. 'Some.'

'Wilf says he's a poof.'

'Who's Wilf?'

'A friend.' She shrugged. 'No one at school.'

Prompted, he set one of the albums playing. *Aladdin Sane.* So this is what one did instead of toys.

There was a telescope on a stand beside the window.

'What can you see through that?' she asked.

'Everything,' he said with an odd smile. 'Every sin so far except murder. Take a look.'

She sat on the end of his very tidy bed to look.

'You have to shut the other eye,' he said, 'or you'll never focus.'

She looked. It was trained on a house further down the hill, a large, modernist place with a lot of plate glass and very few curtains. Leaning in so close beside her she could smell his *Eau Sauvage*, he turned a handle which minutely ratcheted up the angle of vision so that she saw first the living room, then a large bedroom above and part of a bathroom.

'They have sex every Saturday,' he murmured. 'After *Match of the Day*. And their son wanks on the sofa sometimes once they've gone to bed.'

'Do they have a daughter?' she asked, continuing to stare down the telescope to hide her shock.

'No. Just the son. But he has a girlfriend. She doesn't stay over or anything but they kiss for hours and if she has a bit to drink she takes her bra off and lets him feel.'

'What? Right off? Can you see?' She giggled.

'No,' he laughed. 'Just under her blouse. She sort of reaches in like this and undoes it for him then lies back like a monument while he feels.' He mimicked the girl to show her, batting his eyelids to make her giggle again.

She wound the handle for herself, taking the view back to the downstairs. The woman had arrived home from shopping and was walking around with plastic bags and cartons. Far more food than a family of three could eat in a week. She seemed so close it was impossible not to start back in alarm when she glanced up, apparently looking straight into Sophie's eyes.

'You don't seem very shocked,' he said, sounding disappointed.

'Sorry,' she said, pleased. 'Were other people?'

'You're the first person I've shown. They've got no idea.'

He didn't need to say who he meant.

She sat back on the bed. She couldn't believe that this morning he didn't know her and now she was sitting on his bed. He had a continental quilt, which was far more sophisticated than at school or Wakefield House, where sheets and blankets were still the norm and every week they did top-to-bottom-bottom-to-wash.

Lucas sang along with a phrase in a song.

'It's no wonder I don't bring anyone home,' he said abruptly. 'The way she carries on. Giving you the third degree like that. Honestly.'

'She didn't. Not really. She was just being nice.'

'Being nice to people is her job. It's how she draws them out and gets their secrets.'

'I like her.'

'You'll learn.'

'She looks like Audrey Hepburn.'

'Do you think so?' All the scorn left his voice. 'She can look amazing sometimes. If they really get dressed up for a party. But she's not very good at dressing down. Did you see how she walked on her toes still, as though she was still in heels? That's typical.'

She had never heard anyone talk like that about his mother. But then she had few intimates with a family life. 'You're very lucky being a dayboy.'

He shrugged. 'It's not like getting back in time for *Blue Peter* and a glass of milk. I'm never back before ten and I go straight to bed.'

'To look through this.'

He grinned. 'Sometimes.'

'Who do you like watching best?' she asked. 'The parents or the son?'

'The son. But only because it's so risky. It's like TV. Someone might interrupt him any second. I worry for him and . . .' He broke off and fiddled with the pile of books on his bedside table, aligning their spines.

'What?' she prompted him.

'Because he's on his own, I don't feel so bad watching. It's as if he needs an audience.'

'Maybe he knows,' she suggested. 'That you're watching.'

'How could he? He can't see.'

'I could put a note in there telling him.'

'Then I'd have to kill you.'

'But you'd never know. He'd come and kill you, maybe.'

Lucas did not seem to mind the idea. There was a sort of buzz in the air between them. He sang along to the song again which started to embarrass her.

'Don't you see many people in the holidays, then?' she asked.

'Not really. I'm the only dayboy in my house. Actually,' he confessed, 'I don't see anyone.'

'How about people from your last school? You must have had friends there.'

'It wasn't near here. I boarded.'

'Weird. Why?'

'Simon – that's my father – thought it would be good for me. To spend more time with boys.'

'Where was it?'

'Sussex. Near the sea. It was okay.' He scowled.

'You hated it.'

'Yeah.'

He had a fancy electric clock with a radio inside and numbers that flicked over with a sound like fingernails softly tapping on paper. It was getting late. She had missed lunch and Margaret would be worried.

'I should go,' she said. 'They'll be expecting me. Big day tomorrow and I've got to pack.'

'Okay,' he said, not moving. 'Do you want to see Carmel's room?'

'Who's she?'

'My sister. She doesn't live here any more but there's still a room full of her stuff. I'm not allowed in. Come and see.'

Carmel's room was next door. There was a sign on the door saying 'Keep Out' and a poster of a woman dressed in black cowboy gear and pointing a gun but they went in anyway. The room was the same shape as Lucas's but dramatically different. The ceiling and walls, even the windows, were hidden by Indian bedspreads. There were candles and ashtrays and heavy scents of dust and joss sticks.

'Carmel's much older than me,' he explained. 'She lives with her boyfriend in Clifton. They're not married or even engaged. Heidi likes to be thought of as cool but she finds it really hard to talk about. She's terrified Carmel's going to get pregnant and come back to have it up here or something.'

They giggled.

It was a shock to find a space in the immaculate house that felt not quite clean. The bed was neatly made, the books tidy on the shelves, evidence of a visit from Heidi, perhaps, but everything spoke of unresolved conflict, not just the anti-war posters and the Che Guevara and Jimi Hendrix pin-ups but the way both the idyllic view and the house itself had been smothered with gaudy, musky cotton. Very rarely Sophie had been admitted to one of the older girls' rooms at Wakefield House and had struggled to affect nonchalance at their blatant flouting of house rules against alcohol and cigarettes, but they had never felt like this, so compellingly sticky with genuine sin.

30

Lucas opened the walk-in wardrobe and held things out for Sophie to see – white zip-up boots, a floppy black hat, a long ash-blonde wig, a cigarette-rolling device, a green all-in-one swimming costume with impressively stiffened cups – in such a way that it was unclear whether he asked her to join him in admiration or disgust. Perhaps it was enough for her merely to bear silent witness for before long he folded away the last relic and led her back to the landing.

'Do you like school, then?' he asked, lingering at the top of the stairs.

'Can you keep a secret?'

He nodded.

'I love it.' She laughed.

'I'll sit behind you in div,' he said, 'and you can pass me back the answers.'

'Don't be stupid,' she said. 'You're far brainier. You've been in that div for a term already.'

Their conversation retreated to a safer, more mundane level.

She had fantasized about them kissing – nothing wilder than that – but felt far more rewarded by his showing her the secrets of the house. She liked the way he let her out like a grown-up, without involving his mother again.

'In term-time,' he said, 'this place is off-limits but maybe they'd let me ask you back for lunch one Sunday.'

'Yeah,' she said. 'Maybe. That would be nice.'

That evening, after supper, Wilf came to sit in her room while she packed. There was a sudden sense that she had not spoken to him enough during the holidays and had missed her chance, which was strange since he was a boy of few words. And yet the bond between them ran very deep without ever having been discussed.

'You've got more stuff than when you arrived,' he said, tugging off his desert boots with a thump so he could pull his feet up on to her bed. 'I'll never forget that. You only had that big blue book and your bear and you had to have them with you all the time or you cried. You didn't speak to anyone for a week. Then that picture showed up.'

If prompted, he would rehearse the whole familiar story, how he had looked after her, how he had been the first one she spoke to, introducing him to the bear and the picture, offering to read from the book. She gave him no encouragement. Surprised by a wave of homesickness, the last thing she needed was nostalgia.

She glanced up at the bear dismissively. She had discovered too late that it was unnatural of her not to have named him; he was called simply Bear. She had outgrown him but could no more have given him up than thrown away the battered blue book Wilf had mentioned, a copy of *Our Island Story*. They remained on the top shelf of the rickety bookcase Wilf had found her in a skip. Like the Puffin editions of Cynthia Hartnett and Rosemary Sutcliff stacked beside them, she could not imagine reaching for them again now she was a teenager yet did not feel ready to throw them out or give them away. Reading *The Lion, the Witch and the Wardrobe* as a small girl she had suffered nightmares, not about the death of Aslan or the silky temptations of the White Witch, but at the thought of passing through a wardrobe into an enchanted world then being unable to find the route back to her bed. These childhood remnants were a means of groping back to innocent normality, perhaps, fixed there should she ever need them.

'Seems like we've hardly seen you,' Wilf added because she had fallen quiet.

'I know,' she sighed. 'Sorry. It's this fucking Greek.' She always swore when she was alone with him. She feared going to Tatham's would change her speech, iron out her accent. The least she could do was continue to swear. It was one of the things she and Wilf had always done together, one of the things he had taught her, along with riding a bike, sitting around and appreciating the finer points of *The Trigan Empire* and Marvel comics.

She stopped packing and flopped on the bed beside him, tossing her Greek grammar onto the bedspread. 'I've got two more terms to catch up or they'll make me switch to German!'

Wilf flicked through the book, frowning at the alien alphabet.

'Why can't you use English letters?' he asked.

'God knows. It's not as though there are any extra sounds. Here. Look. That's how you write Sophie. She pointed to where she had practised at the back of the book. 'It's Greek for "wise".'

He laughed, a little sadly, so she showed him how to write Wilf, or rather 'Ouilph' but his mind wasn't in it and he was disappointed that it meant nothing.

'I met that boy with the Jew's Canoe and the turntable today,' she said. 'And his mum.'

'Yeah?'

'Yeah. We're in the same div, I mean class, this term.'

'What's he like?'

'Okay. A bit posh. He's called Lucas.'

'Like the headlamps.'

'Yeah.'

Their laughter was interrupted by an outburst. A new girl, Elaine, had arrived only days after Christmas and was having trouble fitting in. Nobody liked her yet and there was a tacit agreement to drive her out. She had a record of running away. Wilf had found out about her already in one of his raids on the office filing cabinet.

'Elaine the Pain,' he said.

'She fancies you.'

'She does not.'

'She does. She watches you when you're not looking and whenever you say something, she does this with her hair.' Sophie mimicked Elaine's way of twisting her hair round a forefinger while staring through her fringe.

'Well I don't fancy her,' Wilf insisted. 'She's got junkie arms.'

'How'd you mean?'

'Too thin and all bruisey and veiny.'

'What are skellies and cutters, Wilf?'

'Search me.'

'So who *do* you fancy?'

'No one.' He gave her a shove.

'No, come on. Who'd you fancy at school? You must have someone by now.'

He smirked. 'Safety in numbers.'

'So have you . . . ?'

'What?'

'You know. Kissed anyone?'

'Course. Look.'

He tugged down the Christmas polo neck Margaret and Kieran had given him to reveal a livid purple love bite.

'That doesn't count,' she said, hot with envy. 'Who gave you that, anyway? I bet it was only Jo Cross. She gives those to anyone who buys her a Caramac.'

'It was Jane Bursley,' he muttered. 'At the party the other night.'

'But she's a fucking slag.'

'I know,' he admitted. 'She . . . No. I shouldn't.'

'What?'

'No . . . Well . . .'

'What, Wilf?'

He was obviously bursting to tell. He seemed to have grown while Sophie was away. His lanky frame was filling out and she saw black hair on his leg where his jeans were too short. He was wearing Brut, too. He never used to wear anything like that.

'You won't tell anyone?' he asked, frowning.

'Who am I going to tell? I don't know anyone who knows Jane fucking Bursley apart from you.'

He picked at the bedspread with stubby fingers. 'She can pick up a wine cork off the pavement without her hands . . . using just her . . . you know.'

Sophie pictured Jane Bursley, whom she remembered from St Bonnie's as a bully and a loudmouth, crouched on the pavement outside Timothy Whites in an admiring circle. 'No she can't!'

'She can.'

'Have you seen her?'

'No, but . . .'

'Wilf, trust me. I'm a girl. It's not physically possible.'

'Oh.'

He seemed crestfallen and Sophie suffered a moment of uncertainty. For a girl she was, after all, completely inexperienced. But she had felt a momentary imperative to defend all girls against such a grotesque misunderstanding.

'So does she fancy you?' she asked.

'I reckon.' He grinned.

'But she's a slag.'

'So?' He lay back against the wall with his hands behind his head. 'She's a good kisser. She's had practice.'

'Are you seeing her again?'

'Doubt it.'

She prodded him with her Greek grammar so that he wriggled.

'Maybe,' he admitted.

'So were you standing up or lying down?'

'Sort of half-sitting. We were on the stairs.'

'Tongues and everything?'

He just smiled a big, fat, slag-snogging smile.

'Was it good?'

'It was all right.'

'Show me.'

'How?' He stopped smiling.

'Show me how she kissed.'

'Soph! I can't!'

'Why not? It's just a lesson.'

'But it's you.' He sat up, perturbed now.

'Exactly. You don't want me to make a fool of myself when my turn comes.'

'But you're only a kid.'

'I'm fourteen in a couple of weeks.'

'Shit. You are too. Why haven't you got tits yet?'

'Shut up,' she said.

'Fourteen,' he said, marvelling.

'Come on,' she told him, shutting her eyes. 'We can both shut our eyes and you can pretend I'm not me. Please, Wilf. It can be my birthday present.'

'Well, okay.'

She was used to his body. They'd played Batman and Robin and The Tomorrow People and Trigan Empire plenty of times. They'd seen each other in swimming gear times without number. So just sitting on her bed, fully clothed, and kissing with their eyes shut need not have felt so odd.

But Wilf had grown. And after the first tentative mouths-shut-no-tongues kiss he felt the need to hold her and suddenly

36

he seemed really big, more like a man. His tongue slipped in and seemed to fill her mouth. She could taste shepherd's pie and the bitterness of his last illicit cigarette. She tried to imagine it was Lucas pressing into her and making the bed squeak but sensed he would taste and feel entirely different.

She dared to push her tongue into Wilf's mouth in turn and was startled to feel him gently sucking on it. She opened her eyes and found he had kept his obediently shut. She had never noticed how long his lashes were before. She pulled back slightly, not because she was ready for him to stop – she was curious for him to continue – but in order to take a breath, without snorting through her slightly blocked-up nose. Wilf responded as though Margaret and Kieran had just walked in. He rolled off her, red in the face, swore, apologized and stumbled from the room.

She probably should have followed him, if only to give him the chance to rebuff her. But his kiss was having after-effects; her face and ears felt hot and tight and when she rose to follow him after all, she saw herself in the mirror over her sink and froze, amazed. They had not kissed for long but something – his stubble, his spit or the one acting on the other – had left the skin around her mouth looking so sore and pink that her lips had lost their neat line of definition.

She finished the last of her packing then dropped back on her bed to reread her notes on that morning's chapter on the Greek middle voice. *Reciprocal use,* sprang off the page at her, *Where middle voice used in the plural implies a reciprocal reflexive pronoun as in they embrace one another – aspazontai – or they talk with one another – dialegontai.* She said the Greek words aloud, slowly, enjoying the exotic sensation of them in her mouth. Even a shopping list in this language sounded like words of binding enchantment. As she studied on, the fingers of the hand not holding the book brushed the tender skin about her lips.

Wilf was the only one not to put in an appearance at break-fast so she knocked on his door before she left the house. There was a big Alice Cooper poster on the door with 'Wilf' written on Alice's forehead in magic marker. He had tried to do it in Gothic script.

'Wilf?'

He grunted in reply, as though half-asleep, but she had heard a soft scuffle after she spoke so knew he was pretending. It was a house rule never to open a bedroom door unless invited so she waited.

'I'm off to school now, actually,' she told him, feeling self-conscious as Elaine the Pain and some of the others were passing on the stairs.

'Actually,' Elaine echoed.

'Okay,' he grunted. Sophie stood on until he added, 'See you, then,' dismissing her.

LENT TERM
(thirteen years, eleven months)

Returning to life in Tatham's was a shock after a Christmas at home because, for Sophie at least, it was so constrainedly feminine. At Wakefield House everyone had their own room but there was no differentiation between genders. To Margaret and Kieran they were all simply *the kids*. Margaret would occasionally take a girl aside for a confidential moment or Kieran might drive some boys somewhere to watch football but most of the time the inmates were a pack, singled out by character traits, not as boy or girl.

Sophie had never been close to any of the girls in the home. This was probably Wilf's fault. She began by trailing around after him then became his best mate, the exception to his belief that cruel early experiences left most girls in the place too damaged to be anything but dangerous liabilities. Independent in most of her thinking, Sophie had absorbed this attitude unconsciously. Certainly some of the older girls there had been terrifyingly unpredictable at times, some of the younger ones too unapproachably miserable or uptight, but Sophie might have befriended some of the saner ones among them had Wilf not got to her first. As it was, she could not remember ever being interested in the things girls were meant to like. Dolls were spooky, The Bay City Rollers and Donny Osmond grotesque, and she had never seen the point in mastering the thin, breathless art of skipping. She was not a tomboy. She had no objection to dresses and had once grown her hair halfway down her back. She took a watchful interest in her appearance and resented her failure thus far to sprout breasts. But given a contest between watching Wilf dismantle his bike or going out with the girls to play with testers in Boots and raid the Pick'n'Mix counter in Woolies, Wilf had always won the day. If she preferred to read in silence, Wilf never treated it as a personal betrayal. Theirs was a basic loyalty whereas friendship between girls seemed always subject to analysis, qualification and revision, to an extent disproportionate to the emotional rewards rendered.

The others in the home teased them often enough for being like a married couple but they had always been able to laugh it off, secure in the knowledge that they were more like siblings. Had she ruined all that? From the moment she was back on the Daughters' Staircase Sophie felt she had been pushed across an invisible line into the female camp and could think of no reason but the kiss.

Returning girls, even Kimiko Matsubara, swapped stories of their Christmases and flashed photographs and all the talk was of holiday romance – older brothers' gorgeous friends, glamorous male cousins, actors drooled over during Christmas trips to the RSC – and Sophie found herself implicated in it.

'What about you, Cullen?' a normally sullen older girl asked, who had just slapped up a poster of Ian McKellen as Richard II over her bed. 'Anything to report?'

Sophie was so stung by the dismissive way the girl flicked her eyes over Sophie's continuing lack of chest that she muttered something about having had a festive snog. Of course she was then expected to tell all so she gave them a mildly upgraded version. Wilf became William, a boy she'd known from childhood, suddenly lust-husky and tongue-tied. Yes they'd kissed, and on a bed, but she had called a halt when he wanted to go further. (Was that a lie, she wondered as she said it.) When asked if he'd be writing to her she scoffed that he could barely spell, truthfully enough though the admission gave her a pang of guilt. When they asked if she had his picture she shrugged and said she knew what he looked like.

For some reason her offhand treatment of a barely literate stud won her far more maturity points than mere breasts would have done and the hierarchy in the Daughters' Chamber subtly shifted to accommodate her. Purvis and Weatherall, two middle-school girls who had never acknowledged her, began to involve her in their more public conversations and Kimiko, who had mustered no more than a new, shorter hairstyle for the show-and-tell session, humbly assigned herself to a wanly studious first-year from Aberdovey whom they had spent their first term ignoring.

Upstairs, room was mysteriously found for her to sleep in an older dormitory. Climbing the steps to Hall for dinner on the first evening back, Weatherall and another middle-school Daughter Sophie didn't know engaged her in conversation long enough to imply they invited her to sit at their subtly bad-girl section of the Daughters' table, midway between the seniors and where Nurse presided over the youngest.

But all this fresh acceptance only served to make Sophie feel more constrained by femininity. In Chapel, the Daughters sat in their own pews in a sort of Lady Chapel, like so many worshipping villagers screened off in a monastery church. She had keenly looked forward to her new div because Lucas would be there and Kimiko wouldn't, but she had to sit in the front row with Purvis and Weatherall, both of them hothoused through the scholarship exam but flagging now that they had to study under their own steam. No boys sat in the front row with them but social freaks. Boys were actually placed there as a punishment for inattention. And Lucas sat two rows back, out of her view, and gave her only a muffled, oh hello sort of greeting on the first day, as though they had barely met.

She looked about her at Scholars doing their Wilfish boy things, kicking footballs, flicking bread pellets, ignoring girls and seethed in impotence. She was prepared to understand Lucas's standoffishness; whatever his good intentions, befriending her in the holidays did not automatically entail being her friend at school. Different rules applied in term-time, overpowering personal preference. For all he knew, she might turn out to be div freak. What she could not understand was the hypocrisy of the other Daughters. To hear them talk amongst themselves was to suppose them boy-mad, barely intellectual. And yet in classes they were all studious conformity and, far from being grateful, appeared to react to any social approach by a male classmate with disdain. Perhaps it was a matter of age and only boys two or so years older, or even men, were worthy of interest? Or was it rather that the Daughters prized themselves so highly, or so lowly, that they could not conceive of a male friendship uncoloured by romance?

Things changed in the sixth-form, apparently. The thirty or so girls admitted to the sixth-form without scholarship had their own common room, wore their own approximation of the boys' relaxed uniform and went about with what seemed to Sophie a daunting social aplomb. They were there because their parents paid handsomely. They went home every evening after lessons, not staying on for prep like Lucas, and rarely had the peaky, unpampered look of the sixth-form Daughters. They had first been admitted in 1970, in a two-pronged mission to raise money and stamp out vice, and had been causing trouble ever since, breaking boys' and teachers' hearts and winning prizes that had previously been the preserve of boys. Sophie had small hope of befriending one when her turn came. Meanwhile she had two years of respectable isolation to endure.

At lunch on the second day of term, however, liberation was granted her. Jonty Mortimer was a kind of god, being Senior Scholar and thus Senior Prefect. A keen footballer, son of a union activist, his retention of his Lancastrian accent in a school where the Iranians, Nigerians and Russians all swiftly acquired the school's drawling version of received pronunciation implied a moral vigour his fellows lacked. All this, his Byronic head of hair, the rumour that he had sired a child off one of the kitchen staff and the extreme rareness of his smiles meant that the Daughters' table fell silent as he approached. Even Nurse paused in doling out Queen of Puddings.

'Cullen?'

It was not the fashion among the boys to use Miss as the dons did. Sophie had so not expected to be addressed by anyone so important that she had just taken a large mouthful of pudding which was too hot to swallow in a hurry so she merely raised a guilty hand to shoulder-height as everyone at the table turned to look at her.

'Christ, you're a bit small, Cullen! What do you weigh?'

She told him, sitting up straighter.

He shrugged. 'Well, rules are rules so you'll have to do. But do try to grow. You're the new bell-ringer replacing Jansen.'

'But I don't know how,' she said, bewildered.

'Which is why you're meeting me at Cloister Gate at two.'

'I've got netball.'

'Damn. Who else has got netball?'

A flurry of hands answered him.

'She can't do netball,' he told them and strode away back to top table.

Sophie was rounded on at once by her new friends, who were suddenly less friendly.

'You're so lucky,' Purvis sneered.

'But I don't want to ring bells,' she assured them.

'You'd rather play netball?' Even Kimiko was faintly hostile in her envy.

'Well, no. I'd rather stay indoors and, I dunno, read.'

'Being a bell-ringer,' Weatherall explained, 'is like winning the Pools.'

Chapel had a ring of eight bells. Each bell was assigned to a Scholar (or Daughter) for the duration of their career in the school. There was neither choice nor volunteering in the matter. In homage to the patterns beloved of change-ringers, each new ringer was selected on a purely mathematical basis according to his or her exam rating in their year's intake. There were always twenty new Scholars chosen each year, including Daughters. Their twenty positions were taken to correspond to the notes of a chromatic scale ascending from middle C. Each bell-ringer was someone who simply happened to score marks that put them in a position corresponding to the next note in the school song. When four bell-ringers left, the four new scholars corresponding to the next four notes of the song were assigned their bells. Because few of the Scholars were musical as well as clever, the Bell Captain had long since been issued with a reduction of the song to its numerical equivalents. The Nurse before the Nurse before last had worked this up into an arcane sampler which hung in the ringing-chamber beside the long roster of bell-ringers past.

Quite apart from the time it bought her, quite honourably unchaperoned in the company of boys, being a female ringer was prized as access to a kind of licensed Hellfire Club. Thanks to their required presence in a chamber beside but not quite *in* Chapel, a tradition of free thought and religious unorthodoxy clung to the Captain and his band. They were exempt from attending the church services they announced, from serving in the school army corps, from playing for any Schola team against their will. Bell-ringers traditionally went on to study classics, maths or philosophy.

Sophie was so nervous that she wolfed down her pudding and hurried through the Slipe, the passage that led under Hall to the cloisters and the rest of the school. She was at the gate to the cloisters ten minutes early for fear of keeping Jonty Mortimer waiting but he was there ahead of her. As he nodded his greeting and led her through the cloisters to the foot of the bell tower, she caught a whiff of cigarettes off his velvet-edged gown.

'Go on up,' he told her. 'I'll bring the others when they come.'

Of course there were others. Jansen would have been only

one of several Scholars leaving last term after sitting Oxbridge. Relieved, but also obscurely disappointed at not being as singled out as she had thought she was, Sophie made her way up the spiral stairs.

Pools of wintry light were shed by narrow, cobwebbed windows. The soft stone of the narrow steps had been so worn that she had to tread on their outer edges to avoid slipping, clinging to the grimy rope looped through hooks in the wall which served as a rail. The stone around each window slit was as thickly carved as the cloister pillars with initials and dates going back to the fourteenth century. The later, nineteenth- and twentieth-century carvings tended to be slapdash and shallow, as though executed in a hurry with only penknives or compass points but some of the really old ones were expert and seemed to have been chiselled with professional tools. Possibly some of the early Scholars had been masons' sons.

The stairs wound on and up until Sophie began to fantasize that they had no end and that she might turn around and run down and down to find they had lost their beginning. At last she arrived at a point where an iron gate blocked the steps. She tried the gate but it was locked. There was a low wooden door in the wall a few steps further down. She went back and tried that. It gave onto a short walkway, open to the sky but enclosed by a head-high parapet on one side and, dizzyingly, by one of Chapel's stained glass windows on the other. Walking gingerly because the duckboards were wet and slimy, she reached the door on the other side and let herself into the ringing-chamber.

After the stairs, this was dazzlingly bright, lit by great windows in front and to her left. The wall to her right gave onto the perilously steep Chapel gallery where Sophie felt compelled to sit at once, assailed by vertigo and the strange scents of Chapel; candle wax, old hymn books and the leather of several hundred kneelers.

Unless one counted the annual Mayor's Carol Concert in the Guildhall, life at Wakefield House was innocent of religion and Sophie found all church interiors oppressive and rather frightening as a result. Worrying though the fat, stripey bell ropes might be – she had recently read *The Nine Tailors* so knew how bells might kill a man – she had not relished her first term's experience of Chapel and would be glad to be spared it. There were baffling, oddly hearty sermons, often by members of staff rather than the Chaplain. The choir music was all right but she hated both the miserable and triumphant hymns and hated still more the inexplicable attempts to encourage more congregational singing by the regular inclusion of mass renditions of, alternately, the 'Libera Me' from Fauré's *Requiem*, Gounod's 'Ave Maria' (which came across like a rugby song) and the 'Chorus of the Hebrew Slaves' from *Nabucco*.

Jonty Mortimer arrived with two other first-year Scholars, whom he didn't think to introduce, and set about a lightning first lesson in bell-ringing. His instruction was lent an extra edge by his pointing out that they would be tested on their knowledge this time next week and be given an hour's detention if they failed to score a hundred per cent on the theoretical side at least. They were each assigned a bell – Sophie was number one, the highest and smallest – and a sort of raised hassock to stand on when ringing. The striped ends of each rope, he explained, were called sallies. Each bell was attached to a sort of bar called a headstock which could pivot through three hundred and sixty degrees on a stoutly fixed frame. During a ringing session, the resting position of a bell was upside-down, where it was said to be rung up. So their first task was to ring the bells up. Then, when the sally was pulled, the bell would swing down and up again, taking most of the rope up through the cast-iron guides and through the ringing-chamber ceiling. One then tugged the rope again to bring the bell back to its starting point. At the end of a session all bells had to be rung down again to make them safe to leave.

'So it goes "ding" once in each direction?' one of the boys asked, earning Sophie's immediate gratitude. She was as nervous as if they were about to start a race. Mortimer gave him a withering glance.

'Very good, Bunsen. *A ding in each direction.* Any other questions?'

'Is it . . . ?' Sophie began.

'Hmm?' Mortimer asked.

'Is it dangerous?'

'Of course. Potentially. The rope moves fast and hard but you let it play through your hands when you're not pulling on it – so no rope burn or getting lifted off the ground – and obviously you wouldn't go winding it round your ankle or neck. So. A first go each at ringing up then we'll try some basic calls. Bunsen, you first. You're going to set it rocking then pull it down and let it rise up on the other side. Ideally just one ding on its way up then it rests there. Like this.' He rang the tenor bell up. One tidy ding. 'Okay? Off you go.'

Bunsen pulled manfully and his bell rang out overhead several times.

'No need to pull so hard,' Mortimer told him. 'You see? Gravity and momentum will do the work for you.' He rang his down, paused then rang it up again. 'All you do is set it in motion. Clitheroe, show us what you're made of. Pretty good. Now you, er . . .'

'Rix, Mortimer.'

'Rix. Good. Off you go.'

Sophie's turn seemed to come and go in seconds. She pulled and the rope flew up through her fingers as the treble bell rang out. She laughed with surprise to realize she had succeeded in ringing it up first time, which made the others smile and she saw that this was to be her role in this group. Jonty Mortimer made them all ring down then up again then had them ring properly, more quickly this time, in an ascending phrase from his tenor to Sophie's treble. Then he pointed out the number embroidered on the front of each hassock and, by calling out the numbers in sequence, four at a time, he had them ringing a Westminster chime like the clock in Margaret and Kieran's rooms; 1326, 6213, 1236, 6213.

Sophie had never learnt to read music, having done no more than tap the odd chime bar or tambourine at St Bonnie's. She knew what written music looked like and instinctively shied away from it. This music by numbers suited her, though, especially since, as Mortimer pointed out, they would be assigned to the same bell number until they left the school or were expelled. He handed out four sheets of ten simple call changes. They were to circle their bell number whenever it appeared then memorize the sequences, paying special attention to how their bell fitted into them.

'Obviously you can't practise on your own or you'd make a fucking awful din, so you'll have to learn on the job from now on or when we practise on Friday nights. We ring every Saturday night from eight forty-five to nine, for quarter of an hour before and after every Sunday morning service and for ten minutes before every congregational service on Wednesday mornings. Always get here a few minutes early. Get here late or don't get here and it's a detention for you. So. See you all up here tomorrow night. Well done. And Bunsen, take a tub. You smell like an otter.'

Bunsen, Clitheroe and Rix ran off across the duckboards and down the stairs, shouting as they tried to trip one another. Mortimer held the ringing-chamber door open for Sophie then shut it behind them. She slipped slightly on the damp wood and proceeded more slowly.

'Do me a favour,' he said and steered her firmly towards the parapet and away from the stained glass. 'I fell here once and went flat against that window.'

'What happened?'

'The whole thing bowed inward slightly – see there?' He pointed to where Saint Catherine's wheel had become concave. 'It held but I've never been so scared in my life. I don't think it would hold a second time either. You settled in?'

'Yes,' Sophie said, nodding.

'Enjoying it all?'

She nodded again.

'Liar,' he said and laughed. 'You're from the children's home, aren't you?'

Her surprise must have showed.

'Don't worry,' he said. 'I won't tell. People here can be bastards and Scholars are the worst because they tend to be chippier. If no one's twigged yet, there's no reason they ever should.'

'But how did you –?'

'Spot of burglary on Micheldever's study to read all your admission notes before deciding who to appoint.'

'But I thought it was all done on mathematical principles.'

'And people thought the Delphic Oracle was the voice of Apollo. Useful myth. If I'm going to be stuck up here with freaks, at least they can be interesting.'

'What about Bunsen?'

'Every group needs a hate object.' He had taken hold of a
chain on his waistcoat as they spoke and she assumed the chain
held a watch as a piece of dandyism to match his velvet-edged
gown but it drew out an old key from his pocket with which
he unlocked the iron door that barred the upper reaches of the
spiral stairs. He creaked the door open and stepped through.
'Want to look?' he asked. 'I won't ask you again.'

She followed in his wake, catching again the waft of his cigarettes and a citrus trace of some aftershave.

'Senior Prefect's perk,' he explained as the steps opened out
into a tiny room. There were two arrow-slit windows, each sill
crusted with dead flies and the ash of joss sticks embedded in
lumps of Blu-Tack, and a low door which he unbolted and
flung open. She saw with a shock that it gave directly onto the
leaded slopes of Chapel roof. 'You can walk all over it,' he
said. 'Fucking brilliant when it's not raining, like now.' He
tugged it closed again, grimacing against the drizzle that had
started since lunch.

She took in the rest of the room. There was a venerable
armchair, which could only have been lugged up with difficulty,
a campaign stool and a card table which served as a desk. He
had a luxurious bar fire, around whose grille someone had twined
paperclips for holding toast in place. There were two posters, a
topless woman in hot pants and stripey socks, paper breasts puck-
ered from damp in the masonry, and a Greek temple on a sea-
washed cliff. 'Sounion,' he said, following her gaze. He didn't
introduce the woman. 'I watched a sunset there last summer. Get
to be Senior Prefect one day, Cullen, and you could have this.'

'How? There'll always be the others ahead of me.'

'Not if you take classics A levels and do better than any

other Scholars who take them with you. Classicists always take precedence over humanities and both over sciences. You're in the same div as that boy, aren't you?'

'Sorry, Mortimer. Which?'

'Behrman.'

'Lucas Behrman. Yes, I am.'

'Is he a mate of yours?'

'Sort of. We're both local.'

'He's a dayboy?' He asked it as though it were a useful revelation.

'Yes,' she said. 'His dad's a QC and his mum's a shrink.'

'Clever Jews.'

'Yes,' she said, less certainly, thinking of the Mercedes on the turntable. 'Suppose so.' It had not occurred to her until now that of course the Behrmans were Jewish.

'Bring him up to watch next time,' Mortimer said. 'If you like.'

'Oh,' she said. 'I'd better go. Netball,' she added. 'I might still be in time for the second half.'

'You're a bell-ringer now,' he said. 'Sod netball.'

'Okay,' she said. 'I will. Thanks, Mortimer.'

She hurried down the stairs, clutching at the greasy rope, but as she reached the bottom and the usual clutch of fifth-form smokers clustered where the oil tank was squeezed between Chapel and the cloister walls, she slowed to a saunter, savouring her small improvement in status.

The next morning was a Saturday, which meant double physics, with practical, double Latin, with a prose and unseen, then div. Saturday mornings always ended with a div class so that each div could be set the Saturday-night essay known as a task. Sophie's

first div don, who made the class plod through Shaw's *Saint Joan*
and bits of *A Portrait of Europe 300-1300*, was uninspired
compared to her new one. Mr Micheldever, who was also Master
of Schola, effectively Sophie's housemaster, was vivacious and
unpredictable, which was possibly how he had bagged a much
younger wife. He approached his chosen texts – Kafka, Frazer,
Eysenck – not as untouchable classics but in the same ironically
sceptical way one might read a newspaper or in which he preached
his occasional sermons. He skipped large bits of *The Golden
Bough* he said were out of date, encouraged wild interpretations
of what *Metamorphosis* was actually about and warned them he
thought most of Eysenck 'stimulating bunkum'.

Most of the div rooms were on the Victorian polychromatic
Brick Quad. They were painted in extraordinarily nasty colours
made worse by being paired, one up to dado height, the other
above. Last term's had been violet and khaki. Mr Micheldever's
was salmon and olive, the grey sort of olive. Commoners had
to wear straw hats as part of their uniform, with differently
striped silk bands depending on their house. These too tended
to feature ugly colour combinations and she had thought at
first that each div room colour corresponded to a different
house. But no house wore salmon and olive so perhaps some
bursar had merely acquired unpopular colours cheaply then
combined them according to a theory that startling colour pair-
ings would combat drowsiness.

Last term's room had enjoyed a view into a horse chestnut
tree. This one's gave onto a dank, brick-lined passage up which
came regular streams of dons on bicycles and pupils on foot,
the pupils raising their hats in a ripple of courtesy marking the
passage of any don that rode along its length. A few people
were already leaving for lunch although there were twenty

minutes to go. Sophie was on the verge of nausea with hunger. Her vast breakfast seemed hours ago.

'Right,' Mr Micheldever said, abruptly slapping shut his copy of the Eysenck book. 'Tonight's task. Write me something about disgust. However you like. Fiction, psychosocial analysis, historical or anthropological, even a poem would be welcome.'

'How long, sir?'

'Foolish question, Brewer. Time-wasting. At least three sides, as always. Though I'll accept two sides for a poem provided it has metre and rhymes. If you want to write your usual cod-Eliot, Pickering, you can do three sides like everyone else.'

Then he passed around a dead cockroach and a magnifying glass as inspiration while reminiscing about how he got shrapnel wounds in Italy during the war.

Sophie was beginning to realize that it was the div classes, not the excellence in maths or Greek, that made Tatham's special. Div classes broadened horizons, gave essay practice, and averted the tunnel vision that too close a focus on exam syllabuses might have induced. Most importantly div kept the teachers fresh by encouraging them to indulge their own interests and pass them on. Not every French teacher wanted to spend their life teaching nothing but Anouilh and the subjunctive.

As Mr Micheldever began to rhapsodize on the exquisite pain of having shrapnel and gravel tweezered out of his unanaesthetized thighs, there was a tap on her shoulder. Lucas had left his desk to pass her the cockroach and magnifying glass. He smiled.

'Catch you afterwards?' he whispered.

'Sure,' she said.

Everyone in the lower half of the school had to fit in at least seven hours of leisure activity a week, known as ekker. This could be 'changed' – sport – or 'unchanged' – music, art, hobbies – but at least half had to get one sweaty. Lucas hated sport and suffered the torments of the damned trying to make up his three and a half hours. She had spotted him in the school pool on a rare occasion, apparently. Lucas was a good swimmer but not as keen on relentless length-swimming as she was. An anomaly in the rules allowed an hour of the three and a half to be taken up by supporting a school match, provided one did so changed into clothes appropriate for the game. Presumably cheering and stamping to keep warm were deemed exercise of a sort and exposure to the feats of the school's better sportsmen might be thought to prove an inspiration to the sluggardly. Thus the almost pathologically unsporty Lucas would be found on the touchlines of one match a week. His cheering was often ill-timed, such was his ignorance of the rules, but his sports kit was always appropriate, if suspiciously clean.

That afternoon Lucas met up with her to watch the first big Tatham's College Football match of the term. Known as TatCoFo, the game was a peculiarly dangerous hybrid of football and rugger. Two teams played on a narrow pitch, bounded by nine-foot-high nets on its long sides. The goals were the unnetted ends. In addition the long boundaries were marked by thick ropes, winched tightly across metal uprights two feet from either net and four feet off the ground. Whenever the ball – a rugby one – passed beyond these, players piled onto the rope and one another in a wild struggle to resume mastery of it. Legs, arms, wrists and ankles were broken every season. Broken necks had been known. There appeared to be few foul rules. TatCoFo was the school's equivalent of gladiatorial combat, not least since the indefinite suspension of school boxing matches after a public outcry when a boy was killed. Played every Lent term, it was necessarily a licensed civil war since no other school had been tempted to take up the game. Inter-house rivalries were wildly illustrated in graphically insulting fly-posting, chants, even 'corpses' dressed in an opponent's colours and hung from prominent high places.

There was no girls' equivalent but Daughters were expected to turn out to support any Schola match and this afternoon set Schola against Dougal's – Lucas's house. Lent courage by her new, freethinking status as a bell-ringer, Sophie left the Schola supporters to join Lucas on the Dougal's side. They had been unable to talk much after div that morning, made shy by witnesses. Now, though still surrounded, they were given a licence to chat by the cheering and jeering of the crowd.

She asked after his mother and he said something formulaically brutal. He asked about life in Schola and she told him about being made a bell-ringer.

'That's him. There.' She didn't point but indicated Jonty Mortimer with a flick of her head. 'With the mud up the back of his shirt.'

'Oh,' he said as Mortimer seized the ball from a Dougalite and turned to race with it towards the Dougal's goal. 'I knew the face but I hadn't linked it to the name.'

She told him about Mortimer showing her the Senior Prefect's enviable eyrie.

Mortimer lobbed the ball back to a team-mate as he was tackled then disappeared beneath a pile of bodies. The team-mate let the ball go out just in front of where they were standing so they found themselves so close to the ensuing scrum against the rope that gobbets of mud were kicked over them.

'Finally,' Lucas said, looking at his shirt appreciatively. 'This was far too clean. She washes *everything*. I have to hide stuff from her.' He broke off to cheer an attempt at a Dougalite goal.

Some other Dougalites walked past them. They greeted Lucas with an odd mixture of contempt and affection. On the one hand they bothered to greet him but on the other they called him Grobber Yid and put on parodic Jewish accents. He countered with, ''Ello dere, Wog,' and the boys passed on.

'Are they friends of yours?' she asked.

'God, no!'

'Why'd you say that to him?'

'It's what people do. Wog's his name.'

'But he's white.'

'Yes, but he has curly hair and his father lives in Lagos.'

'Oh. And they call you that because you're Jewish?'

'Yes.'

'Don't you mind?'

He shrugged, pretending to watch the match.

'They don't hit me. It could be worse. There's a boy called Spaz who everyone kicks. He's perfectly nice. Not spastic at all. But if you don't kick him, well . . .'

'What?'

'I dunno.' He frowned.

Just then Mortimer came by, following the action from a distance. 'Pass!' he shouted. 'Pass, you moron!' Then he noticed Sophie there, gave a quick smile and a gruff, 'Cullen,' before heading back to the fray.

The Dougalite called Wog mimicked Mortimer's accent loudly, substituting Yorkshire for Lancashire. 'Ey-oop, Jonty,' he shouted. 'Ey-oop.' Other Dougalites laughed.

Sophie kept her eyes on the game but she sensed Lucas was turning to look at her.

'You've got a crush on him,' he said.

'I have not.'

'He's got a crush on you, then.'

'He hasn't. Everyone knows he's seeing Emma Acheson. He took her to the upper sixth dance.' Emma Acheson was the tallest and blondest of the sixth-form Commoner girls and a prefect. Their names were linked like Venus and Mars and the pairing was so obvious a match of seniority, brains and looks that evidence was no more required than it was for gravity. She saw Emma Acheson at the far end of the Schola supporters, standing in a huddle of well-wrapped sixth-form girls. One of them waved a football rattle. 'See? She's over there,' Sophie told him.

'So you're jealous.'

'Are you always like this?'

'Like what?'

'Fuck off,' she said.

That stunned him into silence. She had barely met Heidi but Sophie could tell she never swore. She had shocked him. Good.

For a while they watched the match in silence, dutifully applauding as the teams changed ends at half-time. Then, by way of apology, he began to offer up funny stories and gossip about the other people around the pitch, the don whose children were said to belong to his head of house, the one whose wife lost her eyebrows and fringe by lighting an oven too slowly, the boy who had to cut his hair whenever his father was due to buy him lunch, the one known as Wendy for his Wendy Craig profile and the one unwisely obsessed with Olivia Newton-John. As he chatted on she accepted his implied peace offering and took covert glances at the goose bumps on his mud-spattered legs.

'Your football shirts are a much better colour than ours,' he said suddenly, briefly holding his brown-striped arm alongside her blue-striped one. It was the first physical attention he had paid her.

'So buy one,' she said. 'You could wear it in the holidays.'

'Oh no,' he said, disapproving. 'I couldn't.'

As the match ended with Schola the victors, he tried to persuade her to join Glee Club, the school choral society, which had its first meeting that term at five.

'It's not really my thing,' she said and he seemed to believe her because he lightly changed the subject.

'Well I want to see where you live.'

For a terrible moment she thought he meant Wakefield House and pictured the gawping reactions of Wilf and her housemates, Paula, the new girl who cried at strangers, Nikki, who had fits, Steve, who still wore nappies and wet the bed at eleven. But of course he meant Schola. 'Sure,' she said, wondering who would be there, praying the worst of the gossips would be out shopping or playing games. 'But you'll have to deal with Nurse.'

The stifling presence of Nurse as chaperone was why so few boys bothered to visit the Daughters' Staircase. It was easier to meet Daughters outside, under cover of watching a match, as they had just done, or merely walking. There was no rule against happening to meet someone while walking from A to B then continuing to walk with them from B to C. Another gaping loophole in the rules was that there was no ban on meeting up in one of the school libraries or in any of the numerous class-rooms that were left unlocked because they contained nothing stealable unless you wanted light bulbs or chalk. But no one seemed to take advantage of this. Or perhaps they did. Sophie had no way of knowing because she found the gloomily painted classrooms sinister outside school hours.

Kimiko was the only one in and she was busy writing her long weekly letter to her diplomat father. He required her to write the same letter twice, once in English and once in Japanese, and she made rough drafts first to avoid crossings-out. Nurse was off in her own rooms on the other side of the Hall from the chamber, where Sophie could hear she was watching the races on television. She was tempted to break the rules and leave her in peace but Kimiko took one wide-eyed glance at Lucas, put down her fountain pen and slipped across to summon Nurse with all the air of doing Sophie a favour.

Lucas was introduced and immediately engaged Nurse in amiable conversation. While Sophie was despatched to make tea with toast and red jam – the standard afternoon snack and free, unlike food in the tuck shop – Kimiko returned demurely to her letter-writing. Nothing about Nurse was beneath Lucas's interest. He admired the needlepoint glasses case she was making, the ivory brooch she had on, even the little buckles on her boring brown shoes. He asked her how long she had worked there, how she could bear the lack of privacy and she quizzed him in turn. She was immediately able to place his father because she was an avid reader of courtroom news items and had been following one of his recent cases at the city's county courts which had been reported nationally. For the first time Sophie saw Nurse was a terrific snob, forever frustrated at spending most of her time among girls from undistinguished, unmoneyed families. But his questions were also humanizing Nurse for her, making Nurse a person in a way she had not seemed before.

'What made you take the job here?' she asked her abruptly, surprised at herself.

'I was living with my sister,' Nurse explained. 'Out towards Wumpett. But she got married suddenly and I was left feeling rather *de trop*.'

'So here you are,' Lucas added.

Such was his charm assault upon her, he even persuaded her to give him a little guided tour round all the areas to which boys were not usually admitted, quite as though he had been a prospective parent. Nurse showed him upstairs to the three dormitories and cluster of studies. Sophie's dormitory, the largest, enjoyed a view away from the quad, across the Warden's river-trimmed garden. Sophie indicated her bed, when he asked, and he sat on it, bouncing slightly to make it squeak. Nurse led him back down past the bathrooms to the chamber. She baulked, laughing, when he cheekily asked to see where she lived but did so in a way that implied she might show him on another visit.

Back in the chamber, Kimiko made more tea and toast and Nurse returned to *Grandstand* but left her door ajar, 'Not that I expect any mischief.'

Munching toast in a triumphant way that made him momentarily less attractive, Lucas was fascinated by it all. 'I'd always imagined it would be completely different,' he said. 'With elegant, ladylike furniture and a piano – like something out of *Mansfield Park*. It's the mythology, I suppose, and having Nurse and that rose garden.'

The only difference between Sophie's accommodation and the boys' was in the more civilized washing facilities. Boys' quarters had communal washrooms known as tubs on account of the tin baths which one filled at a shower or taps then upended onto the tiled floor when one had finished bathing.

The chamber was marginally tidier than the big one he knew at Dougal's and certainly less anarchic. There were no dustbin fires or bad milk bombs. But Daughters had identical burrows, the curtained-off wooden cubicles where they did their home-work, known as burrowing-down, and stored their private possessions. As in Dougal's, each burrow had a light fitting which most extended with a cluster of wires and adapters, once the fire officer had made his termly inspection, to run cassette players and tiny, in-cup water heaters.

A group of older Daughters came back, loud and filthy from hockey practice and, whether sensing Sophie's discomfort or feeling shy himself at their teasing comments on his apparently unchaperoned presence, Lucas began to leave. He winked at Sophie before knocking on Nurse's open door.

'I'm off now, Nurse,' he told her. 'Thank you for the tour.'

'My pleasure, Master Behrman,' she cooed, lurching out of her armchair to turn down the volume on the television.

'I've been trying to persuade Sophie to come and sing in Glee Club,' he told her.

'What are they doing this term?'

'*Messiah*.'

Nurse had let it be known that she used to sing principal roles with the city's opera society and so found mere choral singing a crude, herdish experience. 'Far harder to sing well than people allow,' she said, confirming Sophie in her resistance.

'I've got to work, anyway,' Sophie muttered.

'Coward.' Lucas grinned, admitting defeat.

'Are you going to cheer her on tonight?'

'Oh no,' Sophie began. 'You really don't have –'

'Why? What's happening?' he asked Nurse.

'Someone's bell-ringing debut. You could go up to the gallery.'

'Is it allowed?' he asked. 'I thought only Scholars went up there.'

'Evening service,' Nurse said. 'Only a quarter full. No one's going to mind. Oh. Sorry. I've got quite a bit riding on this one.' She hurried back to turn up the volume on a race.

'Would you mind?' he asked Sophie as she walked him back out to the quad. It was nearly dark already. A shifting flock of starlings passed overhead like strange, swift smoke. 'It won't embarrass you?'

'Course not,' she said. 'But it's just bells.'

She leaned in the shadow of a buttress, discreetly watching until he had passed through the pool of yellowish light from the light over the entrance to the Slipe and been swallowed up by the dark passageway. Then she returned inside to brave the inevitable quizzing from the other Daughters.

She was studiedly cool. 'It's no big deal,' she said, taking out her task book to make a start on Disgust. 'I know his parents.'

Kimiko looked up from the last Japanese page of her letter, eyes momentarily wide in shock, but her gratitude for Sophie's occasional companionship still outweighed any sense that she was being superseded and she said nothing.

He came. It was five to nine so they were already ringing when he let himself in. Sophie's ringing spot, on number one bell, meant that her back was to the door. She heard the soft clunk of the catch lifting, felt the draught, and caught Jonty Mortimer's raised eyebrows and quick nod of acknowledgement before Lucas passed into her field of vision as he slipped around the edge of the ringing-chamber and sat on a pew just inside the gallery to watch.

Sophie was glad he had come late. For all Nurse had implied

that it was usual, none of the other new ringers had friends to support them. She would have felt awkward if he had been there before they started but now she was concentrating too hard on translating Jonty Mortimer's muttered changes into action and sequence to feel anything much.

She had made no allowances for the realities of bell-ringing in conjunction with a church service. The organ pipes were only yards away, albeit on the other side of a thick stone arch, and even the fairly soft improvisation with which the organ Scholar ushered in the congregation was loud enough to make the bells sound far more distant than they had during their induction session on Friday afternoon. And it wasn't just the organ music. Other, closer sounds overlaid the simple peal they were trying to ring: Jonty Mortimer's quiet instructions, the soft sound of each bell's sally forming a temporary mound on the floor before flying up again, the ominous creaking of floorboards under Rix's and Clitheroe's hassocks. A bell's ring sounded moments after its rope and wheel were set in motion so Sophie soon understood that listening to the rings was off-putting as it tempted her to pull too late when her turn in a sequence arrived. With the organ increasingly muffling the sounds coming down as the improvisation grew in confidence, she found she was taking her cues from her eyes not her ears. Their scant ten minutes of ringing felt more like half an hour.

The evening service was very short, an embellished compline. A psalm, a plainsong *nunc dimittis*, a reading, some prayers and a hymn barely filled forty minutes. The atmosphere was quite different from the crowded morning services Sophie had been obliged to attend last term, partly because people were there because they chose to be and could sit where they pleased in little, prayerful pockets about the building, partly because night transformed the place and made it less sinister than romantic. With the windows blackened, the gaudy martyrs could no longer glare down over their instruments of death and the eye was drawn instead to candlelight and the faces of the living.

The other ringers had all left as the service began, duty done, except for two of the upper-school ones, Crabbe and Weir, who stayed on in the ringing-chamber to continue an interrupted chess game. Sophie had assumed that Lucas would want to leave too, being Jewish, but curiosity held him there, so she slipped into the gallery to watch beside him. They were resolutely spectators, however, remaining seated in silence throughout. She had half-hoped, half-dreaded him singing the hymn but he merely read it during the first verse and spent the next three flicking and reading as though the school hymnal were no more than a book of poetry.

The organ voluntary began so loudly and close at hand that she jumped, which made him laugh. They hurried, giggling, through the ringing-chamber as the choir were filing out of their stalls. She slipped as they crossed the scary duckboards outside the window and he grabbed hold of her to steady her which made them laugh the more.

Mortimer was sitting on the steps to his study as they entered the staircase. Automatically wary, they fell silent but he made no attempt to hide the fact that he had just been enjoying a glass of wine and a cigarette so a reprimand seemed unlikely. 'Not bad,' he told her, 'for a novice.'

'Thanks,' she said. 'It was odd with the organ playing but then it made it easier.'

'It does,' he said, wincing at the taste of the wine. 'Jonty Mortimer,' he said and held out a hand to Lucas, who shook it and said,

'Lucas Behrman.'

'I know,' Mortimer said. He had pulled a disreputable-looking sheepskin coat on for warmth.

'Sophie's told me about your amazing study,' Lucas said. 'Do you sleep up there?'

'Sometimes,' Mortimer said. 'Fucking parky, though. You'll have to come up some time.'

'Thanks,' Lucas told him. ''Night,' and led the way down.

Most of the turret was in pitch darkness so they spooked themselves, clambering and tripping down to the cloisters, clinging to the rope as they went. There was a clang above them as Mortimer shut his gate though no descending footsteps so perhaps he had more work to do on his task. It was hard to imagine someone so cool and confident sweating blood over an essay as Sophie was still doing. Lucas had already written his and was going to post his task book through the Micheldevers' letterbox on his way home.

He dared her to walk round the darkened cloisters with him first and she wondered if he might take the opportunity to kiss her. As they walked, eyes growing accustomed to the dark, she thought of Wilf's kiss and his grinding weight on her and imagined the contrast of kissing Lucas. His lips would be cold, and his fingertips, and he had no stubble yet like Wilf's. She caught a whiff of his *Eau Sauvage*. Would he hold her in his arms or merely cup the back of her head in his hands? They were of a height so perhaps it would be arms. As he spoke, she could feel his breath on her face.

But they didn't kiss. They simply walked as he chattered about this and that, the service, a rumour he had heard about the Chaplain, the scandal that Mortimer was leaving after A levels to go to Durham instead of sitting Oxbridge. He was shivering slightly and sounded excited, almost feverish, but it was probably just the cold.

They left the cloisters and, as she prepared to leave him to head back through the Slipe into Schola, he kissed her quickly on the cheek, careless of the fact that the chess players were passing.

''Night,' he said. 'Do you want to come round tomorrow afternoon for a bit? Escape Nursey?'

'Your mum has to write a letter,' she said.

'Oh. Well how about next weekend? If I get her to write. Could you face a Sunday lunch with Heidi and Simon? Carmel's never there but we could watch TV and stuff.'

'Sure.'

'Okay. See you, then.'

''Night.'

He had put on lip salve earlier. Touching her cheek, she could feel the sticky patch it left.

And so, for a term at least, Sophie enjoyed improved status on two counts, as bell-ringer and as somebody's girlfriend. The fact that Lucas was Jewish, a swot and made physically sick by the prospect of team games was outweighed by the glamour of their daring to be linked in the public mind while still so junior. The social rebellion this might constitute was balanced by his being so diplomatically astute when he visited her in Schola. He continued to charm Nurse, he won over Weatherall and Purvis by bringing cake and his mother's cast-off copies of *Vogue* and *Paris Match* and by dropping these off with suffi-cient casualness for it not to seem as if he expected anything in return, not even that the tributes be acknowledged.

They were cool when they coincided in English lessons and div classes and he continued to sit out of her view. But they met up on most afternoons and he called on her in Schola two or three times a week. Most importantly, he had his mother go through the formal channels to liberate her for lunch at his house every Sunday for the rest of term. This became a kind of ritual between them. As a Jew he was exempt from having to attend Sunday Chapel but he would be waiting for her in the cloisters when she came down from bell-ringing once the service was done. At the non-religious lecture that replaced Chapel every third weekend, they sat together. He would walk her back to Tinker's Hill for a delicious, rather formal Sunday lunch at which she would have to make conversation with his dauntingly clever father whom she liked more and more as she began to appreciate his dry wit and scrupulous lack of personal curiosity. After lunch Heidi and Simon invariably went upstairs for a 'siesta' during which, to Lucas's revulsion, their love-making would often register as a decorous sympathetic squeaking from a floorboard or piece of furniture yards from their bedroom door. The siesta was probably intended as a liberal cue for the young things to get to know each other better but they invariably spent it sitting on Lucas's bed listening to music and talking.

Then they would reconvene for tea and one of the three cakes in Heidi's repertoire – Dutch Apple, Honey Spice or Baked Cheesecake – before Lucas walked her home. In many ways this was her favourite part of the day out. They took their time and circuitous routes. There was a wintry melancholy to late Sunday afternoons, which she relished, and there was talk.

Before meeting Lucas she would have described herself as quiet. She still was quiet around other people. Wilf and she had passed hours in companionable silence, but Lucas had awakened in her a love of chat. The source of talk between them was inexhaustible and seemingly unlimited in scope, from *Henry V* to Sian Phillips as Livia in *I, Claudius* to recurring dreams, birth defects and the social crudity of President Carter's younger children. When Nurse accused them of being like reunited twins separated at birth and separately institutionalized, Sophie found she was more proud than insulted.

Not that they had no quiet times together. The timetable was peppered with quiet periods in which students were expected to study on their own. Most returned to their burrows to brew coffee and listen to music. Sophie and Lucas took to spending the periods in the library, where they worked across a table from one another, *their* table, only occasionally passing notes.

She was inexperienced but not ignorant; she knew this was not a romance. She worried sometimes that this was her fault and that there was something encouraging she was omitting to do. But the next moment she would sense that what there was between them was too delicate to bear scrutiny and that, whatever it was, they both subtly benefited from its being given a romantic gloss by their peers. It was unthreatening and it made people leave them alone. From things Lucas let slip and from glimpses offered her in div of the way some people treated him, she knew this was something he cherished.

By the second to last Sunday of term – the last when exeats were allowed – she found she was thinking of Heidi and Simon as friends, her first adult friends, which in turn made her feel mature. They displayed a nice combination of sympathy and discretion. By the second visit to their house, she had assumed she would be obliged to start answering questions about her family and home but the questions never came. They asked about the books she was reading, the Greek lessons, the Eysenck and what she felt about current affairs but they never probed deeper and, out of a kind of delicacy, withheld from discussing their own families with her, although she knew from Lucas that they each came from large ones.

Lucas was similarly sensitive, so that she cracked one Sunday as they were sitting on his bed, listening to an astonishingly sad Billie Holiday record he had found in his father's collection. She challenged him.

'You never ask about my family,' she said.

'Doesn't interest me,' he replied. 'I'm interested in you but families are a bore. I think it's a basic human right to be treated as your own person on your own account. Don't you?'

'Oh. Yes. I suppose so,' she said and it became a kind of creed between them that they knew when the other despised someone because they would start asking probing questions about their family in the other's hearing.

Heidi wanted it to be a romance more than anyone. In the way she stage-managed brief, just-we-girls moments, in the cakes she baked, in the little compliments she paid, there was an inexplicable sense of crossed fingers and clutched straws. This puzzled Sophie because Lucas might have been sensitive and bookish, a reader rather than a footballer, but he was hardly a pansy. To her outsider's eyes, at least, he was exactly the boy a marriage like Heidi and Simon's would produce.

Simon wasn't handsome – Lucas's looks came entirely from Heidi – but he had a worldly polish and an attractive combination of confidence and attentiveness she had not encountered in a man before. In their quiet conversations he taught her that good looks were not the only way a man could attract. He would never have been so crude as to flirt with her but in a myriad small ways – wrinkling his eyes when he smiled at her, filling her glass before he filled Heidi's, coming out to the front path when she and Lucas left – he stirred a sense of the adult she might become. Given time and felicity.

EASTER HOLIDAYS
(fourteen years, three months)

Her second holiday from Tatham's came as even more of a shock than her first. The atmosphere in Wakefield House had changed as completely as if more than half the inhabitants had been replaced. Wilf had gone off the rails, wrecking his bike, getting drunk, being excluded from school for punching a teacher he accused of being a poof and, as part of this rebellion against his gentle former self, had unearthed a girlfriend, Jackie, whom nobody liked.

Jackie was scrawny, ginger-haired and older than him. She was at least nineteen. She worked in MacFisheries and drove a clapped-out VW Beetle, the distinctive roar of whose engine seemed to cause the household to take a sharp intake of breath whenever it entered the street. She called Wilf Willy. She wore so much of the scent she called Reeve Gorsh that it lingered in a room long after she had left. It lingered on Wilf so that even in her absence he was marked out as hers.

Jackie made the tactical error of treating Margaret and Kieran like borstal warders rather than offering the courtesy due someone's parents. Visitors were not encouraged because there were all the other children to think of and when they had asked Wilf to bring Jackie for a meal she squandered the privilege, spending the visit kissing him and playing with his hair, which had wound everyone up. So he went out with her and stayed out. Margaret and Kieran's powers of veto were limited by law and common sense. There was a house curfew, for the oldest, of ten p.m., which Wilf regularly broke now.

'I can't keep him in against his will or he'll just run away,' Margaret said when Sophie complained. 'And he's too old to punish by saying no TV or no ice cream. He'd just laugh at me.'

Instead the adults were pursuing a policy of stifle-by-encouragement, greeting Jackie's every appearance with cries of welcome and asking so many friendly questions about her when Wilf was around without her that she appeared to have taken up the share of their interest that should rightfully have been his.

Far from being pleased to see Sophie back again, Wilf barely greeted her when he passed her on his way out and it was left to Kieran to introduce her to Jackie. But it wasn't just Wilf who was cool. There was a distinct reserve in Margaret and Kieran's manner towards her, as though they had agreed in advance not to make a fuss of her or single her out in any way for the scant month she was back home. It took a week for her to realize they were upset at her not having spared one Sunday in the term to come home.

It had not occurred to her she would be missed. She was tempted to make up some lie about visits home having to be instigated by letter from the adult involved – which was half the truth – but decided not to insult Margaret's intelligence. Instead she simply apologized and said there had been a lot going on. Margaret was aghast at the thought of appearing manipulative and hugged her and said of course there was and asked her about it. Instinct had warned Sophie off talking about Lucas and his parents so she talked about Greek and bell-ringing and TatCoFo while peeling potatoes for that night's supper. Something of their old, comfortable relations was restored.

With Wilf taken up with the demands of Jackie, and Lucas on holiday in Venice with Heidi and Simon, Sophie consoled herself with the Mary Renault novels Lucas had lent her. She had been too busy with set texts to read them during term. For the next three weeks, as the gardens and parks of the city gave themselves over to spring, she lost herself in the loves and rituals of ancient Crete and Sparta. As he had promised, the novels were well researched enough to spare one shame at their slightly trashy blend of sex and danger.

She had no idea when the Behrmans' trip to Venice would be over and didn't like to turn up uninvited and risk being seen by neighbours – the girl from the wrong side of town peering through the letterbox of their empty house. She had no phone number for them and they were ex-directory. She never needed to ring Lucas during the term because they ran into one another every day and it had not occurred to her to make other arrangements.

She received just one postcard from him, a detail of a painting by someone called Giorgione that showed a bunch of young men from behind as they leaned over a parapet. It said only *Weather is here, wish you were lovely. Too many bells. Making me homesick. L.*

Missing him, hooked by the books he had lent her, she sought consolation in the city library, scouring the fiction shelves for more of the same but found only Henry Treece's equally sexy but less ambivalent *Electra* and a hauntingly violent novel by James Reeves about Hephaestos. However it was Renault's *The Bull from the Sea* that coloured her dreams. By the time she called in at Jago's for the new term's books, she was dreaming about being the one lithe, flat-chested, pre-pubescent girl in a team of beautiful bull-dancers at the court of King Minos.

'*Bleak House, Authority and Challenge, French Idioms for Today, Catiline, Mr Johnson* and *Things Fall Apart*,' announced Miss Jago, ticking off the titles against Sophie's name with one hand as she slid the stack of dog-eared volumes across the counter with the other. 'Whatever do you read for pleasure?'

'Mary Renault,' Sophie told her brightly.

She received a look of unmistakable pity in return, which stayed with her as she carried the loot back to Wakefield House and set her worrying that Lucas had lent her the novels for some purpose she was too dense to pick up.

She began to read *Bleak House* on her last night home. She was swiftly irritated by the dutiful pieties of motherless Esther Summerson and mentally resisted the violent shift from the pre-Christian Mediterranean to smog-bound, Dickensian London. She used Lucas's card as a bookmark. It was the first piece of his writing she had received and the picture seemed a small window onto another world.

CLOISTER TIME
(fourteen years, four months)

In the Tatham's calendar the summer term was called Cloister
Time because, weather allowing, it was the term when dons were
permitted to conduct classes in the open air, and the fourteenth-
century cloisters by Chapel and the School of Voysey memorial
cloisters thrown up in the thirties were the most popular venues
for this. Impromptu classrooms also sprang up on the verandas
of the greater and lesser cricket pavilions, beneath the towering
plane trees across from Brick Quad, in the Warden's Garden and
on the rowing club's landing stage.

This was the time of year when Sophie had first seen and
been smitten by Schola and, after the chill and mud of Lent,
the romance of the place was revived for her. Biology classes
seemed to revert to Nature Study. The jacket and tie rule was
waived for dons and boys, which made everyone look younger

and happier. Whereas in the Winter terms, afternoon school didn't begin until 4.30 to allow daylight time for sport and was conducted largely by artificial light, in Cloister Time afternoon lessons began, rather sleepily, after lunch and were done by four. With the long, light evenings this gave the impression that every day, not just Tuesday and Saturday, was a half-holiday.

Schola lost much of its sternly monastic atmosphere thanks to the custom of lugging chairs and sofas out of chambers to follow the sun around the quad, where swallow dung was added to coffee and other upholstery stains. Being outside, the sofas created spaces where Daughters were free to socialize with Scholars, but many preferred the chaste pleasures of the rose garden. There they lounged in old deck chairs whose baked mildew scent was overlaid with Ambre Solaire as girls tried in vain to revise and tan simultaneously.

Because of the flesh on display, these garden sessions were entirely off-limits to boys, which drove them, Lucas included, to a crazed pitch of fantasy and left Sophie torn. But there were compensations. Sixth-form Daughters shed their hauteur and mystery with the season, drawn down from their studies by nostalgic habit and banana sandwiches. Their presence checked the surliness and cruel tongues of the fifth-formers and it was like being part of a large, dauntingly clever family. Sunshine gave Nurse prickly heat so she sat in the shade in sunglasses and a wide-brimmed hat, offering counsel or correction where required, basking in youthful collusion and her own, hinted-at wealth of worldly experience.

It was repeatedly pointed out to Sophie that this would be her only summer without exams so she should make the most of it but she found herself envying the revisers their shared sense of purpose and apprehension and enjoyed allowing herself to be roped in to test older girls on the long lists of quotations or data they had memorized. The nuggets of Homer, higher maths and art history awakened a kind of covetousness in her. People moaned, because moaning was expected and confidence was as frowned upon as smugness, but the underlying tone was essentially happy and excited.

For a Saturday morning div class, the last of the morning as usual, Mr Micheldever limped out ahead of them to sit in the sweetly scented shade of a lime tree in the Warden's Garden. He set them a relatively easy essay for that weekend's task then had them spend the rest of the class taking it in turns to read *Bleak House* out loud. The book was starting to draw Sophie in and she did not know how long Lucas had been watching her before she noticed. They exchanged half-smiles then she lay back to stare up into the tree's canopy because she wanted to smile properly and wondered if she had ever felt so entirely and simply contented. That was all. It was no more than a moment but within a few hours it was haunting her like a dream image that refused to yield its significance.

Lucas was busy that afternoon, unable to avoid a house athletics meeting and then she had a bell-ringing practice where Mortimer made them play through hundreds of changes until her head was dizzy with the effort of concentrating and her arms ached. Then Lucas had to sing in Glee Club, which she had once again refused to join, so she didn't see him again until that night when, as usual, he sat in the Chapel gallery while they rang before the evening service.

He seemed preoccupied. She sat beside him and twice during the short service found him staring across to the ringing-chamber where the chess players were hunched over yet another game. Unusually for him there was a greasy red spot coming up on his chin and she sensed how bitterly he resented it. He prided himself on his good hygiene, she knew, and seemed to regard spots as a moral shortcoming.

As they walked down the tower afterwards, she had to hurry to keep up with him. She was suddenly stupid with insecurity because nothing had been said about her coming home with him for lunch the next day and she couldn't mention it unless he did. And he didn't. He said nothing until they reached Cloister Gate then, instead of his usual cheek-peck, he gave her an awkward sort of rub on the shoulders and muttered, 'See you tomorrow, then,' and turned away.

Itchen, the porter, had already turned off the few lamps around Schola Field leaving only the dim one that lit the Slipe until morning. The night had clouded over.

'Okay,' she said as Lucas disappeared. ''Night.'

But then she was angry, as she had never been with him before, because suddenly his turning up tonight to watch her ring and his inviting her to Sunday lunch seemed like a tiresome obligation for him, not an honest pleasure. He had avoided her eye as he spoke. And he was right. There was something deadly in the repetition of family lunches. What was it for? Who were they fooling? He had never said he loved her. They had never kissed properly. Not like her and Wilf. She had a glimpse of herself as a wretched, clingy friend, like Kimiko had been with her. Just like Kimiko; a friend whose clinginess was somehow a convenience.

So she hurried after him. She would lie, pretend she hadn't managed to finish that night's task and needed tomorrow to work on it. One lunch cancelled would break the deadly pattern for them both and make it easier to cancel the next. She could send a postcard to Heidi apologizing.

Then she froze. He had abruptly changed direction. His way home lay along the flint-edged path up an avenue towards the art school and sanatorium but instead he had turned left and was skirting the cloisters, following their high wall towards the gateway that led to the concert hall, the rowing club and the Warden's Garden.

Growing accustomed to the darkness now, she tailed him as far as the gateway and the sounds of the river that separated the garden from the Schola buildings. Beside the gateway the river was noisily channelled into a mill race under what had once been the school's combined flour mill and wash house. The building was now the damp accommodation of a junior staff member, a groundsman or lab technician. Lucas had barely passed through the gate when a light came on above the mill house's door and a man emerged to dump a bag of rubbish in a nearby dustbin. Sophie remained stock-still, pressed into the shadowed side of a tree. Lucas must have frozen too for the man noticed nothing. Looking up as a slow rent appeared in the cloud, he lit a cigarette and inhaled with narrow-eyed relish a few times before tossing the rest of the cigarette into the mill race and returning inside.

She waited for the light to turn off but the glare continued for what felt like minutes. Unable to wait, she edged forward into the gateway and looked around her. Ahead, across an elegant bridge, lay the modern concert hall and the footpath that followed the river to the rowing club. To the left lay the dark shapes of the Warden's Garden which she could fill in from memory: scrupulously flat lawn, a lush herbaceous border, trees whose boughs brushed the grass and made sticky chambers behind curtains of leaf. To her left stretched the east wall of the cloisters, then Chapel's Jesse window, then the backs of

Schola buildings that included the Daughters' Staircase and, beyond that, the Warden's Lodgings. The only doors onto the narrow riverbank path on the Schola side were the Warden's own and a small arched entrance into the cloisters that was always bolted from the inside.

There was neither sign nor sound of him. He was in a strange mood, she decided, and perhaps had clambered over the gates beside the concert hall to take a long route back to Tinker's Hill. Or perhaps he had taken the river path and was sitting on one of the wooden bridges in a fit of poetic melancholy.

She stole back through the gateway to the safer darkness and walked briskly around the cloister walls. Schola was rarely quiet before midnight. A sort of peace descended during the hours of burrowing-down but even that was regularly broken by outbursts of hilarity or the sudden shouts or jeers of duty prefects. The moment these study periods ended, music took over, a cacophony, as heard from Flint Quad, of warring record players and tape decks. From nine-thirty, when the first years were meant to head up to bed, a headphone rule was enforced but this merely meant that recognizable music was replaced by the enigmatic, too loud bursts of singing-along from the people listening.

Many of the chambers were adapted cellars or store rooms and had vaulted ceilings that magnified the human voice and threw it out into the night in confusing ways. There was often laughter, rarely kind, and as she passed Cloister Gate on her way back into the quad, the short laugh she heard might have only seemed to come from behind her.

It was nearly ten-thirty. She was breaking several rules being out here and would have to use all her cunning to make it up the stairs to her dormitory undetected; the freedoms accorded bell-ringers stretched only so far. But the laugh was unmistakably Lucas's, dry and rather high and unrelaxed.

She glanced into the Slipe but there was no one there but a small boy of no account bouncing a tennis ball on a racket. As she turned towards the cloisters there was a short burst of 'Bennie and the Jets' from the nearest chamber swiftly drowned out by some indignant swearing then relative silence. Cloud had covered the moon again but the light at the foot of the bell tower staircase was on and reached a small part of the cloisters nearest Cloister Gate, enough for Sophie to get her bearings and follow the rest of her mental plan of them. She had walked around them so often she knew where the old statues were that leaned against one wall and where to step out from the wall to avoid walking into the huddle of empty sarcophagi.

The moon came out again, like a stage effect, and she saw Lucas in the corner farthest from the entrance, just yards from the little door that gave onto the river bank. Lucas had his back to her. He was standing very still, facing out through one of the cloister arches into the little garden around the Chantry in the centre. She had stared for a few seconds before she saw there were arms holding him in place. He was kissing someone, she realized, who was sprawled within the arch, back braced against the stone.

She froze, unable to move until she could see more and understand. Then they broke off to change positions.

He was kissing Jonty Mortimer. Jonty Mortimer was kissing him.

It wasn't the kissing though that drove a piece of steel into her heart. Kissing at their age, even kissing between boys, she imagined, could be unfeelingly experimental. She had demanded Wilf kiss her with the same scientific curiosity with which she had once repeatedly touched the poles of a radio battery to her tongue. But when Lucas reached up a hand and touched Mortimer's cheek with a tenderness that made the older boy take the hand in his and bury his face in its palm, she knew she was spying on love, not sex, and had no business to be there.

As she turned to retrace her steps, one of her soles squeaked on a flagstone and she saw them springing apart. They seemed almost as frightened as she was. She froze again till she was certain they were blinded by the deeper darkness around her. She had started to back away in slow motion when Mortimer said, 'Shit,' very clearly.

Then she heard Lucas tell him, 'It'll be Sophie. It's Cullen.'

'Cullen!' Mortimer hissed. 'Wait! Sophie?' But now she was running.

She didn't turn until she was halfway up the Daughters' Staircase, safely past Nurse's rooms. There she paused on a landing to peer out through a window across the quad. Mortimer was standing in the mouth of the Slipe, beneath its yellowish light, looking straight back at her. His expression was unreadable at such a distance. There was no sign of Lucas, naturally.

As she lay on her bed, mouth sour because she hadn't dared brush her teeth for fear of waking someone, she lived the scene repeatedly, helpless before her mercilessly exact recollection. The thing that set her free to cry at last, to release the tension and let her sleep, wasn't the kissing or the tender touch or the fear of the chase but the small, keen betrayal implicit in hearing Lucas, alone with somebody he loved, call her by her surname.

She wasn't naïve about such matters. Homosexuality was as inevitable in a largely male boarding school as in prison and she heard semi-coded or blatant references to it every day, mostly defensive or mocking. She saw graffiti too. On one of the pews in the gallery someone had scored 'Bailey is Gilks' little man' and someone else, Gilks possibly, had scored out 'Gilks" and carved 'Everybody's'. She had yet to hear it acknowledged by the Daughters but it was impossible to ignore. Inferences and outright accusations pinged over their heads like so many bullets. But the words always seemed playful, or not entirely serious, like the endless crude references the boys made to farts and masturbation.

What she had glimpsed in the cloisters was different: serious, exclusive.

Staring up at the sunlit curtains, tuning out the usual round of complaints about the girl who had talked in her sleep and had to have things thrown at her, Sophie aimed at the sense of betrayal she had felt in the night and fell short. Sunlight had brought with it sense. He had never lied to her. Never, if she was honest with herself, offered her more than friendship. But she *had* been a convenience to him, she perceived, and for that she felt used and angry. She was mortified too at first, until she realized that no one need know unless she blabbed.

She could not avoid Mortimer for long, of course, because bells had to be rung before matins, but she contrived to arrive and leave in a group with Bunsen and the others and found she could meet his eye with equanimity. When she looked, he was the one that looked away and she felt an unfamiliar flicker of power.

Matins finished earlier than usual too so she was also able to give Lucas the slip. In case he tried to find her, she hid in the best way she could imagine, by trailing Kimiko for a change and spending the rest of the morning at the Christian Union meeting.

This was convened every Sunday morning after Chapel by a youngish maths teacher, Dr Liphook. Most weeks there was a guest speaker. Every week there was a discussion group. Coffee and biscuits were served. There was no talk of farts or masturbation or little men. There were about thirty boys and ten girls of all ages and she was surprised to see so many familiar faces. She was welcomed in a nice, polite way that did not draw attention. The guest was a white-haired American man who spoke about continence and the way it enhanced 'the vision thing'. Sophie was baffled until she saw the fierce blushes about the room and realized he was talking about sex.

Over coffee an amazingly clean and vital boy introduced himself as Ali. He was a sixth-former but appeared to have found a way to pass through puberty without a glimmer of unease. He asked her when she had been confirmed and she lied with abandon.

'I was very young,' she told him. 'Too young, probably.'

'And you lapsed,' he supplied.

'Yes,' she said. 'For a bit.'

'Well it's good to have you back,' he said. 'If ever you have any questions about anything, don't bother with the Chaplain, just ask Tony, Dr Liphook. He's amazing.'

'Okay,' she said. 'Thank you. I will,' and she caught Kimiko watching her from across the room and beaming.

Mortimer cornered her after lunch, catching up with her on the stairs coming down from Hall. 'We should talk,' he began. He looked stricken. She wondered if he had slept at all.

'It doesn't matter,' she said.

'It wasn't what you . . .'

'Really,' she said, 'it doesn't matter.'

She found she was smiling quite kindly at him. There were shadows under his eyes, bristles on his chin and his hair needed a wash. He was the image of sinful humanity.

'You won't . . . ?'

'I won't tell,' she said.

'But you must let me –' he began

'What?' A few people came past, two steps at a time. Sunday lunches were quiet affairs when the usual hierarchy sagged because most people were out with parents or friends and those left behind were seated at random on two or three tables. 'What?' she asked when they were alone again.

'What do you need?' he asked.

She saw that, despite her promised discretion, he needed to be able to do something for her so as to pay off a debt of gratitude and let his seniority and the usual order reassert itself. Or perhaps to bind her in a pledge. She thought hard; granted wishes could prove malignant.

'I like swimming,' she said, 'but I hate all the other stuff and I hate the whole ekker book thing.'

'No problem,' he said. 'Just fill it in with whatever you like and bring it to me to sign each week then the duty prefect can't touch you.'

'Thanks,' she said and added, 'is Lucas worried I'll tell people?'

Mortimer was staring across Flint Quad, scowling at some boys who were using the space between two buttresses as an improvised fives court. He glanced back at her and she saw the pledge was already wound about them. 'Sorry, Cullen. I don't know what you mean,' he said and sauntered off.

It was unlikely Lucas would show up now but, just in case, she spent the afternoon working with Kimiko in the rose garden. She was gaining confidence in Greek by now and was starting to enjoy it as unreservedly as Kimiko enjoyed maths, as much for the pleasure of forming the letters, of filling a page in her exercise book with their neat, strange shapes as for the ancient meanings they whispered to her. She liked the fact that her name was Greek and could be rendered in Greek letters with no call for crude transliteration. In the back of a notebook she had begun to list the Graeco-English words with her name hidden inside them. Her favourites thus far were pansophy, *the pretension to universal knowledge*, deipnosophist, *one learned in the arts of dining* and helicosophy, *the geometry of spirals*. She liked the way fairly simple Greek words were giving her confidence in understanding and using complex ones in English.

As though responding to a relief in pressure or to a decision to start afresh in a new direction, her first period began that evening. She was embarrassed and disgusted at first and tried stuffing her knickers with folded layers of the absorbent lavatory paper that was one of the luxuries peculiar to the Daughters' Staircase. But this soon proved untenable and she was obliged to present herself to Nurse.

Resentful at being taken away from *Songs of Praise*, Nurse made an entry in a little red diary on her desk, opened a drawer and wearily presented her with a small packet of Aspirin, a Dr White's sanitary belt and a handful of neatly packaged paper towels to go with it. There was also an oddly unhelpful diagrammatic instruction sheet about how the belt and towels fitted together.

Sophie shut herself in a bathroom to do the necessary, missing Margaret keenly for the first time that term. She was appalled. The belt thing tickled, looked repellent and, scariest of all, didn't seem to fit very closely. As for the so-called towels, wearing one soon felt like having a sizeable dead hamster tucked between her legs. She understood now why Daughters having what Nurse called the Curse were obliged to be off games for the duration. It was all she could do to walk upstairs to bed.

She coincided in several Monday lessons with Lucas and had worried he would come after her the way Mortimer had, to apologize or force a discussion. They had already established a routine of coolness, sitting well apart, walking and talking with others in between classes, however, so she realized it took little exaggeration to avoid close contact with him altogether.

He seemed as uncomfortable as she was, avoiding her eye or seeking out company he did not normally choose. Perhaps he was angry at her for not coming home with him on Sunday.

'He seemed ashamed,' Kimiko said.

Sophie took her into her confidence. She hit on a way of explaining that at once choked further questions from one quarter and raised Lucas's reputation in another.

'The nerve of it!' Kimiko hissed.

'He wanted to,' Sophie sighed. 'When we went home to his parents'. It's a big house. It would have been perfectly easy. But I . . . I didn't feel ready for that.'

'Of course you didn't,' Kimiko said, trembling slightly at the thrill of being so confided in. 'We should pray for him.'

'If you like. But it's not just him. I was, you know . . . *tempted*.'

Kimiko's pretty eyes grew wider. More than ever, her companionship became a sort of force-field in which Sophie could travel safely from class to class.

Kimiko confided that she had been tempted too, once, in Osaka, where the son of her father's driver had shared his cigarette with her by breathing the smoke into her mouth. 'We kissed for hours,' she admitted. 'I wouldn't do it now, of course.'

'Of course not. But . . .'

'But it was amazing. My lips got really hard. And my earlobes and my . . .' She glanced down at her chest by way of illustration. Kimiko's chest was almost as flat as Sophie's still but her mother bought her things called training bras which at least allowed a rehearsal for maturity. Margaret regarded these in the same scornful light she did infant bikinis and kept Sophie in vests, telling her to enjoy the freedom while she could. This was all very well in midwinter but now the days had heated up, Sophie hated the extra layer of cotton under her shirts. Even more, she hated the contortionist's trick she felt obliged to perform whenever changing before a swim.

She remained queasy about the whole breast thing. She wanted them, but only in order to be like everyone else. And now that she was having her first period, she suspected they too would prove more penalty than reward. There were girls with magnificent breasts, like Weatherall, which apparently gave them the power to unsettle and excite a group of boys merely by entering the room. But Sophie had noticed that the excitement was about the breasts to the exclusion of their owner's other characteristics. Blessed with breasts they risked becoming nothing but. And yet there was a power to them, and not just over men. Breasts seemed the source of Margaret's calm assurance and Nurse's worldly wisdom.

For all the stinks, bangs and Bunsen burners in chemistry, biology was far more popular among the boys for the simple reason that most of its teachers were women, whose breasts, rustling beneath their white coats, caught a class's attention

more consistently than anything Mr Otterbourne could do with
a puddle of mercury.

For the rest of the term, Sophie's flat-chestedness along with
the regular indignities of dead hamster syndrome and her secret
knowledge of the thing between Lucas and Mortimer constantly
checked her enjoyment of the summer. Compared to how she
had been, she felt overcast, reluctant, prickly. When she could
have been lolling with friends under the plane trees or enjoying
banana milkshakes and chips at the cricket pavilion café, she
shut herself away with her books, determined that one area of
her life, at least, should be without blemish. But this merely
introduced another anxiety into her waking hours and another
dark element to her dreams. Until she had begun to study so
hard, the possibility of failure had occurred to her but now it
was joined by the possibility of mediocrity, which seemed almost
worse.

Worrying so, she developed hot, bumpy patches of eczema
behind her knees and inside her elbows, which she scratched
in a delirious fury until she drew blood. The sight of blood
would shame and check her for a while but then her clothes
or bed sheets would stick to the tiny scabs, dragging on them,
rubbing in tiny traces of laundry soap, making them itch the
more. Her scalp itched constantly too but in a different, oily
way. She used ferociously medicated shampoo that stank of hot
tarmac and caused temporary, agonizing blindness when it
trickled into her eyes, but even though she used it every day,
where she had previously only had to wash her hair once or
twice a week, her questing fingernails still found great scales

and bumps on her scalp from which, sooner or later, she would start teasing out flakes of dead skin that was often orange with dried blood and matter.

All these sufferings she now found she could offer to Jesus. Religion started to work, she discovered, once you had a big enough problem to drop in the collection bag. When Old Testament readings spoke of blood sacrifices, she no longer thought with disgust of bleating ewes and the ripe steam from slaughtered heifers but of Dr White's clotted hamsters, the hot itch where she pressed the back of her knees against the pew and of the hair she hardly dared comb for fear of the shaming flakes other girls shrank from and pretended were infectious.

She began to receive communion. She would ring the bells with the others, then, while they read comics and played chess in the ringing-chamber, go to her pew in the gallery and take part. She sang the hymns, her small voice drowned out by the din of the organ above her. She joined in the prayers, making herself think about what they were saying. When the Chaplain summoned them to the altar, she hurried out, through the ringing-chamber, down the spiral staircase and in at the back of Chapel. She appreciated the fact that this meant she was always at the back of the queue, a woman of Samaria, picking up crumbs, she liked to think, from under His table. The wine and the wafer, the forgiveness, the small, sweet rush of alcohol then the real coffee and biscuits and bright-eyed zeal of the Christian Unionists brought her a peace that lasted a few precious hours. Like the tar shampoo, however, its effects wore off once she regained the privacy to scratch.

She gave Mortimer her ekker book to sign each week, but largely because it made things even and easier between them. A discreet word from him to Nurse saw her spared the horrors of the athletics track as it no doubt would the hockey pitch. But she had no trouble fulfilling her weekly exercise quota because the daily luxury she allowed herself was an hour-long swim. After the brief, cynical idleness her friendship with Lucas had fostered, she rediscovered the release of swimming lengths until her legs were almost too tired to kick and her arms began to tremble when she allowed them to rest at her sides.

SUMMER HOLIDAYS
(fourteen years, six months)

Summer holidays felt even longer to Wakefield House children than they did for most because there was no trip away, no holiday within a holiday to break the eight weeks into intervals of expectation, excitement and winding-down. Kieran organized long, heat-frazzled daytrips in the minibus, to Stonehenge, to the seaside, to a funfair, but otherwise the children and teenagers had to make their own amusement. Some of the older ones found pitifully paid holiday jobs, serving in coffee shops or delivering Sunday papers but, unlike some parents Sophie was now hearing of, Margaret put no pressure on them to do this.

'Time enough for work when you're older,' she would say. 'Time enough for everything.'

Wilf was out all day running errands and making tea at a

firm of lorry mechanics where he hoped for an apprenticeship when he left school and in the evenings was still bewitched by Jackie so was rarely around. On her first few days home, Sophie had sat in his room a bit, playing with his things, surprised to be missing him so cruelly. Then, inspired by Kimiko if not directly by Jesus, she aspired to be good. She found a certain pleasure in becoming one of the house's 'big girls'. She took smaller children swimming in the town baths. She rallied them into playing board games or splashing in the padding pool or larking under the garden hose. She helped Margaret in the kitchen.

Glad to have her back, appreciating the support perhaps, Margaret took her to the GP for some powerful steroid cream for the eczema. Sophie was defensive when Margaret tried to winkle out of her what might be the worry behind it and hid behind a story she had heard that most eczema was caused by laundry bleach or the new biological washing powders everyone was using.

'There's no point you sticking at that place if it makes you unhappy,' Margaret said. 'Just say the word and we'll move you out of there and into the girls' grammar in time for the autumn.'

'No!' Sophie said, horrified. 'It's not making me unhappy. I'm fine. I've just got itchy legs and stuff.'

She wasn't meant to apply the cream anywhere her skin was broken but as soon as she saw how fast it worked, she spread it even where her nails had recently lifted scabs, wanting only to be whole again.

When she admitted to her scalp problem, Margaret gave her a head massage, which didn't help the itching much but relaxed Sophie enough for her to mention Nurse and the Dr White's belt. Margaret roared with laughter, apologized, hugged her, kissed her itchy head and showed her a Tupperware box on the top of the first-aid cupboard which she said was always kept well stocked with all sizes of tampons. Dr White's, she explained, were favoured by the sort of mothers who thought ignorance was bliss and masturbation a sin. 'And I'm the nearest you have to a mother and I'm not like that so you're to come and see me if there's anything you want to know. Anything at all, Soph.'

While she gave Sophie a lesson in how to make apple charlotte, she subtly ascertained that Sophie knew what contraception was and knew she only had to ask Margaret as and when she felt the need of it. If the conversation made Sophie feel grown-up, the realization that she was shielding this older woman by not telling her about Lucas and Mortimer made her feel older still.

Sophie had become one of the oldest in the house without noticing it. Nikki and Gill, who had both been there for years, had left during the term, now that they were both seventeen, and found jobs with Marks and Spencer and a flat to share. Wilf was sixteen, still around but barely. Elaine the Pain had been driven away to the care of a foster family. There was one other older boy, Randall, who was fifteen, and a girl, Paula, also fifteen, so a year older than Sophie, but so disturbed and unsociable still that Sophie hardly knew her and was wary of befriending her. Before she started at Tatham's, Sophie would have been fascinated by each new arrival and found out all about them – largely indirectly, through Wilf or one of the girls – but several children had arrived since she went away who still felt like strangers to her. This and the respect they showed her made her feel old and responsible, which left her torn. On the one hand she felt an old, familiar jealousy, wanting to regress to needily occupying a principal space in Margaret and Kieran's preoccupations, on the other she felt flattered.

One of the new arrivals, an eight-year-old boy called Zacky, had latched on to her when she last took a group of them swimming because she helped him blow up his water wings and let him change in the ladies' with her because the bigger boys were bullying him. Now he followed her like a dog with a runny nose. In the spirit of aspiring to be good, she fought down the impulse to drive him off with a harsh word or two and took him on so as to lighten the burden on Margaret. 'He misses his mum,' was all Margaret had said about him. 'And he's got a bladder like a sieve, so if he says he needs to go for God's sake let him and fast.'

That afternoon Sophie had been going to the city library anyway so when Zacky started trailing after her, asking what could he do now, she took him with her. He had never been to the library before and was touchingly awed by it, not least by the fact that it was free.

'I can take any books I want?' he asked repeatedly.

'Borrow, not take. From the children's library, yeah,' Sophie said. 'Any six. But you have to bring them back in time or there's a fine. Money to pay. And Margaret won't lend it to you . . .'

She enrolled him in the children's library and for a while he was quite happy poring over the books he had chosen at one side of a table while she took notes from a reference-only history encyclopaedia at the other. After a while he grew restless in a way that couldn't be solved by a trip to the ladies'. He kept staring at her instead of reading – from the childishness of the books he had picked, she suspected his reading was not very advanced – and he asked her questions about her history project so loudly that people stared and shushed.

So she packed up their things and took him for a stroll by the river, then to the swings and slides. Unfortunately this made him want to piss again, urgently, so they had to hurry back along the river to a grubby little park near the bus station where she knew there were conveniences. He flatly refused to go into the ladies' with her, as he had been happy to do at the library, and made so much noise about it that a policeman asked them what was wrong.

'He needs to go to the loo,' she told him, 'but he won't go in the ladies' with me.'

'Best take him home, then,' he said. 'You don't want him going in there on his own.'

'I'll wet myself,' Zacky shouted. 'I will, you know.'

'I don't suppose . . .' she started

'Come on, then,' the policeman said. 'Don't keep your mum waiting.' He winked at her so she knew he didn't really think she was a teenage mother. Rather sweetly, she thought, Zacky took his hand as they headed into the dingy gents'. Almost immediately she saw Lucas.

He emerged, tucking in the skinny, purple-striped cheesecloth shirt he had on. His hair seemed to have grown a lot since term-time but perhaps he was merely brushing it differently. He saw her and blushed so deeply and was in such obvious discomfort that every shred of animosity or awkwardness she had been feeling about him evaporated and she smiled.

'Surprise!' she said.

'Hi. Er . . . what are you doing down here?'

'A little friend needed a leak.' She nodded towards the gents' where the policeman was already coming out again, Zacky in tow. 'Thanks,' she called out as Zacky dropped his hand and ran over to her.

'Who's this?' Lucas asked. 'Your brother?'

'I'm Zacky,' said Zacky.

'Not exactly,' Sophie began.

'She's my mum,' Zacky said and laughed when Sophie hotly denied it.

'Zacky's just come to live with us,' she said. 'Still settling in.' And the three of them walked back up to the High Street. Her instinct was to send Zacky down the lane to the home on his own then walk on somewhere else with Lucas but Zacky and his chatter and tugging inexorably drew them both back there.

Pride made her resist explaining anything.

Let him ask, she thought.

She could see him working to piece evidence together. It must have been obvious to him the moment they arrived back and were on the short path that cut across the scrappy garden that surrounded the house. This was obviously neither a normal family house nor the house of a normal family. There were far too many clothes on the washing lines. There was an industrial bin on wheels instead of a small domestic dustbin. Had it been a winter afternoon, he'd have seen too, at a glance, the expanses of fluorescent lighting glaring from all the downstairs rooms that shrieked *institution*.

There were rules about bringing outsiders back so most people didn't bother. If they made friends at school, they rarely wanted to risk sharing them in any case so visited them rather than bringing them back. You were only allowed one visitor at a time. They had to be signed into a book, introduced to either Margaret or Kieran and they weren't allowed to penetrate further into the house than the communal areas, kitchen, dayroom and hall. (It wasn't so different from the Daughters' Staircase.)

As it was sunny and miraculously there wasn't a gang of

children messing about out there for once, Sophie kept Lucas in the garden and brought them both a big mug of tea and a handful of Jammy Dodgers. Margaret came out, tailed by Zacky, to take in the washing and came over to meet Lucas briefly. Sophie watched him taking her in, her tired, unmade-up face, her scrappily cut, home-dyed hair, and watched his automatic charm soften her expression as he admired her Chinese blouse.

'Okay,' Sophie sighed as Margaret left them alone. 'So I know your dark secret and now you know mine. We're quits. It's not exactly Tinker's Hill, is it?'

'It's okay. Which is your room?'

'You can't see my window from here. It's round the back, over the kitchen.'

'So is this an orphanage?' he asked and she laughed.

'Children's home is the correct term. We're a mixture. Kids in temporary care, while their parents are being sorted out or getting out of custody or whatever, kids waiting for adoption or fostering and several like me.'

'Orphans.'

'I lied about that. My parents are alive, I think. I just don't know who they are. Bastard, not orphan.'

'Wow.'

'Sort of.'

They laughed but she could tell he was a bit nervous. He had never been in a situation like this before. Life with Heidi and Simon had given him no training in it. Apart from whatever glimpses his wicked sister had granted him of counter-culture, this was probably a thrilling first glimpse into the dark underbelly for him. It was lucky for him Nikki and Gill had moved out or they'd have been over there by now asking him questions and putting the bad-girl frighteners on him.

'Have you been here all your life?' he asked.

She shook her head. 'I was four or five, I think. I don't remember my dad at all, so he probably didn't stick around. I don't remember my mum either. Not really. Just her voice and being on my own a lot with lots of books. I think she was quite old. Not a teenager or anything like that. Or maybe she wasn't my mum at all but my granny and then she couldn't cope.'

'Weird.'

'Yeah. But Margaret's nice and Kieran's okay too. He's taken all the others out somewhere. It's not normally this quiet.'

'Do you mind me asking questions?' He looked at her, pushed his new, longer hair off his eyes.

'Nope,' she said, grinned. 'My turn next.'

He pulled a Jammy Dodger in two, scraped at the filling with his front teeth. 'Sorry,' he said, 'bad habit,' and he munched the rest of the biscuit. 'Why weren't you adopted?'

'People adopting want babies, I suppose. I must have been too old. And I stopped wanting to be. I mean a social worker comes once a year to check we're all happy and so on and one of the things they always ask is do we want to be considered for adoption or fostering into a family. As long as I can remember I've been saying no thanks, I like it here. It's a kind of family and I know where I stand. And the things you hear from some of the kids they bring in – stuff about unhinged foster parents and nightmare step-brothers – it's enough to put you off. I'd show you my room but it's not allowed.'

'Why not?'

'Perverts. Weirdoes. Whatever. Some of the little ones especially are really messed up about strangers, the ones who've been taken away from their parents, and they need to feel safe here. So. No strangers upstairs. Ever . . . Lucas?'

'What?'

'I'm sorry. You know. About last term.'

'No, I am. I should have said something. I was a coward and then I just thought . . .' He pushed at his hair again then looked away at Zacky who was sitting on the doorstep with a half-deflated spacehopper and aching to join them. Sophie glared at the child and firmly shook her head. He dragged the spacehopper off to the yard at the back.

'What?' she asked.

'I thought you were disgusted.'

'How do you know I wasn't?'

'Well . . . We're talking so . . .'

'Were you in love with him?' she asked.

He shook his head then sighed and said maybe.

'You were kissing as if you were,' she said.

'Did you watch for long?' he asked, beginning a mischievous smile.

'Long enough,' she said. 'Can you see him again?'

'Hardly. He's doing VSO in the Sudan for a year then he'll be up in Durham and . . . He didn't give me an address or anything. We never discussed anything. I think it was just a 3D wank for him.'

'Have there been others?'

'Said the jealous wife.'

'Sorry. But have there?'

He shrugged.

'I mean,' she asked, 'do you think it's just a sort of phase or is that who you are?'

'Oh, it's who I am.' He flicked his hair out of his eyes and looked at her levelly.

'No question?'

'Never the slightest.'

'What's your mum say?'

'Christ! Heidi'll never know. Not till I leave home at least. Thanks to Carmel, I've got to be the good one. It'd kill her.'

'Lucas, I think she knows already.'

'She thought you were my girlfriend.'

'So did I!'

'You didn't! Not really?'

'No,' she said. 'Not really. But it was fun kidding myself.'

'We could carry on, if you like.' His offer was half-suggestion. 'Pretending to people.'

'I'm not being your fucking disguise.'

'Sophia Cullen, you swore!'

'What? I've sworn at you before. I swear all the fucking time.'

'You don't.'

'I do when I'm home. They think I'm turning all poncy at the poncy school.'

'Well you probably are, darling.'

She rolled over on her back on the grass. 'So were it good?' She dropped her voice a tone or two and mimicked Jonty's accent. 'Sex wi' Mortimer.'

'It were fucking fabulous, pet. He carried me up those steps once. And we did it on that roof of his, under the stars.' He sighed. 'The only reason you caught us that night was he was too horny to wait to get upstairs.' He laughed shortly.

'You miss him,' she said. 'You must do.'

Lucas shrugged, nodded glumly then pushed his melancholy aside like an old curtain. 'So are we friends again? Will you come round to play?'

'Of course! Aren't you going away?'

102

'Last two weeks of August, while the new kitchen's put in finally. Till then Simon's in chambers all the time and Heidi's stuck in there with the skellies and slashers so we can't even go on daytrips. I'm bored to death, splishing around the pool to keep cool. And if I don't distract you you'll only work. What are you doing tomorrow?'

'Oh. Hundreds of things. What d'you think?'

'Come for lunch. Bring your swimmies and we can loll by the pool and pretend Tinker's Hill is Bel Air.'

'You're on.'

'Heidi'll be happy. You're not going to tell her, are you?'

'I'm not going to pretend to be your girlfriend.'

'No, no but –'

'But I won't tell her you're a poof.'

'Thanks.'

'If you don't go telling people about this place.'

'You're not ashamed or anything, are you?' He frowned.

'No but . . . Oh. I dunno.' She sat up and picked at her feet with a twig. She remembered the eczema that was still showing behind her knees and tweaked her skirt to cover them. 'I don't like people jumping to conclusions, that's all. If they know, I want it to be because I chose to tell them. Okay?'

'Sure.'

The minibus pulled up outside and brought with it the noise of shouting children, slamming doors, music and Kieran's growly requests for good sense.

'I'd better go.' Lucas stood, looming over her for a second and she remembered that now that it was established he could never be hers, she was at liberty to find him beautiful again.

'Why don't you ever get spots?' she asked.

'I do.'

'Hardly. Not like Wilf. You get them so rarely it's like a siren going off.'

He raised an eyebrow. 'My blemishes are all internal,' he said. 'Actually I scald my face with TCP most nights. I'll probably erupt in weeping sores in my twenties. See you tomorrow.'

She enjoyed watching his awkwardness as he crossed the grass, eyeballed by the others as they came shambling in.

There was a noisy party in the house next door that night which normally would have infuriated her but she enjoyed lying on her bed – it was too warm for covers – happily contemplating the summer ahead, listening to the music and laughter through the open window and indulging in fantasy.

One day, after they had each independently enjoyed a profound but ultimately too scorching love affair, they would live together. Or not together but pleasantly side by side in some glamorous city, like Paris or New York, where there was street life, music on the night air like this and where they had strings of interesting lovers but were always there for one another. As she finally fell asleep, she was mapping in her mind the small, perfect house where they could have a floor each, with a kitchen in the middle perhaps, where they might meet by the fridge for gossip after a night of delicious parties. She could wear the top halves of his pyjamas and they would cut one another's hair sitting in the bath and share a brace of Abyssinian cats with wittily paired names and people would be excited to know them.

She apprehended with a jolt of rebellious joy that, however virtuously she studied, her life was not after all to be conformist and continent and polite. It would follow an uncharted route somewhere between the life paths of Kimiko's Christian Union friends and the Wakefield House bad-girls.

It would be interesting and vivid in ways that would earn her both disapproval and envy. As she fell asleep her future seemed briefly offered to her as something she could seize unapologetically like a greedy child and taste till its juice ran down her chin.

MICHAELMAS TERM
(fourteen years, nine months)

For four glorious weeks of the Michaelmas term, everything was perfect. The weather was golden, her set texts were good (*Learning to Philosophize, The Doors of Perception & Heaven and Hell, L'Etranger, Aeneid Book One, Thucydides Book Six*) and she had only one frightening teacher. (This was Mr Headbourne, for maths, whose dulcet sarcasm gave way without warning to losses of temper so violent that neighbouring classes would fall silent out of respect.) With Jonty Mortimer gone and writing no letters, Lucas's friendship with Sophie was re-established on a far stronger footing. There was new knowledge and honesty between them. He shared his passing crushes with her, reducing them to unthreatening entertainment, and opened her eyes to the network of unofficial romances around the school, including a notorious one carrying on between two

106

x

Scholars of which she had been entirely unaware. He sought her out for snatched, hilarious bulletins between lessons. He began to play with her name and tried out Sophie, Soph, So and Phi. Phi was her preferred one, as he pronounced it like the Greek letter, but no one else seemed to take it up and she suspected it wouldn't stick. She called him Lou, which he seemed to like, but his failure to find a nickname that fitted her was like a small warning that something between them remained unsettled.

She let Kimiko believe that she had arrived at some mysterious, adult rapprochement with him but, with the memory of last term still raw, she did not repeat the mistake of exclusivity. She maintained her quieter relationship with Kimiko on a lesser footing but in a separate part of her life: along with Jesus, Tampax and the occasional ache in the breasts she was, at long last, acquiring.

She continued to slip down from the ringing-chamber to receive communion but it began to feel too routine to work much magic on her. She decided not to go home with Lucas for lunch every Sunday and not to go to Christian Union every Sunday but to keep them both appreciative of her feminine right to withhold herself. Stung by something Kieran had said as he and the youngest ones waved her off at the start of term, she made an effort to stay in touch with Wakefield House, writing the occasional letter to Wilf and sometimes breaking the rules on a half-holiday by using a licensed trip to the shops as cover for straying beyond bounds to surprise Margaret and Kieran with a quick visit home.

By chance – she happened to overhear the singing one morning and walked in out of curiosity – she discovered that on three days a week there was a tiny, untrumpeted matins service in the Chantry in the middle of the cloisters.

Accompanied by a piano, the sixteen Quiristers, who were trained at the cathedral's choir school but still part of the Tatham's foundation, sang the day's morning psalm and a hymn. There were a few prayers and a Bible-reading in between. It never took longer than twenty minutes and was slotted into the slovenly, burnt-toast half-hour between breakfast and the day's first period. There was no one there but the Chaplain, Reverend Harestock, Mr Sutton the choirmaster at the piano and a don she did not know who always gave the reading. He was younger than most, very tall and suited with a quiet elegance that seemed to elude his colleagues. His voice was thoughtful, easily floated in the echoing, vaulted space, and it was almost as though he were reading to himself or, indeed, as though the service were happening purely for him, a restrained celebration for the good of his aristocratic soul.

As it wasn't communion, little was required of Sophie but to sit or kneel where appropriate and to listen. It was meditative and peaceful and she found herself keeping it a secret from both Lucas and Kimiko. The second time she attended, the mystery don nodded to her in acknowledgement as she sat across the aisle from him. He looked, she decided, like a dark version of Peter O'Toole. Once she had been several times, she began to worry that she might be apprehended, as the only other congregation member, to give the day's reading but she never was so perhaps the service was the don's peculiar after all.

Lucas grabbed her one morning during the long walk from Stinks to the language labs, bursting with news. A boy in

Dougal's had been called out of class and sent home to London the previous afternoon because his father had died from a heart attack.

This was news in itself. People's parents or siblings died rarely enough during term-time for it to mark them out for the rest of their time at school as boy whose sister died of Hodgkin's or girl whose mother had a fatal car crash. Because of its rareness, bereavement conferred a sort of glamour on the afflicted, akin to the whispered spell cast by the equally rare blow of divorce.

More newsworthy still, however, was that Mr Headbourne, the ferocious maths teacher who was also housemaster of Dougal's, had called Lucas into his study last night to impress upon him that when this boy returned, Lucas was to take steps to befriend him.

'But you can't just say *Boy, be that person's friend!* You don't even know him, do you?'

'Well,' Lucas confessed, 'I know him a bit. We're in the same year so we're on the same table at meals so we talk a bit. But he's not a friend. We've got hardly anything in common. He plays cricket, for Christ's sake, and likes going to Deb. Soc. and he sings in the choir. He's a bit of a hearty. But maybe he doesn't have any other friends or something. Headbourne said he's going to bend the rules for us so I can take him home for tea in the afternoons and stuff.'

'You're joking!' Sophie heard how envy made her voice squeak.

'And there's worse. Headbourne had rung up Heidi and without either of them consulting me first, probably because she assumed he was a friend, they've agreed that Somborne-Abbot can live with us and be a temporary dayboy until he feels ready to board again.'

109

'Are you pissed off?'

'Well I think they might have asked me first. He'll be sleeping in my room because Carmel still won't let anyone use hers, selfish cow. Actually she probably doesn't care and it's just Heidi not wanting to drive her further away than she feels she has already.'

His words were indignant but she heard the excitement in his tone that he had been swept up in a drama. He had been brushed by bereavement and acquired a touch of its glamour without the grief.

Charlie Somborne-Abbot. She could not put a face to the name, whatever prompts Lucas gave her over the next few days, that Somborne-Abbot sang in the choir, on the right as you faced the altar, that he was blond and apple-cheeked, that he had played the bingo caller in *The Dark Tower* last year. The surname was familiar but in a school run on surnames, where lists of the things were everywhere, painted on honours boards, carved on memorials and written in the front of second-hand textbooks, it was easy to be familiar with many without knowing their owners by sight.

The only detail Lucas was able to supply that was sufficiently intriguing to flesh out Charles Somborne-Abbot as something more than a generic, stuck-up hearty was that he had already been linked to a scandal. Before coming to Tatham's he had been at the cathedral choir school, enjoying the virtually free private education that came with winning a place as one of Tatham's Quiristers. So from the ages of eight to thirteen he had been coming into daily contact – through choir – with older boys at the 'big' school. Apparently one of these had become obsessed with him to the point of writing him compromising letters. The child Somborne-Abbot had either been sly or flattered enough to hoard the letters and his parents found them. There was a red-faced enquiry and, although nothing was proved and the older boy was punished with no more than a caution, a dramatic clampdown ensued, stifling any further fraternization between Quiristers and their elders. The choirboys, who had previously moved around as an exuberant gang, chatting with any older boys who came their way, showing off and getting wildly overexcited, took to passing between Chapel and choir school in a silent crocodile, like so many pious novices.

Inexplicably, no change was made in the plans laid down for young Somborne-Abbot and he remained marked down for the same Tatham's house as the youth who had written the inappropriate letters. And as Lucas.

'Naturally when people heard he was coming, they expected some kind of pint-sized Delilah, a sort of Lolita in flannel shorts, so they were a bit put out when this big, fat –'

'*Fat?* You didn't say he was fat.'

'Well, no. Not fat. But big-boned. When this big boy arrived with his clompy shoes and cricket bat and . . . Not a temptation. A Labrador, not a Saluki. And he hasn't really fitted in yet. He's a bit keen to please and, well, you know how people are. And I expect it's only now he's here that he realizes the boy who wrote him the letters is a completely weird, sociopath spaz and not at all a good character reference. Oh Christ. But who knows? Maybe you'll like him.'

The moment she saw Charles, when Lucas brought him across to Schola for tea, she recognized him. They had never been in the same class for anything – he was three divs below them and something of a plodder, apparently – but she had noticed him in the choir stalls when she joined the end of the queue to receive communion and should probably have been staring reverently at the altar or humbly at her feet. He had a

111

lot of straight blond hair, very white skin, dark, bovine eyes and full, rather feminine lips. He wasn't as overweight as Lucas had cattily implied, but he had childbearing hips and one of those teenage faces that was going to be in a transitional phase for longer than most. Just when she thought, *Oh yes, really quite goodlooking*, a kind of plump ripple passed over it and a sulky, dim little boy was revealed.

'Sophie, this is Charles,' Lucas said.

'Charlie, please,' said Charles and shook her hand, which felt a bit odd in someone of their own age. 'How do you do?'

'Fine, thanks,' she said, laughing at him and letting go. 'Have you two come for tea?'

'Please!' said Lucas. 'Hello, Nurse.'

Lucas had become such a regular visitor by now that if he found Sophie out when he called, Nurse took him into her rooms for tea and a lemon cupcake.

'Hello, Trouble,' she said and looked enquiringly at Charlie. 'Hello,' she added.

'Nurse, this is Somborne-Abbot.'

Her face crumpled up in sympathy.

'Oh yes. I'm so sorry about your father.'

Rather than saying that's quite all right or something else blandly subject-changing, Charlie stammered something and raced back out into Flint Quad.

'Oh dear,' Nurse sighed. 'Shouldn't I have said anything?'

'Don't worry,' Lucas told her. 'He's like this a lot.'

'Shouldn't you go after him?' Sophie asked, amused despite knowing better.

'It's exhausting. He can't cope with anyone mentioning it and he can't cope with anyone saying nothing and treating him like normal.'

112

'It does seem a bit soon to send him back,' Sophie said.

'His mother insisted, apparently. She and Headbourne agreed it was best for him to get back into the swing of things as soon as possible. But he's terribly tense. I'd better go.' Lucas pulled a face. 'Fancy helping me with him a bit?'

'Isn't three an awkward number?'

'Not when one's a girl, surely? Please.'

'Oh. Okay.'

So they left Nurse and went in search of him. He had stalked off but not so far that he couldn't be found. She saw, to her dismay, that he had been crying and suddenly felt sorry for him. He was on the burly side and his sports jacket had been chosen with an eye to leaving room for growth, which had the effect of making him look overwhelmed by tweed.

Lucas's instinct in bringing her along was a cunning one. Unlike Lucas, whose mother had made him at ease around women, Charlie seemed stuffed with old-fashioned, chivalrous ideas about putting women first, walking between them and traffic, deferring to their opinions in everything. When she was around it was out of the question for him to *play up*, as Lucas put it, because of his duty to entertain Sophie. Rather than make him endure Nurse and the curiosity of the Daughters' Chamber with his eyes still puffy from grief, she suggested they go to the tuck shop. There she ordered a milkshake and the boys, who had reached the age of being permanently hungry, asked for milkshakes and plates of egg and chips.

The tuck shop was run by two middle-aged women, one stick-thin with a wheedling, flirtatious voice at odds with her stony, smoker's features, the other so fat with dropsy that her ankles overflowed her shoes and she could not walk and talk simultaneously for wheezing. They greeted Charlie by name and he drew them both out, asking the thin one what flavours of milkshake she had and bringing a worrying flush to the fat one's face by admiring the charm bracelet that was puckering her wrist. Seconds after they left, he began imitating them with raspy accuracy.

'Raspbwy, Stworbwy, Chocklik, Poynapil, Furniller, Lemming or Loyme. Daren't take it off or I'd never [wheeze] get it on again.'

His face looked nothing like either woman's but he had a professional impersonator's blandness and mobility so that he somehow suggested first one then the other by subtle modulations of eye and lip. In the light of his hypocritical friendliness towards them it was monstrous, reprehensible and one of the funniest things Sophie had ever seen. Building on their laughter and shouted suggestions, he worked the two phrases up into an impromptu sketch of the women's home life. They were sisters, he had decided, and the thin one waited on the fat one's every need and was actually plotting to kill her with over-consumption.

'She'll feed her till she bursts!' Lucas suggested.

'No,' Charlie said quietly. 'Just the once, and very fast, she'll find a way to make her run.'

And Sophie saw at once what the dynamic of their relationship was to be; however hard Lucas tried, Charlie was officially the funny one.

She did not warm to him at first but she at least tried to dismiss her indifference as petty jealousy. The boys were in none of the same classes apart from Latin, Lucas's weak spot, whereas Sophie still saw plenty of Lucas on her own during teaching hours. Charlie developed a technique, however, for popping up between them when they were changing classrooms.

114

He also came to monopolize Lucas's Sundays. He had politely declined the offer of becoming a temporary dayboy, about which Lucas was so relieved that guilt made him vulnerable and he let Heidi invite Charlie for lunch time and again.

Sophie went to Tinker's Hill with Charlie just the once but found the worry that he was forever on the brink of satirizing the Behrmans, whom she sort of loved by now, was unbearable. He would go back to London in the holidays, she reminded herself. She could see lots of them then and have Lucas to herself again.

But then Charlie began to seek her out on her own. He found out her favourite corner of the library, in the classics section, which was comfortable and sunny and usually deserted. He always checked his presence would not disturb her then sat, quietly working, across the table from her. Sometimes Lucas came with him but Lucas was bending the rules and slipping home to study more and more because he found the rustling of other people's papers distracting. When he did try working at their table, Charlie could madden him in minutes by sighing in a certain way or subtly sliding Lucas's books out of the neat order in which he liked them stacked. Sophie tried not to find his teasing funny but she was so glad it wasn't aimed at her that she couldn't help smiling. He brought out a side to Lucas she hadn't seen before, a fussy, old-womanish side she supposed must be connected to his being gay.

When they were on their own Charlie often just watched her taking notes or making calculations. From the corner of her eye she could see him turn to her and it made her self-conscious and extra neat. But if she then looked up and caught his eye, he would smile with a sweetness that disarmed her, or even shake his head with a kind of wonder.

Surrounded by clever people now, she had grown unused to admiration.

As she had guessed from his placing in relation to his age, he was not one of the clever ones. The choir school had been an efficient forcing house and drilled him for the Commoners' entrance exam successfully enough but now, like a lot of the wealthier Commoners, he was beginning to flounder.

One Saturday, when the two of them were working in the library, she caught him poring and sighing over the same page of maths problems for nearly an hour. At last, when he slipped out to go to the lavatory, she grabbed his textbook and saw he was on a chapter she had covered two terms ago, on algebraic fractions. She tore a sheet from her exercise book and worked quickly down the page, scribbling down the answers for him. His shifty delight when he saw what she had done reminded her unexpectedly of Wilf, whose homework she had often completed as a matter of course.

'But now you've got to work out why they're right,' she said, the way she would with Wilf. 'They'll know you've cheated if you don't show your workings.'

He made her promise not to tell Lucas and then it all came out, how he was under tremendous pressure from his mother, who would not hear of him doing any A levels but scientific ones when the time came.

'But if you're no good at those –'

'I've got to get good. I have to get good enough Os to go on the C ladder to do sciences.'

'What if you refuse?'

'She'd put me in a state school. She did that to Tim. That's my brother.'

Sophie was about to ask if state education would be so very

bad then saw his expression and knew it would. Even she would find it difficult going back after a year of all this, and Charlie Somborne-Abbot with his clompy shoes and cricket bat would be eaten alive.

So she took him on as a sort of challenge, figuring that teaching him what she had already mastered was a good form of O level revision. When she pointed out simple truths, such as a fractions being just another way of expressing a division sum, he laughed for the pleasure of suddenly understanding something and she saw how he had learnt his maths parrot-fashion, crippling his understanding of it by storing the information as a series of formulae – fractions are done this way, algebra is done that – without ever daring to relate the contents of one compartment to another.

When she finally succeeded in making him work a problem out correctly for himself, he was so delighted that he leaned across from his chair to kiss her. It was only a shambling sort of kiss, on her cheek, and nobody was around to see them but there was something defiant in the look he gave her as he sat back that suggested it wasn't so different from the kiss she had demanded of Wilf. Something about his look stopped her telling Lucas, as she might easily have done to win back some territory at Charlie's expense.

It became a Saturday afternoon fixture. He would find her in the interval between his playing football and having to meet Lucas at Glee Club and she would explain something he didn't understand and when they were done, or nearly done, he would kiss her.

The second kiss was on the lips and the third, partly at her instigation, was a full-on, Wilf-style snog. There was no one around but they were taking a crazy risk. Someone might have come in. A don might have been watching from the path below the window where she liked to sit. The risk made it all the more exciting and they kissed and kissed, half falling out of their chairs, then leaning against the bookshelves, heedless of how they sent copies tumbling. They were both sufficiently detached to break down and laugh occasionally at the over-dramatized ease with which they could excite one another, mimicry blurring into clumsy lust. His tracksuit and football things were not spotless like Lucas's but smelled of mud and sweat and his skin had a smoky, slightly hammy smell like the fancy delicatessen near the Butter Cross where Lucas led her sometimes to buy German chocolate biscuits and things Heidi liked. And in her excitement and confusion, this taste of the meat the Behrmans never ate, or even mentioned, for all their sophistication, became part of the secret's flavour.

By the time mid-terms tests had shown Charlie's maths performance to have improved impressively, Sophie had started to wonder whether the kisses weren't a grateful payment at all but a way of binding her to silence about the help she was giving him. She began to be afraid of him sometimes now, of his power to expose through telling secrets or throwing off corrosive mimicry, of his effortless social confidence and ability to be arrogant where Lucas always felt the need to charm. This time she told Kimiko nothing.

After their last kiss of term, she saw that she didn't desire him. She didn't, if she was frank, even like him very much. She only thought of him as someone to be appeased and, in his absence, he played no part in her happier fantasies the way that Lucas did. But she had enough of a killer instinct to want a part of whatever it was that gave him confidence despite his intellectual pallor or lack of popularity. So when he caught her before she went up to ring bells for Illumina, and said, 'Come and stay in London. Meet my family. Once Christmas is over. Lucas needn't know,' she readily agreed.

CHRISTMAS HOLIDAYS
(fourteen years, eleven months)

Charlie agreed dates for the visit with his mother on the phone. He spoke of her with such respect that Sophie sensed that if Mrs Somborne-Abbot said No that would have been that. No holiday visitor. Lucas had told her in amazement how Charlie's mother expected her son to compile a list of news items or requests so that once he had queued to make his weekly call home from a phone box and she went to the expense of calling him back, there should be no costly waffle or sentimental hesitation. The message came back that Sophie was welcome to visit and should arrive on January third and leave on the fourth. She was to catch the 9.35 train to town and would be sent home on the 6.30, thus avoiding peak-time travel costs.

No one from the home ever went away to visit friends because friends were always local. Margaret warned her to present it as a joint revision trip to avoid arousing envy in the others. Sophie did tell Lucas, defying Charlie's wish that they keep it secret from him. Charlie was addicted to conspiracy, she thought, and anyway Lucas was going to be away with his family skiing so would hardly care.

Wilf was home with a vengeance because Jackie had dumped him for her best mate's brother. When he wasn't at work at the lorry garage which had finally offered him an apprenticeship, he was lying on his bed, scowling, smelling of diesel fumes and playing his music too loud. Despite his outward fury at the world in general and Jackie – whom he would only call The Slag – in particular, he was plainly miserable. When he got involved with Jackie and then got taken on by the garage, he thought his life was going to be a steady climb out and away from all that Wakefield House represented and to find himself back in his room with nowhere to go and no one to see felt like a cosmic rejection. He was genuinely keen to hear Sophie's news but she gave him only an edited version so their paths would not seem too divergent.

They treated one another with nostalgic kindness, taking refuge in comforting rituals and safe subjects but, for the first time, neglected to conspire in rigging the Christmas present lottery so each ended up buying for near strangers. Sophie drew Randall's name. She hardly knew him so gave him soap-on-a-rope. Her name was drawn by Zacky, who gave her a packet of Callard and Bowser toffee.

Because she was poor and Lucas was Jewish, they had agreed to celebrate Christmas in only a small way, buying one another books from the paperbacks section of the town's second-hand bookshop. She gave him Mary Renault's *The Charioteer*, which she knew he would be too cowardly to buy himself and would probably hide under his mattress. He gave her an English translation of *Bonjour Tristesse*. He was going through a phase of being in love with all things French and Françoise Sagan had recently ousted Jean Rhys from his pantheon just as a record of someone called just Barbara breathily singing Jacques Brel songs had driven David Bowie off his bedroom stereo system. He also had some very bouncy blue Kickers which looked rather fetching when worn with his Guernsey, an ensemble which Charlie said made him look like Florence off *The Magic Roundabout*.

The late Mr Somborne-Abbot had done something for Shell. For most of his marriage, so all of Charlie's life, he had been obliged to live abroad in Oman, Nairobi and then, most recently, in Kuala Lumpur or KL, as Charlie called it. The children – Charlie was the youngest of four – had all been sent back to boarding school in England from the age of seven. Mr Somborne-Abbot had died in the throes of taking a senior desk job at the London office. His widow found herself cut adrift socially. She had lived abroad too long to have maintained close ties to either family or friends at home. She had also become used to cheap domestic staff and a certain, pseudo-colonial style of living. Returning to London obliged her to settle in a western district beyond the Circle Line, where nice girls never went when she was last a Londoner. She found herself widowed at an awkward age, with two hulking teenagers yet to fly the nest and only a twice-weekly cleaning lady to help her cope.

She let slip most of this in the stream of chat she kept up

when collecting Sophie from Waterloo in her little apple-green car.

They were standing side by side as Sophie approached the ticket barrier. Mrs Somborne-Abbot was so pale and thin she might have been carved from bone. Her blonde hair was swept tightly back off her humourless face by a silk scarf. Sophie didn't really notice her clothes beyond their being well pressed and generally smart. The eye was drawn first to her face, which seemed tightly drawn back along with the hair, then to her hands, which were beautiful and long but held out curiously from her body, as though still dripping from a plunge in a sink or as though their nail varnish were still wet. She inexplicably had a patent leather handbag over one arm which seemed far too small to be useful. Beside her Charlie looked pinkly chubby. Shaking her hand, Sophie was similarly blighted by comparison and felt brown, busty and indelicate.

Well trained, Charlie took Sophie's bag while his mother clicked along the concourse on Sophie's other side, chatting. She persisted in calling her Sophia, which was probably the result of a simple misunderstanding but seemed to imply a judgement against the unsuitability of Phi, which was what both Charlie and Lucas tended to call her. Not having corrected her at first made it impossible to do so later. Unlike Heidi, Mrs Somborne-Abbot did not offer a first name, although Sophie knew it was Christine.

'I thought I'd drop you two off in the centre of things to enjoy yourselves,' she said, 'then see you at home for dinner.'

Sophie did not like to admit she had only ever been to London twice before, on group excursions with Margaret and Kieran, and had seen only the Tower, Madame Tussaud's and the Science Museum. She was terrified it was going to be expensive as she had only ten pounds spending money for the whole trip, which was her Christmas present from them, along with the train ticket. Luckily Charlie was as economical by training as she was by necessity. Their morning's entertainment – a walk round the National Gallery – was free. They then had a cheap lunch in a new place called McDonald's. Then, as it began to rain, they spent the afternoon watching a film which was also cheap because it was a matinée.

Once his mother had dropped them off, Charlie became far more relaxed than he ever was at school, as though only here, deep in anonymous crowds, did he feel unobserved or unjudged. He was funny, copying people, pointing things out to her, telling Christmas horror stories. But as the time came to catch the Tube west, he came to talk more and more about home and family and she started wishing it was only a daytrip and that Waterloo not Fulham Broadway was their destination.

Charlie was the family's great white hope. His older brother, Tim, had disappointed everyone by recovering from a bad start at school only to drop out of Exeter after one year (he was reading Geography) without telling his parents, to go to join an Indian ashram. The ashram's monks had eventually thrown him out because he never did anything. He had returned to England on the morning of his father's funeral, moved home and was showing no signs of finding work or moving back to university. The eldest two – discounted, Sophie noticed, because they were girls – were non-identical twins. Jenny and Emma had left home but were still belittlingly coupled as the Girls in family speech, and were not high flyers either. They had trained as secretaries at somewhere called The Ox and Cow. Jenny, the more level-headed of the two, had worked as a typist at Sotheby's and was getting married that summer. This was a cause of general relief as she had been living 'in sin' with her wealthy fiancé, something their mother had difficulty acknowledging, although he was 'a catch'. The other sister, Charlie's favourite, was giddy and fun-loving and showed no signs of settling. She worked in an estate agent's, to her mother's mortification. Both Girls were coming for supper.

Sophie fell quiet with nerves long before they reached Eel Brook Common but Charlie didn't seem to notice. The house was in the middle of a terrace in a street made to feel doubly crowded by the cars squeezed into every available parking space. When they came through the door, Sophie could see straight through to the kitchen at the back. The immediate impression was of too much furniture purchased for a larger space.

Mrs Somborne-Abbot, Christine, was arguing with the Girls in the kitchen but all Sophie heard was her spitting, 'I am not to be spoken to like that!' before the three realized they had an audience and came hurrying out for an inspection. Tim, a taller, leaner version of Charlie with blue eyes and floppy black hair, a brooding Celt among noisy Saxons, slouched out of the sitting room. It seemed to Sophie that for a clear two or three seconds they were all, Charlie included, looking at her in silence but that was probably her nerves.

If not, it was the only silent instant of the entire evening. The talk was incessant, all of it overlapping, barely a sentence allowed to reach its end uninterrupted. They were extraordinarily bossy with one another. It was all do this, do that, pour it this way, not there you goose, what you ought to do is this. The bossiness even extended beyond those present. When conversation strayed towards public figures the Somborne-Abbots all had opinions about who should do what and why. For the most part they were completely self-sufficient and self-obsessed, entertaining themselves with stories about the Somborne-Abbots and their funny ways they must all have heard before. Tim was the only one to say little, possibly because when he did he was brutally shouted down and, from his contemplative period in India, had lost the technique of interrupting.

Shown to the spare bedroom so she could unpack the small, borrowed holdall she had not intended to unpack at all, and more or less ordered to 'freshen up', Sophie took the chance to lock herself in the hot, claustrophobic bathroom for as long as she dared. She washed her face in cold water and stared at herself. Collar-length brown hair, funny, feline eyes, bumpy nose, tits that seemed to belong to someone else. Not a Somborne-Abbot.

When she had told Lucas where she was going and confessed it made her nervous because she had never stayed with someone's family before, he said the crucial thing was to take a little something.

'Like what?' she'd asked, even more worried now.

'Tea towel. Hankies. Nothing much. Just something to say thank you. Here, Heidi'll have something in her present drawer. I'll do a raid.' Explaining how Heidi kept a stash of unwanted presents for just such moments, he presented her with two floral handkerchiefs in a little box done up with a ribbon. 'There,' he said. 'Perfect. You just hand it over to her when you arrive and she'll say oh you shouldn't have and you say it's just a little something. She'll probably stick it straight in her present drawer without opening it but that doesn't matter. You'll have done the right thing.'

Sophie handed the handkerchiefs over when she returned downstairs. Mrs Somborne-Abbot said oh you shouldn't have, the Girls both had a good look and said very pretty and the box was spirited away in exchange for a tray of drinks and nibbles as the evening began.

Sophie ate and drank several things for the first time: olives, red wine, avocado pears and prawns. Her hostess made a strange fuss about the small white dishes in which the avocados were served.

'I know they're probably N.Q.O.C.D.,' she said, 'but nothing else keeps an avocado quite so still. But I draw the line at those plastic-handled spoke things for holding corn on the cob.'

'You wouldn't if Peter Jones did them in wood or china,' one of the Girls said but her mother was impervious to teasing, apparently.

'If you're so worried, I say, don't eat corn on the cob in public. Don't you think, Sophia?'

Sophie nodded, baffled. She had never eaten any corn but tinned. Margaret sometimes made delicious fritters with the creamed kind to serve with chicken drumsticks. She had no idea what N.Q.O.C.D. meant either beyond inferring it was something bad.

Tim passed her tiny roast potatoes to go with her chicken and winked as though he understood her confusion. This was some comfort because Charlie had barely spoken to her since introducing her but seemed to be regressing into some long-established routine with the Girls. They kept speaking in funny voices, imitating accents of people they had known abroad or in Cornwall, where their father's family lived. She liked Tim best, she decided. She liked his long hair and his relative silence.

The Girls were as loudly confident as Charlie and only the certainty that they were both profoundly undereducated stopped them being frightening – that and their complacent lack of curiosity. They were neat and clean-looking rather than beautiful, with the same thick blonde hair, big jaws and spookily little-girly taste in clothes. One – Sophie was already confusing them – wore a tartan Alice band and, when the other began to show signs of impatience with the way her own hair kept falling across her face, slipped the band off and fixed it onto her sister's head. It was like watching them exchange faces.

Tim topped up her wine and winked again so perhaps it was a twitch, not friendliness. Soon the chicken plates were whipped away and Mrs Somborne-Abbot produced a board of French cheeses. The unaccustomed wine was making Sophie relax. Television families were plainly artificial. Lucas's diminished household didn't really count either. She wondered if this was her first typical family. Besides the bossiness, the thing about them that struck her most forcefully, in the light of how Charlie's behaviour changed now that he was home, was how needy the children were, even Tim in his enigmatic way. Three of them were adults and Charlie nearly was and yet they seemed not have left their childhoods behind. They were forever remembering this or that incident from when they were small and became nakedly competitive in encouraging their mother to remember how sweet they were as babies.

But perhaps this wasn't normal. Perhaps it was an effect of their having all been sent to boarding school when they were small. Or an effect of their being recently bereaved.

There was a prominent photograph of Mr Somborne-Abbot, showing him at the oars of a rowing boat. His were the apple-cheeked, big-boned genes and the dominant ones, which was why his wife looked such a birdlike alien among her strapping brood, fosterer to four cuckoos. On the television stood a silver-framed wedding photograph, with her looking wonderfully delicate but triumphant and him looking like a startled, less confident version of Charlie.

Mrs Somborne-Abbot abruptly took exception to an especially fruity impersonation one of the Girls made of their Nigerian driver, whom apparently they had campaigned to tease to the point of a violent outburst so as to get him sacked. She swung the conversation smartly aside to schoolwork. She was worried about Charlie's maths still. Maths was so important if he was to take science A levels.

'This again,' Tim muttered and brought down howls by cheerfully cutting the pointy bit off one of the cheeses.

'Do you *like* maths?' the Girl now wearing no Alice band asked, wrinkling her nose.

'Sometimes,' Sophie admitted. 'It's satisfying. I suppose, once you've got the hang of something, when it becomes clear, it stays clear. Whereas plays and books and history are sort of cloudy.'

Mrs Somborne-Abbot said that she was sending Charlie for extra maths coaching at a nearby crammer's because he had to get at least a B in his O level to be allowed onto the C ladder.

And suddenly Tim cracked. Why couldn't she just accept they were all thick and were never going to amount to anything much? All she'd ever done was push, push, push. The way she had their father. If anyone was to blame for giving him a heart attack then –

At this point the siblings objected, trying to tease him into calmness as their mother turned white then dangerously pink but Tim pushed back his chair, said, 'Oh just fuck off the lot of you. Not you, Sophie,' and stormed upstairs and slammed his door.

Sophie didn't know where to look, so concentrated on lining up her remaining cutlery.

'And stereo on,' said Charlie, 'and headphones on and . . .
cue groaning . . .'

Sure enough, right on cue, they could hear Tim groaning
along to a song. To Sophie's surprise, Mrs Somborne-Abbot
stifled a giggle and said, 'Don't.'

'The Lord of the Manor,' Charlie said.

'Don't, Charlie!' said one of the Girls then they all laughed,
breaking the tension for a few seconds. But then their laughter
died and the only sound was Tim's tuneless singing. Sophie
looked up at the ceiling.

'I'm so sorry,' Mrs Somborne-Abbot told her. 'He has no
idea how to behave.'

'That's nothing,' Sophie told her.

'Are your brothers *worse*?' one of the Girls asked.

'You could say that,' Sophie suggested. It seemed to fall to
her to rescue them from awkwardness. She imagined what Lucas
would say at that moment. He was always so tactful. She said
it. 'I expect Tim feels he disappointed his father,' she offered.

Perfect response, apparently. All at once they opened out, to
her now, rather than each other. Charlie's Lord of the Manor
quip had been a statement of fact, apparently. Mr Somborne-
Abbot came from an old West Country family. There was a
fine old house in Devon – Sophie was shown several images of
it, the latest being estate agents' details from when it was last
on the market – where the family had lived for hundreds of
years. And there was a title.

'Sorry,' Sophie said, not understanding. 'Was he a lord?'

'No, no,' his widow explained hastily. 'Lord of the Manor
just means the family had duties in the community and would
have received tithes.'

'Landed gentry,' Charlie said, with a curious tightening of

his mouth. 'I mean it was all long ago. His grandfather was the last to own the house and even he didn't live there but we retain the title. Americans have tried to buy it.'

'And those awful people who live there now,' one of the Girls said.

'And as the eldest son,' Charlie finished, 'Tim is now Lord of the Manor and I think it's only just dawning on him.'

Sophie was fascinated. It all made perfect sense now. Charlie's combination of confidence and subdued resentfulness. They were like marooned officers losing sight of their glorious ship. She looked at the pictures again. It wasn't a castle but the house was very old and fine, a manor house, a house that would immediately confer standing on its owners. But they lived in this house in a Fulham terrace, where small rooms had been knocked together to produce a long, thin room that was still, somehow, small.

'Goodness, we've been so rude!' Jenny exclaimed, stifling a yawn. 'We've talked about nothing but us all evening. Tell us about your family, Sophie.'

Sophie tried to focus but realized she was a little drunk. She pretended Jenny was one of the inquisitive Daughters at school and gave her standard reply. 'Oh, you know. Nothing very interesting.'

But she hadn't worded her response quite right or must have looked sad or something because Emma chipped in, 'Have you got lots of brothers and sisters?'

'What is it your father does again?' Mrs Somborne-Abbot asked.

'Well . . .' Sophie started.

'Hey!' Charlie said. 'Don't interrogate her. Who wants coffee?'

131

'Oh but it's fun,' Jenny said. 'I love families. They're always fascinating, like novels, even when people think they're normal and ordinary, they're always odd in some way.'

'Mine really isn't,' Sophie assured her.

Jenny's eyes were gleaming and dark, like a hawk's. 'I bet it is,' she said.

Sophie found she could hardly answer. Her tongue felt thick. The candles seemed to have burned up all the air in the room. 'It really isn't all that . . .' she began.

'Sophie's parents are both dead, okay?' Charlie suddenly said. 'Happy now?'

'They're not dead,' Sophie told him, startled.

'But you . . . You're in an orphanage, aren't you?' he challenged her.

'Yes,' she said. 'But it's called a children's home because lots of us aren't orphans.'

There was an appalling pause during which Tim distinctly groaned that Layla had got him on his knees.

Sophie had looked down at her cheese plate as she spoke but looked back at Charlie now, suspecting two things: that Lucas had betrayed her and that to bring an illegitimate girl to stay was an offensive in a private family battle. He was suddenly absorbed in scraping the pip from a grape which seemed to confirm the second.

'I'm so sorry,' Mrs Somborne-Abbot asked at last, all concern. 'Are there many of you in there?'

'No,' Sophie said, forcing herself to smile, 'it's not like Dickens. There are never more than ten, so it's just like a very big family.'

'And your parents aren't dead?'

'They could be. I don't know. I can't know anything about

them until I'm older and I'm not even sure I'll want to know when the time comes.'

'Oh but it would be fascinating,' Emma said. 'Aren't you dying to know?'

'I don't think they'll turn out to be Lords of the Manor,' Sophie told her. 'Life isn't like that, is it?'

Somehow she managed to deflect the conversation back off herself, perhaps through mention of landed gentry, then pleaded tiredness to escape them all to soak in a bath.

Charlie was sitting on her bed when she came back to her room. The bath had been too hot and she was sweating.

'Sorry about that down there,' he said.

'How long have you known?'

'End of term.'

'Lucas.'

'Yeah.'

She thought of the lies she had told him, the implicit lies, the veiled, fleeting references to Wilf and the others, her prac- tised way of describing days out to the seaside in such a way that they could be mistaken for references to holidays with a smallish family.

'You shouldn't be ashamed of it, you know,' he said.

'I'm not ashamed. But it's a private thing. I just don't like being different from everyone else.'

'But you are different. You're rather amazing.'

'Crap. You won't tell people, will you? Other people?'

'Why on earth should I?'

'Same reason Lucas told you . . .'

'Phi! Of course I won't. As you say, it's private. Lucas isn't very . . . Well, he doesn't always know how people should, you know, behave . . .'

Listening to this cool disloyalty, she considered kissing him. It felt even riskier there than in the library so would be exciting. If she kissed him and his mother caught them it would punish Charlie for using her so callously to score points against his family and would punish his mother for being a snob. There was also a good chance he would find a way to brag about it to Lucas, which would punish Lucas. She needed to hurt Lucas badly.

However, Charlie looked ridiculous in dressing gown and pyjamas, more deserving of a bedtime story than a snog, so instead she sat at the dressing table and told him, as casually as she could, pretending to be more interested in towelling her hair, 'Lucas was Jonty Mortimer's little man all last summer. But I expect he told you. Didn't he? Oh Christ, he didn't!'

This felt good, better than one of Charlie's slobbery kisses. Better yet, Charlie didn't know and it was hard to tell whether he was more shocked at the news or at his friend keeping it from him. The well-fed pinkness of him drained away and he actually paced the room. He was nervous, she saw, more than disgusted, worried for his own reputation.

'I'll tell you what else he's been doing that's really creepy,' she said. 'You know that telescope in his bedroom?'

'Yeah?'

'Well he uses it to spy on a family in the next house down the hill from them. He watched them having sex, and watches the son playing with himself.'

'You are kidding!'

'It's pretty weird. Actually it's a bit pathetic,' she added, setting aside her towel and proud of managing to sound so like Weatherall at her most dismissive.

Now Charlie was even more anxious in case people would talk about him in the same way, or think him gay too because of all the times he'd gone home with Lucas so she reassured him.

'Everyone knows you're not really friends. Even Kimiko knows you go home with him to be polite to Heidi and because Headbourne expected it of him.'

Distancing himself further, he did a deadly parody of Heidi, a kind of improvised riff in which she talked about eating disorders even as she encouraged Sophie to eat the luxurious contents of her double-doored fridge. He was brilliant. He turned the wardrobe into a walk-in larder. He even made himself look a bit like Heidi, suggesting the plucked eyebrows, the raised-heel walk. Even though Heidi had nothing like the Yiddish accent he was putting on – her voice was as elegantly neutral as a newscaster's – he somehow suggested that this grotesque version was her real voice, the voice of her thoughts.

Sophie laughed as she hadn't laughed all evening, knowing they were trampling on something precious to her, and when Mrs Somborne-Abbot suddenly opened the door without knocking, she felt as guilty as if they'd been caught in a full-on snog.

'Now, now, Charlie. Give this poor girl some rest and let her sleep,' she said. Ignoring his protests, she herded him from the room as though he was four, not fourteen.

The next morning Charlie had to go for his extra maths lesson. Used to idleness and solitude, Sophie had assumed she would be left to amuse herself or given a chance to spend time with the mysteriously attractive Tim. She had started an interesting conversation with him about Hindu mythology over breakfast

– he was reading *Siddartha* – and sensed he was not far off inviting her up to his room to listen to records. Instead of which she had the alarming experience of being taken under Mrs Somborne-Abbot's bony wing. Even Charlie protested loyally that Sophie would be fine just reading or watching TV.

'Nonsense,' his mother replied. 'We'll go to the sales.'

So Charlie was dropped off at his crammer's which, judging from the girls gathered on its steps, was full of people just like his sisters, only younger, then Sophie was whisked off in Mrs Somborne-Abbot's car. She drove extremely fast and, it seemed to Sophie, aggressively.

'My father was a racing driver – not professionally you understand – and we all had to pass our advanced tests. I can handle a lorry through a skid pan,' she added darkly. 'Get out of this lane, you stupid little man!'

Superficially they went to Regent Street, to the New Year sales, to Jaeger's and Liberty's and Dickins and Jones. Superficially because, had anyone watched them, that was what they were doing. Actually Mrs Somborne-Abbot was subjecting Sophie to a gruelling combination of etiquette tutorial, interrogation and warning.

'Somborne-Abbots have no imagination,' she began, twitching through a bin of clothes. 'No, it's true,' she insisted, although Sophie had said nothing in the family's defence. 'We have no imagination. It's why we've always produced scientists and engineers or administrators. Charlie's much better off on the C ladder. The other artsy subjects are too . . . What's the word?'

'Subjective?' Sophie suggested.

'Exactly. All that interpretation and choice. Far too difficult. At least with maths and science there's always a right and a wrong answer so once you've done the revision you know where you stand. But Charlie lacks application sometimes. And this maths O level is so crucial. It's really most important that he has no other distractions or demands on his time.'

'Mrs Somborne-Abbot, I'm not Charlie's girlfriend,' Sophie told her. 'If that's what's worrying you.'

'You're not?' Mrs Somborne-Abbot looked up, lovely hands twitched clear of bargain underwear.

'No.'

'Oh. Oh!' She laughed and came over quite girlish. 'Oh, I'm so glad. I don't mean that . . . It's just that . . . You'll think me so foolish. As I say, Somborne-Abbots have no imagination. So you're just his friend?'

'Yes,' Sophie laughed.

'Well, isn't that fun? I think it's so exciting nowadays the way boys and girls can be just friends without it meaning more. Though with the chain of men Jenny's introduced over the last five years, I do get rather confused, I must admit. It's so good, you know, that you're a Daughter at Tatham's. People like to be able to place people. They like to be able to say *He's Dick Somborne-Abbot's boy* or *She's Christine's daughter*. And having you there means that people will be able to say *She's a Daughter at Tatham's, you know, fearfully bright!* and that will help balance out the awkwardness of your not knowing who your parents were. Did she give you up because she was unmarried, do you think? Your mother?'

'Er, I don't know. Probably. People do. I'll know when I'm older.'

'But you might not want to, you said.'

'Yes. I mean, what's the point? So I can turn up on their doorsteps and say remember me?'

Charlie's mother laughed at that. Now that they had established that Sophie was not about to lure her great white hope off the true path to a sensibly unimaginative science qualification and a career in industry, she became entirely frank and, with it, almost likeable. Curiously, given that she was no longer dealing with a potential daughter-in-law, she also began to give Sophie pieces of blunt social advice. They slipped out between comments on clothes and special offers. Don't say serviette, say napkin. Don't say toilet, say lavatory. Don't say pardon, say what. Anything, anything but pardon.

'Don't ask me why, but it's the kiss of death.'

Sophie had the strange sensation of being taken in hand for no other reason than that this woman recognized something in her that made her protective, something of herself perhaps. As she moved the car to a new spot to avoid a traffic warden, parked with speedy precision and whirled Sophie through more shops, she went through the motions of asking Sophie's opinion of this or that item of clothing she would twitch off a railing and hold against herself or even, with a critical stare, against Sophie. But under cover of that she offered her countless little nuggets of sisterly advice. She told her to grow her hair longer and wear it back off her face in a chignon or Alice band.

'Either that or switch from Phi to Sophia so people know where they are.'

She showed her how wearing shoes with a little more heel would appear to narrow her calves and ankles while adding that soupcon of height. She suggested Sophie wear pearls, once she was eighteen, to show off her skin tone, and bought her a string of false ones to demonstrate. She taught her a little cluster of deadly acronyms, not just N.Q.O.C.D. – Not Quite Our Class Darling – but P.L.U. and non-P.L.U., U and non-U. She referred several times to something or someone as 'a bit Petey M. Whitey', which Sophie later learned from Charlie stood for Pleased to Meet You, Toilet.

'Why can't you just say common?' Sophie asked. Mrs Somborne-Abbot, flicking through a rack of silk blouses with a hunter's quick eye, was so shocked she hurried Sophie on in case someone had overheard.

'People used to,' she explained. 'My mother's generation. When people still had maids and so on. But you couldn't now. It wouldn't do.'

As they wove through the crowds and more gloves, belts and dresses than Sophie had seen in her lifetime, she painted a picture of the world as a place full of traps and pitfalls, at once exciting and terrifying, where no one was 'out of your league' but where people – always those omnipresent, omniscient 'people' – were noting and remembering one's least lapse.

'The hardest thing for a girl,' she said as they tore out of Liberty's and made through the crowds for Jaeger's, a shop she spoke of as a kind of safe haven of good taste and good tailoring. 'The hardest thing for a girl is to have to rely on beauty. You're so lucky to have brains. This way!'

Trailing behind her, missing the floury solidities of Margaret and her kitchen, Sophie wondered if she meant to imply an 'instead'.

Mrs Somborne-Abbot found what she said was perfect for Sophie. It was a dark blue woollen skirt. Sophie protested that it wasn't her and that besides she had no money, to which Mrs Somborne-Abbot murmured that it wasn't P.L.U. to speak about money. if you didn't have it, people would know and if they were the right people, would understand and not make you uncomfortable. This was a lesson she had learnt imperfectly herself, it seemed, for she then bought the skirt and insisted Sophie accept it as a late Christmas present.

Sophie was dismayed by both generosity and garment. The skirt seemed ridiculously middle-aged and she would have been far happier with a pair of jeans for half the price or a cheese-cloth dress for even less but she knew better than to say so. When she drew it from its bag however to show Charlie back at the house, he was quite serious in saying how well she looked in it, how grown up and so on. She was curious enough to try it on again on her own, in the spare room, and the self that looked back at her was unfamiliar and older-looking, still a schoolgirl with no family but a schoolgirl with a certain poise. She resolved to beg Margaret for some shoes with a little more heel once her current pair wore out.

That afternoon she and Charlie made an excursion to Hampton Court. Sophie had never been and neither, he admitted after he got them to jump off at the wrong bus stop, had Charlie. They had agreed to be back by five to leave time for Sophie to be escorted back to her train but they were late home, as much from talking too much as from the rush-hour traffic. Mrs Somborne-Abbot was not pleased. While Sophie raced to stuff her few things back in her borrowed bag there was a sharp-edged exchange of views downstairs and it was decided that, because there was not enough time for Charlie to go with her and be back for that evening's engagement, a cab must be called for Sophie to go safely on her own.

'We can't set you loose on the Underground on your own at this time of day if you've never ridden it on your own before,'

Mrs Somborne-Abbot announced. 'The cab will take you almost onto the station platform. Much safer and you've plenty of time.'

In the rush nobody checked to see if Sophie had enough money. She was simply bundled into the taxi which headed off over Wandsworth Bridge because south of the river would be quicker apparently.

Sophie had rashly treated Charlie to a cake and tea at Hampton Court in return for his buying their entrance tickets. She had only four pounds left and the meter soon reached that. She explained her problem to the driver who said only, 'Better let you off here, then, while you've got enough for a bus.'

He left her on a pavement somewhere, in front of a line of boarded-up houses.

She didn't have enough money for a bus but it wasn't raining and she decided to walk, because what else could she do? She remembered noticing that Waterloo was near the Thames so decided to follow the river as closely as the roads let her. She also discovered that there were tiny maps at some of the bus stops which she could use to check her bearings. She set off cheerfully enough, glad simply to be free of Charlie's mother and her traps and judgements but she soon slowed. It was bitterly cold, her windcheater was thin and the big roads she found herself on had few glimpses of the river and fewer bus stops. It was far further than she had realized and, when she finally made her way along the embankment from Vauxhall to Lambeth Palace and from there to Waterloo, she had long since missed the train she had told Kieran to meet. The train she eventually took was a seedy, late one, full of drunk commuters and smoke, which stopped at every station.

Margaret was livid when Sophie eventually walked home

from the station. She had met one train, Kieran another then they had rung the Somborne-Abbots' house, where there was no reply, and decided Sophie was not coming home that night after all. She was even angrier when she heard why Sophie had missed her train and how she had walked across South London on her own.

'I've a good mind to ring her up and tear a strip off her,' she said and Sophie found herself in the funny position of springing to Mrs Somborne-Abbot's defence, blaming herself, blaming Charlie, apologizing abjectly until the subject was dropped and everyone went to bed.

But the subject was not forgotten. Long after Sophie had posted a carefully penned and worded thank-you note on a postcard of the cathedral, Margaret continued to fume about the incident, rehearsing her indignation at the least prompting until Sophie, too, began to feel a sense of grievance that she had been financially presumed upon and even physically endangered. She didn't dare show the new skirt to anyone, not even Wilf, but hung it carefully in her cupboard, a compromised promise of a person she was not yet ready to become.

LENT TERM
(fifteen and a bit)

'I will lift up mine eyes unto the hills,' Reverend Harestock murmured.

'From whence cometh my help,' Sophie, Mr Compton, the sixteen Quiristers and Mr Sutton, the choirmaster, mumbled in reply. Mr Compton was the don she had thought to resemble Peter O'Toole, identified at last by a discreet, offhand enquiry of a bell-ringer in his div.

'My help cometh even from the Lord.'

'Who hath made Heaven and Earth.'

Reverend Harestock announced the psalm, adding as he always did, 'The congregation may sit until the Gloria.'

Sophie and Mr Compton and the Chaplain sat. Mr Sutton played the day's chant through once on the piano which, as usual, was made to sound fractionally out of tune by the

Chantry's cavernous acoustic. One of the smallest boys seemed unable to sing but merely stared up at the altarpiece, eyes red, twisting a sodden handkerchief in his fingers while the others sang around him. It was icily cold, the sun had yet to melt the frost in the cloister garden and the boys' breath rose in little clouds. As ever, Mr Compton had fetched his elegant calfskin psalter out of his overcoat pocket and was following the verses so the Gloria should not catch him unawares.

Sophie tightened her scarf a little and sat back against her pew corner to admire the effect of sunlight on a little school of fish that swam along the border of her favourite window. She drew in chilled air and breathed out peace.

Several notable things had happened already that term. Sophie turned fifteen, which she succeeded in keeping a secret even though Wilf posted her a gigantic bar of Fruit and Nut inside a spangly card in which he had written *Nearly LEGAL!! Love Wilf*. She mastered indirect statements and questions in Greek and the subjunctive in French. Her set texts included *Gormenghast, Language, Truth and Logic*, Paine's *Common Sense* and, in translation, the *Phaedrus* of Plato. And Charlie turned gay.

There was no other way to describe it. There was no discussion or announcement or scene. He was just suddenly talking incessantly about which boys he had crushes on. They were always sporty, older boys, of the Jonty Mortimer mould, inaccessible and godlike. There was no suggestion his crushes were being acted upon or encouraged. But the minutiae of this one's appeal over that one's, of the significance of a glance bestowed in Tubs or a comment let slip in a corridor now absorbed all the energy he had once devoted to talking about his family.

Thanks, perhaps, to all the extra hours he had put in at the library the previous term, he had edged – by a hair's breadth – into the same div as Sophie and Lucas. The boys had become inseparable. With Lucas's gossip and Charlie's mimicry now shorn of whatever restraint had been necessary while each felt the need to persuade the other of his relative normality, they were a noisy gang of two, co-opting Sophie whenever their paths crossed.

She was embarrassed at first, glad to be sitting two rows in front of them in div. She was not a lawbreaker or boat-rocker and would always tend towards behaviour that drew no attention. Then the third time Mr Micheldever had to reprimand them for giggling, he made them move forward to the front row 'with the other Daughters' and they were so delighted to have a chance to sit on either side of her that they stayed on there, choosing infamy. She was made a helpless party to their jokes, their surreptitious messages, passed on scraps or flashed from book margins. Even the gentle rocking of the desk that betrayed the fact that Lucas was laughing at something and trying not to let it show was infectious and she would find herself laughing too, merely at the memory of things they had already found funny several times before.

She resisted it at first, tried to sigh with impatience, to pull herself metaphorically aloof, but they always teased her out of her superior stance with a sneer or a poke or a devastating silent impersonation. She felt excluded by their gayness as much as by the jokes they would often elaborate without her so that their insistence on including her physically – sitting by her, seeking her out, sending her notes through the pigeon-hole system – left her feeling twitchy and even slow-witted. Thanks to the time she had spent alone with one or the other of them, they knew all her hiding places. Nurse adored them – *such charming boys* – and they were quite capable of inviting themselves to tea and telly with her while they waited for Sophie to return from hiding, passing on all manner of information she did not want Nurse to know. The only spots she could remain free of them were the dormitory or bathrooms, where Kimiko could nonetheless seek her out with a message that they were waiting, and these brief morning services in the Founder's Chantry.

Sophie was pulled out of her reverie by Mr Compton standing for the Gloria and stood too, then they all sat down again except for Mr Compton who exchanged his private psalter for his private Bible and announced that day's reading from the book of Judges. As always he paused a little before he began, for the choir to stop fidgeting, coughing and rattling throat-lozenge tins. As always his delivery was tantalizing, intimate, so that the reading had an air more of storytelling than of proclaimed truth.

She was glad of an Old Testament reading. She had fallen out of love with Jesus. Two Sundays previously she had attended her last Christian Union meeting with Kimiko. Instead of a guest speaker, the talk had been given by Dr Liphook, the maths don who ran the group.

'Today,' he said, 'I want to put you all on your guard.' He spoke about homosexuality, with no pussyfootings like *continence*. He cited texts from St Paul and Leviticus to show that it was a sin and warned them not to be swayed by so-called liberal apologists or psychiatric fashions or dangerously appealing pop stars. They were Soldiers of Christ, he reminded them. They were not only to resist approaches made to them by other pupils but to reason with them and persuade them, frighten or threaten them if necessary, into abandoning sin.

'They'll tell you they were born that way. Well I'm sorry, my friends, but we were all born that way insofar as we were all born into sin. To err is human and sometimes to repent and reform takes superhuman strength. Which is where you can help them and Jesus can help you. Help them aim for resistance, for abstinence, for chastity if normality seems too high for them to aim at.'

If evangelizing failed, they were to have no hesitation in reporting any boy or girl known to be indulging in homosexual acts. 'It's not only against the rule of God but against those of the school and, given that they're under twenty-one, the laws of the State.'

Sophie became uncomfortably aware of Kimiko's eyes on her and not only Kimiko's. She raised her hand, irritated, when the time came for questions and asked him some awkward ones. What of Jesus's failure to set an example by marrying? What of the repeated references to his love – *philia* not *agape* – for the disciple John? What of his signal failure to mention homosexuality in the Sermon on the Mount or in his other teachings?

There were murmurs of dissent, even laughter. Dr Liphook fixed her with his watery blue eyes, taking off his glasses for that sincerity effect, and said that perhaps he and Sophie should have a private talk afterwards since the subject was clearly bothering her personally.

Despising him for not mustering the courage or arguments to talk with her publicly, she ignored his suggestion and hurried away afterwards, giving even Kimiko the slip. She spent a happy Sunday at Lucas's house with Charlie, eating Heidi's cookies and watching *The Robe* on television, distancing herself slightly from the boys' guffawing by encouraging Simon to teach her how to solve the *Listener* crossword.

She had forgiven Lucas his betrayal. She had said nothing about it to his face. Having avoided him for what remained of the Christmas holidays she found that her rancour had evaporated. He said nothing to her, either, of her betrayal of his secrets to Charlie. Her indiscretion had apparently admitted a new, mutual openness into his friendship with Charlie. It was just possible that Charlie's betrayal had done the same for her. Shorn of secrets, in their company at least, she felt more completely herself, her school and home personae brought a step nearer alignment.

While Sophie was loading the tea things into the dishwasher for her, Heidi let slip a reference to Wakefield House, discreetly making it clear that she too was fully informed. 'Jumping between that life and Tatham's can't be easy for you,' she said. 'If ever you want to talk, you know I'm always here for you.'

'Thanks,' Sophie told her. She blushed and changed the subject but rather than feeling betrayed yet again, realized she was experiencing something like the encompassing love of family.

Later, when Kimiko passed on the message that Tony, Dr Liphook, had encouraged the group to pray for her, Sophie realized she had broken the habit of a lifetime and taken a stance on a selfless point of principle.

In their way, she decided, Lucas and Charlie were being amazingly brave. She told Kimiko they were like the early Christians daring to be counted. But unlike the early Christians they weren't thrown to the lions or used for target practice. Perhaps because they weren't otherwise perceived as bad boys what with Charlie doing his bit in sport, albeit on an inter-house rather than on an inter-school level, and Lucas working hard and appearing in plays and writing pieces for school magazines, their courage went unpunished. Certainly some boys and girls jeered but equally some dons happily played along with them and found ways to acknowledge their difference without mockery or opprobrium.

Armed with honorary membership of such a gang, she realized that she too could cultivate a reputation for outrageousness provided she tempered it with good marks. So she stopped slipping down from the ringing-chamber to receive communion.

She was quizzed by Charlie about this. He had been confirmed in his last year at choir school and she realized he saw no hypocrisy or strangeness in continuing to endorse an organization that truly despised him. When she tried to broach the subject, he reduced it to mockery, saying, whatever the theory, he would always feel welcomed by men in frocks.

After a couple of attempts to bring her back to the fold, she persuaded Kimiko to give up and agree that they should differ. She knew Kimiko was secretly drawn by their company and was developing a quiet appetite for what might ruin her. She dipped and blushed when Charlie or Lucas complimented her. She kept a wary distance if she encountered them out of doors or in class but when they dropped in on the Daughters' Chamber she hovered nearby, not quite participating, not quite withdrawing, delighted to be shocked. Lucas, who had developed a taste for opera, nicknamed her Suzuki, which was sometimes abbreviated to Sukey or Sue.

Dr Harestock announced the morning's hymn, 'Awake my Soul and With the Sun.' He evidently despised truncation or imprecise delivery. In the evening collect, she had noticed, he never said 'that both our hearts', but always, 'that both', long pause, 'our hearts', to make it clear there was a comma in between and, when announcing a hymn, he never treated the first line as a title but read until the first full stop. This suited

Sophie, who barely sang but liked to listen to others singing while she followed the words in the hymnal, returning them to poetry. She found it almost impossible to perceive sense and sing at the same time in any case and, judging from where they paused for breaths, so did most Christians.

Mr Compton and Reverend Harestock sang, however, lent courage by the hearty singing of the Quiristers. Reverend Harestock had a breathy, nasal voice that faded in and out of audibility like a badly tuned radio. Mr Compton, who looked as though he would have a quiet, even effete tenor tone, produced an unexpectedly hearty baritone, a spirits-raising, campfire sort of voice. Peter O'Toole again.

They all knelt for the Grace then Mr Sutton struck up some cheery piece on the piano and the Chaplain marched out, noisily followed by the Quiristers. Usually Mr Compton swept out on their tail as though smartly whipping his cloak of worldliness back about him, leaving either Sophie or the choirmaster to shut the door. This morning, however, he sat on in his pew, gently tapping his fingers in time to the music.

Sophie felt she should sit on too though she knew it to be an irrational fantasy of hers that these little services were held at his behest. Mr Sutton abruptly finished his voluntary, locked the piano lid and went out with a nervous cough.

'That's better,' Mr Compton said quietly, implying devastating mockery of Mr Sutton's sausagey fingers. 'Silly, isn't it, how one never finds time to come in here when there isn't a service on? It's extraordinarily peaceful.'

'Yes,' she said. 'But I like the morning service too.'

'So I see. You haven't been in one of my classes yet. I'm Compton. Who are you?'

'Cullen,' she told him. 'Sophie Cullen.'

'Miss Cullen. A pleasure. You must hurry or you'll be late for div and so shall I.'

'Yes, sir.'

They stood and he ushered her before him with a minute inclination of his handsome head.

'Would you like to come to tea?' he asked. 'Nothing frightening.'

'Thank you,' she said. 'Yes, please. When should I come?'

'You don't play in either orchestra, do you?'

'No, sir.'

'Thought not. Well come this afternoon, then. I'll expect you at four. Come through the back entrance. It's the wrought-iron gate in the wall to the right of War Cloisters if you're walking from Schola.'

Lucas was off sick with 'flu that day so she could not discuss the invitation with him. Without Lucas there to whip him on, Charlie was unusually quiet and thoughtful but even so some instinct held her tongue with him.

Mr Compton was a keen gardener. He oversaw the upkeep of the Warden's Garden and, over the last few years, had bought and planted himself the hundreds of bulbs that emerged in late winter and early spring in swathes around the trees that marked the paths between Brick Court and Stinks. The high-walled garden behind his house was lush and almost entirely without flowers. She only learned later, from an art history student, that he had ripped out old roses and lilacs to make it and had modelled it on the jungles painted by Rousseau.

Arriving from the back, one passed through a narrow, wrought-iron gate in the school's original flint-studded outer wall then followed a winding gravel path through dense planting. Plants she could not name soon hid wall and house with huge leaves or tropical spikes. It was unlike any garden she had ever seen, not obviously pretty, not even obviously nice. Its aim was to disorientate rather than simply to please, although it was pleasing too. Just not pretty. Giant silvery fish stirred the face of a deep pond set in the garden's heart, where the foliage was cleared to provide the one sunny area, then the artificial jungle closed about one again as the path wound on to the big glass porch on the house's rear.

Mr Compton let her into what felt like a heated extension of the garden, a marble-tiled room dotted with seven-foot potted palms, and waved her onto one of the comfortable rattan sofas draped with sun-bleached rugs and cushions. There was a tang in the air she could not place until she realized that, unlike any of the dons she had met so far, he wore aftershave.

'*Eau Sauvage*,' she said without thinking.

He looked startled.

'Sorry, sir,' she said, confused to be so abruptly reminded of Lucas. 'A friend of mine wears it.'

'House rule,' he said. 'While you're in here, I don't "Miss" and you don't "Sir".'

'But what do I call you?' she asked and he smiled.

'Since there's only the two of us here, I think we'll know who we're talking to. What kind of tea would you like?'

'I don't know. I never normally have a choice.'

'I'm having karkady. It's Egyptian hibiscus. Bright red and tastes of lemons. Very refreshing.'

'That sounds great.'

There was music playing from somewhere, outrageous, lush music with opera singers and what sounded like an orchestral army. Sophie was used to people's stereo systems being proudly displayed. As he disappeared between the palms to make their tea, she craned her neck in vain to see the huge speakers that must been generating such an intensely textured sound.

She had been into dons' houses before. Essays often had to be delivered that way, left on hall tables or handed to exhausted wives. In the upper sixth, she knew, it was common-place to be taught in dons' studies or drawing rooms in groups of four or fewer. But the interiors she had seen so far had all felt like extensions of the school, public spaces the dons and their families were briefly inhabiting but on which they had left little mark. There was something provisional and battered about them. Whether because she had entered through the jungly garden or because there were no books or papers on view, in this room she felt admitted to somewhere personal and private where she might gain knowledge of the room's possessor.

He turned the volume down somewhere before coming back to serve the tea Egyptian-style, in brass-handled glasses on a big brass tray he balanced on a squat carved table. There was a plate of tiny spiced biscuits he said were flavoured with cardamom so would taste of orange. The tea was strange, not really tea at all, blood-red and tart. He watched for her reac-tion as she took a sip.

'I can get you something more normal if you'd prefer,' he offered. 'There's Ceylon.'

But she shook her head. 'No. It's good. Thank you.' She sipped again. It wasn't good. It was strange but she wanted to prefer it to the normal stuff so drank more, thinking of it as hot lemon squash so that her palate didn't react against its not being tea. She suspected he knew she was making an effort. 'I like your jungle,' she said.

'Thank you. It's not really mine. The house was radically

remodelled by Fulke Winnall, who founded the art department in the 1900s. The house was his so he did what he liked with it – he obviously wasn't short of a bob – and then he left it to the school in this state. He knocked down so many walls that it's quite unsuitable for dons with wives and children. I just happen to be the current lucky bachelor. It's a good retreat. When these windows are open in the summer and the fountain's on, the splashing water seems to block out any sounds from beyond the walls. There used to be orange trees in here but they were forever getting infested by whitefly so I gave up and bought these instead.' He batted at a palm leaf with his hand. 'You're going to be a classicist, I gather.'

'Am I?'

'Judging from your marks, you are,' he said. 'Would it please you?'

'Yes.'

'Why?'

'I'd like to be Senior Prefect.'

'For that study?'

She nodded so unthinkingly that he smiled.

'I didn't think it'd be for power,' he said, then thought a moment. 'You've got good friends, haven't you? I've noticed you together a few times, you, Behrman and the other one.'

'Somborne-Abbot.'

'That's the one.'

'Oh dear. Were we being noisy?'

'Not especially. It's good to have friends, especially outside your own house. But you like to escape them sometimes too, I expect.'

'Yes.' She looked for a way of explaining herself. 'I'm not . . . They have strong personalities and I'm not used to being in a gang. Sometimes I need time apart to . . . Well, in a funny way, to be myself again.'

'Odd, isn't it,' he said, 'how friends can project an idea of you back that isn't quite you? And rather than set them right, you work harder and harder to be that person they expect. Parents do the same thing. They're often too busy driving to get the child they want to notice the one they've got. That friend of yours, Behrman. I expect his parents assume he's going to leave here to go to Cambridge then up to the Bar like his father.'

'They've never said.'

'They don't need to. It's an assumption. And in fact he probably wants to go to Glasgow and be a painter.'

'Actor,' she said. 'RADA. He hasn't dared tell them.'

'Hmm. More?'

'Yes, please.'

He reached across from his sofa to refill her glass.

'So how do you escape these friends of yours when you need to be yourself again?'

'I go to the library,' she said, 'or take a long bath or lie on my bed with a book.'

'And you come to morning service.'

'Yes. But I'm not really a Christian. I tried to be but . . .'

'Me neither.'

'Aren't you?' To her surprise she found that she was profoundly shocked at this.

He looked wistfully out at the garden and sighed. 'Not really. But I went along to morning service a few times out of curiosity then the Chaplain asked me to read the lesson and all at once the rest of the regular congregation seemed to die or drop away so I rather felt I had to keep going. But the peace is good and the contemplativeness of it. Organized religion can be as over-whelming and unsatisfactory as organized friendship. I dare say I could hand over the reading duties to you, now?'

'Don't you dare!' she said without hesitation, which made him chuckle.

'Do you like this music?'

'I don't know,' she said. 'I've never heard it before.'

'Wagner. *Tristan*. Act Three.'

'Oh.'

'Not a good place to start if you know nothing of opera. He had trouble with religion too. He liked religiousness – the feel-ings that religion can induce – but wanted to find ways of arousing those feelings away from church through music drama. I only discovered the other day that he had dreams of writing a Buddhist opera because Buddhism appealed to him with its apparent lack of churchiness. Astonishing idea! A bit like Lord Britten's dream of adapting *Mansfield Park*. One of those pleas-ures we shall never taste. Ah well. It's been a pleasure meeting you, young Cullen.'

Sophie stood, understanding herself dismissed. She worried that her expression had revealed her lack of comprehension but, as he opened the garden door for her and she thanked him for the karkady, he added, 'You must come again. Feel free to drop in any weekday afternoon. If it's not convenient, I lock the gate or simply don't come to the door.'

'Thank you, sir. Sorry. I mean, thank you.'

She said nothing about the visit to Lucas or Charlie after-wards. Or even to Kimiko. It might have felt like smugness. She told herself she would mention it if the subject arose natu-rally but it never did. For fear of proving a bore, she went back several times that term but always on different days of the week.

On her second visit they sat out in cool sunshine by the pond and talked about the *Phaedrus*. He was actually an English don but he took a deep interest in every subject and gave the impression of having read more widely than any teacher she had met so far.

Thereafter she never had him to herself on visits. She was one of a select band, she realized – *ma Petite Bande* he called them – quoting yet another book she could not place. They were all students who had caught his eye or ear for some reason. She was flattered. All the others seemed to be extremely clever and all of them were older than her. But house rules applied. So long as they were drinking his karkady there was no sneering or teasing or pulling of rank and ideas and discoveries were batted about as though they were equal members of a symposium, not vastly unequal representatives of a hierarchy.

Time spent in Mr Compton's garden room left her inexplicably euphoric, even though she often did little there but sip and listen. At times the conversation made her feel that everything was connected, Greek, maths, opera, Lucifer, Mrs Somborne-Abbot and the redness of hibiscus tea and that she was teetering on the brink of a point, maturity perhaps, where the artificial divisions between subjects would tumble down and she would begin to make calm connections for herself without effort.

She never met other girls in the house, something that gave her a pleasure she could not explain to herself, given that she would not have liked to be the only girl in somebody's class. A boy brought a girl with him just once when Sophie was there. Because he had to introduce her, it was immediately evident that she was uninvited. Nobody said anything unwelcoming and Mr Compton was his usual self towards her but Sophie could tell from the way the boy talked more to the girl than to anyone that he had broken an unwritten rule. The two of them sat apart on an old swing seat, like a faintly ridiculous courting couple in an H.G. Wells novel. She saw neither of them there again.

EASTER HOLIDAYS
(fifteen years, three months)

Dear Lou,

You get no sympathy at all. If Jean Luc's big brother is so beau you can't dormir for dreaming of him, practise your best boudoir Frog and tell him so. At best this means the two of you live happily ever after, at worse, he tells their maman and your fucking exchange trip comes to an early end and we get to play again. It's Jean Luc I feel sorry for. No wonder he's sulky if you're pining after Christophe all the time. Would he do for me? Not even a little bit?? Oh. Okay, then.

Revision going to plan. Naturally, because there's nothing else to do. You'll have to help me with the French, though Ça m'agace!! I'll trade you for Latin.

This place is going to get even quieter soon because my only real mate here leaves tomorrow. Guess that just leaves Heidi. I can go and see her and pretend to be pining for you and we'll have a long, girly heart-to-heart about your needs.

Keep your hair on. Joke.
Kiss me there but mind the zit. Miss Phix.

Sophie reread the letter. It was a prepaid aerogramme and she had written too large and run out of space. She sealed it and carefully copied out the address in Poitiers Lucas had sent her. Then she turned to the postcard Charlie had sent her from Cornwall.

He wasn't in love but complained of being bored from spending time with horse-faced girls whose brothers were all too young to be interesting.

Sturmführer Christine says to bring you and Lucas when she rents this place again. Would you like that? Surf and stuff to celebrate finishing our Os? She has painted her toe nails cerise and decided she likes The Bee Gees. Spare me. Next stop: hot pants and disco dancing on dad's grave. Kisses, Brown Girl in the Ring.

She started a suitably non-committal reply. The thought of being trapped in a Cornish holiday house with Christine Somborne-Abbot and the Girls was too frightening to contemplate just then. She had been promised a waitressing job in the summer holidays. Charlie, like Lucas, had an allowance and would fail to understand the preciousness of the five pounds a day she would be earning.

The landing creaked, then there was a light tapping on her door in the pattern – two short, two long – she had agreed so long ago with Wilf that she didn't need a moment's reaction time before calling out hi. He was still flushed from his afterwork bath. Now that he was an apprentice mechanic at UBM, no amount of washing quite removed the air of diesel and oil that hung about him but it was not unpleasant. The effect was similar to the contradictory, tarry-clean smell of the anti-dandruff shampoo Sophie used.

He flopped in the armchair between the table where she worked and the window. Both were pieces of furniture Kieran and he had found in skips and dragged back to the house.

'You all packed?' she asked.

'Yup,' he sighed and looked at his hands in the way he did when upset.

He had broken his nose during term-time, when he and some mates from work were drawn into a drunken brawl outside a disco. Far from spoiling his face, the new, broader nose was the making of it, providing an air of craggy resilience that suited him better than his old one had done. His other new look was a chunky silver identity bracelet he had bought with his first pay packet. He was forever fiddling with it, as he did now, turning it around his wrist, still unused to the sensation of it flopping down onto the top of his hand.

'It's going to feel so weird without you,' she said. 'I hope you'll still come and see us.'

'I hope you'll come and see *us*,' he countered.

'Well, sure,' she said, dropping her pen and pushing back her chair so she could face him properly.

But she wasn't sure. Tomorrow Wilf's mother, Elsa Franks, was coming out of prison and he was going to live with her. He had always complained about her, dismissing her as stupid and irresponsible and a lousy mother. But from the day her letter came saying she had a release date it was as though he had never said a word against her. A great store of filial respect had been revealed in him.

With help from his social worker, he found them a brand-new council flat in the town centre and busied himself getting it ready. He let slip details about her he had never revealed before, that she had a bad knee now and couldn't manage stairs, that she loved music, that she was nearly sixty – far older than Sophie had always pictured her. He checked himself occasionally, as if remembering, under Sophie's gaze, the number of times he had called Elsa 'useless scrubber' and 'poxy witch'.

'I'm all she's got, Soph. I've got to do right by her. I won't be there for long. Three or four months max and we'll be driving each other up the fucking wall. She's a filthy temper. She killed a bloke, don't forget.'

And Sophie didn't need to point out the obvious rejoinder, that his mother was all he had too.

So tonight was his last in the home and tomorrow his first in ten years out of its shifting tribe and back in a family of two. Sophie knew she would have to meet his mother and was unaccountably apprehensive. His leaving the home to move in with Elsa threatened to define him, to fix him in a way that would also accentuate the unconnected paths they were taking.

'This your revision plan?' he asked, suddenly rolling out of his chair to tweak the two sheets of A4 off her table. He sat down again at once to examine them but the comforting smell of him reached her, diesel and Dettol. He persisted in turning his bathwater milky with disinfectant in the belief it would clear up the spots on his shoulderblades.

'Jesus H, Soph,' he breathed, looking over the neat table she had drawn herself. 'No wonder you didn't want a holiday job yet. When's your first paper?'

'Oh, a few weeks into term, but I figured it was easier to revise before term starts so I can spend the time that's left going over whatever's still giving me trouble.' She had been rigorously methodical, dividing the days in the holidays by the O level exams she would have to sit, discounting the general paper, so that each paper should have an equal share of revision time. 'There's something nice about ticking stuff off,' she told him. 'And when the time runs out for something, the time runs out and I have to move on. That's quite nice too.'

'Sounds fucking awful.'

There was laughter from Kieran downstairs. He rang the bell for supper and the house was full of hurrying footfalls, flushing loos and chatter. They could hear Margaret arguing with Zacky, who was still kicking a football around the garden. It was a house tradition to make supper a bit special on anyone's last night. The leaver got to choose the main course and the newest arrival, the pudding. This was Margaret's way of knitting new arrivals in and, Sophie supposed, subtly reminding the leaver that the tribe would carry on without them. Choices had to come from Margaret's repertoire. She kept a box of index cards showing well-thumbed recipes she had successfully scaled up for bigger numbers.

Used to the time it took to call in and settle the youngest ones, Sophie and Wilf made no movement to go down just yet.

'What did you choose?' she asked.

'Shepherd's pie,' he said.

'You're joking! We have that every week, nearly.'

'So? I like it. I like the way she gets crunchy bits round the edges.'

'Does your mum cook?'

He shook his head slowly and looked at his hands again. 'Not unless she's learnt inside. The last meal I remember her making was one of those horrible meat pies from a tin and a tin of beans and a tin of carrots.' He snorted, amazed. 'I'm going to have to teach her how a freezer works. Soph?'

'What?'

'If you suddenly heard from your mum, whoever she is, and she wanted you back, you would go?'

Sophie thought. 'I dunno. I mean, it wouldn't really be *back*, would it? I don't remember her. I remember books. Nothing but books. And being very quiet. And looking out of a window into trees. Maybe there's a good reason I remember that but not her. Or him. Maybe there was just a dad and he couldn't cope on his own.'

'But would you go if they asked?'

'I'd be curious,' she said. 'I can't pretend I wouldn't.'

'You'd probably be pissed off too,' he said, grinning.

'Yeah. Give 'em a piece of my mind. Oh. I dunno. It's not going to happen, anyway. I'm fifteen. No one wants a fifteen-year-old.'

'I thought you were sixteen now,' he said.

'Next birthday.'

'You could pass, you know.'

She caught his covert glance at her tits. 'Thanks,' she told him.

'I'm going to miss you,' he added. 'It's going to be weird, isn't it?'

He looked tragic suddenly and she knelt on the floor in front of his chair so she could hug him. He hugged her back and gave a fruity sniff, so she knew when she next looked his eyes would be red and cloudy with tears.

'Here,' she said. 'It's not the end of the world,' although there was a wrenching in her heart too. She bent to kiss him on the side of the face but he turned at the same moment so they kissed on the lips. Properly, as they would have said a year ago.

Margaret called up the stairs so they had to pull themselves together and go down. He blew his nose and she brushed her hair, avoiding his eye, then they went down. She didn't feel all churned up as she had when Charlie had once cupped her breasts while kissing her. She felt only sad, a desperate, hungry sort of sadness like her salty homesickness when she had started at Tatham's, a sadness that could only be answered by touching him.

The spaces left for them at the kitchen table were far apart, which was probably a good thing. She sat between Kieran and Zacky. Zacky had stopped trailing around after her, brutally cured of his fixation by her absence during term-time, but he still saved her a place at meals when he could and liked to sit on the floor and lean against her legs when they were all watching television.

In answer to someone's questions, Kieran said how he had been in care too, as a boy, raised by very strict monks in Ireland. 'Like a boarding school, only we never went home,' he said. 'And the only women we ever saw were the statue of the Blessed Virgin in the playground grotto and the laundresses who collected the dirty clothes and sheets once a week. They were in care too, poor girls, only they were older.'

'Were you unhappy?' she asked him.

'Miserable,' he said. 'As sin itself. I had good friends but I was miserable. They were very tough with us.'

'Did they beat you?' Zacky asked with a disturbing kind of relish.

'Sometimes,' Kieran said uneasily. 'I used my psalter to count off the days.'

'How was that?' Sophie asked.

'We worked our way through it day after day, night after night. In Latin, mind you, which I never really understood. A psalm for morning and a psalm for evening, sometimes more than one, sometimes just bits if it was very long. Every day. So

I worked out how many weeks till I'd be sixteen and allowed to leave and how many times we'd sing each psalm till then and I started counting them off. I made a tiny dot in the back of the psalter each time we finished Psalm 150 again.'

It was one of those occasions – their birthdays and wedding anniversary were the others – when Sophie received a strong sense of the degree to which Kieran and Margaret had sacrificed themselves. Or if not themselves then the things which constituted a life for so many people: home, family, friendships, travel. They had a home within Wakefield House – a bedroom, sitting room and bathroom that were off-limits – but they were rarely in them. They had no family of their own. They seemed to have few friends who were not ex-residents of the home. They never took holidays. Because one of them was always required to cover for the other, they never had simultaneous days off and when either was taking time off they seemed invariably to gravitate back to the kitchen to see if the other needed help or company.

Kieran had been married to someone else before he met Margaret and it hadn't worked out. Perhaps he was sterile? Sophie could not imagine asking him and she had never dared enquire of Margaret. Given that she spent so little time in private, Margaret had a necessarily fierce sense of privacy. She had a knack for sharing her character but not her life and Kieran was much the same. Revelations like this one about his miserable childhood were rare and Sophie even thought she saw something flash between them as though Margaret were warning him to change the subject. She wondered idly what would happen if society did not regularly throw up these childless, patient people, monks, nuns, Margarets and Kierans, to take on surplus children.

She felt Wilf's eyes on her. She glanced down at her plate

then looked back and he gazed back, hard and unsmiling, so she knew to expect him later.

The meal seemed to go on for hours, although they could not have been at the table for more than two, even allowing for Margaret's inevitable reminiscences of the bad things and good which Wilf had got up to in his ten years under their roof.

There was the usual sense of anticlimax as the celebration supper segued into the social diminuendo that ended every ordinary day: television, ping-pong, embattled bathtimes and dolings-out of medication. Sophie started watching *Sapphire and Steel* with the rest but she could not focus her mind on it so slipped upstairs. She found the normality of it all upsetting, the realization that Wilf's leaving meant almost nothing to most of the other residents.

Taught by boarding school, she had grabbed a shower earlier in the afternoon, when hot water was plentiful and there was no one about. So now she simply brushed her teeth, washed her face extra carefully, scrubbing at her nose with TCP the way Lucas had taught her, and went to bed. She did not try to sleep because Charlie had opened her eyes to the risk of waking up with bad breath. Instead she banked up her pillows and sat up against her rickety headboard and revised her physics.

Work equals force times distance, she read in handwriting that no longer matched the way she was writing now. *Or joules equal Newtons times metres.*

Someone came up the stairs but carried on past her door.

Power equals work done divided by time taken, she read on. *Or Watts equal joules over seconds. Energy can neither be created nor destroyed. Energy can be converted into different forms but total E always stays same. Law of Conservation of Energy.*

She put the book upside-down and, as she had been doing

since she was eleven or so, pictured the page she had just been looking at and read aloud the information on it. But she got something wrong. She was checking what it was when an ultra-quiet version of two shorts and two longs sounded on her door.

'Hi,' she said softly and he came in.

'You awake?' he asked.

'Course.'

She slid her physics notebook onto the lino as he came over and sat on her bed. She reached up and touched his broken nose, feeling the slight bump in the bone. He kissed her hand. Then she touched the side of his face and drew his head down so they could kiss.

'Is this okay?' he asked after a while.

'Course,' she said, mentally explaining to Kimiko, Margaret, Dr Liphook and the Christian Union that she knew what she was doing and she was ready. Quite ready. 'Are you going to get in properly?'

'Okay.'

They kissed some more and he was still outside the bedding.

'Maybe if you locked the door . . . ?' she murmured.

'Oh,' he said. 'Yeah. Maybe,' and he went to lock it.

As he was coming back, she sat up and switched off the bedside light so they had only the wash of streetlamp across the window and could see shapes but not expressions. He kicked off his shoes and started to unbutton his shirt – it was his best one, she had noted – but she said, 'No. Let me.' She slipped out of bed to stand before him and took off his clothes one by one, releasing small, warm wafts of diesel, Dettol and hot boy skin and noticing how he always kept one hand on her as she worked, on her face, or breast or back of her head. They laughed as she tweaked off his socks, which made it easier to manoeuvre off his underwear and draw him back into bed with her.

He kissed her differently once he was naked. He grew impatient with the boy's pyjamas she slept in and didn't apologize when one of the buttons clattered off as he tugged the jacket over her head. The rest happened rather fast and for a few minutes she was in bed with a quite different version of him from the one she knew.

When he came he said her name as though his life depended on her and he clutched her tight against him, a hand on either buttock, as though anxious she catch every drop. 'God,' he sighed, returning to himself. 'Jesus, Soph!' and she heard the usual Wilf come back to her. 'Was that okay? Did it hurt?' He pulled away as though straining to focus on her in the dark. She saw his eyes glitter.

'Not much,' she lied. 'It was nice.' She drew him to her again, shifting his weight between her legs and wondering if it was normal to begin to feel pleasure afterwards rather than during. 'I wanted it to be you,' she added truthfully.

He was very gentle with her then, kissed her, kissed each breast in turn. Then he fetched a handkerchief from his jeans and used it to form a kind of pad between her legs.

'Dead hamster,' she chuckled.

'What?'

'Nothing. Hold me.'

'You're not on the pill, are you?' he asked.

'I'm fifteen, Wilf. I'm still at school.'

'Some blokes say you never get pregnant your first time.'

'Yeah, well, half the kids in here are living proof of what balls that is.'

They fell asleep together. It was only a single bed, of course, so they had to lie close. Several times in the night she turned over and felt him turning and settling too, warm against her. She liked it best when she was facing away from him but holding one of his arms about her, his hand pressed under hers, his bracelet marking the skin beneath her breasts.

She had no sense of his leaving, only a sudden awareness, after dawn, that when she rolled there was no more resistance, no more answering warmth.

Because she had only slept fitfully so long as he was with her, she fell into deep slumber once she was alone and over-slept by hours. She could hear Kieran mowing the grass when she next opened her eyes. When she finally dressed and came down, Wilf had left for his new life. His belongings were all gone and the room at the front that had been his for as long as she could remember, had already been claimed by Zacky.

Sad but also a little reassured because she did not trust Wilf not to betray by some word or gesture how they had passed the night, she was drawn to the kitchen and Margaret. She ate two bowls of Shreddies at one end of the table watching Margaret make a steak and kidney pie then an apple crumble at the other. There was something deeply comforting about nibbling a flour-dusty chunk of cooking apple and watching her at work.

'You missed seeing his mum,' Margaret told her. 'She came by in a friend's car to pick him up so they could arrive at the new flat together.'

'What's she like?'

Margaret concentrated on spreading crumble mixture over a dish of apple chunks without spilling it. 'He looks just like her,' she said at last. 'Only she's blonde. Out of a bottle, mind. She wanted to meet me and see where he'd been living while she was . . . away.'

'In prison.'

'Yes.'

'Did she really kill someone?'

Margaret shrugged and turned to slide the crumble into the oven. 'I don't think she planned to. She was desperate for money. She thought Wilf was going to be taken away from her if she couldn't provide for him properly. She'd stolen before but only in a small way. Then she got involved in this robbery that went wrong. She shot a policeman, I think. Or a store detective. Tragic really, losing him by trying to keep him. It was great seeing them together again.'

'Was he pleased?'

'Oh, you know Wilf. Never likes to let much show. But he obviously loves her. She's got herself quite a son. Are you okay, Soph? You look worn out.' She felt Sophie's forehead briskly.

'I'm fine,' Sophie said. 'Slept badly, that's all.'

'You've been working too hard. Have a day off.'

'Can't. Physics today.'

'Just a day though?'

'I'd get behind. Why did my mother give me up, then?'

Margaret sighed, brushed the flour off her hands with a tea towel and came over to sit by her. 'I wish I could tell you,' she started.

'Why do I have to wait? It's not as though I'm going to turn up on her doorstep. Not after all this time.'

'It's not fair, is it?'

'No it fucking isn't.'

Margaret tutted and gave her a warm, floury hug. She gave her the scant comfort of the explanation she had offered so often before, that girls often got pregnant when they were too young to cope, by boys too young to bear responsibility or by men not free to marry them. 'Whoever she was, whoever she is,' Margaret assured her, 'she won't have given you up lightly, anymore than Wilf's mother wanted to give up him.'

There was an outburst from the dayroom, where a fight had broken out over the ping-pong table. Sophie took advantage of Margaret being called away to steal a few squares from the block of cooking chocolate in the temporarily unlocked larder before she returned to her room and the day's portion of revision.

An envelope had been pushed under her door but had slid under the lino instead of above it so she hadn't noticed it earlier. There were some tightly folded photocopies inside and a little note from Wilf, with oily fingerprints on it.

> Thought I'd copy these for you before I moved out. Didn't see you getting round to doing it for yourself. I didn't read them and the originals are back under lock and key in M&K's office. Be good littlun. William xx

He had crossed out two attempts to spell original. She noted the way he signed himself. Only his mother still called him William.

The papers represented the slim contents of her personal file. They gave her name, date of admission and the brief reports made after her annual review by the social workers. Settling in well. No wish expressed to be considered for adoption or family fostering. Enjoying school. Et cetera.

Sophie curled up on her bed reading them closely.

Just one paper stood out from the others. It was far earlier, dating from when she was not quite two and recorded an application to foster her, pending their hoped-for adoption of her, by a married couple. Their names and address were given. Mr and Mrs Adrian Pickett, The Old Vicarage, in a village just outside the city boundaries. His profession was listed as civil servant, hers as cello teacher.

She cursed Wilf for the snippet of information, however kindly meant. She had never wanted it, or not much, but now that she had it her mind had difficulty focusing for long on anything else. Through the *Henry V* choruses, the Reform Act, the sexual organs of flowers and the scandal of Alcibiades and the herms, she kept imagining the house, the woman, the man. Adrian Pickett was an older husband by ten or even fifteen years, who worshipped his young wife and did all he could not to make her feel too bad about her failure to produce children. He had bought her a lapdog or a greyhound as compensation. Yes, a greyhound was best; she had met one on the street recently and it was the first large dog that had not scared her. The decision to adopt had been the wife's, she decided, instantly, lovingly supported by him. His only condition being that they adopt a girl first and that it be named after his late grandmother.

At last she could bear it no longer and, lent courage by a ninety-five per cent score on a physics self-testing, she wrote a letter.

Dear Mr and Mrs Pickett,
    You won't remember my name, I expect, but we have met at least once, when I was a baby. I have discovered that you applied to foster me but that your application was then cancelled. Either that or you did foster me then gave me up again. Don't feel bad. All I can remember are your bookcases. I still love reading. But naturally I am wondering why. Perhaps you could let me know. I have so little information about my origins that every small detail is precious.

She only realized the truth of this as she wrote it. Damn Wilf! Damn him!

As you can see from my address, no-one else adopted me.

She crossed out the last line, rejecting it as too crudely pathetic, then decided to reinstate it. Then the letter looked too messy so she copied it out again perfectly, just as Kimiko would have done.

No reply came but the writing of the letter stilled the curiosity Wilf's research had aroused. Perhaps they no longer lived at the same address? Perhaps they were dead? Perhaps her letter had been daintily chewed up by the imaginary greyhound on arrival?

The summer term was starting and Sophie left her vulnerable, no longer virginal self at home to resume her carefully constructed school persona. All that mattered for the next ten weeks was exams.

CLOISTER TIME
(fifteen years, five months)

At a sign from the umpire all the players began to leave their places around the cricket pitch. For a brief, lovely moment Sophie thought the match was over then she realized the fielders were not leaving the field but transferring to their mirror positions in relation to the facing batsman.

'End of an over,' Lucas interpreted for her, reading her mind.

As he changed positions, Charlie looked across at where she and Lucas were slumped in deckchairs beneath a mulberry tree. He inclined his head slightly and pulled the subtly disapproving face that was a standing joke between them; one eyebrow raised, mouth a thin line, superhumanly impervious to all answering smiles or laughter. He had been pulling it in exams and had twice succeeded in earning Lucas an invigilator's shush for snorting.

Sophie and Lucas raised hands in gleefully uncool waves just before he had to turn his back on them, then they subsided, oppressed by the heat. A series of balls followed, each neatly chipped to the grass by the batsman in a way that scored him no runs but couldn't be caught.

'Do you understand cricket?' Sophie asked.

'Not really.'

'But you used to have to play it, you said.'

'That's one of the mysteries of the game – that you can be made to play every summer from seven to thirteen and still be a little hazy about the rules. You just go where you're told and try not to be upset when people get cross with you.' He yawned. 'It hurts like hell if you make the mistake of trying to catch the ball – that I do remember.'

'But is Charlie any good?'

'Not really. Keen, though.'

She had a sheet of Latin revision on her lap, carefully folded several times so it would look like no more than scrap paper and she would not be thought a swot.

'Test me,' she asked and Lucas took the sheet and stared at it a moment.

'Which way round?' he asked.

'English into Latin's hardest.'

'Okay . . . Buffoon.'

'*Scurror.*'

'Dandy, jester or parasite.'

'*Scurra.*'

'Rubbish.'

'It's not!'

'No. The Latin for rubbish.'

'Oh. Sorry. *Scruta.*'

'To examine or find out.'

176

'*Scutor*. No. *Scrutor*.'

As he ran through the vocab list, she took care to flunk several words she knew perfectly well so that he wouldn't know she knew them all. The school was founded on the perfectibility of mind and body and yet it was only feats of the body that were countenanced as a source of pride. It was a kind of good manners, she reflected, to bluff and fumble like this until faced with an exam paper, rather than revealing too much knowledge, but also a kind of guerrilla warfare.

'You'll do,' he said eventually and flicked the list back onto her lap with a touch of peevishness.

Anyone who claimed to have lost count of how many papers were still to be sat was lying. There were just six to go, including the Latin prose and French dictation, the hardest exams to prepare for since revision for them had to take in everything knowable in either subject. Lucas had been trying to make her speak French earlier but she had rebelled because her accent made him giggle.

The country was suffering a heatwave and a hosepipe ban. Charlie did not know it but half the reason for watching him in this match was the honourable excuse it gave to leave the airless library for the refreshment of sitting in shade and looking on grass that had not cooked to yellowness. The cricket pitches were the only green grass left in the city. They were watered by a Victorian pump system running from the nearby river. Legend had it that small dried-out fish could sometimes be found on their sacrosanct turf.

There could not have been a crueller time for exams. A levels took place in the concert hall where there was the luxury of a string of doors open onto the Warden's Garden. O levels took place in the school's gym at rows of little folding chairs and tables stacked in a barn the rest of the year. Although the room was as large as a large church it became insufferably fuggy by late morning with the sun on its roof and a hundred or more students fretting, sighing, fighting to concentrate. The doors and windows remained closed to keep out noise from a nearby street. Someone fainted every day. During the first history paper this had been one of the invigilators and chaos had broken out on his side of the gym just long enough for a flurry of blatant information-exchange. The only advantage of being in the gym was its proximity to the swimming pool; Sophie and Lucas had celebrated the end of each afternoon paper so far with a glorious, hour-long plunge.

Charlie did not come swimming, and not just because he swam like a frightened child. Where they approached papers with a kind of quiz-show relish, serene in the knowledge that they could not have done more to prepare, he became grey with second thoughts and apprehension and had to be treated as gently as in the weeks after his father's death. It did not do to discuss papers in any detail with him once the test was over. Several times he had emerged early from a paper, crowing about what a doddle he had found it, what a relief, only for some chance remark (or, indeed, put-down) to make him see how wrong he had got an answer or how badly he had misinterpreted a question. It was not until getting to know Charlie that Sophie understood the necessity of teachers repeating the banal advice to *remember to answer the question.*

Asked to describe the changes in tone in *Henry V*, he wrote an essay about the changes of scene. Asked to define metaphor, he had defined simile. The worst occasion had been when they came out of the first maths paper, which Sophie had surprised herself by finding quite tough, to find Charlie boasting that he had spotted the trick question. Panicked, Sophie had turned at once to the question paper, only to reveal that the so-called trick question had been a perfectly straightforward one which Charlie had misread in his haste to be finished. In her relief at being right after all, she had laughed. Charlie stormed off in a white-faced fury – her first direct experience of him being in what Lucas called a bait – and had not spoken to or acknowledged her for days. Apart from the social awkwardness caused when they tried going somewhere as a group, it had felt nearer respite than retribution and his abrupt, unspoken forgiveness when he needed to borrow the tidy notes she had taken summarizing the different meanings of and cases taken by *cum* had been a disappointment. She saw the relief on Lucas's face, that they were getting on again, however, and was glad, if only for his sake.

The two boys were more than ever like twins this term since Lucas had persuaded Charlie to buy painter's jeans to match his, with a little strap on one thigh for a paintbrush, a non-uniform they made more uniform still with the addition of white-on-blue striped Breton tops. During the one surreptitious teatime visit she had managed to pay to Mr Compton's gloriously cool garden, he had slyly remarked that her friends had 'taken to dressing like the hands on a rather louche commercial liner.' Recalled when their double act was becoming a trial, the remark lent her strength.

She had been aching to tell Lucas about losing her virginity. He had long since lost his, after all, so would have been unlikely to disapprove. But the knowledge that he would feel compelled to tell Charlie, the way he told him everything sooner or later, and the certainty that Charlie would somehow find a way to pass on the intelligence to his mother, the Girls and Heidi, blocked the urge to confess to a boy. Instead she told Kimiko, her ever-loyal Suzuki, who was gratifyingly shocked, saddened and hungry for intimate details.

Fifth-form Daughters escaped the Daughters' Chamber and dormitories to live higher up the staircase in shared bedsits. These were allocated by a lottery process but Daughters were expected to express a preference in study-mate. Sophie could not imagine sharing with anyone else but felt she ought to ask Kimiko before putting their names together on the list.

'Oh sure,' Kimiko said. 'We'll have such a great time. Just the two of us.'

Only then did Sophie wonder how she would have felt if Kimiko had said oh, no, sorry but she'd said she'd share with someone else, and she realized with a start that Kimiko was one of her closest friends.

Kimiko had become a genuine friend, as opposed to a convenience, by degrees so small Sophie would have been hard-pressed to say precisely when the promotion had occurred. Possibly it had something to do with Mr Compton's gentle mockery of her spending all her time with Charlie and Lucas. Possibly it arose from a need for an exclusive female friendship to balance out their male one. Compared to the dramas and vicissitudes between the boys, friendship with Kimiko was a placid affair. She was calm, level-headed, loyal. But she was also, in her way, as much of a misfit as Sophie. It was easy to imagine that, once free from necessary obedience to parents and school, she would become eccentric or even subversive in ways of which her sympathies now gave only hints. What Sophie had taken for subservience was merely, she was starting to appreciate, the reticence of a careful foreigner. As Kimiko gained in cultural ease, casually abandoned religion and started dabbling in wild rock music and extreme literature, Sophie saw she had much the louder personality of the two of them.

Someone, not Charlie, had caught the ball. Lucas stretched then lay back on his deckchair. Everyone but Sophie and he clapped as the defeated batsman walked back to the pavilion and the next man in walked out. There was a trace of white powder around Lucas's nostrils, from where he had last used his anti-hay fever puffer. The rims of his eyes were red and sore. When it was really bad, he said, it felt as though he had sand in his eyes. The drug made him woozy so he did not like to use it before exams, relying instead on the gym's closed windows and Heidi's old solution of smearing Vaseline thinly around each nostril to trap the worst of the pollen before it was inhaled. Plunging into the swimming pool when a paper was done was thus doubly a treat for him and he would dose up with his puffer while waiting for her to emerge from the changing room. They had swum after this afternoon's chemistry paper, secure in the knowledge that Charlie never bowled and that even if the Dougalites batted first, he would only be the last man in.

'He has Dice Cricket,' Lucas said suddenly.

'Is that a board game?'

'You mean bored game.'

'So amusing,' she said – their current put-down for jokes that were clever but not remotely funny.

'No, it's dice. Little alloy dice. One gives runs and the other says things like *caught, bowled, L.B.W.* It lives in a little tin and it's the dullest thing I think I've ever seen. The idea is that you make up your imaginary teams then have them play an imaginary match by endlessly throwing the dice and scoring it all, just like a real game.'

'Only less interesting.'

'He thinks I despise it because I don't know how to write the scores down but he's wrong; I just despise it. He loves knowing something I don't.'

'Well be kind. It's a fairly rare occurrence.' She hesitated. Perhaps she had gone too far? Just as there was an unwritten rule that only each boy was allowed to mock his own mother, so mocking Charlie was dangerous territory unless Lucas led the way, and even then Sophie wondered if he were merely humouring her. In one of her rare moods of open bitterness, Kimiko once said that Lucas would say anything to anyone for a snatched alliance.

'I can't wait for next term,' he sighed as the new batsman whacked the ball for six and sent Charlie running. A change of subject. She *had* presumed too far.

'You're sick,' she retorted. 'I can't wait for the holidays. Eight whole weeks of clearing tables, earning tips, eating leftover gâteau and NO BOOKS!'

'I know you. You'll have Catullus tucked in your apron.'

He was right, of course. However well her O levels went, she still had a sneaking fear she would be below standard for the classics ladder and that her brain would atrophy over eight long weeks with no more stimulus than other waitresses' chitchat. Only last night she had suffered an acutely plain and accurate dream in which she arrived in her A level Greek class only to have the don turn to her with sly pity and say, 'Oh, Miss Cullen. I don't think so. Do you?' which was when she noticed that her scholastic gown and waistcoat had become a frilly French maid's uniform and her exercise book a greasy order pad with Ratty's Tunnel on the cover.

'It's the thought of no more maths and chemistry ever, no

more of *that*.' He flicked a hand at her Latin vocab list. 'And a lot less of *him*!' To her astonishment he indicated Charlie, smiling at him even as Charlie caught his eye between overs. 'I mean, we'll have to share a study – there's no one else I could share with and live – but we won't be in a single class together.'

'I thought you'd become inseparable,' she said, cautiously.

'Doesn't mean I like him. Oh. Well. I don't hate him. Not really. But. Well.'

'What?'

'The moods are exhausting. He loses his temper at least once a week. Really loses it. So that a whole roomful of people falls quiet. There are so many forbidden subjects. I feel I'm walking on eggshells half the time. And he's so competitive. He can't stand it that he never comes first or wins a prize.'

'Nothing to take home to the *Sturmführerin*.'

'Something like that. You know that Eng. Lit. thing I won last term with the essay on *Typhoon*? Well he was so angry I'd won, he had to go all around house telling people I'd copied it from a book.'

'But he copied his. I remember him showing me.'

'Exactly. We went to the library after Allsford announced the competition and it was sort of fun choosing writers we weren't studying but just liked.'

'I took Salinger.'

'And I took Conrad, and Charlie, for some reason, took Tennessee Williams. He found a book that had only been out a year, for heaven's sake, and just copied out a chapter on *Streetcar*. He didn't realize we were just using the books to give us a head start. He copied it out very neatly. He even asked me what I thought some bits meant.

'Me too. Hetaira, he needed, and catharsis.'

'And he was so pissed off when he saw I wasn't just copying too. He tried to make out I wasn't playing fair by not cheating. And when I won the bloody book token that did it. Turkey shut him up though. Turkey and Dago. I could've kissed them. He was going on and on about how I'd won the prize by copying something from a book and they just told him, "But he still won, which is all anyone cares about." He's such a girl! Sorry. But do you know what I mean?'

'Fights dirty,' Sophie said, 'takes spiteful, nasty little revenges and keeps a tally of all your weak points.'

'Exactly.'

'I thought you adored him, Lou.'

'You didn't!'

'But you're such good friends.'

'Huh. Just remember I didn't know him until Headbourne said I had to be nice to him and take him home and stuff.'

'Do you think he's even gay? I mean deep down?'

'Oh. Completely.' But he paused for thought. 'I mean he really *is* a girl. He's far more of a girl than you.'

'But he hasn't . . . done much, has he?'

'Nobody fancies him. He thinks it's like prison or something and all these men are desperate for a woman so they'll fall for a bloke who looks womanly. He doesn't understand it's a different thing involved. It's a buffet where one of the dishes has run out. No more chicken. So they think, okay, I'll have beef. They don't want chickenybeef.'

'Chickenybeef. Suits him.'

They laughed and it was a while before they were able to stop.

'So pale and colourless yet somehow beefy,' Lucas stammered which set them off again. A Dougalite fielder turned round and glared. They stopped laughing because it was a boy Lucas had always had an inexplicable thing about and who was said to be persuadable if one caught him at the right moment. But nobody fancied gigglers any more than they wanted Charlie.

'He used to kiss me,' she admitted. 'In the library.'

She half-expected him to say that Charlie had told him but he simply looked astonished and sat forward in his chair.

'No!' he breathed, using one of their catchphrases. 'Tell me it's not true, Tina.'

'I thought he'd have told you. Maybe he was ashamed.'

'So . . . What was it like?' he murmured, wincing in anticipation.

She looked at him, looked out at Charlie, who was now facing them again in silly midriff or whatever and frowning because the sun was in his face. From this distance, too far to register his mood, he looked handsome in a gold-haired, school of Rupert Brooke fashion, greatly helped by the cricket whites.

'It wasn't,' she began thoughtfully, 'terribly nice.'

'How? Wet? Smelly? Some men's spit smells really odd.'

Some men? How many men had Lucas kissed?

'It was always a bit sudden,' she recalled, 'and then it was, I dunno, too complete. It was as though he lacked whatever bone in your skull holds your faces apart from each other. He sort of swamped me and I couldn't breathe. It was like kissing someone with no teeth, I suppose.'

Lucas was beginning to giggle again.

'But the worst of it,' she said.

'Yes?'

'Well . . . You should shut your eyes when you kiss. Shouldn't you?'

'I've no idea, actually.'

'They always do in films so one assumes it's usual. But I checked once or twice and he never shut his. He just stared. As though he wasn't involved at all but wanted to see the effect on me. As though it was an experiment.'

'Which I suppose, in a sense, it was.'

'He's going to be handsome, though. One day,' she said. 'When he loses his puppy fat.'

'You think?' Lucas stopped laughing, stung.

'Women will fancy him. He'll be a vet or a doctor and he'll get a reputation for being good with children and old ladies, and women will want to sleep with him.'

'But he's gay.'

'Actually I think he's just very unhappy and he wants to be on whichever team is currently winning.'

'So what about me, Oracle?'

'Oh, you.' She looked briefly at Lucas then back at her Latin. *Caelebs*, she reminded herself. *Bachelor*. 'You're a poof.'

'I know that but what else do you see for me?'

'Oh,' she said, airily. 'You'll be very international.'

'Chinese boyfriends?' He wrinkled his nose.

'Grow up. Nice, easy international. Italy or somewhere. New York.'

'Christ, that would be fun. You could come too.'

'Huh.' High on confession and won-back intimacy, she was on the point of telling him her old fantasy about them sharing a little house and all of life but bed, then remembered he would be sharing a study with Charlie all through fifth-form so said, 'Huh,' again.

They fell to watching cricket for a while, Lucas made briefly studious by a strikingly handsome cricketer from the other team who threw himself into the empty deckchair beside them. The stranger made a few comments on the game then, somehow sensing he was talking to quite the wrong people, excused himself, leaving Lucas to sigh.

'Don't,' she told him. 'Sighing's almost as unsexy as giggling. No one fancies boys who sigh. At least, not initially. I'm hungry.' She was inspired by the sight of a woman emerging from the pavilion café with a cup of tea and a polystyrene tray of chips.

'I'll go.' He rocked out of his chair. He was always generous with her, knowing her funds to be far shorter than his. 'What'll it be. Banana sandwich or chips?' He paused. 'Or both?'

She watched him strolling towards the café, his hair still tousled from swimming, hands thrust deep in the new jeans pockets because he never knew what to do with them when he walked. She saw him cast a look of spaniel hunger at the impervious batsman who had just left their side, and she discovered that an ache could be a kind of pleasure.

SUMMER HOLIDAYS
(fifteen years, seven months)

'More chicken, Sophia? Lucas? No? Or a crab sandwich? Delicious crab, only caught yesterday apparently. I'd never have made so many if I'd known no one was eating. Good, girl, Sophia. Put some flesh on those bony knees of yours. Me too. Mmm! Crab. So good!'

Sophie and Lucas were sitting in a sand dune in Cornwall with Christine Somborne-Abbot, several polystyrene surfboards and a large, green cold-box. Charlie was playing rounders with his sister Emma and a clutch of female non-relations whose friendship his mother was so keen he cultivate that she had insisted on coming over here every day although there was a far more exciting beach on their doorstep. Tim, Charlie's interesting brother, was not with them. He was free to come – he still hadn't returned to university or found himself a job – but

188

apparently preferred a few weeks' hard labour on his uncle's farm in Dorset.

Lucas liked Polteath because it was aglow with men and so crowded one could ogle undetected. Sophie liked it because it faced the open Atlantic so had magnificent breakers and she enjoyed trying to surf with the boards they had found in the holiday house's garage. But Charlie had intimated to them, after one afternoon of such treats – made bliss by regular visits to a circling ice cream van – that Polteath was not quite the thing. This bay, on the other hand, was 'Sloane-Square-on-Sea', whatever that meant. So they had come here this morning, Sophie bringing the surfboards on the off-chance that they could still use them.

The girls Charlie was intended to befriend were younger sisters or cousins of schoolfriends of Emma and Jenny and Sophie had no sooner met them than she knew this trip was a Big Mistake. They were all roughly sixteen and gave the impression, quite unfairly, of all having thick, waist-length hair and being called names that ended in A. Lucas was still trying nicknames on for size. Rubellas. Viyellas. Salmonellas. It might well become a party game. The Vanillas was the most successful collective noun for them so far. When Mrs Somborne-Abbot introduced her as Sophia, Sophie saw they were prepared to give her a sporting chance, on account of the A-ending and Tatham's, but were mystified by her because she was short-limbed and smiled. None of them smiled. They made sounds of merriment often. They chuckled and harrumphed and hoorayed. Yet they did it all with hidden teeth and an over-riding air of boredom.

They had never knowingly been on holiday with someone Jewish before, anymore than had Charlie's mother.

'So let me see if I've got it right, Lucas,' Mrs Somborne-Abbot was saying. 'No pork ever, no bacon, obviously, or ham. No shellfish. And meals either have to be dairy or meat, not both.'

'Er, more or less,' Lucas said. 'But we're not kosher at home. Not really. We don't have two fridges, for instance, to keep the meat and dairy apart. I wasn't barmitzvahed and Carmel wasn't batmitzvahed and we only go to synagogue for weddings and funerals.'

'Ha! Just like us, then, and since my husband died I've become an utter pagan. There's the most brilliant way of slow roasting a pork joint in milk until it forms a delicious crust. I must find it for your mother.'

'She'd like that,' Lucas said carefully and Sophie knew that, like her, he was picturing Heidi and the Sturmführerin face to face. He looked paler than anyone else on the beach, an effect heightened by his black hair, black Speedos and thick sunglasses. He said the last were drop-dead fashionable but Sophie thought them a bit Sophia Loren and he had been quite petulant after Emma Somborne-Abbot admired them and said she had a remarkably similar pair at home.

Sophie had brought dark glasses too, cheap tortoiseshell ones, and loved the way they let her stare or even scowl unobserved. They also helped hugely in the struggle to pass among the Vanillas or to tune out Mrs Somborne-Abbot's more offensive chat.

Their hostess had retained an excellent figure despite her love of rich cooking and was showing it off in a navy blue one-piece that rather worryingly, Sophie thought, had no skirt so that it was like meeting her in her underwear. Sophie found herself staring at the spider veins around her ankles or the crepiness

190

on her thighs, anything that might make her less intimidating. Even more than when she was dressed, the swimming costume made her seem all hands and jabbing, sharpened fingers. Sophie thought of Margaret's comfortable folds on a daytrip to the Isle of Wight two weeks ago and wondered what she was doing now.

'Do you want to swim?' she offered. 'I don't mind watching the picnic.'

'No. You two run along,' Mrs Somborne-Abbot told them. 'I'm warming up nicely and swimming would make my hair completely impossible and frizzy for tonight. You run along. But do tell Charlie and those girls to come back here and eat something or this will all go to waste.'

There was to be a birthday party that night at the big house near Rock belonging to the parents of one of the Vanillas. She was a smart, thin girl, called Serafina but content to be known as Saggy and Sophie was dreading it. Unwarned, she had nothing good to wear. Not that she had anything smart to wear at home, beyond the winter skirt Mrs Somborne-Abbot had given her, but the lack of warning was the excuse on which her feeble hopes were pinned and fluttering.

Charlie was especially keen on Saggy, but from the way he went on and on about how big her house was and how fabulous her friends were and how she'd invited him to play croquet with her at the Hurlingham when they got home, one could be forgiven for thinking she frightened him.

The beach faced across the mouth of a broad estuary so, although one could see the Atlantic off to one side and although the water was salty, the waves were what Lucas dismissed as 'plishy' rather than thundering and there was always a strong current to right or left, depending on the direction of the tide.

Holidaymakers tended to stake out their small territories in the dunes around its fringes and leave the wide, flat expanse of beach for ball games, kite-flying and dogs. Following Lucas across it, Sophie wondered why it felt familiar then realized it filled her with the same fear as crossing a playground, only with adults hurling the balls one was dodging.

Charlie, Emma and the Vanillas had established a rounders match at the beach's middle so the Vanillas could socialize and play at the same time. They seemed to know everyone and everyone's dogs. Because the mere proximity of a ball game he might be expected to join made Lucas physically sick, she assumed he would give them all a wide berth and leave her to pass on the message about crab sandwiches. They all waved and cheered and called out to him to join the fun, in the unmistakably mocking way she felt sure would drive him into the sea, so she was amazed when he duly allowed himself to be bossed into a fielding position by Saggy. When he was thumped on the back and called 'Good Man' by a hunky blond in rugger shirt and cut-offs, immediately recognizable as Saggy's brother, she understood. Lucas would put up with any amount of humiliation, she had noticed, if rewarded by a certain kind of male approval.

'Hiya!' Charlie ran up to her. He was tanned and it suited him, even though his nose and ear-tops were peeling. He claimed he always burned before he went brown. 'You got away.' Did he regret kissing her now?

'Yes. But your mum's worried about all the food. She said to tell you all to go back and eat something.'

Emma had overheard them. 'Oh she doesn't want us interrupting her,' she said. 'Not now.'

Sophie glanced back and saw that Mrs Somborne-Abbot had

no sooner been left alone than she had three older men standing around her eating the picnic and chatting. As Sophie watched, Mrs Somborne Abbot waved girlishly and tucked her legs under her like a woman on an old-fashioned holiday poster. One of the men hunkered down beside her and the other two followed suit.

Sophie excused herself from playing. 'I can't catch,' she told them. 'And I need to cool off.'

'Sophie's a demon swimmer,' Charlie said by way of excusing and explaining her.

The beach shelved swiftly into the deep channel formed by the estuary so, once she had waded out through the ranks of barking dogs and splashing children, the sounds of the beach were muffled by the inhuman sea sounds, gulls, boat engines, the sorrowful dinging of a buoy placed to warn of a sandbar. The sea was far colder than Lucas's pool but not unbearable, especially once she remembered Margaret's trick of plunging in for a few minutes, coming ashore just long enough for the breeze to raise goose bumps then plunging back in. The second time the sea felt warmer than the breezy air above it.

She stayed in, undisturbed for nearly an hour, now swimming vigorously, parallel to the shore, now content to drift on her back, enjoying the warmth of sun through shallow water. One advantage of having no breakers was that swimming required less of an effort. She might have been in an extra-buoyant pool.

The more she thought about it, the stranger it was that she and Lucas had been invited to visit. When Charlie wrote from there during the Easter holidays the Vanillas were clearly getting on his nerves. When Lucas told her the Sturmführerin had rung Heidi to ask them both down, they assumed it was because Charlie needed reinforcements. The novelty of working as a waitress in the gloomily subterranean Ratty's Tunnel was wearing off and it was dawning on her that, if she kept it up, she would miss the summer entirely. Courage bolstered by the prospect of having Lucas for company on the long train ride, she swallowed her misgivings and said yes. She told a white lie to Kieran and Margaret and said she was going to Cornwall for a few days with the Behrmans. They had yet to forgive Mrs Somborne-Abbot for casting her adrift in London with no cash.

Charlie was pleased enough to see them – although he didn't come to Bodmin to meet their train but sent Emma on her own – but they had not seen him alone in two days. Either he or his mother intended this as some kind of demonstration, Sophie decided.

'I'm normal. I'm popular. These are my Right People. I've made friends with the sort of girls a man ends up marrying and we're happy precisely because we're not bothered about being clever.'

Both Charlie and his mother had mentioned the party that evening but nobody had specifically said Lucas and Sophie were invited. Sophie's spirits lifted at the idea that they were not. They'd be quite happy to stay behind in the holiday house. They could lounge in its sparsely furnished, sun-baked sitting room, watching the sunset. They could cross the beach to Polteath for fish and chips. They were nearly fifth-formers now. They no longer needed child-minding.

But if Lucas was content to play rounders, and his shell-shocked intellectual routine was all a pose, he'd be sure to want to go. She could picture him overcoming his initial shyness with a glass or three of scrumpy then charming Saggy's brother – who was probably a bad dancer so would have gravitated to the kitchen too. He'd express a flattering interest in going out on the family's little crabber, then let slip how well he'd known Jonty Mortimer, who was at Durham with Master Saggy, and generally play on his nostalgia for boarding school. Then he'd catch his eye in a certain way as all the Young People set out for the inevitable midnight dip.

She spied on the rounders game from the water in time to see Lucas racing for the home mound, which meant he had actually hit a ball, which meant he was fitting in.

Her imagination was running away with her, fed by the glimpse of Mrs Somborne-Abbot being chatted up by three men simultaneously. It was making a kind of satanic orgy from a gathering that would probably be no more intimidating than a pineapple-cheese hedgehog.

Restraining herself, Sophie swam back into the shallows and waded out. A big, wet Labrador took a keen interest in her and followed her closely, trying to ram its nose between her legs. Big dogs scared her. Most dogs did. She was unused to them. She tried shooing it away but it only licked her, so she swore at it, which made it bark at her. She knew running was probably the worst thing to do but she ran anyway and the beast pursued her, getting in a few, humiliating nose-shoves before she reached the others.

She was rescued at once by Saggy's brother, who knew the dog, of course, and spoke fluent canine so was able to round on it furiously and send it away.

'My God, you've been in for hours,' Saggy said. 'You're amazing! Don't you feel the cold at all? There's nothing to you. Not like some of the whales around here, like my mum.'

'Actually I am quite cold,' Sophie said, newly aware of her damp costume and lack of a towel. Her teeth began to chatter.

'Charlie!' Saggy commanded. 'Get the poor girl a towel and a jersey, for Pete's sake.' Charlie ran off obediently. 'Now we've got to head back and start getting the place ready,' she continued. 'You can come, can't you? You and Jeremy?'

'Lucas. Yes. We'd love to.'

Damn! She had missed the perfect chance to say well no, nothing to wear but shorts and anyway I've got double pneumonia.

'Great. Super. Bye all.' Saggy turned away, shouting, 'Tisha, I'll drive over to pick up the wine if you can clear the downstairs out a bit.' And marshalling Vanillas and brother, she strode away towards the car park.

'You can tell her father's a General,' Charlie said, draping a towel around her shoulders.

'Yeah,' Sophie said. 'She's amazing.' But Saggy didn't strike her as amazing at all, simply brimming with upper-class aplomb and even bossier than Charlie's sisters. She recalled, with an inner chill to match her outer one, that she would come up against a lot more Saggies now she was entering the upper school. Mercifully few of them entered on the classics ladder. Lucas was taking French, English and history of art so would acquire an abundance of new girlfriends.

Spirits were high in the car as Mrs Somborne-Abbot drove them back to Polteath. This was partly because it was a squash and Sophie and Lucas had to travel in the boot, which seemed to remind everyone but Sophie of childhood and other happy holidays. Mrs Somborne-Abbot was especially happy, high on sunshine and harmless flirtation and the anticipation of more. Sunshine suited the Somborne-Abbots.

'Saggy's got a brilliant dress for tonight,' Emma said. 'Fiorucci. She showed me yesterday.'

'Oh good,' Sophie said feebly.

'Now you're not to worry about dressing up, Sophia,' Mrs Somborne-Abbot called from the front.

'Yeah,' Charlie agreed. 'It's not like London. It's actually a bit infra-dig to get all done up.'

'Everyone's on holiday. No one expects anyone to have their best clothes,' his mother echoed, waving merry, sharp fingers at a woman with two barking dogs who just stared back from the sandy verge.

Perhaps she was right for when they reached the house Charlie and Lucas simply showered off the sand in the 'boys' bathroom' downstairs and were soon out on the patch of sun-scorched grass under Sophie's window playing a game of Swingball wearing jeans and T-shirts as they might have on any evening. The women, however, were clearly making more painstaking preparations. The upstairs was busy with baths and pattering feet and bossy arguments over who could wear what.

When Lucas eventually burst in on Sophie, flushed from their game, to see what she was up to, he found her huddled on the bed, turning in on herself in dread.

'Are you sick, Phi?' he asked.

'Just a bit chilled,' she said. 'There's been rather a rush for the bath.'

'They've probably had all the hot water. Our shower's electric. Wash downstairs.'

'I've got nothing to wear,' she said.

'That doesn't matter.'

'It's different for boys. I really don't want to go, Lou.'

'No one can make you. Stay here. Say you're sick.'

'I can't.'

'It's just a party.'

Could she tell him? 'Lou, I've . . . I've never been to a party before.'

There. She'd said it now.

'But you must have!'

'Well I haven't. And I hate these people. I don't want the first one I go to to be –'

She was cut off by Charlie's mother coming in. She had on a flowery skirt the colour of Granny Smiths and a crisp cream blouse that brought out her tan. 'Come on, Sophia,' she said briskly. 'We'll be late.'

'She's got nothing to wear,' Lucas said.

'But that doesn't matter. We told you.'

'No,' Sophie added. 'Really nothing. *No dresses.*'

Mrs Somborne-Abbot glanced from one to the other, sniffing conspiracy. 'But that's easily fixed. Let's see what Emma's got. She's not so much bigger than you.'

She brought in three equally unSophie dresses on padded hangers. They were puffy, Laura Ashley things that would spend all evening sliding off her sloping shoulders and bagging out around her waist and bottom if she dared do anything but stand still in a corner. One glance at a label told her Emma was at least three sizes bigger than her.

'Out you go, Lucas. Respect a young lady's privacy.' Mrs Somborne-Abbot was relentless. 'This one, I think. The turquoise will do things with your eyes. Emma always looked lovely in it. Come on. Skin a rabbit and we'll see how it looks.' She was speaking as though Sophie were a child, not a teenager, but perhaps Sophie deserved it for acting like one. She slid to the edge of the bed and pulled off her borrowed baggy jersey she had tugged on for warmth and reassurance. Her bra was her second-best and none too clean but she couldn't change it with Christine Somborne-Abbot and her spiky hands looming over her.

'Actually I really don't feel very well,' she said.

'Are you sick? The crab was fine, I thought.'

'No, I . . . I just think I must have spent too long in the sea. I think I may have caught a chill. Sorry.'

Sophie had never been quite sure what symptoms catching a chill involved beyond getting too cold but the words worked like a charm. The impending dress was lowered. She could see Mrs Somborne-Abbot making rapid calculations. There were fresh men waiting for her, Vanillas for her only satisfactory son to dance with. The door opened and Emma came in.

'Any luck?' she began, then saw there had been no progress and sensed an atmosphere. 'Oh,' she said.

'Honestly,' Sophie pleaded. 'I'll be fine here. I will. I'll just get into bed and go to sleep.'

'But someone should stay with you.'

If she hadn't been so miserable, Sophie would have been amused at how nakedly the older woman's selfishness was showing. Someone should stay behind and she really didn't see why it should have to be her.

'I'll stay,' Emma offered. 'They're all a bit young for me anyway.'

'You can't,' her mother reminded her. 'What about Olly?'

'No one stay,' Sophie said. 'I'll be fine. I'm sixteen,' she lied. 'I won't burn the place down. Promise.' She gave them her best, sunny orphan smile.

'We're going to be late,' Charlie shouted from downstairs.

'Coming!' his mother shouted back crossly. 'Honestly! Well . . . If you're quite sure, Sophia . . .'

'Certain. Have a great evening both of you. Sorry to be a killjoy.'

The door was closed on her. The rejected dresses were left draped on the bedstead as a reproach. As their voices receded along the landing, Sophie heard a brisk flare-up of indignation in Mrs Somborne-Abbot's explanations but she didn't care. She had been reprieved and nothing else mattered. She heard the front door banging to, footsteps on the gravel path, the clicking of the gate catch and the impatient departure of the little car.

She remembered childhood mornings when a half-fabricated fever had been enough to persuade Margaret to keep her back from St Bonnie's for the day, and the delicious sensation of lying on in bed on a weekday hearing the house grow quieter and quieter about her.

She pulled the jersey back on and tugged the bedding about her. She *had* been quite chilled. Perhaps she would sleep for a little then slip downstairs after a safe interval to visit the kitchen. Eating up some leftover crab sandwiches would risk her less disapproval than raiding the fridge for anything new.

There were steps on the stairs suddenly and along the landing.

'You're not really ill, are you?' Lucas asked.

'Course not,' she said, sitting up. 'Why didn't you go? I thought you were getting on with them.'

'That was anthropology, not getting on. I could tell they'd feel happier leaving you if I offered to stay behind. Come on. Get dressed.'

'What for? I'm so comfy now.'

'I just ordered us a taxi. There's a train to Plymouth then we can change and get as far as Bristol. We can crash at Carmel's for the night.'

'Your wicked sister!'

'Yes. Come on. The man said he was just dropping someone

off in Polteath. Cab'll be here in ten minutes.'

'But we can't just go!'

'We can. I've written a note. Family crisis – hence the sudden visit to the sister. I took you with me so you wouldn't have to travel back on your own on Tuesday.'

'They won't believe it. Charlie certainly won't.'

'Do you care? Do you care if you never see any of them again?'

'No. But it's very rude.'

'Rude schmude. Carmel's much more fun and she won't make you wear hideous hand-me-down frocks.'

'I love you, Lucas Behrman.'

'Yes but hurry up about it or I'll go without you. God, that bra's filthy!'

As they waited for their connection in Plymouth and she ate the rest of the pork pie he had bought from the canteen out of curiosity, he asked her, 'Was that true, what you said back there? Have you really never been to a party?'

'Not unless you count those ones in primary school where the whole class went and there were games and jelly and bossy mothers and stuff. No. Not since I started having a choice in the matter.'

'You're not normal, Sophie Cullen. You do know that, don't you?'

She shrugged, still happy and high from the adrenalin brought on by behaving disgracefully.

'You're going to love Carmel's squat,' he went on. 'You'll fit right in. They steal electricity from the mains and grow their own drugs. Mum would die if she knew we'd spent a night there.'

'So? I won't tell her.'

They didn't arrive in Bristol until nearly midnight then had a long walk from Temple Meads to his sister's squat on the rougher side of Clifton where they had to bed down, fully clothed, on dusty sofa cushions on the floor but she doubted any refugee had ever slept so soundly.

MICHAELMAS TERM
(fifteen years, nine months)

Lucas told her he was in love and, in one of those rare pieces of real-life pathetic fallacy, a huge minor chord blasted out on the chapel organ from the other side of the study wall.

'Nah-nah-nah!' she echoed, joking.

'What?' Lucas frowned, perplexed and she saw at a glance that he was in deadly earnest. Love with a big L.

'Who is it?' she asked him. 'Sit down. Move those. Tell. Who?'

But he carried on pacing around. He had managed to appear his usual debonair self until a prompting of tact sent Kimiko out of the study on a mumbling errand, whereupon he had become jumpy, walking around, picking things up, realigning books and pencils, flicking the surprisingly tough leaves of Kimiko's money plant.

'I've never felt like this before.'

'Not even with Jonty?' Jonty Mortimer was acknowledged between them as the high water mark for grand passion, despite or perhaps because he had offered a relationship with so few of a relationship's usual trappings.

'Oh, doesn't even compare. He just came into the room and our eyes met and bang! Look at my hands. Look!'

He held out his hands and Sophie saw they were shaking.

'Christ,' she said. 'So who is it?'

'The weirdest thing,' he rambled on, 'is how I never seem to have seen him before. I mean of course I have. I've seen everyone in this place before but maybe I've just never focused on him or he's never focused on me. Ow!'

Sophie had thrown a copy of Gibbon at him.

'Who?!' she demanded again now that she had his attention.

'Compton. Mr Compton. I don't even know his first name yet. We just had our first English class with him this morning.'

'It's Antony,' she said dryly. 'Spelt the Roman way with no H.'

At last he sat. 'Of course it is!' he sighed. 'The perfect flawed lover, the gifted orator, the noble soldier. Antony Compton. *Oh happy horse*. Perfect.'

'He's not a soldier. Oh. Yes. I suppose he is.'

Now that she thought of it, she had seen Mr Compton in uniform several times on Wednesday afternoons but had put it from her mind because it interested her so little. Girls could join the Cadet Corps too but only in order to become worryingly mature girl guides, in effect; learning map-reading, first aid and semaphore, and how to be radio operators. As soon as Kimiko had told her girls received no rifle-training Sophie lost all interest. She had chosen the 'soft' option of Wednesday afternoon social work instead and had been assigned an old lady to visit. Because he could act, Lucas had been assigned to the Happy Brigade – a group who toured singalongs and cabaret to geriatric wards and old people's homes. Kimiko volunteered at a special school Tatham's ran in one of the suburbs. Only Charlie played toy soldiers. Sophie secretly thought the uniform did wonders for his sex appeal, much as cricket whites or a dinner jacket did. He had that sort of face.

'Why did you have to persuade me out of doing Corps?' Lucas rounded on her.

'I did not!'

'You sneered. You called it Toy Soldiers.'

'Well it is. But you couldn't join because of your eyes.'

Lucas's astigmatism was such that if he looked down the barrel of a gun he saw two targets, neither of them in the right place. They had discovered this at a local funfair.

'But he's Senior Officer. And he takes the shooting classes.'

'Oh well,' she said. 'You'll just have to shine in his English class. He's meant to be a brilliant teacher. His house is incredible.'

'How do you know?'

'Oh . . . I go there sometimes for tea. Several of us do.'

'You never said.'

'There's a lot I don't tell you now you share a study with the Mouth of England.'

'Can I come?'

'He has to ask you. It doesn't go down well if people just bring friends along. I've seen it happen.'

'So how do you know him? He's never taught you.'

'We just got talking once. Nothing sinister. He's lovely.'

She continued to see Mr Compton in the Chantry three mornings a week. This was precious territory she was not about to share merely to fan the flames of Lucas's latest crush. Either because he had become too obviously gay and therefore a social risk or because of Charlie's competitive friendship, Lucas had enjoyed no significant involvement since the one with Jonty Mortimer. Instead there were these crushes, innumerable, minutely analysed and agonized over. Their objects were usually unattainable or impossible in some way; an ex-policeman, married with two toddlers, who taught gymnastics, the captain of a visiting fencing team, Perry Rees, the older half of a pairing already so long established it had become a kind of romantic paradigm in school lore, like Achilles and Patroclus.

The crush on Compton would not pass. She had observed that it was in the nature of crushes never to pass, because they were unrequited and therefore, in a sense, never a disappointment. Instead it would be superseded by a fresh one and added to a collection. Charlie had crushes too, and Kimiko, these days. When the three were together and the mood was upon them, they could indulge themselves for hours at a time analysing the finer merits of their respective heroes much as some boys discussed football teams or guitarists.

Sophie had crushes too. She was only human. But she had seen too many people subjected to humiliation when friends had revealed a crush to its object to want to risk that herself. Both Lucas and Charlie had it in them to race across a quad to some idol of hers and say my friend Sophie thinks you're a god, simply for the flirtatious pretext such phoney altruism gave them to speak to the boy themselves. So she allowed her friends to think her above all fleshly trivia. She was the wise one, the controlled one, the one to whom others made their confessions of weakness. If she thought of anyone in the minutes before sleeping, it was of Wilf, not in any fantasizing way but simply to rehearse the details of the one night she had spent with him.

Crushes on anyone outside the school were indefinably low, on a par with crushes on actors or pop singers, not to be paraded.

Kimiko returned and Lucas changed the subject at once, quizzing her, as a fellow-linguist, on what she made of that year's French *assistante* and the Anouilh play they were reading with her.

Sophie wondered if she was right to dismiss his feelings for Mr Compton as just another self-dramatizing infatuation. Normally he would not have kept such a thing back from Kimiko since she was a far more patient, less openly critical listener than Sophie.

'Did you tell Charlie about . . . ?' she began as he was leaving.

'God, no,' he said. 'Not the Mouth of England.'

And he continued not to tell Charlie. She knew it for a fact. Even if sworn to silence Charlie would have been sure to have found a moment to take Sophie aside to say, 'Look, I promised not to tell anyone but . . .'

Now that they were in the upper school, the four of them led far more separate lives than they had done. With Charlie studying sciences, Lucas studying humanities and Sophie one of just eight fifth-formers taking Greek, Latin and ancient history, there was no longer a single class in which they coincided. In study hours, Kimiko now saw more of Lucas than Sophie did, to the point where Sophie felt obliged to tease him about his New Best Friend.

As planned, Sophie and Kimiko now shared a bedsit. High up in the upper attics, hard against Chapel, its lofty removal from the toast and chatter of the Daughters' Chamber brought with it a sense that they were less subject to rules than they had been. They no longer needed to complete a set amount of changed ekker every week and no longer troubled to register their visitors with Nurse. Thanks to Kimiko's parents, they had their own toaster, kettle and record player. There was also a Baby Belling on the landing where they could heat baked beans or make a stink reconstituting Vesta dried meals.

In Dougal's, Lucas and Charlie had acquired similarly adult privileges. That Lucas was not confessing despite all the new opportunities they had to talk in privacy commanded Sophie's respect.

In their ritualized morning encounters in the Chantry, she found herself looking at Mr Compton with new eyes. Despite the resemblance to Peter O'Toole, she had thought him monastic, but there was something romantic about him, she saw that now. It lay in the conjunction of his perfect skin, permanent five o'clock shadow, subdued courtesy and the sense that he carried a burden of suffering that would remain private. Lucas caught her elbow one Wednesday afternoon when he spotted Mr Compton in his immaculate Corps uniform and hissed, 'I've got it. It's Guy Crouchback!'

Waugh's *Sword of Honour* trilogy had been among the last books they had studied together when they were in the same div. She forgot the novels within weeks of finishing them but retained a strong sense of the flawed hero's essential decency.

Heidi took her aside before a Sunday lunch on the pretext of needing her opinion on the saltiness of a sauce.

'What's wrong with Lucas?' she asked her in an undertone. 'Is someone bullying him? A teacher? Another boy?'

'I don't think so.'

'You can tell me, Sophie.' Those Disney eyes bored into her.

Sophie shook her head. 'I really don't think so,' she said. 'Honestly, Heidi. He'd have told me.'

'He tells you everything,' Heidi said.

'Eventually, yes.'

'That's good. I'm glad it's still you and not . . . someone else. He's not eating properly. And look how pale he's getting!' She gestured through the kitchen's serving hatch to where Lucas and his father were laying the dining room table. It was true. Sophie tried to look with a mother's gaze and saw he had dark shadows under his eyes. He looked far more careworn than he had even during O levels.

'It's just winter,' she said, to comfort Heidi. 'He just needs a little sun. Maybe when you go skiing at Christmas . . .'

But Heidi had turned aside, sighing. 'You give them a mother's love but you're always the last to hear. His sister was the same. I had to hear it from him when Carmel moved in with . . . into that *place* in Bristol.'

Sophie had enjoyed her short visit to Carmel's squat and had seen nothing wrong with her boyfriend, Klaus, who clearly cared for her deeply. Lucas said he suspected that what upset his mother was not the living in sin but the living in a place without paying rent; property irregularities threatened some deeper moral dereliction. That and the fact that Klaus was Austrian and not Jewish.

Heidi was whisking tiny cubes of softened butter into a sauce. The smell of hot butter, vinegar, peppercorns and tarragon was making Sophie faint with hunger although she had eaten a whole packet of Dutch shortbread during Chapel that morning. Heidi had just tossed four steaks onto a big griddle and was sprinkling them with sea salt. She was mesmerizingly confident when she cooked – like a beautiful witch – not like Margaret who, despite years of experience, was incapable of cooking anything without much cursing and hesitant reference to her recipe cards.

'He's in love, isn't he?'

Sophie froze. She could not lie to this woman. Seemingly her trapped silence was confirmation enough.

'I knew it. I *knew* it!' Heidi turned back to the stove. She whisked the sauce furiously with one hand and shook the steaks with the other. She flipped the steaks over with the point of a little steel knife and turned off the stove. Then she seized a tissue from a nearby box and dabbed at her eyes. 'Vinegar,' she said. 'Always makes them run. Oh, Sophie, Sophie, you've been very good to him but it was never going to be enough, was it? Right. *A table* everyone!' And she whisked off her apron and, with it, the brief spasm of grief that had shaken her elegant frame.

That week Sophie remembered Heidi's words as a challenge and resolved to do more. Pursuing Mr Compton as he left the Chantry one morning, she said, 'Sir, please say no if it's not on but I was wondering if I could bring one of my friends to visit you this afternoon. I think he'd . . . I think it would mean a lot to him.'

'But of course.' He stepped onto the grass to let the choir-master pass. 'I'm surprised you haven't asked before. I hope he likes Wagner. I promised Paston I'd play some of the Solti *Ring*.'

'Oh yes,' she was able to say quite honestly. 'He loves music.'

'Really? I knew he sang but I thought cricket was more his thing.'

'Oh. Not Somborne-Abbot, sir. I was thinking of bringing Behrman.'

'Ah. Yes. But of course. The clever one. Much better idea.'

'He knows who you are,' she told Lucas, who was so excited he could hardly breathe. 'He called you *The Clever One*.' She kept quiet about the flash of disappointment she had detected in Mr Compton's manner that she was not introducing him to Charlie.

They turned up promptly at four o'clock. Lucas was impressed by the exoticism of the garden and the house and she was pleased to see that the prospect of Wagner had scared off the more earnest of the regulars. There was only Paston and a couple of owlish music scholars who were planning on starting a Wagner Soc and discussing what symbolic colours would be best for the society's scarf.

Lucas was far more attractive and socially able than any of them and she assumed he would be his usual, charming self. He was all but silent, however, almost dull, for all the pointed cues she gave him to sparkle. She worried that Mr Compton would be gaining a false impression. It was a relief when their cups of karkady were done with and music and reverent listening took over from conversation.

They heard the last side of the last LP from the great, gold-papered boxed set in which Mr Compton had recently invested a huge amount of money. Sophie freely admitted to not knowing the *Ring Cycle* at all. She didn't think Lucas did either so was surprised when he quietly explained to her that the music they were about to hear portrayed the death and rebirth of the world.

'Brünnhilde sacrifices herself and all worldly power for love,' he told her. 'She rides her horse onto Siegfried's funeral pyre and so gives up the ring, which would have given her that power, back to its rightful guardians, the Rhinemaidens. Her act destroys Valhalla and the old gods but there's a hint, right at the end, that something good and new is coming of it.'

'Oh,' she said. 'Thanks, Lou.' She had never glimpsed Wagner in his record collection so suspected him of swotting up.

The music was huge, even allowing for Mr Compton's fondness for playing it loud, and it filled the room like the fire and floodwaters it depicted. When it subsided they all sat there, a little stunned, until Lucas spoke again.

'It's curious,' he said, 'how Loge's music, that glittering fire music, is happy despite the death and destruction it's bringing.'

Paston snorted. 'You mean it's in a major key.'

'No,' Lucas corrected him with a smile. 'It's happy. The two aren't the same. Brünnhilde's love motif is in a major key as well but it's far too restless and yearning to be happy. The fire theme is just that; happy, self-contained. But Loge never belongs, does he, sir?' he went on. 'He's a god but not one of them. Even at the beginning he places himself apart from them. He's elemental, true to himself. Fire can't help the things it burns. Maybe the happiness is because he knows he brings a sort of purity and release?'

The music scholars tittered but Mr Compton nodded and asked the group to choose another passage to hear.

'Are you taking music A level?' he asked as he showed them out afterwards.

'No,' Lucas said. 'Only history of art.'

'Pity. We never get any non-musicians to take it but they'd bring clearer vision to the subject. Come again, won't you? Cullen, here, will show you the form.'

Before they had emerged through the garden's rear gate again she could hear Lucas's teeth chattering. She was about to make some quip about him having it bad when he apologized and ran ahead, and around the corner into the War Cloisters, where she found him in the darkness, moments later, leaning between a pair of limestone pillars to be sick into a lavender bed.

Awestruck, she said nothing beyond offering him a peppermint and readily resigned herself to the idea that he would become a regular at Mr Compton's afternoons and that she might attend less often.

One of the effects of night falling hours before afternoon school was over was that the gap between lunch and supper came to seem impossibly wide. Mid-afternoon trips to the tuck shop for egg and chips became a winter routine among them. Sophie, Lucas and Kimiko had just placed an order there when Charlie ran in, full of news.

It was not yet official, he said, but he'd just heard from a reliable source that Mr Compton had been implicated in a scandal and had been given the choice of discreetly handing in his notice and leaving at once or waiting for the police to become involved.

'Sex or drugs?' Kimiko asked because it was always one or the other.

'Both.'

'No!' they all gasped and Charlie had to shush them because people were looking over and the skinny waitress with the stony face was showing an interest.

'Who's your source?' Lucas asked. The colour had drained from his face. Charlie seemed not to notice.

'Hush-Lara,' he said. This was Dougal's equivalent of Nurse, so nicknamed because that was what she said whenever her dachshund flew out of her room barking, which it did, Charlie had discovered, if you whistled through your teeth. He had demonstrated the phenomenon for Sophie once. The funny whistling, the manic dachshund skidding on parquet floor and the matron waddling out after her, her hands clasped under her bosom while she chid, 'Hush, Lara. Hush!'; everything was precisely as he had predicted. Hush-Lara had a sister – same bosom, Patterdale terrier – who worked as secretary to the Undermaster, so was a reliable source of information, especially if one caught her during lunch, while Mr Headbourne's South African sherry was still active.

'I don't believe it,' Lucas said.

Charlie shrugged. 'Are you going to eat that?' he asked. Their food had arrived and Lucas wasn't touching his. Lucas gave the plate a minute shove towards Charlie who said, 'Thanks,' and broke the egg yolk with a chip.

'So what happened?'

Charlie munched a little, playing with them. They had earned a punishment for showing no jealousy when he recently started spending time with a sweet, unwary chemist and photography enthusiast called David Crisp. Then he related how, according to Hush-Lara's intelligence, Larding and Dahl had been back to visit Mr Compton.

This was ominous in itself. Sophie had always disliked Larding and Dahl, two self-consciously decadent and rather frightening sixth-form Scholars in her first term. They were so obviously bad that everyone had assumed they would be expelled, if only for smoking or vandalism, and it had been disappointing to realize each had lasted through their Oxbridge term and moved on, undisgraced, to the college of his choice.

During the visit Dahl was said to have produced some dope, which they shared, then Compton led Larding off to his bedroom. Piqued at not being so singled out, Dahl had gone to the Headman. He sneaked.

'So when's he going?' Kimiko asked.

Charlie shrugged again, glanced at Lucas. 'Tomorrow? Soon, anyway. I doubt they'll let him do any more teaching.'

'I'll have to go and see him,' Lucas said softly.

'You can't, Lou,' Sophie told him.

'I have to tell him,' he insisted. 'I can't just let him go and never know. I'd never stop wondering.'

'Know what?' Charlie asked.

Everyone looked at Lucas. Lucas glanced at Sophie and shrugged, which she took as permission.

'Lucas is in love with him,' she said quietly. 'Really in love.'

Charlie laughed. 'But you can't *tell* him!'

'Why not,' Lucas asked, 'if it's true? He needs some friends at a time like this.'

'Yes, but . . .'

'It's after four,' Sophie reminded him. 'There'll be people there.'

'So? I'll go in through the front. I'll wait for everyone to leave.'

'Think,' Sophie told him. 'What do you want to happen?'

'What do you think?' Charlie asked with a smirk.

Sophie ignored him. 'Okay,' she said. 'So. Say he loves you back or is grateful or whatever and sleeps with you. Then what?'

'Sleep with him again?' Charlie suggested and spluttered. Kimiko laughed too, damn her.

Sophie tried to block them out, tried to make Lucas focus on her. 'He's a don,' she reminded him. 'And it's illegal. Where's it going to go?'

'I dunno,' he said and stood. 'I don't care, really. I might leave. We could go away together. Maybe we'll just write letters. I . . . I've got to tell him.'

215

And he walked out.

'Raspbwy, Stworbwy, Chocklik, Poynapil, Furniller, Lemming or Loyme,' the waitress was telling someone.

'Well fuck me,' Charlie said. 'Who'd have thought it?'

'You don't think he's really going?' Kimiko asked. 'Not really?'

'He is,' Sophie said. 'He's serious. He's seriously in love.' She found she was shivering with adrenalin as though she, not Lucas, was about to bare her heart.

'Let's go and watch.' Charlie jumped up.

'Charlie!' Sophie protested but he was leaving so she and Kimiko followed.

The tuck shop was on one end of Queensgate Row. Mr Compton's house was four hundred yards away. Dusk was falling. They tailed Lucas in silence in and out of pools of light that fell from house windows and fanlights. There were no proper street lights but here and there lamps were fixed on wall brackets over entrances. Mr Compton's house was in darkness. Perhaps he had already packed his bags and fled to the Continent? They stopped in the shadows twenty yards away and watched Lucas mount the steps and reach for the bell.

It was so strange that the school was going about its normal half-day business – people returning muddied from football matches, dons on bicycles, two small boys dwarfed by cello cases hurrying to rehearsal, a housemaster's wife walking her retriever – unaware that this illegal drama was unfolding in its midst.

Like many of the houses, Mr Compton's still had an old bell pull rather than an electric buzzer. Lucas reached for the brass knob and hesitated.

'No,' Charlie breathed. 'He's not going through with it. He's chickening out.'

Lucas pulled.

'Jesus! He is,' Charlie shouted. 'I've got to stop him! Lucas?'

Lucas turned to see them at the moment the fanlight above him lit up and the door opened. Mr Compton was there. Lucas turned, they spoke and Mr Compton let him in. The door closed.

'Jesus fuck,' Charlie said. 'Bloody hell. I was only kidding.'

'What?' Kimiko hissed.

'I guessed something was up from the way he kept mooning about the place and not paying attention when we were talking. And he was putting all his energy into his English and listening to all this fucking Wagner and . . . If I'd said about Compton going and there was no reaction, I'd have known I was on the wrong track.'

'You are such a moron,' Sophie said. 'You'll have to go after him. I can't believe you'd be so stupid.'

He hadn't been stupid, though. She thought back to his narrative in the tuck shop, his excited entrance, the telling details; he must have planned it all like a short, cruel play. He had revealed an uncharacteristic psychotic cunning.

'Well it's a bit late now,' he said.

'Charlie!' She was amazed to see him shrug it off. One moment he had been exploding with nerves, now he actually seemed amused at what he had done.

'Well it is. I've done him a favour.' He sauntered on, walking boldly up to and past Mr Compton's house. 'Either he tells him and Bingo, or he tells him and Compton sends him for a little chat with Rev Harestock but at least I'll have stopped him mooning around being such a bloody bore. But he probably won't get around to saying anything. He'll wimp out and just stammer something about music or Milton or something.'

They adjourned to Charlie and Lucas's study to eat toast and wait.

A former housekeeper's room, the study lay on a remote, unpoliced branch of the building near a discreet staff entrance. They had hung one wall with a tattered Union Jack, another with a striped horse blanket, and had plastered a third with a collage of images from magazines. Most of the images were of women but Sophie's trained eye had swiftly spotted the handful of men they were chosen to disguise. A young Paul Newman warming his hands at a brazier was a particular favourite, promoted to the wall from its former hiding place in Charlie's burrow cupboard. There had been a furious row the previous term when Charlie refused to believe Paul Newman was Jewish.

Sophie noticed that, as time wore on and a whole hour passed, Charlie's bravado began to fray at the edges, so she avenged Lucas a little by winding him up.

'They're going to the Headman together,' she told him. 'He's making Lucas repeat what you told him.'

'Shut up.'

'And even as we speak, a call's being put through to Headbourne and your mother.'

'Shut up, Sophie!'

'Or maybe they're having sex already?' Kimiko picked up Sophie's lead. 'Maybe Compton is buggering him and it's really, really hurting and Lucas has changed his mind and it's too late. Maybe we should call the police?'

'Nonsense!' Charlie was close to tears or losing his temper or both and Sophie tasted the bloodlust of a tease about to go too far.

Suddenly there were footsteps up the stairs outside and Lucas burst in. He was transformed, glowing, happy, breathless from running.

'Well?'

Now he tortured them by making them wait. He just stood there, panting.

'What?' Charlie asked, throwing a cushion at him.

'I should murder you,' Lucas started.

'Yes. But what happened?'

'Nothing.'

'For a whole hour?'

'There was no one there for once. He'd locked the garden gate because he was working or something. When I saw the house so dark, I thought he'd left.'

'But he hadn't.'

Lucas sat on one of the beds and pulled his legs up. He took his time.

'No. I . . . I asked him if we could talk about something and he said of course and sat me down and made me a pot of karkady and, I dunno . . .' He giggled. 'I just came out with it.'

'Tell me it's not true, Tina!' Kimiko said. She was fluent in their talk.

'I told him I'd heard he was leaving and I couldn't bear him going without me saying how I'd fallen deeply in love with him.'

'Which was when he said he wasn't leaving,' Charlie started. 'Ssh!'

'No,' Lucas said. 'He didn't tell me that. He came over and sat on the sofa next to me and said he was very touched and flattered but that of course I knew it was completely impossible because he was far too old and a teacher with responsibilities and *in loco parentis* and so on. And I said yes, I knew,

219

of course and the funny thing was that I did. Just saying it out loud made me see it was impossible but I felt so happy to have told him! And then he played me a bit of *Rosenkavalier* – the bit where the Marschallin sings about the clocks and her fear of getting old – and he held my hand.'

'He never!' Charlie crowed.

He had sounded pleased but as he listened to Lucas rattle on Sophie saw an expression flit across his face that frightened her; a glimpse of the side to him that Lucas jokingly called The Monstrous Child.

'He did,' Lucas was saying. 'Just held it, because my hand was shaking so much. I said was he going to tell anyone and he said why on earth should he since I'd done nothing wrong and saw how impossible it was. And then he asked me other things, about home and work and did I want to go to Oxford or Cambridge and what books was I enjoying and . . .' He paused, blissed out, regaining his breath. 'Well. He was just very, very civilized. And he said I'm to go round there whenever I like.'

There was a stunned silence then Charlie slammed down a geometry case he had been fiddling with and stamped out. Lucas glanced at Sophie before following him.

'Time for supper,' Kimiko said. 'We should hurry back.'

'Yeah,' said Sophie but having followed her onto the landing she lingered.

Charlie had stormed into the washroom a few doors along the corridor. Lucas had followed him in there but left the door ajar.

'You don't know what you all put me through,' Charlie was raging. 'I thought you might have gone to the Headman. I thought they were calling my mother!' He sounded like a jealous wife.

'I don't know where the time went,' Lucas said. 'I love him, Charlie. I really do.'

'You're so fucking inconsiderate,' Charlie said and it sounded as though he had kicked out at a loo seat.

'I'm sorry,' Lucas said. 'I didn't realize. Charlie? Come and eat something. You'll soon feel better.'

Aware Kimiko was holding the back door open, Sophie hurried out to join her but she was haunted by Lucas's appeasing, almost cringing tone and by the dismayed affection in his words. Their friendship was far more complex, she realized, than either Lucas or Charlie let on and compromised them both in ways she could not understand.

CHRISTMAS HOLIDAYS
(fifteen years, eleven months)

'Pinch me, Phi,' Lucas murmured happily as they followed Mr
Compton and his mother along a plush opera house corridor.
He was wearing a dinner jacket for the first time, bought
expressly by Heidi when the invitation came, and looked at
once grown up and about six.

Sophie flicked his bow tie.

'Hey!' He clapped a hand over it protectively. He had insisted
on buying a real one and it had taken the two of them half an
hour to tie it, using the enigmatic diagram that came in its box.

Sophie had on her only good skirt, the dark blue one Mrs
Somborne-Abbot had given her, and the black silk blouse and the
tiny silver crucifix and chain she had bought with her earnings
as a waitress. She had on brand-new, very sheer tights that would
be lucky to last the night without laddering, a pair of second-

222

hand court shoes Margaret had helped her dye and a peacock blue Indian shawl Heidi had given her on semi-permanent loan.

Lucas was even happier, she could tell, when they were ushered through a door not into ordinary seats but a box with four little gilt chairs, wine on ice and a tray of tiny sandwiches.

'Oh good!' exclaimed Mrs Compton, a serenely pear-shaped woman. Beneath her fur coat she had on the sort of comfortable, floor-length Indian cotton frock they sold in the market at home and, Sophie sensed, equally unpretentious and comfortable underwear. She was not at all the glacial priestess one would have imagined for Mr Compton's mother and Sophie warmed to her the moment they shook hands in the opera house porch. She put her in mind of a scene in an Irish novel she had read for fun recently that described dowagers at a hunt ball shamelessly sporting high-necked, yellowing woollen vests beneath their décolleté gowns.

Mr Compton had sent her a Christmas card of a Botticelli virgin. (The only other posted ones were from Kimiko, Charlie and Lucas.) This was surprising in itself but then she found the brief note he had written on a piece of notepaper folded inside.

My mother and I are going to Der Rosenkavalier at Covent Garden on the 3rd and would be delighted to take you and Lucas too.

The opera did not appeal to her greatly. She could see it was popular – there was not a free seat in the theatre – and guessed that Mr Compton had chosen it for its comic story and sweet melodiousness. But the music was *too* sweet to her ear, its textures cloying. Added to which, the plot was an uneasy blend of adult material with pantomime. There was a principal boy, sung by a woman in breeches and open-necked shirt, but one who slept with the leading lady. The lecherous comic baron merely made her long for the women to sing again and she resented the music's implication that, deep down, he was lovable. Kitsch was fun, usually one could laugh at it, but this was kitsch of a disturbing and sticky kind, perhaps because it was so nakedly a piece of early twentieth-century escapism.

The others were enraptured, however, so she said nothing. There was much to enjoy, the glamour of the sets and costumes, the other people in the audience, the novelty of finding herself in such a place. She noted the way the nymphs holding up the lights began as little more than cherubs up by the cheapest seats and became larger and more voluptuous by degrees until, near where they were sitting, they were full-blown naked women.

'Only the grandees merit nipples,' Mr Compton said, following her gaze. 'My mother came here during the war to go dancing with soldiers.'

'Not soldiers in the plural, Antony. You make me sound much faster than I was. I came here with your father.' She turned to Sophie, eyes sparkling at the memory. 'They used to cover the stalls with a dance floor. It was *heaven*! Mind you, it was pretty shabby, then.'

'It's fairly shabby now,' Mr Compton observed.

'Do you come here regularly?' Lucas asked them.

'Not as often as we should,' Mrs Compton said. 'It's up to Julius.'

'My older brother takes this box for each opera of the season,' Mr Compton explained. 'But he can't abide anything in German.'

'Not even *The Magic Flute*,' she added. 'Imagine! So my daughter-in-law gives us his cast-offs.'

In the first interval they stayed put for wine and sandwiches. In the second Mrs Compton led Sophie to the ladies', though the way she put it was, 'Perhaps Sophie would keep an old biddy company to powder her nose.'

She bowed and twinkled at several people she knew on the way and, in the queue, introduced Sophie to some friends simply as 'my young friend, Sophie Cullen', which had a certain thematic, Sapphic flair.

Sophie noted the old-fashioned way Mr Compton and Lucas rose when they re-entered the box and made way for them to reach the foremost pair of chairs with the best view. Normally she would have offered to swap with Lucas but she could see he was far too happy to want to move.

'I'm longing for supper,' Mrs Compton said, as though the opera were a chore. 'So I can find out all about you both. Now. Act Three. The comic business at the start goes on rather but you'll find the last ten minutes make the whole thing worthwhile.' As the lights dimmed, she reached into her bag and brought out a battered pair of army binoculars. 'My late husband's,' she whispered. 'Not very delicate but most effective.'

They went on to a big hotel for what the Comptons called supper, but for Sophie was the grandest dinner she had eaten in her life. They were evidently familiar faces there because several of the older waiters greeted them like friends and, when Mrs Compton was chatting amiably with one of them as he shook their napkins out in their laps, Sophie was horrified to hear him address her as Lady Droxford.

'I'm sorry,' she said as he left them. 'I've been calling you Mrs Compton all evening.'

Lady Droxford twinkled. 'And I couldn't bear to put you right,' she said. 'Mrs Compton sounds so *comfortable*, like a favourite chair, whereas the other's always put me in mind of an Isle of Wight ferry. Julius is Droxford now because he inherited and Antony stays Compton unless Julius dies without getting a son.'

'Oh. I see.' Sophie didn't see at all but found herself re-arranging her mental furniture and realizing Charlie's family wasn't nearly as grand as she'd thought.

Lady Droxford looked about the glittering room then out at the lights on the river. 'I love this place,' she sighed. 'I associate it with treats. Antony tells me your background is *much* more interesting.'

'But I don't have one.'

Lady Droxford laughed. 'Maybe that's what he meant. Families can be a terrible burden. At least with a husband you get some choice in the matter, see what you're taking on. Do you think you'll ever try to find out who they were?'

'I don't see why. I found out about some people who were going to adopt me then didn't. I wrote to them.'

'I bet that startled them!'

'They never wrote back.'

'How rude!'

'Are you close to your mother?'

'Oh, my dear, she's long dead. And no. I wasn't. I think I worried her because I wasn't pretty. She worked very hard at making me vivacious instead, which was rather cruel. We only found common ground once I'd married and started gardening. Lamb cutlets!' she exclaimed to her elderly waiter. 'How lovely! Thank you.'

All evening their conversations seemed to have divided along gender lines, but with the arrival of the main course, as if on cue, mother and son turned their attention in the other direction and Sophie found herself gazed at by Mr Compton. He looked extremely handsome, as if he'd been polished. The

severity of his black and white clothes brought out the darkness of his hair and soulfulness of his expression. Less Guy
Crouchback, she decided, than Mr Knightley.

'I'm sorry I could only bring the two of you,' he said. 'I
know you're normally a gang of three.'

'Oh,' she said. 'Not as much as we were.'

'Really?' He seemed sad.

'We haven't fallen out or anything and Lucas and Charlie
share a study. It's just that we're all on different ladders now.'

'Of course.'

'But don't worry. Charlie will be envious, of course, but,
well, he lives up here so he probably gets more treats.'

'Yes. It's Hammersmith, isn't it?'

'Fulham.'

'Ah yes. With the widowed mother.'

'Yes. I stayed there this time last year, in fact.'

'Is she so very awful?'

'I didn't say that . . .'

He smiled mischievously in a way he never did in school.
'You didn't need to. I heard from another source.'

Sophie glanced across at Lucas but he was deep in conversation with Lady Droxford, who was holding out her ring hand
so he could examine the antique bracelet she had on. She was
saying something about the Holy Roman Emperor.

'He seems an outlandish friend for the two of you to have.'

'In what way?'

'Well . . . He's not a high flyer.'

'Neither am I.'

'You don't fool me,' he murmured flirtatiously. 'I haven't
forgotten the glint in your eye when you mentioned Jonty
Mortimer's study.'

Lucas glanced over guiltily at the mention of Jonty.

'Jonty and Lucas were friends,' Sophie explained and Lucas dived back into conversation.

'Good lord,' said Mr Compton, dropping his voice. 'So Charlie Selbourne Doodad . . .'

'Somborne-Abbot.'

'Yes – so he isn't an anomaly?'

'Oh. No. Charlie and Lucas aren't . . . I mean, they're . . .' Sophie gulped her wine, blushing. 'Lucas was very good to Charlie when his father died,' she explained, recovering.

'There's a lot to be said for friendship. And of course having such different interests means they don't compete.'

'And Charlie's very funny,' she said. 'He's a lethal mimic. He does you very well, sir.'

'Does he, now?' He raised an eyebrow and ate the last of his meat, closing the subject. 'I'm sorry you didn't like the Strauss,' he added later.

'But I did,' she said. 'Some of the singing was amazing.'

'But it's not your thing.'

'I don't think I know enough about it to pass judgement,' she said carefully. 'But from what I've heard, I think I'm happier with earlier operas. I like *The Marriage of Figaro* and Lucas has a record of Handel arias that . . . that I like too.'

'Ah yes. You prefer purity in your music. A clearer line. I should have sent you up to hear Gluck with my brother.'

'Oh, no. I didn't mean –'

'I know,' he said, silencing her kindly. 'I was teasing. A bad habit. Now I don't eat puddings but you both have to or my mother will sulk. The crème brûlée has a good, Handelian honesty to it. Or perhaps you'd find the fruit salad less lush . . .'

Three crèmes brûlées and a brandy later, Lady Droxford

again pretended she needed Sophie's assistance in finding the ladies'. 'Sorry to drag you off,' she said, 'but the men wouldn't understand and it's a joy. It has little armchairs where one could wait for friends, an attentive maid, flower arrangements and a great tray of bottles of delicious scent.'

The facilities were just as she had described. Sophie had no great need but all the mirrors and gilt made her feel under-dressed and waiting in front of the maid made her self-conscious so she shut herself in a cubicle too until she heard Lady Droxford stop whistling and emerge from hers. They washed hands side by side then Lady Droxford reached for a scent bottle.

'Here,' she said, squirting some on Sophie's wrist. 'Shalimar. Far too old for someone young and pretty like you as it's pure sex but it will give you wonderful dreams. God, I look a fright!'

Throwing a smile to the maid she pulled a chair closer to one of the looking-glasses and grimly dragged a comb through her no-nonsense, iron grey hair. Then she repaired her lipstick and powdered her nose.

Sophie disliked wearing make-up. She had messed around a few times recently with the testers in Boots with girls from the home, and had dipped into Kimiko's secret supply, but always wiped it off again. It felt sticky and made her feel too visible. Watching Lady Droxford use it, though, she saw the purely ritual appeal, just as she could see the appeal of having a chic cigarette lighter to click even though she felt no desire to start smoking.

'Lucas is a nice boy,' Lady Droxford told her reflection, wiping lettuce off one of her large teeth with a tissue. 'Funny. Clever. Socially very able for his age. You're both, what, sixteen?'

'Lucas is. I'm sixteen next week.'

Tentatively, because she was not sure she liked the idea of a public hair brush, Sophie took a brush off the table and ran it through her own hair a few times. The various scents left behind on its heavy handle and the Shalimar on her wrist reached her and spoke of bed. She thought of Wilf, then of Lucas, the two interleaving in her mind as they tended to. *I could marry one of them next week*, she thought, *with my mother's consent.*

'And this other friend of yours, the one Antony was rather catty about.'

'Charlie. Charlie Somborne-Abbot.' Declaring Charlie's full name, complete with overtones of feudal tithes or whatever, seemed suddenly an act of loyalty. There had been disloyalty flickering in the air all evening. This was perfectly all right when she was alone with Lucas, but with adults present it made her uneasy. She made a mental note to let Charlie know Mr Compton was the younger son of a peer. It was the sort of information that would give him pleasure. Since A.D., the Afternoon of Declaration as Lucas spoke of it, Charlie's stature in their circle had been unexpectedly reduced. Lucas had begun to be far more assertive around him, leaving him out of things, implying small but deadly failings in Charlie's taste and intellect, just as Charlie had used to do concerning Lucas's religion and class. It made her fonder and newly protective of their absent friend, brought out the Wilf in him for her.

'Could I give you a word of warning, my dear?' Lady Droxford asked.

Sophie was startled, caught day-dreaming. The hotel hairbrush was still in her hand. She felt suddenly weary and wondered if she were drunk.

'Of course,' she said and set the brush carefully down again.

'You need to be wary of getting too close to boys like Lucas and . . . I'm sorry.'

'Charlie.'

'Yes. To, how can I put it? Oh. I'm a hopeless old bat. Let me start again.' Lady Droxford's hand shook minutely as she clicked her lipstick back into her bag. 'Men with a touch of the *exotic* about them. Men who aren't just men. They're very attractive and funny, and they probably make you feel very special. But don't lose sight of the greater scheme of things. Don't let them spoil you for . . . for normality. Especially as you get older, regular contact with normal people can be a great comfort. There are simpler pleasures; it wouldn't do to go to the opera every night. Sorry. Now I've confused you.'

'No you haven't,' Sophie assured her but felt anxious nonetheless.

Lady Droxford stood. 'You're a very dear girl, I can tell,' she said and gave Sophie a quick hug. 'I shall send you Shalimar for your thirtieth birthday, if I'm not quite dead then. You see . . .' She stood back, glancing once more at her big, horsey face. 'I married a man like that. So I know. I couldn't believe my luck at the time. And of course there were compensations. There always are with very charming men. That's how it happens. But don't let them spoil you. Now. We must get you two and this old carcass home.' She tipped the maid with another smile and a 'Thank you, dear.'

Mr Compton and his mother had been doing something in town that afternoon so Lucas and Sophie had ridden up on the train. But Mr Compton was taking his mother back to his house for the night and had assured them he would drive them home. He was driving his mother's car for the occasion, not the mossy Morris he used about school. It was an old Rover or Wolseley. Sophie only caught a glimpse of the radiator as he drove up from the hotel's basement garage.

231

'Now,' Lady Droxford said, 'Lucas can ride up front because he's a man, and feed Antony humbugs if he starts nodding off. Sophie. Tuck yourself in.'

There was a lovely smell of leather inside and the back seat felt like a big old sofa. Lady Droxford had produced hot water bottles which she filled from a pair of huge Thermoses and handed out because the heating could no longer work without filling the car with dangerous fumes, apparently.

As Mr Compton drove along the Strand, past landmarks Sophie remembered from her previous trip with Charlie, Lady Droxford tucked a couple of blankets about them, lay back humming a phrase from the Strauss, and was soon fast asleep. Full of rich music, richer foods and sound counsel, Sophie was not long in following her. Occasionally she woke, hearing Lucas's and Mr Compton's low voices from the front, and stayed awake just long enough to see they were circling an unfamiliar roundabout or crossing an unfamiliar bridge and the Shalimar wafting up from where she was holding the blanket cosily over her shoulders was at once stern reminder and sensuous promise.

LENT TERM
(sixteen exactly)

Birthdays were the one time Sophie continued to feel homesick at Tatham's. She had always rather hated her own birthdays anyway. Even more than Christmas, they carried an impossible freight of expectation. Margaret and Kieran always made an effort for them. Margaret baked the cake of choice, Kieran always made an improvement to one's room, like a new bedside lamp or a ceramic doorplate with one's name on it. But she had seen films, she knew how birthdays were in the real world and no amount of party pudding and games and silly little presents could disguise the fact that she was turning a year older in a fake family made up of people she wasn't related to and didn't necessarily like.

Wilf felt the same, she knew. She had noticed how he would often get into big trouble in the days before his birthday as though hoping to sabotage any celebration by being grounded or held back after class or even moved on to the dread place Kieran mentioned on the rare occasions when boys or girls were completely out of control: approved school.

But birthdays were even worse for her because she was convinced nobody actually knew when she was born, any more than they could be sure her right surname was Cullen. She heard stories of how foundlings were often called after the street they were found on or given the surname or birthday of the policeman or dustbin man who had rescued them. A girl desperate enough to dump a baby – and now that she was beginning to notice girls not much older than her with prams, Sophie increasingly thought of her mother as a girl, not a woman – such a girl would be unlikely to go to the trouble of pinning a little, tearstained apology to the baby's blanket. *Her name is Sophie Cullen. I love her but can't cope.* Or whatever. Star sign. Recognition token. The stuff of romance. The turning point of Roman comedies. The reality would be a girl in pain and fear, racing to put distance and oblivion between herself and the shameful thing she had just dragged into the world.

So her birthday was not only a well-meaning torture, a whole day of making sure she looked happy enough to satisfy the happy faces around her, but probably wrongly dated too.

In St Bonnie's, term-time birthdays were institutionalized by a mention in assembly, the form mistress having everyone sing 'Happy Birthday' and the assumption that when anyone in the class had a party, the entire class was invited. In Tatham's the notice accorded a birthday was left perilously to the pupils. No one could give a party and there was certainly no classroom singing of 'Happy Birthday' but there might be the humiliating horror of being given the bumps or worse, for the unpopular

234

– the smelly or strange – the pointed non-marking of a birthday known of but uncelebrated.

For most it was impossible to keep a birthday secret because of the little pile of extra parcels and cards awaiting them on the post table after breakfast. Sophie was a practised deceiver, however, and intercepted her small clutch of offerings – from Wilf, Kieran and Margaret – at the Porters' Lodge. When anyone asked what star sign she was, she gave a different answer, thus creating a fog of confusion that rapidly became a lack of interest. The trick was to show no interest in other people's birthdays; if you never marked theirs or encouraged them to mark yours, it was surprising how easily friends accepted an amnesty on the topic. Kimiko, Charlie and Lucas were blessed with birthdays that fell in the holidays so the subject rarely arose among them.

But all this left Sophie with a painfully childish, homesickly hunger when the day arrived unremarked. Perhaps, deep down, she wanted pats on the back, silly cards, a little sentimental attention instead of which she had a day like any other, punctuated, at some point, by a surreptitious trip to the library or a bathroom to open the few offerings she had received.

Today, her sixteenth, was the worst of the three boarding school birthdays to date. She had slipped over to the Porters' Lodge well before breakfast as usual and found nothing there for her. Not even a card from Wilf. Then it seemed to turn into one of those days when she was more than usually invisible. Someone bumped into her and sent her books flying on a muddy path. When she put her hand up with questions or answers, dons seemed to ignore her. When she finally saw friendly faces, running into Kimiko and Lucas as her ancient history class came out before lunch, Lucas was going on and on about the latest Charlie psychodrama.

Fate had cruelly arranged that Charlie did rather well in his first term on the science ladder – Fate, and some kind assistance from his new Phot Soc friend, David Crisp – so he had moved up a notch and started the new year in the div run by Mr Compton. He was thus in a position to drive Lucas wild with daily bulletins of Mr Compton's attempts to inculcate an interest in Wagner and Nietzsche into his scientists, of the interest Mr Compton was showing in him in particular, of how Mr Compton had nicknamed him Siegfried because he was big and blond and, as he cheerfully admitted, ever so slightly dim. The latest agony, apparently, was that Mr Compton had invited Charlie – just Charlie, not the whole div – on a trip to London to see *Götterdämmerung*.

'A whole evening. Just the two of them.'

'I bet he won't bring his mother along this time,' Kimiko murmured. She was revealing a capacity for spite.

Lucas groaned. 'Oh, god, yes. Lady Droxford. No, it'll just be the two of them – although he'd love her there because she's a Lady and he's such a snob. Maybe they'll stay at a hotel because it'll end so late.'

'Maybe,' Sophie said, 'it would be nice for Charlie to have all the attention for a change. It's not always about you, Lou.' He looked up, stung. *At last*, she thought, *I have his attention*. 'The way you carry on sometimes,' she added. 'Anyone would think you were an only child.'

'Yeah, well a fat lot you'd know about that,' he shot back.

Kimiko was caught between them, shocked, glancing from one to the other as they glared but then she seemed fractionally to turn to face Sophie more, siding with Lucas, her new best friend.

Sophie turned and walked back towards Schola, face burning, feeling foolish and wretched. She had almost flounced. She never flounced. It was more Charlie's style than hers. She never lost her temper because she hated feeling like this. She couldn't even hint it was her time of the month because Kimiko would know it wasn't.

She passed through the Slipe into Flint Quad. The din of lunch was already starting upstairs. Boys were stamping up the boomy wooden steps to Hall. Kitchen staff clanged trays and yelled to one another. She hesitated at the foot of the steps. Lucas and Kimiko would be gaining on her. It had become a practice among them to exploit the studied coolness and lower discipline of the upper school by insinuating Lucas or Charlie into Schola for meals occasionally. The smell of fish pie reached her, and boiled cabbage and the urinous whiff of carrot steam. Far from revolting her, it made her stomach contract with hunger; school food always smelled worse at a distance.

She started up the steps but was stopped by a familiar voice shouting her name. A rush of first-years, gowns flying as they pounded upstairs on either side of her, confused her senses and it was only when Margaret waved an arm that she spotted her.

She was out of place there, in a dazzlingly awful hat and scarf set she had knitted herself and the padded, cream rain-coat that turned a bulky woman into a tumulus. She dwarfed Itchen, the diminutive, polio-lamed porter, who was hobbling along beside her. Clutching a bunch of daffodils, she managed to appear the model of the embarrassing, inopportunely arriving mother and Sophie had never been so happy to see anyone. Ignoring Lucas and Kimiko, who were just coming through the Slipe, she raced over to her and hugged her.

'Happy birthday, love,' Margaret laughed and kissed her. It might have been the first kiss she had ever given her. Normally she restricted herself to loving hugs, professionally or maternally wary of how anything warmer might be interpreted. She didn't smell of cooking or washing for once but of scent, so Sophie realized she was treating this as an occasion, not just another task.

'Found her. Good,' Itchen said and hobbled back to the lodge, glad to be spared the arduous climb up to Hall.

'I'm kidnapping you,' Margaret said, handing over the flowers. 'You don't turn sixteen every day. These are for you. I invented a dentist's appointment for you so don't look too happy. So this is where you live?'

'Yes. My study's up there.' Sophie pointed at a dormer window, aware that she had never given Margaret a tour. 'Do you want to see?'

'Maybe later. Come on. Your presents are in the car. Kieran's covering for me so we've got just two hours before I have to get back and get supper started. You look well.'

'I don't. I've got zits.'

'Just be glad you're still young enough to get them, my girl.'

Margaret drove her out of town to a small pub on a riverbank. 'My refuge,' she explained. 'Where I come to get away from you lot.'

Waiting for their lunch, she gave Sophie her presents. A very grown-up Sheaffer fountain pen from her and a purple bean bag from Kieran. There was a card signed by all the children in the home and Sophie realized she was really having difficulty putting faces to all the names. The last present, a bulky one, was from Wilf. It was an authentic American baseball jacket, red with white sleeves and stripey cuffs. It was worth far more than they usually spent on each other, embarrassingly far more.

'He's earning now,' Margaret said, reading her mind as Sophie tried it on, stroking the warm fabric. 'Will they let you wear that at school? It looks funny over your uniform.'

'On half-days and Sundays we can wear what we like. And he's got it a bit too big. He knows I like that. Oh, I feel awful!'

'Why? He loves you. Just because he moved out doesn't change that. I'd take it off now though or you might get gravy on it. It doesn't look machine-washable.'

'I don't care. It's fab,' Sophie said then took it off, guilty that she had not made nearly as much fuss about the fountain pen and sag bag.

When they'd reached the coffee stage, Margaret produced another envelope. 'This came from your social worker,' she said.

'She remembered my birthday?' Sophie asked.

Margaret shook her head. 'No, love. It's just been forwarded by her. You'd better read it.'

The letter was rather sad but also indignant. Enclosing the one Sophie had written them, Mr Pickett explained that he and his wife had indeed tried to adopt her when she was just six months old but then had been told there was an administrative error and that she had been adopted already. Disappointed after a long search, they had given up on parenthood only for a miracle to happen and Mrs Pickett became pregnant, something they had been assured was quite impossible. They were aghast to hear that Sophie had not been adopted after all but possibly more so that she had been given their details to contact them. Surely this was a breach of confidentiality rules?

The letter was typed, as though to mask whatever sense of Mr Pickett's personality might have leaked through its careful wording. The signature, in black ink, was illegible but, combined with the typing, suggested a pinched quality, a lack of warmth.

Sophie could feel Margaret's eyes on her as she read the letter again. She tried to imagine the child, her supplanter, younger by half a year, and what growing up in an old vicarage, loved by the writer of such a letter would have made of her. She pictured the clothes of conformity: white lacy knee socks, brown, *vieille fille* shoes, one of those unflatteringly square-hanging tartan skirts with the traditional pin fastening. A life-time completer of holiday diaries and meek wearer of Dr White's towels.

At last she could avoid Margaret's questioning eye no longer.

'Wilf,' she explained. 'He'd been on at me for years about how he knew where all the files were kept in your office and did I want to read mine if he took a hairpin to the lock. I'd always said no but he copied my file anyway, without telling me. He left it as a sort of moving-out present. I don't know why I wrote. Maybe I was a bit angry. I'd given up waiting to hear back.'

'They'd moved, look.' Margaret tapped the pages, drawing her attention to the difference between the address printed at the top of one and the one in her own writing at the top of the other. Some low, feral part of her could not help taking a mental snapshot of the new address – another old vicarage, this time in a Wiltshire village – in the seconds before Margaret folded the letters away.

'I'm sorry,' Sophie said. 'Does this get you into trouble?'

'No,' Margaret told her sadly. 'Not really. I've been onto the council before about the lack of security in the office. Wilf isn't the first kid we've had who could pick locks. It's a stupid rule anyway.'

'Which?'

'Oh. Nothing. Don't mind me. I'm being . . . Oh fuck it.' Margaret never swore. And now she was getting tearful, Margaret who didn't even cry at *Ring of Bright Water*.

'Don't cry,' Sophie told her. 'God, I'm sorry, Margaret.'

'It's not you, love. I . . . I don't care. They wouldn't sack me for it. They wouldn't have the nerve.'

'What? I don't understand.'

But Margaret was all mystifying animation suddenly. 'Come on. Someone for you to meet. Another bit of your birthday present, call it.'

She drove some distance, back around the city's outskirts, then stopped at a phone box to make a call. Watching her through the glass, Sophie could see she was agitated.

'Right,' Margaret said, getting back in the car and driving on. 'You've got half an hour then I'll have to drop you back at school.'

'Who is it? Where are we going? Margaret?'

Margaret pulled over, parked and cut the engine. It was a quiet, entirely unremarkable suburban street of redbrick bungalows. 'Number Twenty-two,' she said. 'Just over there by the zebra crossing. She's expecting you. I'm not here, okay? I never told you anything. But you can't know so much and no more. It's not your mother, though, okay? Don't get your hopes up. She's called Betty. Betty Kirklow. She's expecting you. She's been expecting you a while, I reckon. I'll wait out here, love. Better that way.'

Number Twenty-two was a bungalow, like its neighbours. There was a lawn, punctuated by a cherry tree and a circular flower bed stuffed with winter pansies. Beside it, concrete slabs made a hard standing for a car. A fat tabby cat slunk away beneath the hedge as Sophie came up the path. A little metal basket for milk bottles. A device for removing muddy boots. A stirring net curtain. She told her brain to remember, remember anything it could, but nothing here sparked the slightest recognition beyond a faint echo of the house Janet and John lived in. She realized she remembered Janet and John, remembered turning the pages and learning to read and her frustration that the sentences she was reading were so rudimentary and pedestrian. Just as the memory returned to her, the front door opened and a woman was standing there.

She looked like a piano teacher. Blue blouse, tweed skirt, carefully styled brown hair. A kind, moon-like face. A cameo brooch at her neck. 'Hello,' she said. 'Sophie? I'm Betty.' Her voice shook slightly with nerves as she held out a hand. It was warm, wet even. She was scared. 'Please come in,' she said. 'Come in and sit down where I can look at you.'

She closed the door swiftly behind them and led her to the sitting room. The house smelled of lavender air freshener with an undertow of boiled egg. Its atmosphere was not a happy one.

'Look at you. So grown up! How old are you now? Fifteen, is it?'

'Sixteen.' Sophie held back from telling this stranger it was her birthday. She was too curious to want to deflect her attention.

'Goodness.' Betty Kirklow smacked her hands together. 'Do you want tea? Coffee?'

'I've just had some, thank you. I know your voice.'

It was true. Nothing about her struck any chords but the voice, which was far higher than the face and build led one to expect.

'Really? You remember that?'

Sophie nodded. 'Who are you?' she asked. 'Why should I remember?'

Betty Kirklow glanced nervously at the clock that was ticking on the mantelpiece. 'Sit down, please,' she said.

They both sat.

'I used to run a home,' she said softly. 'Not a children's home,

a mother and baby home. They don't have them any more,
thank God. Girls came to us who were pregnant but not
married. Actually they didn't come. They never came. They
were delivered. By their parents or sometimes by the people
they worked for. The idea was that they stayed with us long
enough to have their babies and we found the babies adoptive
parents so the babies could go straight to a new home that
wanted them and the poor girls could get on with their lives.
They didn't always want to give the babies up.'

'Did my mother come to you like that?'

'No. No, you were bought to us by social services, or whatever they called it then. You were the most beautiful baby. And
so quiet. You never seemed to cry. I'd never met a child like
you.' She broke off to retrieve a handkerchief she had tucked
up her sleeve and dabbed at her eyes. 'The other nurses thought,
with you being so quiet, you weren't quite right in the head.
But I knew better. You were just thoughtful. We found parents
for you, no problem at all, but then you got a fever and I moved
you into my flat to nurse you. I lived above the home, you see,
over the job as it were. And . . . Well . . .'

She twisted the handkerchief into a tight knot between her
hands so that it stopped the blood in one of her fingers then
another. Her hands were very plump and smooth. But Sophie
remembered them too, as she remembered the voice. *Murderer's
hands,* she thought. *The smooth hands of cruelty.* She imagined
them firmly plucking babies from their mothers' laps, remembered
them turning the pages of a book and the way they smoothed
each page as they turned it, with their soft, bed-making fingers.

'I took you into my room to nurse you. It was a Sunday.
You were due to go the following week. None of the other staff
were around. Then, when they were during the week and

243

someone asked after you, I said your new parents had come to collect you at the weekend. Just like that.'

She looked up and her lower lip shook like a child's on the verge of tears.

'It came to me all at once. I hadn't planned it or anything but as soon as I lied and nobody questioned it, it became quite clear to me. I would keep you by me! In the flat! You've no idea what it was like living in that place, surrounded by pregnancy and birth and babies and always handing babies over to happy mothers or taking them from unhappy ones and never having one of my own. I signed the forms and did all the paperwork – not that there was much paperwork back then – to make it look as though you'd gone to your new home and I, oh dear, I rang the couple who wanted you and said I was so sorry but there had been an administrative error and that you weren't available after all because some other parents had a prior claim. I remember I said that, *prior claim*, like an official form, and it worked like a charm. They were upset, obviously, but they didn't want to talk much because they were ashamed. Parents adopting back then often were. A bit hole-in-corner.

'So there you were, living with me. I fed you and changed you and dressed you and you were so good! I've got photographs. Here.'

She rose and went to one of those ugly wooden work boxes that opened out ingeniously into layers. She had a small white album hidden beneath a plastic bag of muddled darning wools. 'Last place he'd think of looking,' she said.

Sophie had not noticed at first but now he had been alluded to she spotted traces of a husband here and there. A set of golf clubs in the hall. A pipe in an ashtray. A library book on the companion armchair to Betty Kirklow's with a picture of a submarine on the cover. Betty Kirklow came to sit on the sofa beside Sophie.

'Look,' she said. 'You were so sweet.' She turned the pages of the album slowly while Sophie looked. She didn't offer to let Sophie hold it and read it for herself. It was too precious a secret for that. More probably, she could not connect the baby in the pictures with the inquisitive, discomfiting young woman on the sofa beside her.

There were no captions, just pictures, first of Sophie as a tiny baby, lying in her cot, or on a rug, then of her crawling and then, quite suddenly, the one Sophie had grown up with, in which her toddler self was learning to walk with the support of a bookcase.

'I've got that one.'

'Have you?' Betty Kirklow sounded surprised. 'Well perhaps there was a spare. They never got this. I kept it hidden.'

'But they got me?'

'I hadn't made any plans. I just took you because I wanted you but once I'd got you it was so difficult. You were quiet as a mouse. You played so quietly. You just stared at things with those big eyes of yours and held them and turned them over and over. I left you in a playpen at first, while I slipped down to work, but then you got bigger and I . . .' The pictures ran out abruptly with a picture of Sophie aged three or four at a kitchen table with a children's picture book open before her. She strained to see what the book was but Betty Kirklow shut the album nervously and went to conceal it again in her mending box. She glanced at the clock.

'Were you arrested?' Sophie asked her. 'How did they find out?'

'You followed me out.' Betty Kirklow shook her head sorrowfully, remembering. 'I always used to lock you in. I'd read to you so often you'd started reading for yourself and I used to lock you in but with plenty of books to keep you quiet while I did my round. But one day I forgot to lock the door. The psychiatrist said maybe I forgot on purpose and maybe I wanted them to find out. Anyway you came toddling out after me, followed me downstairs. You'd never even been out of doors, poor lamb! And when I heard the other nurses talking and saw one pointing I turned round and there you were, in the middle of the room, holding out a book and you just smiled very sweetly and said, "Finished!" No. No, dear, they didn't arrest me. Not exactly. There was an enquiry and I lost my job, of course. Couldn't work in nursing or childcare again, unfit and so on. I never saw you again.' She blew her nose. 'You were so bright and good. I never thought you'd be without a family for long. Some mothers prefer to adopt older children. Don't like nappies.' She pulled a face. 'I was quite shocked when Margaret said you hadn't wanted to move. You like her? Margaret?'

'Yes.'

'She used to work with me. That's how she knew how to find me. Not that I've been very good at keeping in touch or anything but I think she kept tabs. For your sake.'

The clock on the mantelpiece pinged three times. She jumped up.

'I'm sorry, dear, but you're going to have to go now. My husband will be back from his life class soon and he doesn't know about you or anything like that.'

Sophie suddenly fell a hot pressure behind her eyes as though she might be about to faint and realized she was boiling up with unfamiliar anger.

'So?' she asked. 'You messed up my life. Why shouldn't I mess up yours?'

'Did I?' Betty Kirklow seemed startled at the abrupt loss of manners, which made the angry feeling worse. 'You don't seem very messed up. Are you unhappy?'

'I could have had a family.'

'Margaret said you didn't want –'

'Well of *course* I didn't by the time I was seven or eight. I was happy where I was! I had friends and . . . But maybe earlier.'

'I wasn't well. I had to see a therapist and take tranquillizers and –'

'My heart bleeds.'

There were ornaments all over the mantelpiece and tables, hideous, attenuated porcelain women and children with off-white skin and sickly, far-away expressions. Sophie snatched the biggest one, a sort of nun, enjoying the whimper this produced in Betty Kirklow. She thought of hitting her with it, cracking it down on her skull. It felt like a weapon, cold and sharp. But she hurled it against the hearth, instead, where it smashed most satisfactorily. Betty Kirklow flinched.

'Tell him you knocked it over dusting,' Sophie told her. 'And take my advice. Burn that creepy album or I'll come back to haunt you.'

She had never knowingly made anyone cry before but right now she wanted this moonfaced baby-snatcher to break down and wail, to fall on her knees on the sharp shards of porcelain and beg forgiveness. But Betty Kirklow merely walked to the front door.

'If you come back,' she said, 'or ring or anything, I shall call the police.' She opened the door wide. 'You ruined my life too, you know.'

'I did?' Sophie began but then they both saw Margaret

coming up the path. Margaret looked swiftly from the one face to the other, sniffing trouble. She had a sixth sense for conflict, had always shown an uncanny ability to walk into a room just before a fight was about to break out.

'I could shop you,' Betty Kirklow told her.

'You could, Betty,' Margaret told her calmly, 'but you won't. Nice place you've got. Quiet. Come along, Sophie. Time to get you back. Bye, Betty. Be good.'

She put an arm about Sophie as they walked back to the car but Sophie was still too angry to risk conversation or even sympathy. She shook herself free. Her revulsion at her own loss of control must have been palpable because Margaret respected it, unlocking the car and driving her back to Tatham's in silence.

Neither spoke until they were approaching the school gates, when Margaret asked, 'Are you okay going straight back like this? Do you want to talk about it?'

Sophie shook her head. 'No,' she said. 'I need to think about it all a bit. But thanks.'

'I didn't think she'd keep you in there so long.'

'She was showing me baby photographs.'

'She kept them? She's insane! She didn't mean any harm, you know. It's a syndrome, snatching babies. She was a mess. And you *were* very. sweet.'

'Don't you start.'

'Did I do the right thing?'

'Yes,' Sophie told her. 'Thank you.' But she had to hurry away then, clutching her bulky presents, for fear Margaret's brimming concern might make her cry.

When she reached her study, hurrying because it was nearly time for afternoon school, she found a honey spice cake waiting for her with a card from Lucas that read simply, *I'm a pig. Forgive me? Love Lou x.*

Her heart was so full of other things that she stared at it for a good half-minute before remembering they had quarrelled. Only Heidi baked cakes so cake-shop perfect but the fact that it was purloined from a mother's larder not bought in a shop made the gesture all the more tender for her. She cut herself a quick slice and munched it as she grabbed Horace and *Phaedra* and the relevant files and the taste returned her to the melancholy of the morning. But the homesickness had been overlaid with bittersweetness. Hurrying down the creaking stairs, dodging puddles as she ran out across Flint Quad, she had a new sense of the school, of her friendships, as things she would look back on. She briefly saw herself as in the film of her youth, feeling nostalgia for a phase of her life that had not even finished yet.

EASTER HOLIDAYS
(sixteen years, three months)

It was the week after Easter. Sophie, Charlie and Lucas had been invited down to lend a hand at Lady Droxford's Easter Fête and to stay the night. Lady Droxford lived in the dower house on the estate her eldest son had inherited. The big Edwardian house where he lived with the wife nobody liked could be seen in the distance if one walked through a copse at the end of her garden. The original Queen Anne house had been knocked down by Mr Compton's grandfather and replaced with something that looked like a chest hospital. The dower house was far older and prettier. It had begun life as a kind of lunching pavilion, for when the Droxfords came to row or fish on the ornamental canal that stretched before it, then it was extended, for a long-lived and independent dowager, in the Strawberry Hill Gothick style.

Various women from the village set up stalls on the lawns

to either side of the canal. There was an Aunt Sally, a jam stall, a bring-and-buy, a second-hand book stall and a tea stall. Two rowing boats could be hired, from Mr Compton, for ten-minute trips on the canal. Lady Droxford produced a huge fruit cake and had Lucas take money off people who wanted to guess its weight for the chance of taking it home. Charlie, as a scientist, was put in charge of one of those electric games where punters were challenged to pass a hoop along a length of convoluted wire without triggering a bell by letting their hand shake. Sophie had to sit at the entrance with Lady Droxford taking money for entries and plants while Lady Droxford answered queries about things on the plant stall or the few shrubs and trees she had not labelled.

When the last children had been chased from their hiding place in the weeping pear and the last stallholder had been thanked and waved off, they all bathed and changed and a long and extraordinarily alcoholic dinner followed.

The dining room was as pretty as the rest of the house, its painted, panelled walls hung with old flower paintings Lucas recognized as seventeenth-century Dutch. ('Lucas wants to work for Christie's,' Charlie said cattily. 'I think he'd make a brilliant antique dealer.') The adults sat at either end of the table with Sophie on one side and the boys on the other. From the start there was a painful inequality of attention paid. Made honest by gin, perhaps, Mr Compton spoke almost entirely to Charlie, whom he encouraged to tell ever more scurrilous stories about the other dons. The joking comparisons of Charlie to Siegfried had led to his nicknaming him Ziggy. Charlie had saucily taken to dropping the Mr and called him Compton, as if he were a fellow-schoolboy. He was in seventh heaven, flushed with lamb and claret and social indulgence and gaining a deep, inexplicable pleasure from their hostess being the widow of a lord.

Lucas made repeated attempts to break in on their conversation, like a moth on the wrong side of a lighted window.

Lady Droxford was a very private cook and would let no one follow her out to the kitchen to help between courses but whenever she sat again she took pity on Lucas, diverting him with questions that required long and detailed answers, asking him about his mother's fascinating work and so on. Now and then she called her son to attention with a little cough or a comment and he would play the host for her, walking round the table to refill wine glasses or turning to say something to Sophie. But whatever he said would inevitably inspire a comment from Charlie that would draw him back to where he had started.

It was the closest Sophie had seen to him forgetting his manners but he was so obviously a man enchanted that it was more pitiful than offensive. Lady Droxford was palpably pained and helpless. Sophie wondered how he had manipulated her into inviting them all. Perhaps he had wanted to invite just Charlie. Of course he had. And she had insisted on including Sophie and Lucas to maintain decorum. Sophie suspected she much preferred Lucas to Charlie, not because he did not fawn on her and treated her as a human rather than a title, but because she felt kinship with the pain her son was causing him. All her instincts and training were to put people at their ease so she responded to social discomfort in people as spontaneously as she would to suffering in a dog.

The dinner was delicious – a cold sorrel soup, roast beef with purple sprouting broccoli and an intensely garlicky dish of pommes dauphinoises, then rhubarb fool with home-made shortbread – but Sophie found the tensions around the table so uncomfortable it was a relief when Lady Droxford stood, suggesting they leave everything where it was and have coffee in the drawing room. Sophie had worried that she would be expected to retire with Lady Droxford while the men drank port and this was almost what happened. She followed her to the drawing room where, she discovered, some powerful coffee had been waiting in a Thermos jug since before dinner began. Lucas followed hesitantly, but Mr Compton and Charlie remained chatting and quietly laughing at the table. Lady Droxford served coffee but could not relax, watching Lucas who in turn was loitering unhappily near the doorway so as to retain a view of the couple at the dining table.

There was a piano in a corner, a Broadwood baby grand draped in a silk shawl to protect it from sunlight, and displaying a cluster of family photographs in heavy silver frames.

'Do you play?' Sophie asked. 'I mean, of course you do but would you?'

'Oh, yes,' Lucas joined in with a hint of desperation as Lady Droxford began to demur. 'Play us something. Please.'

Perhaps he thought the sound would draw the others in. Perhaps Lady Droxford did too. At any rate she gamely tossed back the scarf, laid bare the keyboard and played from memory some fifteen minutes of unexpectedly vampy old songs like 'Begin the Beguine', 'Blue Moon' and 'La Vie en Rose'. Songs of desire and yearning. Were they not obviously the songs at the forefront of her repertoire, one might have suspected her of irony or mischief. More than anything else in the room – the overmantel so antique it showed more rust spots than reflection, the shelves of old porcelain, the faded silk rugs – her playing conjured an era when girls were still expected to acquire accomplishments, to entertain rather than merely to be. She relaxed as she played and drew Lucas to her side with her skill. Was this, Sophie wondered, how she had attracted Mr Compton's almost too charming father?

Sophie felt a sudden draught against her neck and glanced round from her sofa to see Charlie disappearing out into the garden through the dining room's French windows. Mr Compton was nowhere in sight. Lady Droxford must have noticed it too for she wound her playing up to an abrupt climax minutes later, laughing, 'Enough, enough! I'm so rusty,' to silence their applause. She could not help throwing a look across to the empty dining room where the door to the outside was drifting open again because Charlie hadn't shut it properly. Lucas noticed too but before he could say anything she was jumping up from the piano and leading them both upstairs.

'No more sitting around,' she said. 'I'd completely forgotten I wanted your help with these pictures. Especially since Lucas is such an expert. Bring more coffee if you like, Sophie.'

There had been water damage at one end of the long upstairs landing where some tiles had shifted to let rain in. She had recently had the damage fixed and the landing redecorated, 'But I've got it into my head to change the pictures around rather than just rehang everything the way it was. And something in the way Lucas was looking at the flower paintings in the dining room tells me he has an eye. And if there's something we country mice are good at it's the exploitation of useful guests. You see. Those are the pictures that were up and there are all the others we can choose from. Julius has offloaded rather a lot that *She* didn't want. I mean, I don't want it to look like a shop but at the same time, it seems a pity to let them gather dust.'

There were stacks of pictures leaning against the wall, nearly thirty. There were oils, watercolours, etchings. Everything from sunlit churchyards to moonlit estuaries, lobster pots to great-great-aunts. Sophie could understand her not having rehung anything; the choice and variety would have overwhelmed her. But Lucas seemed as glad of distraction as Lady Droxford was to offer it and swiftly fell to sorting and arranging.

It was getting late, past eleven o'clock, by the time he and Lady Droxford had agreed a scheme involving at least half the pictures and still Charlie and her son were nowhere to be seen and still no one had commented on their absence. Sophie had been set to work with a hammer and picture nails. Lucas had already held a picture in place while Lady Droxford squinted at it critically from a few feet away before he made a small pencil mark. Sophie's task was to work along the landing tapping in a picture nail wherever he had left a little cross for her. She felt light-headed, equally capable of collapsing with exhaustion or riding a second wind until dawn. Margaret had trouble sleeping sometimes and did things like this, not hanging old pictures but making jam or cleaning the larder shelves. As she woke briefly to roll over, Sophie would hear her from her bed and feel selfishly comforted that no thoughts were keeping her so active.

Sophie was sent downstairs to fetch some extra boxes of picture nails Lady Droxford had left on the kitchen dresser. Passing back along the hall she was suddenly aware that the others had come inside again. She heard their voices from the drawing room. They laughed loudly at something then their laughter subsided into chuckles and then to a stillness so suggestive and threatening she didn't dare look in on them but ran back upstairs. Her only thought was that Lady Droxford must not know and that they should all go safely to bed as soon as possible.

If Lady Droxford had heard the laughter, her performance

was flawless. 'Left a little, Lucas. Up a bit. That's it. To cover that rose on the paper. There.' She kept up her instructions as though nothing were amiss. 'Now. Do you really think Aunt Sibyl on the end and not the horses? She's so very disapproving when one's not looking one's best. Of course I'll be guided by you, though.'

Not long afterwards, however, even she flagged.

'What am I thinking of? You must both be shattered after a day like this. Sophie. Stop. Honestly. Stop now. We can always do a little more after breakfast. Bless you both. Good night.' She walked into her own room, inches from where they had just hung the disapproving girl in white, and closed her door.

No longer obliged to play along, Lucas turned towards the stairs.

'Where are you going?' Sophie asked.

'They've come back in,' he said. 'I heard them.'

'I shouldn't, Lou,' she said sharply and he stopped, frowning. 'Why not?'

'I . . . I really shouldn't. That's all.'

He scanned her face. 'Oh,' he said. 'Oh.'

He realized he was still clutching a Norwich School view of Lord Hereford's Knob and walked past her to hang it on the last nail she had tapped in. He stood back to be sure it was hanging straight.

Sophie had never seen him look so desolate and deflated but felt powerless to help so took the cowardly way out. 'I'm dropping too,' she said. 'It's been a very long day.' Conscious of not addressing the matter so obviously at hand, she yawned heavily to veil her treachery. ''Night.' She set her hammer and box of picture nails on a table and headed off to bed without looking back at him.

She had put out her light when he tapped at her door and came in, in his pyjamas and bare feet. The bedroom felt completely unheated.

'You'll freeze,' she said. 'Get in.'

'Do you mind?'

'Don't snore, that's all.'

'Thanks, Phi.'

It was an old bed with a droopy mattress, not designed for sharing, but she was quietly glad of his company. He didn't snore but he twitched violently as he was falling asleep, lashing out at enemies she could not see.

Charlie behaved impeccably in the morning, as if to balance out his delinquency of the night. He contrived to wake before anyone, do all the washing up and make porridge on the Aga. Mr Compton displayed what was either great tact or rank cowardice by taking himself off on an errand to his brother all morning so that it was left to his mother to drive them to the station before church. She insisted on giving Sophie leftover sandwiches and cake from the fête for their journeys home. Her farewells and thanks were opaque and general, hiding whatever she knew or had guessed of the night before.

They rode in the same train for the first twenty minutes before Charlie had to change to a faster one towards London. Sophie had braced herself during the drive to the station, assuming he would behave appallingly once they were all alone, teasing Lucas with brazen denials or, worse, pornographic detail. Instead he was very sweet and even bewildered.

'I behaved dreadfully,' he said. 'She'll never ask me back.'

'Probably not,' Sophie said.

'Lucas?'

Lucas was scowling out of the window.

257

'Lucas, I'm really sorry. I won't even say I was drunk. Although I was. Jesus, I was plastered! They really put it away, those two. Were you both sick in the night?'

'No.'

'I was. Must have been the brandy. Lucas, I'm so sorry.'

Lucas was forced to acknowledge him.

'Don't be,' he muttered, making eye contact for a second. 'I'd have done the same.'

'Yes but, well, that's the point, isn't it?' He sighed. 'Fuck. I don't know what I'm going to do.'

'Pregnancy test?' Lucas suggested and they all laughed, relieved that he'd decided not to sulk.

CLOISTER TIME
(sixteen years, five months)

Calling on the combined muscle and expertise of the army Corps, the art students and almost anyone signed up for carpentry, Mr Compton had converted the school concert hall to a temporary opera house. There was only one woodland set, the brief being to leave room for as many performers as possible and to use lighting tricks and portable scenery, carried by the chorus, to vary the view. At various points what appeared to be solid backdrop or flat was actually painted gauze so that 'visions' could be revealed, as if by magic – a thing technically advanced by the school's stagecraft standards.

Even allowing for Purcell's limited requirements of brass and wind, most of the school's senior orchestra was squeezed into a pit made by removing the front few rows of seats and erecting a low wall of hardboard, artfully painted to blend in with the forest scenery beyond and a few real bushes in pots placed before.

As for what occurred on stage, it was less full-blown opera than a hybrid entertainment involving as many pupils as possible. Mr Compton had interlaced music filleted from Purcell's *The Fairy Queen* with those scenes from *A Midsummer Night's Dream* involving either fairies or rustics. Shakespeare's quartet of mortal lovers was removed entirely and the nuptial celebrations at the climax became a celebration of Oberon's and Titania's happy reunion, at which the rustics were led to perform under a spell cast by the fairies. His cunning was thus to place the dramatic burden of the show on actors and orchestra and to use singers and dancers as spectacle and diversion. Purcell's arias seemed to require sweetness rather than professional dexterity or force and there were enough strong singers to do them credit. With the sixteen Quiristers providing the 'ahh' factor as a troupe of junior fairies in place of Shakespeare's four, and plenty of stirring choruses, marches and familiar tunes imported from other Purcell works, the result was a farrago of tableaux and barely connected scenes but probably true to the spirit of Purcell's hybridized original.

After a fraudulent morning of 'open' auditions for the speaking roles, Charlie had landed the part of Oberon. Lucas was one of a pack of short-horned, shag-pile-legged satyrs in the chorus. Sophie, who did not dance, sing, act or play an instrument had been pressured into being stage manager because Mr Compton said she had a cool head. She in turn claimed Kimiko as her ASM. There were almost as many pupils involved off the stage as on it, in props, make-up, wardrobe, lighting and front-of-house, most of them already experienced from working on other school productions, so the only expertise required of Sophie was to follow the script and marshal people into the right wings at the right time and to cue the various lighting or scenery effects. She had a little lit-up desk in a dark corner of the stage right wings where she followed her script, murmuring cues or performer summonses into an intercom as they came up. She commanded a slanting view across the stage, close enough to see fumbles and giggles that escaped the audience's notice.

This was the first dress rehearsal and already she was hooked on the smells of greasepaint and nerves, of hot lights and dust and on the adrenaline rush from the sense of each act as a big machine that swept them all along. The atmosphere in the wings was electric and not unpleasantly smelly.

The green light on her desk flashed and she whipped a finger to her lips to hush the Quiristers who were huddling on her side of the wings, craning their necks to see across the stage to their colleagues gathered around Kimiko on the opposite side.

'Standby houselights,' Sophie murmured into her intercom, 'and . . . houselights down.' The houselights dimmed to black. The master of music took his place on the podium and the first solemn bars of the overture sounded. Sophie gave the next lighting cue as the faster music began and the junior fairies queued up to light their sparklers at a cigarette lighter held out by Charlie's shy scientist friend, Crisp, who was in charge of stage right props. As each boy's sparkler took, he raced out across the stage, bare feet stamping. Crisp lifted a bucket of damp sand, ready to receive the sparkler's hot wires as the Quiristers Kimiko had launched ran off stage right, chased by the boy playing Puck.

The music changed again. Sophie had never learnt to read music but she could spot a change of tempo or material.

'Oberon and Titania and chorus, please,' Sophie murmured into her mike. 'Standby: light cue three.'

The wings around her were soon rustling with gauze and nylon. She made out two of the four sixth-form girls representing the seasons confused by Oberon's and Titania's quarrel. They weren't really required to dance, more to skip around with garlands and strike statuesque poses but they had all the queenliness of *prima ballerinas*. At the first run-through, Winter had made a prop girl cry so Sophie was watching for further trouble. Oberon passed between them, outdoing them in haughtiness. The moonlight effect now flooding the stage threw a cold glitter on his crown and jewelled doublet. He caught Sophie watching him and gave her a broad wink.

Summer was always Charlie's glory term, partly because it suited his colouring and the cricket season raised his prestige. She would have predicted that the combination of this starring role and Mr Compton's favouritism would have made him insufferable but found herself humbled by his good behaviour instead. (This in marked contrast to the girl in the non-singing title role who had let the whole business go to her head and caused a fuss by announcing she was going to RADA instead of Cambridge.) As though suddenly freed from insecurities or left with nothing to prove, Charlie had spent all term being thoroughly pleasant, catching both Lucas and Sophie in his overspill of affection. Either people had decided to like him or he was being uncharacteristically careful, for not a breath of gossip had linked him and the opera's director.

The first proper scene began and everyone emptied onto the stage. As their singing filled the air, along with the hollow thump of footsteps on scenery ramps, Sophie found she wasn't alone in the wings with Crisp. Jeremy Weir was there, led in apparently by Kimiko with whom he was whispering. They both glanced across at Sophie. He was current Senior Prefect, far too serious even to involve himself in sport, still less a school opera and his sudden appearance there caused Sophie's heart to lurch. Somebody must have died for him to leave his study to come on such a mission. Kimiko's father? Simon Behrman? Surely not Mrs Somborne-Abbot. But it was her he was approaching.

'You're to come with me, Cullen,' he said. He barely bothered to whisper.

'But I can't,' she hissed. 'We're in the middle of a dress.'

'Matsubara can take over for a while. Can't you, Matsubara?'

'Sure.' Kimiko nodded, glancing at Sophie for reassurance that this would be taken as obedience not treachery.

'Headman wants to see you,' Weir added. 'You're to come at once.' He stood aside to let Kimiko take Sophie's headphones and stool. He cast a quick, incurious look at the scene developing on stage then marched out through the flap in the blackout curtains.

'Tell Compton if he asks,' she told Kimiko, 'but only if,' and followed him.

Unlike Jonty Mortimer, who had done all he could – football, loud music, smoking – to dodge the social taint of braininess, Weir was already too isolated socially to care. He was one of the Scholars marked out as such even when not wearing his gown and waistcoat. Tall, thin, bony, inevitably nicknamed Weird within weeks of arrival, he kept highly effective control, not with any display of machismo or popularism but by dint of his ability to make one feel immature and underevolved with one unsmiling glance. He never smiled just as he rarely changed out of his uniform into half-day clothes, because he saw no point. Only when bell-ringing did he show anything like abandon and even that was possibly an optical illusion arising from the rarity of seeing him in rapid motion.

He didn't speak as he led Sophie across the river, back past Schola and through Brick Quad and Lawn Quad to the Headman's house, because he had fulfilled his task in fetching her and his mind was already returning to whatever thoughts the summons had interrupted. He probably resented her, whatever she had done, for being the cause of interrupting him.

Sunlight was dazzling after hours spent backstage and she felt doubly uprooted by being suddenly among people to whom the opera meant nothing, boys kicking a tennis ball, some Daughters lying on a rug beneath a tree, a groundsman mowing one of the cricket squares; most people. This heady, communal achievement that had been swallowing up so much of her time that she had not slipped home or up to the Behrmans' once all term meant less to most people than the Sex Pistols or the impending cricket match against Winchester.

'Phi!'

She turned to see Lucas, still in satyr costume and make-up but with his denim jacket thrown over the top, coming through the arch from Brick Quad twenty yards behind them.

'You're not to talk to him beforehand,' Weir said. 'Headman's orders,' and as he drew her on she saw that Lucas, too, had an escort, the only prefect from Dougal's on whom he had never developed a crush. He was held back as Weir led her on with a gentle pressure on her elbow.

'What's going on?' she asked him as, joylessly polite, he held open the back door to the Headman's house. 'What am I supposed to have done?'

'I've no idea,' Weir said. 'I was simply told to bring you a.s.a.p. without you conferring with Miss Behrman first.'

His routine mockery of Lucas's reputation was the nearest she had seen him come to amusement.

The Headman, Dr Twyford, lived with his historian wife in some splendour on the first and second floors of the house. The ground floor was given over to his study, hall, secretary's office and a function room where he received leavers for sherry and newcomers for tea. He was a mild, even smooth man, an urbane preacher, a champion of the claims of music over sport but said to be implacable in opposition and thus to have several enemies across the lawn in the dons' common room. Thus far Sophie had avoided ever having to speak to him apart from a few brief words at the newcomers' tea because his very mildness made her nervous. So many pupils seemed beneath his notice that, whenever she caught him watching her in passing in one of the quads or corridors, she was convinced he was keeping tabs on her for some reason.

'Sit there,' Weir said, indicating a row of the kind of hard hall chairs designed for tenants waiting to pay rent. While she sat, sharply conscious in such pristine surroundings of her paint-splashed T-shirt and jeans and filthy plimsolls, he tapped on the study door and opened it when the Headman's voice called, 'Yes?'

'Cullen's in the hall, sir,' he said.

'Ah. Good,' Dr Twyford said. 'Send her straight in.'

As she crossed to the study door, Lucas came in from outside, ushered by his prefect. He cast Sophie a hunted look, the sweaty look of the weak one who cracked in a prison camp film. He had grown over the holidays and his wiry swimmer's frame was filling out. With his bare chest, shaggy brown leggings and little horns poking out of his wig, he had looked quite sexy back-stage but in this setting he looked merely ridiculous and vulnerable, a fey woodland creature thrust into a hostile environment. She looked away, ashamed to be connected to the boy with the streaky orange make-up and the silly wig. Weir knocked for her.

'Ah, Phi. Come in.' It was typical of his smooth operation that the Headman both knew her nickname and used it. 'Sit. I think you know Mrs Somborne-Abbot.'

It was a shock to see her there, and yet not a surprise at all. She was if anything, thinner and smarter than Sophie had ever seen her. She had changed her hairstyle, which now looked twice the size, no longer tugged tightly off her face but sweeping up, off and away from it in a lacquered cloud.

'Oh yes,' she said, shifting in her chair to tuck her ankles together the other way. 'Sophia and I are *old* friends.'

'Hello.' Sophie aimed for cheeriness but her greeting sounded frail. 'I'm sorry to come dressed like this, sir.'

'That's quite all right, Sophie. I'm sorry to pull you out of your rehearsal so dramatically. We'll have you back there before the end of Act One. Now, don't worry. You've done nothing wrong. Mrs Somborne-Abbot and I simply need some information – confirmation, possibly – concerning a very serious matter. We need you to be entirely honest.'

Someone knocked.

'Excuse me.' Dr Twyford walked over and opened the door a few inches. 'Thank you,' he said. 'Just wait there, would you?'

Mrs Somborne-Abbot had whipped out her powder compact and was dabbing at her nose. Had she been crying? Sophie took advantage of the momentary dropping of supervision to glance at the papers on the expanse of desk before her. There were several much-folded letters on thick, white paper. Mr Compton wrote a distinctive, cursive hand with black ink and a thick italic nib. Like his garden and marksmanship, it was one of the things that set him apart from the other staff.

Sophie looked at her hands as Dr Twyford returned to his seat, and pretended to pluck at some scenery paint on her thumbnail.

'Now,' he said, 'It's quite simple. Charlie's a friend of yours, isn't he?'

'Yes,' she said, with a glance at Charlie's mother, who had clicked her compact out of sight again and no longer looked like a woman who might once have shed a tear. 'He's one of my best friends.'

'And Mr Compton. How well do you know him? He's never taught you, has he?'

'No, sir. Not in class. But he and I both go to morning services in the Chantry.'

'Do you, by Jove?'

'Yes, er, and I've been to his house for tea. Lots of times. And he took me to the opera with Lady Droxford and then she had Charlie and me and Lucas Behrman to stay once.'

'Lady Droxford is who?' Mrs Somborne-Abbot asked the Headman.

'That's his mother,' Sophie told her.

'Mr Compton is the second son of the late Lord Droxford,' Dr Twyford explained in an undertone and Mrs Somborne-Abbot's posture became doubly alert.

'Oh,' she said. 'I didn't know.' She cleared her throat. 'Not that that changes anything.'

'Quite so,' Dr Twyford turned back to Sophie with a small smile that might conceivably have been satirical. 'And would you say he and Charlie got on well?'

'Yes, sir. Charlie was in his div and he's in the Corps too, so . . . And of course he cast Charlie as Oberon in the opera.'

'Of course. But would you say he takes a . . . a special interest in Charlie?'

Sophie glanced down at the letters. Dr Twyford noticed and calmly rearranged them into a heap on his blotter which he then covered with a large desk diary.

'Yes,' she said and was aware of Mrs Somborne-Abbot's stare upon her. 'But not in the way I think you mean. Charlie's not very . . . academic but he stands up to Mr Compton, which is unusual. A lot of pupils are scared of him but Charlie even teases him. If they were the same age, I think they'd be friends.'

'He took him to the opera,' Mrs Somborne-Abbot said. 'Just the two of them that time. To Wagner.'

'He takes a lot of pupils to the opera,' Sophie said. 'It's one of the things he cares about.'

'Does Charlie write to him, do you know?' the Headman asked her.

'I don't know. Possibly. Probably. He loves sending notes though the pigeon-hole system. And we all write to each other in the holiday. If he counts Mr Compton as a friend, I expect he writes to him too.'

'Do *you* write to Mr Compton?'

I mustn't lie, she thought. Not outright. She remembered the thank you letter she wrote after the trip to Covent Garden. 'I have done,' she said. 'Yes.'

'And as his friend, you've not been worried there was anything unsuitable or inappropriate between Charlie and Mr Compton?'

Sophie's cheeks were hot. Her back, she realized, was streaming with sweat. 'No,' she said. 'Never.' She was sure she was a beacon of deceit but he seemed satisfied. He smiled.

Perhaps he knew she was lying but she was telling the lies he wanted to hear.

'Thank you, Sophie. Now if you'd like to sit over there?' He waved her across to a small sofa near the door. 'I'm going to be a bit tougher on Lucas than I was on you,' he warned her. 'I might imply things. Please don't say a word, though. Unless I ask you to.'

'All right, she said.

As he went to call Lucas in, she realized she was praying to her quiet, not entirely Christian deity.

Lucas walked in, apparently without noticing she was still there. Perhaps he thought she had been released through the other door. Dr Twyford steered him to the chair by the desk so that his back was to her. 'I like your horns,' he said playfully.

'Sorry, sir. Dexter said to come straight over without changing.'

'Quite right of him.'

Lucas said hello to Mrs Somborne-Abbot and got a cool 'Hello Lucas' in reply. He tugged at his costume because the fake hairy leggings were riding up to reveal the real hairy legs beneath.

Dr Twyford sat across from him. He slid the diary off the handful of letters and picked the letters up, turning them over in his pale, neat hands. 'You and Charlie Somborne-Abbot share a study, don't you, Lucas?'

'Yes, sir.'

'He tells you everything?'

'Pretty much, sir. Though now he's on the C ladder and I'm on the B, we don't –'

'I meant besides work.'

'Oh. Yes, sir.'

'Are you more than friends?'

'No, sir!'

Dr Twyford smiled at Lucas's involuntary indignation. 'You see, we know everything really. We have the letters Mr Compton has been writing to Charlie in the holidays, which Mrs Somborne-Abbot has quite properly brought to me, and we have heard all about what Charlie's been up to from your friend, Sophie, here.'

Sophie saw Lucas's back stiffen. So he hadn't noticed her.

'There's nothing between them, sir,' Lucas said abruptly. 'If Sophie told you anything, she was lying to protect me.'

This is disgrace, Sophie thought. *This is how it starts, with a pointed but polite interrogation in gracious surroundings. Then a handshake, perhaps, and an abrupt dismissal.* There had been expulsions in the last year, one for a second-time smoking offence, one for drugs, one for a boy accused of sexually assaulting a younger one. In each case she had been startled by the ruthless rapidity with which the offenders were removed but she saw now how, behind closed doors, Dr Twyford had probably been equally bland with each offender. By tonight she would be back in her room at Wakefield House. Next week she would have to go for an interview about starting at the girls' grammar school in the autumn. If they would take her. Perhaps she would have to go to the secondary modern with the others in the home. Everyone would know about her fall from grace: a sex scandal in which she didn't even get to have sex but was left perverted by association. She would be branded a snob, too, simply from the inference that she had not thought the secondary modern good enough for her in the first place.

'How should her lying protect you?' the Headman asked.

'Maybe not protect exactly,' Lucas stammered. 'I . . . She . . . She's just jealous on my behalf, because of Charlie being Oberon and getting all the attention. Mr Compton has favourites, sir. Most of the dons do. And he invites us to his house for tea and to listen to music and discuss things but I swear he'd never –'

'How can you be so sure?'

'Because I love him. I thought he was leaving. I'd heard he'd been asked to leave. So I had to tell him. I told him I loved him. I laid myself completely open to him and he didn't lay a finger on me, sir. He was very kind and helpful and told me he was flattered but that I'd get over it and I had to see it was out of the question.'

Mrs Somborne-Abbot let out a kind of slow snort. Its violence was enough to make her pearls move against her blouse.

'I see,' Dr Twyford said. He betrayed nothing as he folded the letters neatly and slid them into a large brown envelope but Sophie was sure he was as startled as the rest of them. 'Thank you, Lucas. I appreciate your honesty and your courage.' He handed the envelope to Mrs Somborne-Abbot. 'These belong with you,' he said.

'He's a good man, sir,' Lucas said. 'An excellent teacher.'

'Yes, Lucas. Thank you. And thank you, Sophie. You can go now.'

'Yes, sir. Thank you, sir.'

Lucas rose and turned to join Sophie, who had her hand on the doorknob to return to the hall. But Mrs Somborne-Abbot was standing too, in a white fury.

'Is that it? You take the testimony of . . . the bastard and the Jew as gospel and –'

'Please wait until we're alone again.'

'My son's fine friends! I wouldn't be surprised if –'

'Mrs Somborne-Abbot, please!' he silenced her and turned to the door. 'Thank you.'

Sophie nodded and held the door open for Lucas. They walked out and her relief was so immense she wanted to hurry on out into the sunshine of Lawn Quad but Lucas grabbed her arm and stopped her. He opened the outer door then closed it with a firm thump then gestured for Sophie to follow him back to the study door so they could listen.

'. . . gone to the County Constabulary,' she was saying.

'I'm very glad you didn't,' Dr Twyford said.

'Of course you are. Your precious school . . .'

'Actually I was thinking of your precious son. This way will do far less harm. You can confront him, if you like. I've no doubt you will. And if he confesses then you're at liberty to take whatever action you choose. If, however, you approach a respected member of my staff simply on the thin evidence of those letters, which reveal nothing more criminal than affection for your son and a certain lack of respect for yourself, you might find yourself being sued for libel by an institution that can well afford it.'

There was a terrible pause. Sophie was all for hurrying away in case they had been detected but then they heard Mrs Somborne-Abbot ask, 'Are you going to do nothing?'

'Of course not. I shall speak separately to Charlie and to Mr Compton and tell them that their friendship is inappropriate and that they are to see no more of each other so long as Charlie is a pupil at the school. If either disobeys – *either* – I will have them removed. To make it easier for them, I propose moving Charlie to a higher div, regardless of his academic performance this term. Will that satisfy you?'

She must have nodded.

'Good. Now perhaps you'd like to come across to the concert hall to watch Charlie's dress rehearsal first . . .'

Aware that the door might open any minute, Sophie dragged Lucas away. They opened and closed the outer door in silence then sprinted off around the edge of the quad so as not to be spotted.

'I didn't say a word,' she panted, when they finally stopped running.

He laughed. 'I know! I knew as soon as I started talking. I knew he'd tricked me but what the hell. Do you think he'll throw me out now?'

'Why? What have you done?'

'Well, I . . . I told him.'

'It's perfectly legal to be a poof and in love. You just mustn't act on it. You heard him. He respected your honesty. What do you think Compton wrote about her in those letters? You'll have to ask Charlie. It must have been something wild!'

They hurried back to the concert hall and in through the wings. Far less time had passed than Sophie realized, or there had been some musical hitch that had caused a long delay, for as she slipped onto the stool beside Kimiko she found the dress rehearsal had progressed only as far as the fifth number.

'Okay?' Kimiko whispered.

'Fine,' Sophie said. 'Fine.' And adrenalin began to make her shake at last. 'You're a star, Sukie. Thanks.'

Mrs Somborne-Abbot was not a woman to be outman-oeuvred by a bastard and a Jew and not even by a man as notoriously unflappable as Dr Twyford. She came across to the concert hall with him. Sophie saw them sitting towards the rear during the interval, Mrs Somborne-Abbot looking daggers at the back of Mr Compton's head. She stayed to the end and clapped along with the technical crew and wardrobe mistresses. By six o'clock, however, she had loaded Charlie into her little green car and was driving him back to Fulham with a week of term still to run.

Lucas took his place as Oberon, although he was slightly shorter than Titania, because he already had the speeches by heart from the hours he had spent testing Charlie on his lines. His performance was good, melancholy, different from Charlie's. His manner was less naturally arrogant, verging on petulance at times in a way that was almost a parody of his friend's worst moods.

Heidi was beside herself with pride, Mr Compton grateful, if subdued, in his praise.

SUMMER HOLIDAYS
(sixteen years, seven months)

Sophie teetered up the perilously steep staff stairs with a laden tray and swore as a knife slid off its plate and smeared the front of her apron with cream and blackcurrant jam. Ratty's Tunnel was a purple-painted basement beneath a kitchenware shop. Its booths were decorated with illustrations to *The Wind in the Willows*. The lack of windows made it hugely popular with underage smokers and illicit couples. The lack of ventilation meant that its atmosphere on such high summer days was a toxic blend of nicotine, cheap scent, hot scones and milkshake flavouring. It was run by André, a world-weary former hairdresser who avoided all dealings with the public by staying in the kitchen and back yard, and staffed entirely by teenagers because they were cheap, had the stamina necessary to cope with the endless running up and

275

down stairs from tables to kitchen and could be kept sweet with unlimited slices of the house Black Forest gâteau. When she had worked there the previous summer, Sophie had been wary of André and guarded in what she revealed of herself but during the last weeks he had won her over and she had confided in him about all manner of things from spying on Lucas and Mortimer to losing her virginity. Since he knew nobody who knew her, she was enjoying the luxury of trying opinions and characters on for size with him playing conversational looking-glass.

André was perched on his stool in the small patch of yard outside the kitchen that caught the sun from two to four. He was flicking through the *Daily Mail*. He was ageless, permanently tanned and shockingly unprincipled. The restaurant offered a narrow range of things that could be stored for days and safely reheated in a microwave: two types of quiche, fish pie and something with mince, pasta, tinned peppers and grated mousetrap cheese called Beef Italian. The gâteau was the best-seller, along with the teapots of red wine the waitresses served outside licensing hours for a suitably fat tip. André had perfected the art of fitting most of his work into the two hours before lunch. Every day he cooked and iced a gâteau and made a week's worth of one of the menu staples. And that was his day, apart from dishing up orders, collecting gossip and giving the odd free haircut to favourites. It was his restaurant, he was fond of saying, he could do as he liked.

He glanced up as Sophie emptied the dishwasher, filled it and tipped in a glug of bleach.

'What star sign are you?' he asked.

'Pisces, and I already looked.'

'Yeah but I didn't. Hot date, it says.'

'Fat chance. All I want to do is go home and flop in a tepid bath.'

'So snatch a breather.'

'I can't. It's mayhem down there and table three want their quiche.'

'Tell them it's teatime.'

'André!'

'Fuck! I dished it up, doll, but I forgot to stick it in.'

'Okay. I'm there.'

He made no move so she slung a plate of three quiche slices into the microwave. She didn't like the microwave. Along with the bleachy steam from the dishwasher, it was one of the things she was sure made the tiny kitchen dangerous. She set the timer then stepped outside to wait in safety.

Sophie was now one of André's favourites. (He had admitted in passing that he was a Barnardo's Boy, which was partly why he had a soft spot for her.) He had cut her hair after work the previous night. He was itching to peroxide it, which she refused, but she let him have his way with the cut and she now had a feathery crop that felt deliciously cool. He had also weaned her off the tar shampoo to a mild brand for babies and her scalp no longer raged to be scratched.

'You know you made me look like a little boy,' she said, looking at her reflection in the steamed-up kitchen window.

'Suits you,' he said. 'You've got a neck like Mia Farrow. You've got lovely skin, too.'

'Balls.'

He had met Lucas, who amused him, but typically he was raring to meet Charlie and had decided, purely on reputation, that he was what he called pounceworthy. While cutting her hair he had explained that she was a fag hag, or fruit fly; a woman who couldn't help gravitating to gay men. She was fighting the idea.

'You'll never ever be short of friends or fun,' he said, 'even if you lose your looks or you're over the hill. You'll have lovely birthday presents every year and great decorating tips but you'll have a huge phone bill and a crummy love-life.'

'Well, thanks.'

'Don't thank me, doll, thank your lucky stars. Love is over-rated. Friendship's what counts.'

Sophie didn't want to be a fag hag. Or a fruit fly. Quite apart from the nasty name, she had no desire to turn into Maria. This was a former salon colleague of André's who apparently typified the species. She was a hard-edged, sad-eyed person who, Sophie had noticed, ignored every woman around her to the point of psychosis and grew misty-eyed over the loves in André's past and transparently aggressive towards any possible candidate in his present.

André declared it was impossible to have a sex-life in a provincial city without forever encountering it while shopping so now confined his to three weeks a year of unbridled licence on Mykonos. Maria was never invited but, with low cunning, entrusted with the care of André's precious restaurant instead.

The microwave pinged and Sophie returned to the kitchen, distributed the quiche between three plates. Generous helpings from tired salads would be added downstairs.

'Can you manage?' André asked, not shifting.

'Sure.'

'Don't trip, for God's sake. The insurance here's a joke. Here.'

'What?' She paused, tray in hand.

'You know that mate of yours that had your cherry?'

'Wilf.'

'That's the one. Where's he work now? Is he still on lorries?'

'No. He was taken on by one of the mechanics at UBM who set up on his own.'

'Oh.' André turned a page, dismissing her.

Lucas was standing at the foot of the public stairs looking about him as she came back down.

'Find a booth,' she told him. 'Gâteau or ice cream?'

'Gâteau.'

'Sit.'

André paid them all so little that the staff thought nothing of slipping treats to visiting friends on the side. Knowing André was no fool, Sophie was sure he had factored this into their meagre wages. She served table three their quiches and salad, took two other tables their bills then served Lucas a slab of Black Forest gâteau and a cup of nasty coffee that had been steadily cooking on the machine since the lunch-hour.

'Try the cream first,' she warned. 'It could be a bit cheesy. They haven't been selling so well in this heat.'

Lucas dug in regardless. Since Simon had suffered a heart scare recently, Heidi had stopped all but the most penitential baking.

'You look well,' she said. He did. The sudden burst of glory, stepping into Charlie's shoes at the end of term, had been a turning point for him. He carried himself with a new confidence, like a man with a secret. Well, a boy. He hadn't changed so much. She envied him his shorts and cool, clean, white T-shirt. He always claimed to envy her having a job; Heidi forbade holiday jobs because they interfered with holiday plans and she preferred him to use the time to study. It could only have been for the excuse it gave to flirt with strangers since Sophie had never known him short of spending money and suspected he had a far more generous allowance than Charlie.

'Have you heard from Fulham?' he asked.

She shook her head, glancing about at the customers.

'I thought he might be pissed off at me doing Oberon but if you haven't heard either . . .'

'She'll be tearing up our letters,' Sophie said. 'She's that sort.'

She didn't tell him she had heard from Mr Compton. He was touring Sicily with Lady Droxford and sent a postcard of a Roman mosaic showing girl athletes in what looked remarkably like bikinis.

Cruelly hot, he wrote. *We were mad to come here in high summer. So sorry about your ordeal at the end of term. Your support much appreciated. May the sixth-form see you justly rewarded.*

He had worded it carefully, she noted, so that it might be interpreted as a card referring solely to her work as his stage manager. She guessed he would not risk writing even innocently to either Charlie or Lucas so said nothing to Lucas for fear of hurting his feelings.

'I'm not writing again,' Lucas said.

'No point. It'll only enrage her. The bastard and the Jew, remember.'

'Unbelievable.'

'Not really. She'd have voted Nazi on her way to church.'

'Yeah,' he chuckled. 'Or she'd have collaborated and after Liberation they'd have shaved her little head.'

'Her head is small, isn't it? I hadn't thought of it before.'

'Tiny. It's a clinically accepted sign of violent tendencies. Here. Guess what?'

'Tell. Shit. I have to go and serve. Bev's pulling faces.'

He leant closer in the booth so as not to have to raise his voice.

'Telescope Boy is gay!'

It took her a second or two to realize who he was talking about. Then she recalled her first visit to his house and the family he had been spying on from his room.

'Telescope Man, actually,' he added. 'He's left home now.'

'But he had a girlfriend. You used to watch them together.'

'So? She's probably his wife by now. He's still gay.'

'How do you know?'

'I . . . I'd have to show you.'

'Show me later. Gotta go.'

She jumped up, not trusting her face to behave, and busied herself clearing tables, slinging tips in the jar and carrying another load up to the dishwasher. He had been so excited and eager for her to share in his news and all she could feel was irritation. She scowled as she glugged another dose of bleach into the dishwasher and slammed its door.

'Careful,' André tutted. 'I paid for that.'

'What is it with you people?' she snapped. 'Why does the whole world have to be gay?'

'Only half the world, Sophie,' he batted straight back. 'Women hold up half the sky, remember.'

He was joking, she knew he was, but she could only glare in response and carry two orders of scones back down. It was five o'clock. She hung up the closed sign firmly, without apologizing to the couple who were halfway down the stairs. She squirted cream onto the scone plates, which were still warm so it melted. She served with the minimum of charm so the cream-tea eaters would not feel encouraged to linger. Then she agreed that Bev could take two-thirds of the day's tips in return for staying on to see the last people off the premises.

Lucas was waiting for her upstairs, affecting an interest in a cake-icing kit.

'So show me,' she told him.

He led her down the high street then off down a side road towards the river and a spot where she had run into him once before.

'But this is just a public bogs,' she said.

'Wrong,' he told her. 'That,' he pointed at the ladies', 'is a public bog. This,' he pointed at the gents', 'is a cottage.'

'I don't understand. I'm really tired, Lou. I need a bath.'

'Hang on.' He slipped inside and she assumed he was using it but he came out seconds later and said, 'Coast's clear. Come on, I'll show you.'

'But I can't! I'll be arrested.'

'Hardly. Come on.'

Laughing, he tugged her inside. She had never seen inside a gents' before and, although the smell of disinfectant cubes and dried-out pee was revolting, she was curious. Urinals were shockingly intimate.

'So you actually stand here and pee alongside each other? How do you manage?'

'Not everyone does. Stage fright can set in. But here. Look.' He pushed her into one of the cubicles.

At that moment someone else came in.

'Quick!' Lucas hissed. 'Look your door!'

The walls of ladies' had graffiti – usually along the lines of X is a fat slapper or Y loves Z. She had assumed the scribbles in a gents' would be cruder but nothing had prepared her for this. There were a few cartoons or references to women but the vast majority of what she could decipher was about men. Men looking for men. What exactly they wanted to do to them

or have done to them. And when. It was a kind of appoint-
ments diary. *I'll be here 6–8 every Weds. 7 inches 7 pm.* It was an erotic
palimpsest, layer upon layer of commands, requests, warnings
and descriptions built up over each other. Over years, to judge
from the spread in the dates she made out. Some public-spirited
soul had been busy with white paint at some point, not to clean
it all away, apparently, but simply to clean just enough away
to leave room for a fresh round of clearly legible doodles. Every
available surface, including the back of the door and what could
be reached of the ceiling, had been inscribed but some bits more
than others. The scribbles were most concentrated around holes,
some two inches across, that had been chipped away in the
partitions between cubicles.

Lucas, she realized, was watching her reaction through one
of them. Someone else was moving around beyond the one to
the other side of her and she was not about to take a closer
look. Using a scrap of scratchy council loo paper so her fingers
would not come into contact with anything, she unlocked her
door and ran out, startling three men who were using the urinal.
Even with hair so short, no one could mistake her for a boy.

She was halfway up the street when Lucas caught up with her.
'Wait!' he shouted.

'It's disgusting,' she said. 'How can you? And it stank!'

'Yes, it stinks. But where else can I go?'

'Why d'you have to go anywhere? Just . . .' She was fighting
tears. 'Just . . . Why can't you just *wait?*'

'I only found it by accident, Phi. But it's kind of fascinating.
All these different types. Not just Telescope Boy but that funny
traffic warden with the built-up shoe. They're all at it. I don't
do anything. I only watch.'

'And that's better?'

'I thought you'd think it was funny. I couldn't believe it. I was in there and suddenly in comes Telescope Boy, carrying an M&S bag as camouflage. I nearly introduced myself, then I remembered we'd never actually . . . What? Wait!'

'Just fuck off,' she said. 'You're disgusting. You're all disgusting. Don't follow me or I'll tell Heidi.'

That stopped him, or she was pretty sure it did. She didn't look round once until she was home.

She had a mound of reading to catch up on but she neglected it to spend the evening using two greasy old packs of cards to teach kalookie to Tam, a new girl, a twelve-year-old who had been so abused she would still not come out of her room for fear of meeting one of the male residents. She was even terrified of Kieran, the world's least threatening male. Tam wore a grubby pink sunhat to hide the scabs where she had been systematically pulling out her own hair in an effort to make herself less attractive to her father and brother. Sophie didn't need to visit public conveniences for proof that men were animals.

The next day André asked her to help him out at the cash and carry. It was hardly glamour shopping – three-kilo bags of mix for pastry, chocolate sponge and scones and crates of canned black cherries and long-life cream guns – but any excursion was welcome that took her out of the itchy pit the restaurant was becoming. A ride in any car beyond the city boundaries was a treat and a ride in André's especially so as he drove a tarty, mustard-yellow Triumph Stag with white leather bucket seats and a booming stereo. They listened to Donna Summer and she lit his St Moritzes for him. She said nothing of her argument with Lucas but couldn't resist asking him if he ever went to a cottage.

'As in away for the weekend or down on my knees before a married man?'

She blushed to the roots of her feather cut. 'The second,' she muttered, leaning on the shopping trolley. 'Do you?'

He laughed so loudly people in the other checkout queues looked their way. 'No, doll. I have standards and I hate the smell of wee. And, for the record, the correct usage is I cottage, you cottage, he cottages. It's intransitive. Yes, that's right. I learnt *some* grammar before I got into hair.'

On the way back into town he made a detour to a small back-street garage. 'Just got to see about booking a service,' he said and left her in the car in a yard crowded with vehicles. It took her a second or two to recognize the man with the oily face who was beaming at her as he rubbed his hands clean on a filthy rag.

'Wilf?' She got out of the car.

'Soph? You look great. The hair suits you.'

'Thanks. How are you?'

'Great. Busy. Mum's back at her beautician work. Doing it from home, mind, for neighbours and stuff.'

'That's good.'

'Yeah.' He fell quiet and she realized he was taking in the tart car.

'It's André's, my boss. I'm working in Ratty's again. And I've been helping him at the cash and carry.'

'Ah. Do you fancy going out one night, Soph?'

'Sure. Give me a ring.'

'Okay. Friday, maybe?'

'Yeah. Okay.'

André was coming out of the office chatting to Wilf's boss. She saw his eyes slide over Wilf and then back for a rapid second appraisal but without a word. Only as they pulled up at the next set of lights did his nail-tapping on the wheel reveal his curiosity.

'Well?'

'Friday night. If I'm free.'

'There's something about a man with engine oil under his nails.'

'Oh, shush!' She slapped him playfully with a bag of dried mixed fruit. 'Thanks, though.'

'It's nothing,' he said, vrooming away from the lights to attract the attention of a scaffolder's mate who was dangling his nut-brown legs off the back of a nearby truck. 'Just remember me next March twenty-first.'

'What happens then?'

'Not all mothers are women, Soph.'

Wilf took her out on the Friday night. He bought her a pizza then took her to see *Alien*. They saw each other again on the Sunday, when he took her home for lunch with his mum, Elsa, who was at once much younger looking and more battered than Sophie had expected. She loved Wilf simply and frankly. She always called him William with a touching hint of respect, and wasted no time in telling Sophie he was a good boy, 'far too good for most of those tarts he's been seeing.' She admired Sophie's haircut, said it would look even nicer 'frosted' and offered her a free leg wax if ever she felt the need. But still Sophie kept imagining her shooting a policeman.

That afternoon Wilf drove Sophie out to Wumpett Woods and they made love in the back of his van, listening to the Top Forty.

For the five long weeks that remained of the holidays, she had a boyfriend. They tended only to meet up at weekends, because each was left so tired on working days. Egged on by

Elsa, Sophie experimented with make-up and let him buy her presents. This last seemed to give him intense pleasure. He bought her singles, bits of cheap jewellery, bottles of scent. Now that he had money to spend and had worked his way through a few girlfriends, Wilf was becoming a bit of a peacock and liked to celebrate Saturday, the first of each week's non-oily days, by taking extra care over his appearance and shopping for clothes which he would wear that night. It frustrated him that she usually worked on Saturdays until five but André sometimes took pity on her and set her free at three so that Wilf could take her shopping, consult her opinion and, usually, buy things for her too. They went for a meal, either a burger in the new pseudo-American diner that had just opened, or a pizza, then to a film. Then they went to Bogart's, the city's disco. From there, after a slow dance had got them all steamed up, they drove out to the countryside somewhere and had sex in his van before he dropped her off.

It was having sex, not making love. She was firm about that, at least to herself. Wilf had a way of turning dreamily sentimental afterwards but before and during it was fun. He had cheekily fitted a mattress in the van's rear.

The Monday after their first date, Margaret said, 'We need to get you kitted out,' and drove her to the family planning clinic for the Pill. She was calm about it – inured by generations of early developers passing through her care, and knowing better than to attempt to dissuade a girl happily in the grip of raging hormones. All she said was, 'Remember he's a bit older than you. He may want a bit more than you're ready for. Emotionally, I mean. Don't let him put you under pressure.'

André saw himself as godfather to the liaison and required details as his due. He repeatedly told her to 'just have fun, doll, or it'll get all heavy' and as a result of a hint she dropped about a difficulty she was having with oral sex, gave her more graphic instruction on male sexuality than she had ever managed to glean from Lucas, Charlie or Mary Renault.

She kept it light and it was fun. Normality for a change. She relished the unusual sense of belonging to the greater tribe, the easiness of it. She liked it when they were out clubbing or waiting in a cinema queue and Wilf slung a possessive arm about her from behind, his chunky identity bracelet pressing into her collarbone.

But she had moments of ambivalence, as when Wilf, coming, groaned that he loved her and she felt unable to respond. She liked the bruised, sleep-starved, slightly sleazy way she felt on Sunday afternoons but also she discovered an appreciation for the cool sobriety of her midweek nights when she retired early to her room to study.

On one of the Saturdays where she was let off early, she and Wilf were walking up the High Street towards Miss Selfridge when she saw Mr Compton coming down the pavement towards them. He was directly ahead, on his own, carrying a bag of groceries. Genuinely happy to see him, she smiled, preparing to say hello and introduce him to Wilf. But he looked straight through her.

'Stuck-up git,' Wilf said afterwards and she concocted some excuse about him having chronic short sight.

Mr Compton hadn't cut her dead, she sensed. He simply hadn't seen her; by joining the tribe of the ordinary, she slipped through into a sub-world that barely registered on his senses.

Later, buoyed up by an extended snog in a changing cubicle, she led Wilf down towards the river and made him go inside the gents' to have a look at the graffiti.

She had underestimated how he would react. She thought simply to impress him with a piece of adult knowledge he might not share or perhaps, exhilarated from their zip-straining kiss, to turn him on by revealing a glimpse of her lack of innocence as another woman might discreetly reveal that she had sexy underwear on or none at all.

For half an hour after he came out he was itchy with disgust. He truly had never been in there before – he was instinctively fastidious – and nothing she said could defuse his directionless anger.

'I can't believe he goes there.'

'It's only to watch.'

'Huh! That's what he says. Kids could be in there. Christ! I might have gone in for a slash and . . . Christ!' He kicked out at a drinks can, sending it skittering into the river.

Perhaps because she found herself obliged to take Lucas's part, defending what she still thought indefensible, perhaps because that evening's film turned out to be *Cruising*, she had trouble sleeping that night. Whichever way she lay, with two pillows or one, with the duvet on or off her shoulders, she kept smelling Wilf's sweat and Blue Stratos on her hands and forearms and picturing the horrific things somebody might do to Lucas if he ventured down by the river on the wrong night or unlocked his cubicle to the wrong man. For she was sure he did unlock it. He only said he just watched once he saw how shocked she was.

Wilf was a man now, a young, independent, working man. He could watch horrific films as pure entertainment and without a moment's real fear because it was impossible to imagine him ever being a victim. Lucas, by contrast, seemed suddenly no more than a boy, a trusting, seductive, crazily foolish boy.

She spent her Monday at work with dark stains under her eyes and went around to Tinker's Hill as soon as she could.

It was a beautiful, golden evening, the air full of swallows, pigeon calls and the scent of baked grass. There were no cars in the drive and the garage was shut. The Behrmans were on holiday.

Rebuking her stupidity, she was turning her bike around when she heard a splash and saw ripples in the small slice of swimming pool visible from the front. She drew closer to be sure it was him then watched him for a while swimming a self-absorbed crawl. He had no application when swimming and could rarely stand to stick to one stroke for long. Sure enough, he reached the near end and flipped around into backstroke.

He was so pleased to see her, so delighted to have a caller for whom to mix gin and tonics like a grown-up, she found herself telling him about Wilf. The friendship between them was strong enough for him to suggest and her to accept the lie that she had been keeping away because she was amorously occupied. She paid a friend's dues in offering up every detail he wanted, even things she had refused to tell André, and realized as she did so that she was robbing Wilf to pay back Lucas, objectifying the one in order to resecure her attachment to the other.

'And what about you?' she asked, once they had established that Heidi and Simon had gone to a dinner party in London. 'What have you been up to?'

'I've finally learnt how to do this,' he said and demonstrated a risky backwards dive off the pool's metal board.

'And?' she asked.

He grinned, flicked water out of his ears. 'Oh. You know.'

'It's so dangerous, Lucas,' she said. 'You could get arrested.'

'I'm too young.'

'You're old enough for borstal, trust me.'

'You're not going to start this again,' he said.

'No. Sorry. No, I'm not. Just promise me you'll do one thing.'

'What?'

'Whenever you feel tempted to go down there, you'll leave a note.'

'Oh yeah. *Gone cottaging. Back soon.*'

She flicked his nearest nipple. 'Not like that. A message in code. So if you go missing or something bad happens, I'll be able to tell people.'

'Isn't this a bit melodramatic?'

'Yes. But promise me.'

'Okay. I'll think of something. So. Do I get to meet him?'

'No. Absolutely not. You've got nothing in common.'

'Isn't it . . . ?'

'What?'

'A bit like sleeping with your brother?'

'How would I know? Probably. Maybe that's why it's so easy.'

'You're looking well on it. Tired but well.'

'Thanks.'

'You might have to go soon.'

'Why?'

'You've got me all steamed up about him. I might have to go upstairs and thrash around.'

'Lou!'

'Well, you're a big, sexy girl now. You can handle it.'

'Sixth-form in two weeks.'

'Don't. Do you feel grown-up yet?'

'Not at all.'

'I'm going to be a prefect. So's Charlie. It's grotesque.'

'Did you hear from him, Lou?'

'Nope.'

'Me neither,' she admitted. 'They'll have been in Cornwall with the Vanillas. Do you mind? Not hearing from him?'

'Nope.'

His expression made her laugh. Was he lying? She realized she could not read him as easily as she used to. She wondered if this was part of growing up and whether her expressions too were becoming opaque as she gained practice at discretion.

For what felt like the first time they talked honestly and seriously about UCCA forms and Oxbridge and gap year plans and the suddenly not quite so distant adult future, a conversation she could not possibly have with Wilf.

MICHAELMAS TERM
(sixteen years, eleven months)

A ferocious gust of wind all but tugged Sophie's bobble hat off her head. She swore and pulled it hard down over her eyes then turned to lug her potato sack a few yards on along the wall to where she had just moved her ladder. It was heavy, filled with fat candle stubs. All year Chapel, Chantry and the three churches in the parish saved their candle stubs for this evening. Burned too short for use in candlesticks, they remained ideal for the hour or so's burning time that Illumina required of them. The building of the giant bonfire was the groundsmen's job but filling the hundreds of little niches in the flint and limestone walls around Schola Field fell, by custom, to the bell-ringers. Perhaps it was thought that they would miss out on the party atmosphere otherwise, since they were required to spend the celebration ringing out Christmas carols. Perhaps there had

293

once been a feudal perk attached to the task, like a baron of beef or a tray of honeycomb but, if so, it had long passed into quaint history, like the Quiristers' contractual beer ration. What was left – lugging ladders and sacks of candle stubs around the perimeter wall of an icy playing field – felt remarkably like a punishment.

The bonfire used to build up over a couple of weeks, a mounting promise that the end of the year's longest, darkest term was drawing near. Last year there had been an ugly scene however because someone had concealed a firework in the pile which flew out into somebody's face, nearly blinding them. So this year the groundsmen had been commanded to gather the wood in a separate location and only pile it up at the traditional spot on the day it was needed. The wood was the usual assortment of a year's worth of pruned or wind-torn branches from the hundreds of trees about the place, broken banisters and chairs, a much painted door, part of a rebuilt cricket pavilion, even, near the top like a throne, a schoolroom desk that had finally succumbed to time or woodworm.

She took another handful of stubs and walked up and down placing them in the blackened alcoves she could reach then took another, filling her pockets, and worked her way up the ladder, reaching out to right and left. The Bell Captain had assigned each ringer a fair stretch of wall to work on. By chance, Sophie had the piece that linked the War Cloisters to the first classroom block of Brick Quad, the piece that included the rear entrance to Mr Compton's house. Distributing her second pocketful of candle stubs she rose high enough to see over the wall and across his jungly garden. The palm court where he entertained visitors was forbiddingly dark. Just one window was lit up, showing an expanse of yellow wall and a cluster of pictures in one of the mysterious upstairs rooms. A room Charlie would know intimately by now.

When Mrs Somborne-Abbot snatched him away before his chance for glory in *The Fairy Queen,* their assumption had been that she was punishing him brutally but that he would return in September and be given a second chance. But when their letters and cards to him went unanswered all summer, Sophie and Lucas each began to wonder if she had removed him for good, not only from the school but from all contact with his former friends.

Perhaps it would have been better if she had, for within days of the Michaelmas term starting it was clear that the Headman's ban on further contact between pupil and teacher was producing the reverse of the desired effect. Fired up by a powerfully normal eight weeks away to rival Sophie's – a month in Rock with Saggy and the Vanillas then a month's hard labour on his uncle's farm in deepest Wiltshire – Charlie had returned ablaze with defiance. Mrs Somborne-Abbot had indeed intercepted their letters to him and, indeed, the ones he had written to them. Her assumption being that, once contact was re-established, they might be couriers for communication with their adored Mr Compton. Starved of news, his heart had grown steadily fonder and he came to see himself as a martyr to love.

Being removed from the Corps and assigned to social services instead was a chance for a small revenge on his mother since he promptly volunteered for the Happy Brigade so as to spend Wednesday afternoons camping around with Lucas, singing songs from the shows to bewildered geriatrics – an outcome she could not have foreseen. However, he had been moved a notch up from Mr Compton's div to one full of desperately serious scientists about to sit their Oxbridge science exams and he hated the violent change from Wagner appreciation classes with Mr Compton to sessions with the dour Mr Alton on politics and ethics as preparation for their General Paper essays.

Most galling for him was Mr Compton's punctilious observation of the ban, sitting on the same side in Chapel so their eyes couldn't meet, crossing a crowded quad to avoid passing him, even resigning his position as one of Dougal's two house tutors so as to miss the twice-weekly risk of meeting Charlie at the lunches that went with the post. Thus thwarted, Charlie did his best to hate the man but even as he tried to decry his cowardice and hypocrisy he was deciding Mr Compton loved him more than ever and was suffering profoundly beneath his polished parade of *sangfroid*.

Two Saturday nights into term, as Sophie finished ringing bells for the evening service, Lucas had come up to the gallery to find her, just as he used to do. He looked so worried she did not even go through the motions of sitting through the service beside him but led him directly back out to the belfry staircase as the choir began the psalm. They were out on the gallery just long enough for her to notice that the choir didn't include Charlie, who was usually a regular volunteer.

'Nightmare,' Lucas said as soon as they were outside.

'What's happened?'

'A total fucking nightmare.'

'Tell me. Where is he?'

'He's gone to Compton's. He went there at six-thirty, as soon as we'd finished supper, and he's been there all evening. I think he's staying the night.'

'Fuck.'

'Exactly.'

There was nothing they could do, of course. They could hardly mount a vigil outside Mr Compton's house. Lucas was expected home by ten and even now she was a sixth-former, Sophie was required to be back on the Daughters' Staircase as soon as the service was over. But as a co-conspirator in last term's mini tribunal, it was unthinkable that he should not have shared the news with her.

Charlie was in the choir as usual the following morning but vanished again afterwards before she could have a chance to speak to him. She went for lunch at the Behrmans' and Lucas and she spent the afternoon in his room, listening to Kate Bush records and feeding each other's bleak foreboding.

Charlie showed up late in the afternoon. Lucas's room faced the back so they didn't see him ride up. They were arguing about the meaning of 'The Man with the Child in his Eyes' and broke off, hearing his laugh downstairs. Lucas went down and found him chatting with Simon, whom he persisted in calling 'sir'. He seemed happy enough but when Lucas finally succeeded in drawing him upstairs after five excruciatingly polite minutes of chat about a career in Law – Mrs Somborne-Abbot's latest idea for him – the front collapsed.

He hugged first Sophie then Lucas then he sat heavily on the bed and started weeping.

'What's wrong?' they asked him, Lucas terrified Heidi would hear and want to barge in.

'Nothing. I'm so happy, that's all. And I don't know what to do. I'm such a chump.'

It transpired that when they thought they had been lying to save two lovers' skins they were themselves deceived. That evening at Lady Droxford's house Compton had felt impelled to confess his feelings but had held back from any physical expression of them beyond holding Charlie's hand and, when encouraged, taking him in his arms. And so on, throughout the summer term that followed. He was horrified of forcing himself on him, of leading him in anyway towards something he might regret. But now all that was behind them. Irrevocably. They had, Sophie realized, become a them.

'I only pretended before,' Charlie told Lucas. 'I was jealous. You'd done stuff and I . . . I was embarrassed I hadn't. Shit. Sorry. Bit sore.'

He self-consciously adjusted the way he was sitting then caught Sophie's eye and snorted with teary laughter.

'He could be sent to prison,' she quietly reminded him.

'Only if someone finds out and he's hardly going to chat about it in the common room. And you won't tell. Will you?'

'Course not,' Sophie said. She glanced at Lucas, who had said nothing.

'But what can you do now?' Lucas asked him.

'Be very careful. I was mad going back there today but I had to talk to him. Oh, Sophie, he's incredible! He's so handsome and wise and gentle.'

He started to cry again and had to grab Lucas's box of tissues. (Sophie found it slightly creepy that Heidi bought her son tissues all year round, regardless of whether he had a cold.)

'We've agreed I'll see him twice a week. It's easy enough to wait until late then get out by the fire escape outside our study. Then if I go the long way round, through War Cloisters, I can let myself in through the garden. There are no lights on that side after ten-thirty. The front's too well lit from the street and someone might see. Is this the new album? Can I hear a bit?'

And he adjusted back to his old self, as though what he had

told them and the inflammatory secret he had bound them to were nothing more controversial than next week's prefect roster for monitoring prep.

For the rest of the term he continued to spend part of two nights each week in Mr Compton's house. Lucas betrayed nothing of his knowledge during his English classes with Mr Compton, though he fancied Mr Compton avoided his eye and avoided asking him questions and Sophie betrayed nothing while praying regularly a few feet from Mr Compton in the Chantry. He did not avoid her eye. He always inclined his head politely to her as he left and often smiled in passing but he never now lingered for a short conversation afterwards.

After one last visit, during which one of the music bores had gone on and on about Britten's *Death in Venice* and wasn't it an embarrassment and what did Mr Compton think, Sophie and Lucas agreed to absent themselves from his informal afternoon gatherings.

Curiously, their shared secret, their criminal knowledge, had the effect of making them both become far more earnest and responsible. Lucas took his duties as a house prefect very seriously and Sophie made a special effort to befriend and support that term's new Daughters much as she had taken to helping new arrivals at Wakefield House. They both studied like fiends as though compensating for Charlie, who was failing to hand essays in and talked cheerfully about forgetting Oxbridge and possibly even flunking his A levels. He was late getting off his UCCA form and flew in the face of his mother's wishes by applying for drama courses instead of law or chemistry, only the school secretary queried his form and his ruse was quashed. The only plan he seemed settled on was spending his gap year in Rome living with Mr Compton who would be there on sabbatical.

Kimiko knew nothing, because they'd decided it wasn't fair to burden her too. She sensed there was something she didn't know and was no longer Lucas's new best friend as a result. The fact that she knew nothing meant that time spent with her in their study was a relief for Sophie from the pointless circular conversations Lucas held with her whenever they met.

In the same way, she looked forward to her conversations with Wilf from the payphone in the music block. It was broken, so allowed one unlimited time for a single coin but it wasn't a proper booth, so the knowledge that any passer-by could hear her was inhibiting. She enjoyed hearing Wilf's voice, though, his long stories about nothing in particular. When he said, 'Miss you,' she said, 'Yeah, me too.' She wondered if he still went out on Saturday nights. He was a creature of habit but he was also senti-mental and might be enjoying the weekly sense of sacrifice. It was good to talk to him but when he offered to take her out on Sundays she put him off with pretexts and the cruel threat that he would have to write a letter to Nurse to make the request. She knew there were few things he would find so hard. It wasn't that she didn't want to see him – having his voice in her ear made him feel close again and made her think of slow dances to *Whiter Shade of Pale* and the oil and bodies smell in the back of his van. But she worried that seeing him, even if they simply went for a walk or to the cinema, would leave her weak when she needed to be in control. Her one concession to romance was to steal a near-empty stick of Blue Stratos deodorant from the top of some boy's unzipped kit bag. She rubbed a little on her forearm at bedtime so she could smell it as she fell asleep.

She tugged the candle sack on a few yards then doubled back with a handful of stubs, filling alcoves. It amazed her that every year they went to all this trouble and then two poor groundsmen had to work their way all the length of the walls from opposite ends with little butane-charged candle lighters just for an effect and a tradition. The flickering spots of light about the walls did look beautiful – she remembered from the one Illumina she had been able to witness before becoming a bell-ringer – but few people bothered themselves over who had placed them there and who had lit them. Half the magic of the effect lay, perhaps, in the luxurious assumption that it was Illumina night so of course the walls would be lit as if by magic and the bonfire in the middle roaring up to the fringes of the surrounding trees.

During the last fortnight she had begun to worry about Lucas and his strength of purpose. Precisely because he no longer discussed his own feelings in the matter, she guessed they must run deep. He was reading a lot of Mauriac and Duras and Jean Genet and was in love with tales of black, annihilating gestures, mother-loathing or near-cannibalistic passion. He probably hated Charlie now where before he had only despised or resented him occasionally. If he could betray him without hurting Mr Compton, he would do it, she felt and she was often tempted to warn Charlie to remember to be tactful around him and avoid chafing an unscabbed wound. Bound by the same secret, however, Charlie undoubtedly found it as impossible not to talk about it when he was alone with Lucas as Lucas did when alone with Sophie. She caught a look of real pain on Lucas's face the day before when he said he had discovered Charlie was visiting Mr Compton in the afternoons sometimes now, in shameless daylight.

She had climbed the ladder again and was surprised by the

light suddenly coming on at the rear of Mr Compton's house. The light upstairs had gone out. And now the downstairs light had gone out too and she heard the palm room door closing and footsteps on the gravelled path that snaked between the shrubs.

It was mid-afternoon. They would barely have finished placing the candle ends before the groundsmen began their long circuit to light them. The sun was low but she could see quite clearly as Mr Compton emerged through his garden door to her left.

'Evening, sir,' she called without thinking. Working in the fading light, alone with her thoughts, must have made her lonely for she was surprised by a small rush of affection for him. She missed their earlier, unambiguous friendship and found she was grinning broadly now as she might have done had Margaret walked out of War Cloisters to join in the celebration.

'Good evening.' He spoke as to a stranger. He didn't recognize her at first. In the cold she had forgotten she had the ludicrous stripey hat pulled low on her brow. She tugged it off, clambering down from the ladder, and he looked back at her. 'Oh,' he said. 'Sophie. I forgot you were a light-bringer.'

'Lucifer,' she said, for something to say.

'Indeed.'

There was something odd about his appearance. She couldn't place it. His hair was as tidy as ever. He had on his long, dark overcoat, the one Lucas called his Mephistopheles because of its unexpected, demonic red lining. Something was wrong. Instinctively she took a step towards him. He backed away, as though in a hurry.

'Bear me a message as well as your lights.' His voice was strange. Could he have been drinking? 'Tell Lucas, when you see him. Tell him that I understand.'

Had she said okay or all right or yes, sir? He was walking on, his long, black back to her and she couldn't remember speaking.

'Shift yourself, there!' One of the groundsmen had arrived with his lighter.

'Sorry,' she called back. 'Nearly done. Here.' She hurried along, filling the last few alcoves.

'Don't worry,' he said with a wink. 'Only teasing,' and she realized he had thought she was a boy at first. She watched as he clicked his lighter and set to work. 'I'll take over your stepladder, miss,' he said. 'If there's anything left in that sack, sling it on the bonfire. Help her go up.'

'Okay.'

She furled up the sack and tucked it under her arm. Turning, she saw where the other groundsman was at work. In the distance, through the sweeping skeletons of plane trees, thirty little pinpricks were glowing, then thirty-five, forty, forty-five. The sight caused her the same spasm of strange, bitter joy she had felt four years earlier when she first stood here, enraged at the other Daughters' nostalgic leave-taking and convinced she was in love with a boy she had never met, whom she had twice seen wearing women's clothes.

The bonfire heap lay directly along her swiftest route to the bell tower. The bell-ringers would soon be due to start sounding the ancient Christmas songs that would tell everyone the fire was lit. The others had gone in already, probably to grab a warming drink in the nearest chambers before heading upstairs where it was almost as cold as outside. Last year the Bell Captain had mulled some wine for them on a camping stove.

She was walking briskly, directly towards it, when she realized someone was clambering onto the bonfire's summit, some idiot seizing his chance to hide a few bangers and rockets. As she passed under the plane trees she saw it was Mr Compton and that he had reached the old desk and was sitting on it.

The first match he struck blew out. As he struck a second successfully, shielded it and touched it to his chest, she understood what had been odd about their short conversation. The air between them had been humming not with booze but with paraffin. His suit was soaked in the stuff. By the time she reached the bonfire's base, he was a human candle. By the time the groundsmen realized there was a man on fire and that some joker hadn't simply lit the fire early, it was far too late.

She didn't cry out. She didn't even speak. The shock of it had locked her throat.

Night fell without her noticing. She found herself standing on his big overcoat. He must have thrown it off before he started to climb. The scarlet lining smelled of paraffin but was not wet with it. She imagined he had pulled it on just before leaving the house, to mask the deadly dripping of his clothes from anyone he might meet on his short journey.

Right on time, the bells began to ring without her. Somebody was ringing her treble so Weir must have press-ganged a last-minute substitute. He would be furious with her but Sophie couldn't move. Someone who loved him had to watch until it was over. He burnt astonishingly fast. She remembered reading how young soldiers set to minding the ovens at Auschwitz had difficulty coping with the intense heat generated by melting human fat. She remembered the page on which she had read it. She saw its illustrations with her memory's eye.

A crowd gathered. There were shouts, screams, insane attempts to mount the conflagration to pull him clear. What was left of him. The fire brigade had trouble finding a route through the chequerboard of buildings that stood between Schola

Field and the nearest road and by the time they were unrolling their hose hidden fireworks were going off. These weren't rockets or bangers like last year's but roman candles that sent up glorious hissing fountains of coloured sparks at crazy angles on every side of the pyre. A few late arrivals, who did not understand, let out festive cheers, innocent ooh and ahs. The gunpowder briefly masked the sweet porky stench of roasting man.

The police arrived and tried to disperse the crowd, talking through loudhailers as the firemen doused the flames.

Somehow Kimiko found her. She wrapped the overcoat about her shoulders and led her back to their study where she pressed a hot drink on her and put her to bed. It was she who drew the story out of Sophie in fragments and passed it on to the authorities. At some point before midnight, Sophie was interviewed by two policewomen, then she was sedated and knew nothing until morning.

It was the worst kind of scandal, tainting like smoke everyone associated with it. The only mercy was that term was over so the Christmas holidays could intervene and minimize the informal post-mortems of what could have, should have been done differently. An official enquiry would be held before the school reconvened in January.

The story reached Sophie in snatches, few of them trustworthy. Early on Illumina afternoon somebody had alerted the Headman, via his secretary, suggesting he call at Mr Compton's house. Dr Twyford had obeyed custom and let himself in through the garden gate. Walking in through the palm room, calling out, he surprised Charlie and Mr Compton.

Mrs Somborne-Abbot collected Charlie that afternoon. Mr Compton was sacked without references and told to vacate his house by Christmas. The police were not involved because Mrs Somborne-Abbot was keen not to damage Charlie's reputation and career chances. He was to complete his schooling in the crammer's that had helped him through his maths O level.

It was inevitable that the story would reach the local, then the national press, through the agency of the police or fire brigade or through the same person who had made the fatal call to Dr Twyford's secretary. It became garbled and inaccurate in the process because no one with the facts was available for comment. Fuelled by conjecture and envy, the reports turned the tragedy into a salacious Gothic fantasy: gay lord burns to protest schoolboy sex ban.

When Sophie insisted on attending the funeral, Margaret was no less insistent that she accompany her. She did not say so in as many words but Sophie sensed she was angry with the school and wanted to shield Sophie from further harm at its hands. She had stood back until now, trusting Tatham's to look after her, trusting Sophie to make her own way through the difficult route she had chosen, but now the school had failed in its proxy-parental duties and Margaret stepped in.

The service was well attended. Regardless of the scandal, Mr Compton had been a much loved and respected teacher and a surprising number of old pupils had come at short notice to show their support. High on his misericord, scholarly wife and the braver members of staff beside him, Dr Twyford might have been in a pillory. His pain must have been exquisite, knowing everyone there, from Lord Droxford and his wife and mother in the front row to Sophie and Margaret, was looking up at him over the coffin and flowers to pass judgement.

There was no eulogy. It would have been impossible. His brother Julius, a red-cheeked, fleshier version of the man they were mourning, haltingly read a surprisingly sunny and hopeful passage from the Song of Solomon: *My Beloved spake, and said unto me, 'Rise up, my love, my fair one, and come away.'* Otherwise it was left to Reverend Harestock to shield their shared anguish with the merciful rite of the prayer book.

A jackdaw had become trapped in the Chapel, as they sometimes did, and spent the service, perched and defecating, on one of the carved saints behind the altar. It was attentive and miraculously silent until the sudden movement of everyone kneeling for a final prayer sent it, wildly flapping, up into the gallery and the ringing-chamber. Like Mr Compton's immolation on an old desk, it was one of those details nobody would believe who had not seen it.

There was no choir, it being the holidays, and the Droxfords had forbidden music in any case so the atmosphere of the coffin's silent exit was doubly oppressive. Sophie noticed a flurry of coughing as men strove to master their emotions. Spontaneously, the congregation elected to follow the cortège, peeling out pew by pew as the coffin and family passed them. Sophie was shocked to see Lucas walking out ahead of her. They were the youngest there by several years, local pupils being still comparatively unusual and none of the boarders having parents who were prepared to drive them back just days after they had made the journey to collect them.

She had not had a chance to pass on Mr Compton's cryptic message and when Lucas had not sought her out or rung her up, she had thought through its words in the light of his silence and assumed the worst.

The Droxfords were standing just outside the chapel doors,

heroically shaking the hand of every mourner who emerged. Sophie craned her neck to watch Lucas greet the older Lady Droxford and wanted to shout down his hypocrisy. When it was her turn, she smiled sadly in her face, ready to say something but found Mr Compton's mother dismissing her with a drained, 'Thank you so much for coming,' and no trace of recognition.

'Hang on a sec,' she told Margaret as they came out into Flint Quad and she hurried over to give Lucas a sharp poke in the back. Bewildered, he turned to see her.

'God!' he exclaimed. 'Hi. What?'

'He knew it was you,' she said. 'He told me to tell you he understood. That's all. That was his message to you. How could you look them in the face and live with yourself?'

'What? Phi, wait!'

She threw his hand off her arm. 'Fuck off,' she hissed. 'You disgust me. You always have.' Then she hurried back to Margaret, easily losing him in the aimlessly shifting crowd.

As Margaret drove her home, Sophie pictured his pale, sensitive face above his dapper coat with the velvet collar and thought to herself, *Lou will become a spy.*

CHRISTMAS HOLIDAYS
(sixteen years, eleven months)

She said nothing to Margaret about Lucas's betrayal. Margaret's paper had been too high-minded to carry any version of the story and she did not listen to local gossip. All she knew was that a favourite teacher of Sophie's had committed suicide horribly and that Sophie had seen it all. Sophie told her nothing further, cherishing her unquestioning support. Several times she tried ringing Charlie but each time hung up without speaking when she heard his mother's querulous, 'Hello? Hello?' She could not imagine what he must be feeling. It was unthinkable that news of the tragedy had not reached him. She wrote him several drafts of a letter intended to tell him he must not blame himself but found she could not keep a judgemental tone from colouring her prose. The fault lay with him, after all, even more than it did with Lucas. The fault of his silly, self-dramatizing, competitive passion. Besides, Christine Somborne-Abbot knew her handwriting by now and would be sure to pounce on the envelope before the corrupting letter inside it could reach her precious son.

When Wilf turned up on the doorstep, Saturday-clean, blithe in his ignorance of the story and keen to take up exactly where they had left off it seemed a chance to turn back time and recover from him an earlier version of herself untainted by grief or bitterness.

They went shopping. She helped him choose Christmas presents for his mother, Margaret and Kieran. Then they went to a pub for some lunch and grew boozily nostalgic about how they used to buy one another's Christmas present in the home.

'So who do you buy for now?' he asked.

'I dunno,' she said. 'Whoever's name I pull out of Margaret's pudding basin, I suppose,' and she caught a ghost of sorrow in his face.

'So what about this teacher who topped himself?' he asked. 'Was he queer like everyone says?'

Of course he had heard the stories. He skimmed the papers every day. He heard gossip from half the clients who picked up or dropped off cars at the garage. The only reason he hadn't mentioned it earlier was that he had no inkling of how closely she was connected to the story. The temptation to keep the day on its nice, unthreatening level was strong, to carry on being the happy, normal girl Mr Compton had looked straight through when he passed her in the High Street. All she had to do was shrug and say, 'Yeah. Wasn't it awful, poor sod,' and maybe give Wilf some gory detail, harmless enough now, to pass on to his mates.

But he was so solid and good and dependable and the huge

gin and tonic he had bought her had undone a resolve already loosened by the Sally Army band playing carols outside and memories of their shared childhood. She broke down.

'Hey,' he crooned. 'Hush. I'm sorry, Soph.' He took her in his arms, sloshing their drinks, and rocked her gently against him. She knew he would be glaring at anyone with the temerity to look their way and she relaxed against the bearish bulk of him, clutching his leather jacket against her cheek. She stayed on his side of the table, curled against him in the booth, and, while the juke box played Slade, she told him everything. She told him how first Lucas had fallen for Mr Compton, then Charlie, or rather how Mr Compton had fallen for Charlie and Charlie, once forbidden to see him, decided he was in love. She told how Charlie had broken the ban and the pair had taken ever wilder risks until Lucas, crazily jealous, had betrayed them. As she told the story, from innocent beginning to brutal close, it occurred to her how entirely marginal her role had been in it all. Given confidences to the last, she had been emotionally, even morally implicated yet she could remove herself from the narrative and it would still make perfect sense.

She had expected Wilf to become angry but he listened without interrupting, although plainly disgusted, and his final response was solicitous and protective. 'He used you,' he said. 'That teacher.'

'Mr Compton.'

'Yeah. He only made friends with you to get at the blond one.'

'Charlie.'

'Yes. That's how nonces work.'

'Oh he's not, he wasn't a . . . a nonce.' Her shock was real but it concealed a doubt.

'Well what would you call it? Christ, Sophie! You're well out of there. They should be shot.'

'Who?'

'The school. The headmaster.'

'That's what Margaret said. She wanted someone to blame but I don't think anyone was, really. Charlie was very persistent.'

'Come on,' he said, standing to close the subject. 'Mum's off with mates in London till at least seven. We'll have the flat to ourselves.'

She felt weak with tears and gin and talking and went with him readily but what she really wanted was to curl up in bed with him and have him just hold her safely while she fell asleep. She wanted a guard, not a lover.

Elsa must have cleaned the flat before she left that morning for its air was full of the admonitory smells of cleaning products and Wilf had to move a pile of neatly ironed clothes off the bed before they could lie down.

They had never had sex in daylight before and only once on a proper bed. She found herself shy and inhibited, as if he had become a stranger to her. She kept her eyes closed to make it easier. Wilf had gained weight in her absence, spending more time in pubs, without her to keep amused, and she felt smothered by him. She had stopped taking the pill once she realized she wasn't going to see him during term-time and she wasn't sure how the chemistry of it worked or how soon after she began taking it again it would become effective.

When he finally came, humping into her so hard she was sure she'd find bruises later, he groaned so loudly she thought he was pretending and had felt as unaroused as she. But then he said, 'I love you,' close against her ear. He pulled back to make her look him in the eye. 'I do,' he said. 'I really love you, Soph.'

312

'Oh, Wilf,' she said as warmly as she could and tried to pull him back onto her where he couldn't read her expression but instead he lay to one side, caressing her face over and over until the nerves in her cheek and neck were raw and angry.

And then he reached into the little drawer on his side of the bed, pulled out a box with an Eternity ring in it, and proposed. He hadn't liked to before, he explained, as she stared at the ring, appalled at what it must have cost him, because he wasn't earning enough and because she was doing so well at school. But now he had been offered a full partnership in his mate's garage and was making enough to leave his mother with the flat and take out a mortgage. And after what had happened Sophie wouldn't be going back to Tatham's. And she'd be seventeen in January, old enough to move out of Wakefield House to a place of their own.

She took his hand in hers to stop him stroking her face. 'I can't,' she told him. 'Oh Wilf. I can't! I'm not stopping school. It's my life.'

'I thought I was.'

'You mean so much to me. You've really kept me going, especially last term with everything that was happening, but . . . Oh. Oh, Wilf. It's a beautiful ring. But I can't.'

'Take it. Just wear the ring at least. See how you feel after Christmas. I might not have got the size right. They can alter it, the lady said.'

'No, Wilf. I'm sorry. I can't. I can't leave school yet. I want to go to university, maybe Oxford, and . . .' She shut up, hating how prim she sounded. He was so warm against her, not smothering any more, just comforting, and she wanted to pull him around her and stay there all night, as long as it would get dark soon so she didn't have to see the reproach in his big, gentle face.

'It's that twisted fuck Lucas and his friends, isn't it? And that silly queen at the café.'

'No it isn't.'

'They've turned you.'

'How d'you mean?'

'You're only happy round perverts now, aren't you? I'm not queer enough for you. I'm surprised you don't go the whole hog and turn dyke.'

'Wilf!'

'Go on. Get out.'

'Wilf, I'm sorry. You've got it all wrong.'

'No I haven't. Fuck off.'

He lurched away from her and out of bed and shut himself in the tiny bathroom across the way. She knocked on the door but he ignored her. She thought of climbing back into bed to wait but felt chilled. Instead she dressed quickly, glanced at her pink, teary face through the lettering on his Southern Comfort mirror and escaped.

The Salvation Army band was still playing by the Butter Cross, though only a brave few were singing along now and they were probably drunk. 'In The Bleak Midwinter' followed her halfway home and for the rest of the walk she found she was singing it in her head. *If I were a wise man I should do my part. But what can I give him? Give him my heart!*

The house was full of noise and food smells. Round-the-table ping-pong was that holiday's craze and the hysterical laughter, shuffling feet and the repeated slamming-down of the two bats was booming from the dayroom. She tried to slip up to her room but Kieran emerged to call up to her.

'You've got a visitor, Sophie. Mrs Compton. She's in the kitchen with Margaret. Been here an hour, nearly.'

It was typical of Lady Droxford not to correct them about her name. She would have introduced herself as Mr Compton's mother. She and Margaret were sitting at the kitchen table with empty mugs and a tin of chocolate brownies. The milk bottle was on the table and there were no plates. For a second Sophie found herself looking on with Mrs Somborne-Abbot's critical eye, then realized Lady Droxford was entirely comfortable and that Margaret was too.

'Sophie,' Lady Droxford said. 'How nice. Margaret and I have been having such a lovely talk.' She stood and kissed her, not an air-kiss but a proper one, with a chocolate-scented hug. 'I'm so sorry I didn't speak to you at the funeral. I was telling Margaret here I was completely legless on tranquillizers and brandy. It was the only way I could get through it. But I wanted to come and see you as soon as I could to see how you were bearing up.'

'Oh. I'm okay,' Sophie said, feeling anything but. 'Thanks.' She took the mug of tea Margaret poured her.

'I'm probably terribly in your way,' Lady Droxford told Margaret.

'No you're not,' Margaret said. 'Not really.'

'Actually, I want to see Sophie's room. Is that allowed?'

Margaret winced. 'Against house rules,' she said. 'But since it's you and the dayroom's so heaving . . . Sign Mrs Compton in, would you, Soph?'

'Sure.'

Lady Droxford smiled warmly. 'Thanks,' she whispered. She picked up a big carrier bag to follow Sophie.

'Have you ever been in a children's home before?' Sophie asked her as she signed the visitor's register, wrote Lady Droxford 5.30 and led the way.

'Well, do you know I have, but only once and I was cutting the ribbon on an extension so it was all rather artificial. This is lovely. So warm and colourful. And this is where you live?'

Sophie held the door open for her. She was acutely conscious of how battered the room looked. Posters she had stopped noticing were now glaringly out of date and so very much posters not paintings. Lady Droxford sat on the hard chair, Sophie on the bed. But almost at once Lady Droxford was on her feet again, holding out the carrier bag, looking around her at the room.

'These are for you, Sophie,' she said. 'But you don't seem to have a record player.'

'Well, no. But there's one downstairs.'

'But of course! I'll have Antony's one sent to you. It's far too complicated for me to work – technology's for the young – and anyway I've got one already. But I'm sure he'd have liked you to have those.'

She had put several boxed recordings of complete operas into the bag. *Rosenkavalier, The Marriage of Figaro* and Mr Compton's pride and joy, the almost new Solti *Ring Cycle*.

'I . . . I can't,' Sophie said.

'Ah but you must. You can't say no to the dead. It's a rule.' Lady Droxford smiled in a way that showed she was joking but could not be denied and gave the top of the bag a little pat, half-closing it as she closed the subject. 'And I almost forgot.' She reached into her capacious handbag and brought out her husband's old army binoculars. 'The records were from Antony but these are from me.'

Sophie took them. They were heavy and she had to use both hands.

'You can't say no to those, either,' Lady Droxford said quietly.

'But you'll be using them, won't you?'

'Not any more, dear. Oh, and you can lie in bed here and see trees. That's so important.'

'Lady Droxford?'

'My name's Veronica. Do call me that.'

'Thank you. Veronica, I . . . I know who killed him.'

'He killed himself, Sophie.'

'I mean I know who made it happen by betraying them to Dr Twyford. It was Lucas Behrman.'

'Lucas, your charming friend?'

'Yes.'

'Are you sure?'

'Yes.'

'Because . . . Oh dear. I don't know about you, Sophie, but ever since I heard I seem to keep telling people things I had quite intended to take to my grave.'

'Me too. I split up with my boyfriend this afternoon.'

'And you hadn't meant to?'

'Not really. Only. Oh. It's stupid . . . You were saying. Sorry.'

'I was going to say I hope you haven't broken off with Lucas too.'

'I have sort of. I couldn't believe his nerve, coming to the funeral like that.'

'Oh, was he there? Those pills were strong! Sophie, I wasn't going to tell you but now I'd better. It was me.'

'What was?'

Lady Droxford sat in the chair again. 'I realized Charlie was still in touch with him,' she said. 'I'd guessed because of the way Antony was acting. So morose all through the holiday in Sicily, after the opera debacle, then suddenly so manic and overexcitable when term began again. Then, quite by chance,

I was calling by that afternoon. I love Illumina. I never miss it. Never missed it. It was always the start of Christmas for me. So I'd come over to do a little shopping and hand-post some cards and I was going to see a friend for tea then go with her but she was in bed with flu so nothing doing.'

Unnerved perhaps at having Sophie's stare so intensely upon her, she stood again and started walking about as she talked.

'I thought I'd take Antony by surprise. And I saw that stupid oaf of a boy going in through the garden gate ahead of me. I didn't know what to do at first. I should have called out, I suppose. Stopped him that way. But I dithered so when I eventually went in they were . . . I mean I heard them.' She glanced out of the window, away from Sophie's gaze. 'It was too late. I was so angry.' She looked back at her. 'You have no idea.'

'With Antony?'

'No. With that . . . That ridiculous *schoolboy*! I left the house in such a state. They hadn't seen me and I half-thought I was just going to fetch the car and drive home but instead I called in on Dr Twyford. His wife's an old friend so I know him quite well but I got it so wrong. What I wanted to do was save Antony from the boy. Blame the boy. Say he was laying siege to him or something. But I was angry and you know how it is when you're angry, you lose control of your words rather, and before I knew it Johnny Twyford was marching over there to catch them.'

She had paced to the low window and now stared out, paddling nervously at the thin curtain with her fingertips.

'They say a mother's love is blinder than most and I suppose mine was. I honestly thought it was just a mad infatuation and that a quick, sharp shock would be enough to bring him to his senses. A case of desperate remedies. I knew nothing could be proved and that the last thing anyone would do was involve the police but I thought to lose his job or be forced to take his sabbatical early would be better than, oh, what did I think? I didn't think!' She drew the curtain sharply across and turned back to look at Sophie. 'I had no idea his feelings for him ran so deep.'

Her voice cracked and for a terrible moment Sophie thought she was going to break down. But Lady Droxford controlled herself with a deep breath and a sigh.

'Of course it wasn't just Charlie,' she muttered. 'It was his feelings for the school. He couldn't live without the bloody place.'

Sophie was so taken aback she had no idea what to say.

'What'll you do?' she asked at last.

'Bless you. I shall go on. I shall quietly crumble. I've been thinking of shutting up shop and going to Corrie. It's a sort of female lay community in Dorset. Perfect for stupid, meddlesome old trouts who need to make amends. They'll be glad of my money and Julius can move his mother-in-law into the dower house.'

'He didn't know,' Sophie said. 'Mr . . . Antony didn't. I spoke to him just before he . . . He thought it was Lucas. That's why I –'

Lady Droxford interrupted her. She was all alertness again, jolted out of her sad distraction. 'Does Lucas know?'

'Well, yes. I was so angry I told him after the funeral.'

'Can you go to him now?'

'It's a bit late. Margaret'll –'

'Please, Sophie. Go and tell him? I couldn't bear it if . . .' Her fine old face began to crumple.

Sophie darted forward, leaving the binoculars which she had been cradling. 'Of course,' she told her, understanding at last. 'I'll go now. I'll go on my bike. And thank you.' She kissed her cheek, marvelling at its softness. 'Er . . . Veronica . . . You have to sign yourself out in the book.'

'I'll sign myself out. Go on. Go!'

Sophie ran out through the kitchen. 'Back soon,' she told Margaret. 'Sorry. I'll be very quick.'

She snatched her bike from the shed but it had flat tyres so she hurled it aside and grabbed someone else's, a boy's one, and rode it as fast as she could across town. She laboured up Tinker's Hill, flat-soled shoes repeatedly slipping off the pedals so that she crashed painfully onto the crossbar.

The Hanukkah candles were lit in the big hall window so she knew they hadn't gone skiing yet. She was so breathless when she reached the Behrmans' drive she could hardly speak.

Heidi seemed to catch her urgency off her and dropped her usual routine of offering coffee and biscuits.

'Sorry, Sophie. He's visiting a friend.'

'Oh. Who?'

'Nick, was it? No. Dick! That's it. He said he was visiting Dick. He goes over there quite often these days but hasn't brought him over here yet. Why look so worried? Sophie?'

'It's nothing. It's fine,' Sophie assured her, turning her bike. 'Dick's great. Bye, Heidi. Gotta go. Bye.'

At least the route from the Behrmans' house to the river was downhill all the way. She freewheeled, becoming chilled to the marrow because, in her hurry, she had run from the house without a coat or hat. There were no lights on the bike. Several drivers honked at her.

The lights in the cottage were sinisterly dim, yellowish. She let the bike fall with a clatter on the path and raced in, not caring if she was running in on an orgy.

He was on his back on the filthy floor, his white polo-neck

splashed with the blood that was pooling around his hair. Wilf was standing over him, desperate.

'Get up!' he was urging. 'It's okay now. You can get up. I'm sorry I –' Startled, he spun round and saw her. 'I didn't mean to,' he started. 'But he said he'd –'

'Get out,' she said. 'It's me you should have hit.'

'Soph?'

'Just get out.' She shoved him hard so that he staggered clear of Lucas. 'Lucas? Lou?' she shouted, dipping to the floor. She touched his legs. He cried out and she heard Wilf hurry out. 'Don't move,' she said. 'I'm getting help. Okay?'

She sprinted to the nearest phone box, called an ambulance, then, with her only silver coin, rang Heidi. Luckily it was Simon who answered, calmness personified, and he agreed to bring Heidi to meet them in the hospital. She only told him Lucas had been in an accident.

When she reached him again, Lucas had stood, walked as far as the doorway then slumped to the floor.

'Idiot,' she said. 'I told you not to move, but at least your legs aren't bust.'

'Sorry,' he mumbled and she saw that somewhere under the blood he was trying to smile.

'I've told your dad to meet us in Casualty,' she said. 'I didn't say where you were. *Visiting Dick!* You're the end, Lou.'

He mumbled again, slowly reached up to remove a tooth.

'Jesus!' she said, wincing. 'It was my fault.'

He shook his head and mumbled what might have been, 'Teamwork.'

She put an arm across his shoulder but he cried out again and she pulled back. 'Sorry,' she said and planted a careful kiss on the shoulder nearest her. 'Sorry, Lou.'

She held his hand in the ambulance, talking to him but now getting only faint squeezes in return.

'I know it wasn't you,' she told him. 'Lucas? I know it wasn't. I'm sorry. I saw his mother. Lady Droxford told the Headman. Compton jumped to conclusions and . . . Lou? Stay with me. Squeeze my hand if you can hear me. Good boy. Nearly there. You'll be fine. You'll see.'

Heidi and Simon were waiting, ashen-faced, as he was wheeled in. A hand flew to Heidi's mouth as she saw the state of him. 'Lucas!' she called out. 'Baby? We're here. Dad and I are here, darling!' Then Simon held her back as the nurses swept the trolley off behind a curtain and told them all to sit and wait.

'I don't understand,' Heidi said when Simon had made her drink some water and she was calmer. 'How did you know where to go? Who is this Dick he's started seeing?'

'No one,' Sophie said. 'It's a code to let me know . . . There was a place he liked to go. To be alone. By the river.'

'Hardly safe after dark,' Simon said and Sophie wondered how much his legal work had taught him about the city's seamier side.

'I know who did it,' she told him.

'You *know* them?' Heidi was shocked.

'William Franks. Wilf. I . . . He was in the home with me. He's my boyfriend. He was.'

'But why . . . ?' Simon gestured towards the curtain that was hiding Lucas from them.

'Jealous,' she said. 'I'd split up with him today and he thought . . .'

'Will you tell this to the police when they come?'

'Of course. And his address. Whatever they want.'

Sophie hoped she had told them just enough to give them a story they could work with. There was no shame in a son beaten by a jealous rival in love.

The three of them lapsed into shocked silence. There was a fairly steady stream of admissions. The last Saturday before Christmas was working its spell. Some of them were in far worse shape than Lucas.

Suddenly a nurse was at their side.

'You can see him very briefly,' she said. 'But he was concussed so you'd better just say hi-bye, okay? We've given him a shot for the pain and we'll need him in overnight to keep an eye on him. Two cracked ribs, a front tooth gone, bruised legs and a black eye. He must have had the sense not to fight back. He got off lightly, trust me.'

They jumped up to go over, Sophie with them, but Heidi turned to block her way, her face as hard as her voice.

'No,' she said. 'Not you.'

'But –'

'You've done enough.'

'Sophie found him, darling,' Simon murmured reasonably.

'She's done enough. Stay away from him.'

As Heidi followed the nurse, Simon muttered what might have been an apology, then noticed the police arriving and seized the welcome diversion.

Sophie stood where she was just long enough to catch a glimpse of Lucas, bare chest tightly bandaged, neck in a brace, then Heidi twitched the green curtains across and he was lost to her. She introduced herself to the police and made a careful statement. She told no lies. She told them about Wilf's anger when she had turned him down, gave them his name and address and offered herself as a witness. Her only manipulation of the facts was to say she had found him on the riverside beside the public conveniences rather than in them.

'I'm sorry,' Simon said, shaking her hand. 'Heidi's mind once made up . . . But thank you for finding him and . . .'

'That's all right.'

In the weeks that followed Christmas she kept expecting Lucas to contact her but he didn't. Possibly he recovered soon enough for Heidi and Simon to take him to Switzerland as planned. She heard nothing further from the police so assumed charges against Wilf were not pursued. When she called at Jago's on the last day of the holidays to collect her books for Lent term she picked up a copy of the new Short Roll and found that both Lucas and Charlie had left the school.

Encouraged by Kimiko, she wrote to him at Tinker's Hill, confident that Heidi did not read or steal her son's mail as Christine Somborne-Abbot did. Eventually she received a long, funny letter back. He was in New York, living with Heidi's older brother's family and enrolled in the same High School as his cousins. He was having a ball. He was making new friends he so wanted her to meet. She must come on a visit, he wrote.

Relieved, she wrote back at more length but his reply took weeks and was full of people she didn't know, all of them female apparently, and shiny with an urban sophistication she couldn't match.

As exams once more threatened to engulf them both, her friendship with Kimiko bloomed into warm affection and they studied with the cloistered dedication of nuns. The correspondence with Lucas dwindled from long occasional letters to

324

shorter, rarer ones then to mere, witty bulletins on seasonal postcards. After a while, stung at receiving a particularly thin response to her latest effort, she decided to test him by writing nothing back and seeing how long it took him to contact her again.

After two months of silence, her nerve failed her and she wrote him a six-side letter, closely spaced and straight from the heart, rich with details of her life without him and honest nostalgia for the experiences they had shared. She dared, towards its end, to confess her early fantasy in which the two of them ended up living together but sophisticatedly apart under one roof, shared cats, fridge and all.

The New York post office returned it with an official stamp to say he was now unknown at the only address she had for him. She kept the letter, at first because she had thoughts of sending it to Tinker's Hill for forwarding and then because, without her noticing the alteration, it had become a precious relic of her giddy youth.

LENT TERM
(forty-one)

Sophie arranged the tulips in a vase; rather she put them in one. Her approach to flower-arranging had long been to buy enough flowers to more or less fill a vase's mouth, trim them to the same length then stick them in, let go then give the whole thing a gentle shake to settle it before adding water. It was hardly Constance Spry but it worked for her.

Yellow parrot tulips. One of those extravagances Jack wouldn't notice as such because he had no idea of the cost of flowers. She fancied they looked Hockneyish, although the setting, with its dark oak panelling and antiques lent by Jack's family, made every attempt at ornament look like a poor stab at a Dutch still-life.

She glanced at the kitchen clock and swore. She had a heap of Latin proses she had intended to mark in the gap between

326

her ten o'clock first-year class and now but time had evaporated and they would have to wait.

Lunch was entirely a cheat. Neither Jack nor she had ever
learnt to cook with any confidence. When they first met they
were both postgraduates, living out of canteens, college pantries
and, when they got lucky, at high tables. Once they were married
his sister bought them a microwave and for a while their every
meal had right angles. Then they both took jobs at their old
school and were able more or less to live off school meals
between snacks, especially with the dining privileges that came
with Sophie's becoming Master of Schola. Recently however
their lives had been transformed by an enterprising young couple
taking on the post office and reinventing it as a French-style
delicatessen, selling servings of freshly made dishes as well as
mere ingredients. Sophie and Jack had been paying back old
hospitality debts ever since.

She carried the tulips into the dining room. Jack had been
distracted, halfway through laying the table, by a lost book
found and was stretched in the spring sunshine on the window
seat, reading.

'Oh,' he said as she fetched wine glasses. 'Sorry.' He turned
a page.

'They'll be here soon,' she said. 'Don't you have to change
for the christening?'

'I'm only in the organ loft.'

'You'll still have to shake hands. They'll have a record token
to give you or something over sherry afterwards.'

'Hell. I'm sorry I can't join you for lunch.'

'You love TatCoFo.'

He grinned. 'I do, rather.'

'Just see there are no deaths, okay? Go on. Change. Go.'

She plucked the book from his hand and he lumbered off in search of a presentable suit. She followed him to leave his book on the stairs so he should find it again. *The Lady in Medieval England. Huh*, she thought, glancing at the title, *That's me*, and felt a small surge of love for him.

He was the ideal staff member – organist, sportsman, amateur lepidopterist (founder of the school's latest club, Moth Soc) as well as an historian; far more of an all-rounder than she was. This was one of the reasons they had managed to coincide at Tatham's without becoming acquainted. He was also wonderfully attuned to her needs. If they were driving somewhere and Wagner came on the radio, he had a way of flicking to another channel, making a quiet show of wanting to hear some news. He even changed channels when it wasn't Wagner but nearly, like Bruckner or Liszt. But even he, whom she loved more than anyone, did not know that she sometimes woke in the night with a sweet, sweaty smell in her nostrils and a headful of horror. He was a heavy sleeper and she would slide from the bed without waking him; the smell of his bed-warmed skin, normally a delight to her, made her feel worse at such times. Had he woken, he would have found her in a small, rather hard chair in her study, reading something soothingly remote, in the original. Vitruvius on hypocausts was especially effective.

He ran downstairs again, suited, tugging up a tie, organ music flapping under one elbow. 'People are starting to arrive,' he said in passing, 'and there are some aliens who must be your pals.'

'I'll leave you something to eat in the kitchen,' she told him. 'We might go for a walk as it's so nice.'

'Fine.'

He thundered down the wooden stairs and she crossed to the sitting room to look down. She saw him run lankily across

Flint Quad to the vestry door, saluting the anxious Chaplain as he went. The Chaplain was standing by the Chapel's doors to greet the baby's arriving family and supporters. Sophie leaned against the glass, watching with interest, then spotted her guests. Amidst the drift of black-gowned Scholars milling towards Hall for lunch, they did indeed look like aliens, or even angels, trying to pass for human. On second glance she saw they weren't really all in white, it was only a trick, the contrast between their pale coats and white shirts with their deep tans.

She tapped on the glass and they looked up. The sash was jammed with paper to stop it rattling so she couldn't call out as she wanted to. She ran downstairs then remembered that, outwardly at least, she was forty-one and a housemistress. She threw open the door.

'Lou!'

Lucas ran to meet her and caught her up in a hug. He had put on a bit of weight. He smelled different. Rather expensive.

'You look wonderful,' he said. He sniffed. 'Is that L'Heure Bleue?'

'Shalimar,' she laughed. 'I have a few drops left in a very old birthday bottle.'

Looking at her he shook his head, kindly disbelieving. 'You haven't changed a bit. Heidi said you'd got all imposing.'

'And haven't I?'

'Sorry.'

'Damn.'

He turned to draw over his companion. 'Sophie, this is Rustam. Rustam, meet my boyhood playmate.'

'How do you do?'

'Hello.'

Rustam was handsome, a slightly older man for a change,

forty-five or six to Lucas's forty, and with a beautifully cut griz-zled beard that made him look like an Iranian temple statue. They had met through their work at the United Nations, where Lucas was a translator, and now divided their lives between New York and Mumbai. She had heard all the details by e-mail but this was Rustam's first visit to England, to Lucas's roots.

Lucas had been much married but either to impossible neurotics or to boys so young they bored him. Apparently this relationship with Rustam was the real thing, serious, for keeps. She hoped so. Certainly they fitted together. With age, Lucas's face had revealed a middle-Eastern bone structure like his father's. He and Rustam might have been brothers. She thought of Jack, so much taller than her that the only way of avoiding absurdity in their wedding photograph had been for him to sweep her up in his arms.

Rustam was looking around at Flint Quad as she opened the front door for them.

'I'll give you a tour after lunch, if you like,' she told him.

'That would be great, Sophie. Thank you.' His accent was neither Mumbai nor Yale but a subtle, shifting blend of the two. She felt self-conscious walking ahead of him up the stairs. 'This is all amazing,' he said as they reached the first floor. 'You live in a castle.'

'With early twentieth-century wiring and plumbing that predates George Eliot. The great thing is it goes with the job so we pay no maintenance and when something breaks, the school fixes it.'

'And you were a Scholar here?'

'A Daughter. The girls are called Daughters. Yes. So I lived over there by the edge of the Chapel.' She pointed out of the sitting room window to the staircase on the opposite corner of the quad. 'And it was a lot less comfortable than this.'

'Have you made changes?' Lucas asked, handing them both the wine she had given him to uncork.

'They all have proper baths now, not just the Daughters. And there's more heating. Just a bit.'

'And you send some of them to Heidi, she said.'

Sophie sighed. She sipped her wine. 'Cheers m'dears. Yes. I do. She does wonders. We had an anorexic last year, Rustam, who's now back to eight stone and sitting Oxbridge in the autumn. And Heidi's been helping one of the boys whose brother died recently.'

'They didn't offer therapy in our day,' Lucas told Rustam, pulling a face.

'Christ, Lou,' Sophie said. 'Think of the difference if they had!' and they fell silent a moment, thinking. 'How do you find her?' she asked him.

'Great. I find her great and indomitable and rather . . . She's getting a bit creaky but she's seventy-one so . . .'

'I was so sorry to hear about Carmel.'

'Thanks. She's pulling through, I think. The chemo was hell but she'll make it. She's tough.' Lucas's sister had recently been diagnosed with breast cancer, a family curse which Heidi too had weathered in her time.

'I don't think I'm still friends with anyone from my schooldays,' Rustam said when they sat down. 'Did you two never lose touch?'

'Oh, well,' Lucas said with a shrug. 'We had to grow up a bit.'

'We lost touch for a while after school,' Sophie explained. 'We ended up in different schools and universities but, well . . . It was Simon's funeral, wasn't it, Lou?'

'That's right.'

'So we were inseparable, then we were wrenched apart to

grow up a bit and then we met up on the other side of feminism, you could say, and picked up the pieces. But you two live so far away!'

'So do you. You could always come and stay. Cheap flights and so on.'

'I know. We could. We must. Oh,' she broke off to explain. 'Jack can't join us for lunch as he's playing the organ for a christening service then he has to referee a match but he said please stay long enough for tea so he can lay eyes on you. You don't have to rush off do you?'

'I told Heidi not to expect us till six,' Rustam said.

'Rustam is an inveterate sightseer,' Lucas warned her.

Sophie laughed. 'Fantastic! Chapel-roof tour, the lot.'

They gave her photographs and greetings from Kimiko and her girlfriend, who had recently made it to Manhattan from San Francisco, then they ate lunch. Lucas complimented her on the food even though she insisted all she had done was shop, reheat and arrange. Rustam explained that for New Yorkers, going to that much trouble constituted a dinner party. She heard about his street children initiative in Mumbai and suggested he come back to give the pupils a talk about it.

'They don't have compulsory Chapel every Sunday now,' she said. 'We have so many non-Christian parents – not just Muslims and Hindus, we even have a few Pagans from Devon – that it was getting silly. So every third Sunday now they have an inspiring talk by somebody trying to make a difference. My secret plan is that it will provoke more of them to work for charities in their gap years instead of simply following each other around the same backpacking trail. Do you need volunteers?'

'Graduates only, I'm afraid,' Rustam said. 'Kids can never come for long enough.'

'Huh!' Lucas said. 'Four weeks of you on their case, of course they want to run away to Goa.'

'And they need too much mothering,' Rustam went on, ignoring him. 'Eighteen seems to have got a lot younger than it used to be.'

'Or just maybe,' Lucas said, 'we've got a bit older. I liked Chapel, anyway. And I'm Jewish.'

'You didn't like Chapel,' she reminded him. 'You liked bell-ringers. Which reminds me.' She glanced at her watch. 'Come and see something.'

She left the dining table and went to the window. About thirty feet away to their right people in Sunday best were coming through the Chapel doors. A photographer was waving them towards a sunlit buttress for a group shot.

'What is it?' Lucas asked. 'What are we looking at? Bad fashion?'

'Try these,' she said and handed him her old army binoculars. She found them invaluable when she or Jack wanted to collar a certain pupil after meals and didn't want to hang around the quad in the wind and rain.

'Eurgh!' Lucas said, peering. 'Dodgy hats. Very dodgy. Oh. Are they American? That one's so thin and . . . Oh. Oh my God, Sophie!'

'Yes,' she said. 'It is. Let me look again.'

She grabbed the binoculars for another closer look.

'That's Chris Miller. He was *never* friends with him. And David Crisp, for God's sake. Do you think he's changed? He hasn't got much fatter. You always said he'd get fat.'

'I said women would start fancying him and he'd turn into a vet.'

'Well he's never a vet. The competition is far too stiff.'

'Excuse me?' Rustam asked. 'Translation?'

'It's Charlie,' Lucas told him.

'*The* Charlie? Your friend, Charlie?'

'His son's being christened,' Sophie explained. 'He's got two little girls already but apparently girls don't count.'

'Who did he marry? Let me see.' Lucas grabbed the binoculars again.

'I'm going down. This is an historic occasion.' Rustam unpacked his camera and screwed on a big zoom lens.

'You can't!' Sophie gasped. 'They'll see.'

'They'll see an Indian. They'll assume I'm a tourist,' Rustam said with a mischievous smile and went downstairs.

Sophie found Jack's lightweight birdwatching glasses so they could both watch and each could know what the other was commenting on.

Charlie had married a Vanilla, not one of *the* Vanillas but a woman from the same mould, tall, thin, blonde and as bossy as his sisters – to judge from all the pointing and pushing that was going on. The Girls were there, both in hats. The one with the husband had put on weight and apparently had two teenage boys who didn't want to be in the photograph. The other one was alone but still thin. She had charge of Charlie's first two children, cruelly dressed-up, overlooked little things.

'Which was the thin one? Jenny?'

'I could never tell. She wasn't that thin when we knew them.'

'And where's the brother? I liked him.'

'Tim. You fancied Tim.'

'Do you think he died? Oh God. That would make Charlie Lord of the Manor. Maybe he just escaped. I hope he got well away. Back to the ashram. Or the love of a strong woman.'

Simultaneously they said, 'But I want to see . . .' and simultaneously had their wish granted, a shock that choked the laughter in their throats. Mrs Somborne-Abbot emerged from the Chapel between the Chaplain and Jack, who was clutching a book-token-sized envelope. She had shrunk. She was a little old lady with white hair and a black stick.

'How could we have been so scared of her all this time?' Lucas asked. 'She's almost sweet.'

'You want to go down and introduce yourself?'

'You want a bikini wax? Oh. Oh my God. I love that man.'

'That's my husband, Lou.'

'No, Phi. Him too. But look!'

Rustam was amiably wandering past the family group, taking photographs as though they were an ancient monument.

For a moment Sophie and Lucas lowered their binoculars to look at each other.

'Even in my twenties I used to ring her up sometimes and just listen,' Sophie admitted.

'Me too. "Hello? *Hello?*" I still get bad dreams about her.' *'The Bastard and the Jew.'*

They started looking again.

'What's he doing here? Why have the christening here?' Lucas asked.

They watched Charlie gazing around him at Schola from the middle of the busy group until his wife tapped him to attention for the camera.

'It matters to him,' Sophie said. 'It's a boy. Maybe he wants him to come here one day.'

'Christ.'

'He looks sort of –'

'Normal?'

'Well. Yes.'

'Does she look happy to you?'

'The wife or the mother?'

'The wife.'

'She looks busy. And thin.'

'They were married here too, you know,' Sophie said. 'I checked in the records.'

'And she's called . . . Louisa.'

'Lucia.'

'Lucetta. That's it, Lucetta. Like Hardy.'

'You keep tabs on him too!'

'Of course I do.'

'I thought it was just me.'

Photographs taken, the group was herded out of the quad via the Slipe.

'They've booked Founder's Room for lunch,' she told him. 'Sherry then buffet. Shall we go down? Say hello. Show him we're still alive.'

'Yes. Why not? We're not children, after all. Actually no. I couldn't possibly.'

'Oh go on. How's my hair? Do I look imposing again? I want to look imposing.'

They dithered so long they missed their chance. When they opened the front door and glanced out, the party had vanished, Jack with them, and Rustam was wandering around the quad taking photographs.

Relieved, Sophie linked arms with Lucas and led him over to Rustam so they could begin their tour. They needed him to stop them slipping into a slough of unexpected melancholy. Her lunchtime surprise had backfired. She didn't want Lucas to think it was the only reason she had asked him and Rustam to visit. It was pure coincidence although, in the seconds after she glanced at Jack's desk diary and discovered that Charlie and Lucas were to overlap, she fantasized that destiny was at work. Why did Charlie still fascinate them when all he represented was shame, betrayal, wasted friendship?

'Maybe he'll lose all significance now we've seen him,' she said as they waited for Rustam to come back to them from photographing some Daughters playing cards on a sofa. She knew Lucas knew who she was talking about. 'Maybe. Now that the past has joined the present.'

'Phi? Was there a memorial?' he asked her, changing tack but not exactly.

She shook her head. 'I've looked and looked. Chapel. Both cloisters. Nothing. Maybe he got a tree. There'll be something in the estate church, though. Where the rest of the family are.'

'But the school did nothing with words on it.'

'No.'

They showed Rustam the Chapel, then a typical chamber with its burrows and posters, the traditional mix of scholasticism and anarchy. They entered the cloisters, glancing fearfully across to Founder's Room where the christening lunch was in progress. They visited the Chantry then climbed the tower to the ringing-chamber and gallery. At last, with the Bell Captain's kind permission, they climbed up through his study and onto the chapel roof.

Rustam was delighted and clambered across the leading to take close-up shots of weathered gargoyles and pinnacles.

'He's gorgeous,' she murmured.

'Thank you. It's a shame we can't breed. Parsees are an endangered race.'

'You could adopt.'

'Yes,' he said wistfully. 'Yes, we could. If only we didn't have to travel. Rustam was asking about your mother and I couldn't remember. Did you ever track her down in the end?'

'Yes,' she said, admiring the familiar view. 'You know, I discovered I had two of them.'

'You're joking!'

'Your mother is whoever makes you feel safe and teaches you who you are, gives you that sense of legitimacy. I realized I had Margaret, who'd always been there for me. And this place.'

'Sweet.' Lucas hugged her and planted a kiss in her hair.

There was a click as Rustam took their picture.

'Not fair!' she called out. 'I should be taking yours.' But he was off across the roof again.

'I never asked you,' Lucas said with a nod towards the little door by which they had come out. 'Did you get it in the end, the way you'd planned?'

'Jonty Mortimer's study?' She laughed sadly. 'No way. I worked for it. Christ, I worked in that last year but I came second to bloody Bunsen.'

'Shame.'

'I tried to convince myself they'd marked me down a bit because they weren't ready to have a Daughter rule the roost. And I'd have been a hopeless Senior Prefect anyway. I was an anarchist and I hated team games.'

'Yes, but how about now?'

'This year it's a boy, as you saw, but next year I have plans . . . She'll be perfect.'

'Does she know?'

Sophie shook her head. 'Which is why she's perfect.'

They were leaning against the tower wall rather than one of the outer parapets. She realized they were both reaching the

338

age where good balance could not be taken for granted. Rustam photographed them again, with them looking at him this time, then Sophie took over the camera and photographed them with their arms about each other and the Chapel tower looming behind them.

Rustam kissed Lucas during the second shot and Lucas looked entirely happy which made Sophie feel tearfully mother-of-the-bride-ish. He had been forced to put half the world between him and this place to find happiness, she mused, and still he thought of it all the time. They kissed again. She caught herself glancing around anxiously and was ashamed.

'We should show Rustam the Warden's Garden,' she told them.

'Of course,' Lucas said.

'It's looking wonderful now. No, you first.'

She, on the other hand, had found it was only by coming back that she became free to grow up and grow on. Tatham's was a home and a job to her now, as well as a mother, but no longer a kind of curse.

There were shouts as they came through Cloister Gate.

'Oh God,' Lucas breathed. 'TatCoFo.'

'What's that?' Rustam asked.

'Nothing really. A cross between football and gladiatorial combat. Someone dancing on my grave.'

The day was perfect: late March, blue sky, scudding, cotton-wool clouds and a vigorous breeze in the plane trees. As they skirted the cloister wall, heading for the bridge over the river, they paused to watch a few minutes of Jack's TatCoFo match, the flying mud, the reckless, joyous self-violence of fifteen-year-olds who had yet to see a broken neck or a protruding shin bone.

Turning again, they passed the great circle on the turf where the charring from Illumina's bonfire would last into early summer. She saw Rustam tap Lucas's elbow and ask softly, 'Is that where . . . ?' to which Lucas merely nodded.

It was enough to reassure her that they had a deeply shared life already, a life in which completed sentences were becoming as superfluous as good manners. And that, like her, Lucas was not about to forget.

AUTHOR'S NOTE

This being a fantasy not a memoir, I have seen fit to rearrange 1970s opera schedules and record and film releases to suit the story's purpose.

My heartfelt thanks, however, go to Nick Hay and Rupert Tyler for all the true bits of our shared history they have, wittingly and unwittingly, helped me dredge up, to Celia Gale, who once again was an invaluable source of information, to Ellie Gale for the notebooks and to Susanna Martelli, Ahmed Hussein and Fali Pavri for their cultural input. Patricia Parkin, Clare Reihill and Caradoc King are the best godparents a newborn could wish for.